To Kevin :

Thanks for every

Madynp - is great

Anthony James '09

# SMILES IN AFRICA

## ANTHONY JAMES

Bloomington, IN  Milton Keynes, UK

authorHOUSE®

*AuthorHouse™*
*1663 Liberty Drive, Suite 200*
*Bloomington, IN 47403*
*www.authorhouse.com*
*Phone: 1-800-839-8640*

*AuthorHouse™ UK Ltd.*
*500 Avebury Boulevard*
*Central Milton Keynes, MK9 2BE*
*www.authorhouse.co.uk*
*Phone: 08001974150*

*First published by AuthorHouse 7/12/2007*

*ISBN: 978-1-4259-7116-8 (sc)*

*Printed in the United States of America*
*Bloomington, Indiana*

*This book is printed on acid-free paper.*

# ACKNOWLEDGEMENTS.

My thanks to Dr Claude Evans who over many a late night's carousing, first entreated me to write this book. To Julia Davies who was so kind in helping me get on my way though uncompromising with her criticism. To Loretta McLaughlin-Becker my first fan. Kachi Armony for his help in initial formatting. To all those friends in Africa that I have grown to love over the years, and for Jacqui my late wife, who put up with the trauma of giving this book life with such good humor and unflagging encouragement.

# CHAPTER 1

Africa, - the Dark Continent; Nigeria, perhaps the darkest of all; a venal and dangerous place. Adventure or disaster? Smiles was overwhelmed with excited uncertainty.

Was he mad? Throwing away a sure career, dragging his young family into the unknown? Surely life is for living and the world there to be travelled. In any event; it was too late to go back now......

"We are commencing our descent into Kano." Richard Smiles snapped shut his safety belt and tried to stifle his apprehension as the aircraft lunged gently into its final approach.

All was darkness; then a few dim lights spread like small candles on the black void. Even on landing the airport had a strange unlighted quality as if the airport, aeroplanes and electricity itself had no place here.

He descended the stairs at the rear of the plane; Smiles could not believe that the engines could throw out such heat. Then as he traversed hurriedly to follow the alighting passengers who were disappearing into the blackness of the Terminal, he realized that this heat had nothing to do with aero engines. This was Nigeria, at eight pm. October 20th 1970, and it was hotter than he had ever dreamed.

He trudged, already covered in sweat, trying desperately to pull himself together. He clutched his immigration papers and passport in one hand and carried his weighty briefcase in the other. This heat hit so hard that all his composure deserted him. It sank him in a sea of confusion, made more distressing by the attacks of a thousand insects. He was plunged into an unimaginable ordeal; the sweat poured into his bespectacled eyes, fused his shirt to the flood under his arms and his formerly pristine slacks to his sticky crotch

"For Christ's sake pull yourself together" he urged himself.. He struggled almost blindly to win his way to the front of the line.

Yes, this was Nigeria all right. Mosquitoes and various flying insects bombarded him from every side, he defended in vain, succeeding only in hitting himself repeatedly and painfully with his heavy and hard briefcase.

His race to the Arrivals Hall had been in vain. The hall, or more accurately, 'shed' was already heaving with screaming, scrimmaging crowds. There was much pushing and shoving. Richard took stock, albeit briefly, and set to join the scrum. It was not a place for faint hearts. His first skirmish was with a gargantuan Nigerian who bundled Richard to one side. The uncertainty and strangeness of it all drained his confidence, so he meekly took his place behind his heavier adversary.

The noise was incredible. Languages merged into an incomprehensible din. He was not sure if those around him spoke English or Martian; he just lost the power to comprehend. Here he was in the Tower of Babel, sweating his nuts off and going backwards in an ever-lengthening queue. Was this what adventures were about?

Next to him appeared a tall elegant European; he was polished from toe to the top of his shining head. His shirt was crisp and white; he wore his jacket with kerchief and cuffs smartly and precisely presented. He looked cool. How could anyone look cool? This bugger did and Richard could not avoid disliking him for it.

"Is it always as bad as this?" ventured Richard.

"This, dear boy," smirked the cool one, "is a quiet night. You're damn lucky that Air France is late, then you'd really see how chaos works."

"You can't be serious."

"Your first time, I take it?"

"Yes, actually I'm taking up a new posting in Kaduna." Richard stammered, his voice trailing off, leaking away like his confidence .

"Poor sod." remarked the cool one and that seemed to end the conversation.

A slow thirty-five minutes passed as Richard shuffled to the front of the queue. Eventually, having been bombarded by the sights, sounds and smells of his new adopted home, with his doubts, discomforts, and disorientation overwhelming him; he handed his passport to the Immigration Officer. The officer searched humungous volumes that surely must have the world's population listed inside. He peered into a huge ledger, patently bemused by what he was, or was not seeing. Time dragged on, each second seeming like an age. The official peered at Richard and then with a flurry of hyper-energy stamped the document with almost manic force. The passport was thrust at Richard with a terse and somewhat insincere;

"Welcome to Neejeeriah!"

Richard stuffed his passport into his now grubby jacket and followed the flow that resembled a post match exit from a football game. The baggage claim area was a sight that sent Richard's already depleted resilience to an empty aching low. He thought he would pass out. Where to go? What to do? He began to drown in his misery.

The chaos in the Baggage Hall was breathtaking; bags and parcels were everywhere. People climbed, pushed, and pulled huge bags and parcels, dishing out severe injuries to whomever and whatever was in their way. Everyone seemed single-mindedly focused on retrieving their belongings, obviously convinced that failure to instantly retrieve their goods and chattels would be to bid them farewell forever. The two carousels moved mountains of luggage; huge parcels tethered with tape or string. There were bulging broken suitcases with bloomers, dirty socks, and all manner of personal items spilling off the moving mountains, growing into chaotic volcanoes of junk.

Panic seized Richard, stirring his uncertain stomach, where did he begin to look for his things? He spotted some piles of possessions with a SABENA claim label. He climbed and shoved his way toward them, barking his shins as he went. As much as he searched the piles, the moving, and the floor bound; he saw no sign of his new, smart executive navy blue luggage. Then, as if by magic, there they were; not on the carousel, but neatly stacked on a trolley. They were guarded by a sinister, tall, bald man dressed in what had once been a uniform, even more alarmingly he had deep sinister scars on either side of his face. Richard circled unsurely. Then heart in mouth approached the porter.

He stuttered "Excuse me, I believe these are my bags."

The porter looked coolly at him, sizing him up and down. "Gooood evening Sah! I weel help you Sah." With that, he turned and disappeared at speed into the surging crowd. Richard followed in hot and agitated pursuit, eventually catching up with the man who had joined another massive queue with no apparent end in sight.

The crowd was, if anything, more voluble and anxious. There were dozens of locals who were returning home from Europe. Their luggage was of incredible variety, how it had all been carried in aeroplanes was a mystery. There were all manner of electrical goods, fans, radios, high-fi, TV's, even fridges. There were prams and toys, pots and pans, vacuum cleaners, tennis rackets, and anything else that could be purchased in Paris, London, or Rome. The people were dressed in agdabas of many colors, blues and greens, some of fine lace. The Europeans, with the exception of Mr. 'Cool', seemed to have lost any composure. They all perspired; rivers of sweat which stained their outer clothes. Patience gave way to anxious aggression as people jostled, head down, arms crossed; they stubbornly held their positions in the unending queue.

Tempers began to flare as people pushed and shoved, even Smiles asserted some backbone into the fray, and he held his ground. The porter had somehow found his way to near the front of the crowd and beckoned to the now, cast adrift Richard Smiles to join him. Richard put his head down and went for it. After receiving much abuse and a number of minor, but painful, injuries he arrived breathless, reunited with his luggage and the grinning porter.

The Customs officer beckoned Smiles to a low bench. Everywhere there were opened cases and unpacked parcels.

"Your documents." It was an order not a request.

There was a short silence as the burly customs man noted Richard's passport details.

"How much money do you have?"

Smiles responded truthfully, obligingly, trying to show the man that he was helpful, honest, and delighted to be in Nigeria. It did no good.

"Open your bags!" he ordered. Richard obliged; revealing the meticulously packed cases so lovingly packed that morning by his wife

Joan. The bags contained all that would be expected of a young British gentleman undertaking a tour of duty in the tropics.

The customs man picked out a newly packed, short sleeved, white cotton shirt,

"This is new!" he exclaimed, as though surprised, his eyes fixed on Richard. "There is duty on imported textiles." He stared directly at his prey, daring him to argue.

"They're my personal effects" replied the cowed Richard, meekly.

The customs man dexterously closed the case, neatly placing the new white shirt, now 'white shirt - customs - for the use of", to one side. Richard managed a smile, thought for a second about protesting, thought better of it, and made a hasty dash for the exit.

The porter grinned and needed no further instructions. He was off like a shot. He disappeared once more into yet another crowd of excited welcoming residents.

To Richard's great relief he spotted Edward Regan, head of African operations for United Industries - his new boss. Regan smiled broadly, standing smartly attired in apparent cool detachment. His pants and shirt were immaculately pressed. His brow showed no sign of sweat. Richard felt miserably inferior.

"Richard, welcome to Nigeria." Regan beamed. "Where's your luggage, old boy?"

Richard looked desperately around and caught a glimpse of "his" porter leaning on a battered Peugeot taxi.

"Over there." he stammered.

"Taxi, Sah?" grinned the porter.

Edward Regan, hands on hips, commanded over Richard's stuttering, "Boy! Bring those bags here NOW!"

The demeanor of the porter immediately changed.

"Yassah." He responded. No smile now; as he scuttled to Regan's order.

The three marched in file following Edward Regan to the polished company car, a shining Peugeot, dazzling white even in the dark. A driver suddenly leapt from the invisible interior, bowed, (or was he stooping?) grabbed the luggage from the porter and stacked it into the trunk.

"Adebayo, this is Mr. Smiles, the new Master."

Adebayo, a muscular, round man with a closely cropped head, beamed back a huge smile.

"Welcome Sah, Welcome to Nijeerreea."

For the first time, Richard felt the smile and the welcome to be genuine. He stretched out his hand but Regan blocked the contact, opening the car door. Richard, caught in mid act, couldn't make up his mind if this was accidental or not.

They drove through the unreal candle lit outskirts of Kano. The houses were built of mud, most had thatched roofs, but some had tin. The roads were quiet and shadows danced, illuminated by the many flickering open fires. Regan politely enquired about the journey and, in the ordered quiet of the air-conditioned car, Richard remembered only the good bits - so this was Africa - the continent of mystery adventure and romance.

The journey to the Central Hotel was short. The hotel appeared stark but ordered, at least to a point. It seemed that Edward Regan understood the ways of the place, booking in was quick and efficient, and the room was clean, though Spartan. The shower was cool and refreshing.

Despite his desperate fatigue Richard was keen to make a good impression on Regan, who from now on would order the lives of the Smiles family from on high. So he denied his exhaustion and returned to the hotel bar for a nightcap with his new boss.

A hotel porter had escorted him to his room. The hotel had a number of blocks, all separate from the main building and were all reached through gardens. When Richard emerged from his block he was at once filled with the notion that the garden was alive with snakes and other African creeping things. He stood at the block doorway hoping that another guest would emerge. He waited some minutes but no one came. Eventually he dashed towards the lights of the main building, skipping and leaping like some demented ballet dancer.

He arrived at the bar; his composure once more lost in a sea of sweat. However, his thirst was of a high order and he accepted the offer of local beer from Regan with enthusiasm and genuine gratitude.

It emerged that Regan would stay only a couple of days with Richard in the Kaduna office and then leave Richard to his own devices. The local company was doing well with good people.

Richard should find his first general management role not too difficult and Regan and his staff were only a few hours away.

After a few beers with Regan, who was now a more familiar Edward, Richard retired to his room through the dimly lit gardens. He was exhausted, he had drunk too many beers, he'd lost pounds in floods of perspiration, and he could not wait to get to sleep. As he walked uncertainly to the door of his block, a huge noisy beetle flew within inches of his nose. He leapt in panic and flailed in vain at his unseen assailant. His awareness now much heightened, he accelerated to the haven of his room, once more to shower. He minutely examined the bathroom and bedroom for any signs of creeping things. He donned his pristine tropical pajamas, tip-toed across the insect free floor and dived, or more accurately, collapsed into his damp bed. Try as he would, he could not sleep. The air conditioner groaned and buzzed intermittently, flies and mosquitoes buzzed around him and imaginary spiders big as bats crawled on the ceiling.

He woke early in the bright morning of his first African day. However his first awareness was the intense itching around his neck and wrists. He had obviously been bitten during the night, but so what, this was, after all, Africa.

# CHAPTER 2

He joined Edward for breakfast at the appointed hour. They dined on soggy corn flakes, flabby greasy bacon and rigid, cool fried eggs. The toast was cold and the tea weak. Edward found everything to his satisfaction so Richard suffered in silence.

They set out on the road to Kaduna; there was no sign of the Africa of the tourist glossies, the Africa of Tarzan, the Africa of his imagination. Instead there was mile after mile of scrub. The drive to Kaduna was a huge disappointment to Richard. It was boring. The road was flat and endless. The countryside was dry bush and scrub that extended the wide but shallow horizon. A merciless sun beat down and the road ahead shimmered, it disappeared into a stairway of ascending mirrors. Occasionally they passed enormous trucks which careered at frightening speed towards them, their huge forty foot trailers filled to capacity and on the top of the loads, groups of desperate passengers hanging on for dear life, their robes flying out behind them in the speed stream. Each truck was emblazoned with signs that declared that "God is good" or "Jehovah is our strength" or "Allah is merciful". It seemed to Richard that their Gods had to be all those things if they were to reach their destinations in one piece.

"Those lorries seem to be pushing on a bit,"

"Pushing on? Completely out of control more like it." responded Edward. "These lorries are all hopelessly overloaded they couldn't stop even if there was an emergency." He grinned. "The poor sods on the top have no chance when there's an accident, the statistics are unbelievable more akin to air disasters, often thirty or more dead."

Richard said nothing, just watched as another lorry anointed with thirty or forty frantic passengers passed at an electrifying pace.

"You see, they have no concept of capacity, they fill the lorries till they're full, so a big forty foot trailer can be full of lead or feathers, the problem of course being that the lead load is impossible to stop."

"No surely not." Richard responded.

"You'll soon learn," he ended, "life here is cheap."'

Adebayo drew the car into the Zaria Club, a rather ugly building on the outskirts of a town famed for its university and its ancient heritage as a seat of learning. They took coffee in the brown sofa'd lounge which reeked of its colonial past. The steward greeted Edward with enormous and exaggerated deference; it made Richard feel uncomfortable. It was not so much the steward's attitude, more Edward's response. He did use the word please (just). It was as though he didn't really notice the steward at all.

Here Edward explained the business of "clubs".

Whatever he said Richard decided that it was not for him. This was painfully obviously the establishment's defense against progress. A social ghetto sustained to resist the native climb to equality. This was where the beleaguered whites withdrew to be with their own kind.

Blacks, explained Edward, were of course allowed to join, and increasingly did. Blacks, the 'locals' he called them, were good at sport and most of those joining were professionals and army officers. He concluded by adding that "they" were not too bad "They're welcome."

'Welcome' - you arrogant son of a bitch, thought Richard. No wonder the bloody Empire's dead.

Whilst Richard was conscious of his own ignorance, innocence even, he prayed that he would not develop the supercilious racist attitudes so obviously engrained in Edward Regan. He resolved to remember this moment, to keep it in mind, so that he could in the future hold up the mirror and measure his own frailties.

An hour later they arrived at the house that was to be the Smiles' residence for the next two or more years. The outskirts of Kaduna were much more spacious and gracious than Richard had anticipated. As they swept along Racecourse Road the trees gave a luxuriant shade. There was a cool greenness, with the racecourse itself spread with soft grass and tended beds. The polo field and stands looked pristine and gave an air of an established and ordered community.

The house; that was to be the family home was in Galadima Road, just off Racecourse. The bungalow was set in generous gardens that at one time had been beautiful but had fallen into some decay. On either side there was an empty plot, and then some affluent looking villas. He wondered what the neighbors would be like.

As he entered the house his heart sank; the furniture was tacky and the decoration worse; it was dark dinghy and oppressively hot. At the rear of the property was "the boy's quarters" a separate servant's quarter that looked even filthier than the rest of the plot. The boy's quarters consisted of a solid stand-alone building of one room plus toilet and shower facility.

From this modest abode emerged Joseph, he was short mercurial and scruffy.

Edward announced, "This is the new Master, Mr. Smiles, you must work hard for him."

The delivery was more akin to a railway station announcement than an introduction and it left Richard and the timorous steward quite disconnected. Richard offered his hand but Joseph looked uncomfortable and only after an awkward delay did he respond. His hand felt distinctly unwashed. Edward shifted uncomfortably.

The tour of the house did little to cheer Richard. The place was dirty, the furniture very second hand and the living room was like an oven. The bedrooms were air-conditioned, which seemed the only saving grace of the place. They took tea in the lounge, now slightly more comfortable with the doors and windows open. Richard sitting uncomfortably on a sticky sponge cushioned arm chair, took a deep breath and spoke, the nerves trembling in his throat:

"Before Joan and little David arrive we're going to have to refurnish and redecorate this whole place, I hope you understand." he trailed off.

"Quite so," responded Regan, "'just get your budget approved before you start. Anything we can do to help you settle in, don't hesitate to ask."

"Thank you." The relief refreshed him like cold water.

It was time for Regan to return to his Hotel. He would let Richard unpack and pick him up the following morning and introduce him to his new charges at the 'Universal' factory.

"Tonight, lad, I've arranged for you to be taken out to dinner with Malcolm and Sally Hetherington. You'll like them. Malcolm is the senior audit partner. They'll take you under their wing. See you in the morning." With that he was gone.

Joseph helped with the luggage to the bedroom. Richard could not help but notice the rich acrid odor that drifted from his steward. The little man, for he was much smaller than Richard, was definitely grubby. His fingernails carried a substantial amount of dirt, his hair looked dry and unwashed, and his uniform was grimy. Despite this he was quick and seemed eager to please.

"Joseph."

"Yes, Mastah."

"Don't call me Master, there's a good chap, call me Mr. Smiles, or if you must, Sir, okay?"

"Yes, Mastah." responded Joseph with a grin.

"I am new to your country....." Smiles searched for an opening, "and I shall be relying on you to help settle in. Perhaps it would be good?....... Of course it would be good if we understand each other, what?"

"Yes, Sah." Came the perky response.

"We have a saying Joseph, where I come from, that cleanliness is next to godliness, so we like every thing to be as clean as possible, okay?"

"Yes, Mastah"

"Everybody takes a shower at least once a day, okay?"

"Yes, Sah"

"That includes me and you, okay?"

"I no come your shower." responded the bewildered Joseph.

"No Joseph, that's not what I mean. I mean we.... I mean you shower in your house at least once a day,.... and I shower in my house every day, understand?"

"Mastah, my shower he no work, Sah."

"Well we must get it fixed, as soon as possible. In the meantime have a bath, use the garden hose, but let's be sure that we're clean. Understand?"

Richard was left alone to unpack. He began to notice, with accumulating dread, how dirty and shabby the house really was. He felt miserable, exhausted, and lonely. He doubted that he could expect Joseph, who was a grubby little man, to restore the house to being a clean and comfortable home for Joan and David. They were due to arrive in six weeks and that seemed a very long time away. He lay on the bed and listened to the din of the ancient air conditioner, come to think of it he was a pretty grubby bugger himself, he drifted into the drone of the a/c and slept.

# CHAPTER 3

He was dragged from the soupy depths of his slumber by a banging and cries that he did not comprehend. He sat bolt upright and shook his befuddled and sweaty brow.

"Mastah! Mastah!" the door was being pounded so hard Richard thought it would cave in.

"Yes, what is it?" he shouted grumpily back.

"Mastah, it is Meesta Hetherington and Missy, Sah, they are waiting Sah."

"Shit, why didn't you call me earlier? Shit, shit, shit! Tell them to wait and that I'll be with them as soon as I can. Give them a drink or something."

"Yes, Sah!"

Richard leapt off the bed, whipped off his underpants, and dashed through to the bathroom that was across the hall. He was halfway there when he was conscious that his two guests were looking straight down the corridor at him. He stopped, turned toward them, started to say something but then remembered that he was stark naked. He thrust his hands over his vitals and leapt into the bathroom. No sooner had he turned on the shower and as he tight eyed bewailed his ghastly embarrassment, there was a knock on the bathroom door.

"Yes, what is it now?" shouted Richard impatiently.

"What drink shall I give Mastah and Missy, Sah?"

"Any bloody thing. Beer, gin, whatever, just bloody do it."

13

"Yes Sah." came the resigned reply as he shuffled back up the corridor.

Richard dried himself with haste, wrapped a towel round himself and dashed back to the bedroom and tugged clean clothes over his damp and perspiring torso. He dragged a comb through his frazzled hair. One glance into the mirror, a quick rejection of the wreck that looked back, he took a deep breath, and with gritted teeth set out to meet his guests. He reached the lounge with outstretched hand.

"I'm terribly sorry," he blustered, "just nodded off I'm afraid, terribly sorry."

The Hetherington's sat on the settee drinkless, but relaxed. Malcolm was a well-built man, a little older than Richard. He had a neat black beard that ran like a narrow band tracing the edge of his strong jaw line. Sally, the wife, took his breath away. She was elegant, slim but with enough weight to fill all the right curves. She had lustrous long black hair; sparkling brown eyes, which smiled a flirtatious smile. He was smitten; as it turned out were most of the male community in Kaduna.

"Welcome to Kaduna." They spoke almost in unison. Both seemed genuinely pleased to see him.

Richard apologized for his lateness once more and for the lack of refreshment. He dashed into the kitchen where he found Joseph busily picking his nose, watching an ancient kettle struggling to come to the boil.

"Where are the bloody drinks?" he spat the words through clenched teeth.

"I make tea, Sah." responded Joseph with an air of resigned finality.

"Bollocks." muttered Richard as he span on his heel and returned apologetically to his cool and patient guests. Apparently there were no drinks;

"I'm terribly sorry I'm terribly sorry there doesn't seem to be any drink available, I hope you'll let me show a little hospitality when I've settled in." He gave a nervous giggle.

The Hetherington's nodded with understanding.

The journey to the club was short and although Richard dreaded the prospect of another imperial sham, both Malcolm and Sally, who seemed to be fazed by nothing, charmed him. No reference had been made to his initial nude appearance in the corridor and Richard secretly wondered if Sally's curiosity had been pricked, as it were, by the sight of his pathetic nakedness. On balance he hoped not. 'Get thee behind me Satan, or let me get behind Sally, Oh delicious one.' As they drove into the "club" car park Malcolm reached onto the glove box and brought out two ties.

"Here we are, Richard. Bloody silly I know, but we have to wear a tie, no matter how hot it is, only after seven though. Which one would you like? That one is my Lancashire Regiment tie and this one, Lancashire Cricket Club."

"The two loves of his life." interjected Sally. "You're very honored to be offered either. He's probably secretly mad at me for choosing them. Sorry darling, can never remember which is which"

"Not at all." replied Malcolm without conviction.

"I think the cricket tie seems less sacred" said Richard, hoping it was the right thing to say.

" Good man, just as well you chose that one."

They entered the undistinguished building; through into an equally unimpressive hall which had a desk manned by a huge and jolly Commissionaire. Malcolm introduced Richard to Daniel who, resplendent in uniform, declined his hand but bowed almost imperceptibly and grinned a great welcome.

The bar was a long polished wooden affair that ran virtually the whole length of the room. Along the front of it there were several groups of furniture, all brown leather, grouped around low coffee tables. All the groups were arranged in absolutely straight lines. Each table had an ashtray precisely in the centre and large potted palms decorated the corners at each end.

The floor was covered with a plain beige carpet and the whole impression was one of profound dullness. The one bright spot in the room itself was the shining bar and the brightly clad barman who wore a white robe gathered at the waist with a scarlet cumber band.

"This is Mussa, our counselor and comforter," quipped Malcolm, obviously to the delight of the broadly grinning Nigerian, whose waxed moustache pointed heavenward as he smiled.

"What would you like to drink? Star, Heineken, a short perhaps?"

"A beer would be fine thanks, a Star please." His mind had put away the hangover of the previous night in Kano.

Malcolm wondered off, "Look after Richard for a minute. I won't be long." he called over his shoulder as he disappeared out the other end of the room.

He sat with Sally who nursed an orange cocktail. In a matter of moments he drained his beer and was suddenly embarrassed. "I'm so sorry. It's just that it's so hot and I was so thirsty. May I get you another drink?"

"No, Richard, don't worry about me, you have another one." She smiled. Her perfume was intoxicating; her eyes met his with an intimacy that made his heart skip a beat. His throat dried as he drank in her loveliness. He became alarmed, he straightened, coughed and started afresh. He gathered himself and they settled and talked easily.

"It's all a bit of a blur so far, it's not at all what I expected." He was quiet for a second, reflecting, 'what was it; he was expecting?'

She merely laughed, she touched his hand across the table, "Don't worry Richard all new boys and girls take time to settle down."

The touch of her hand, a flash between them, another shortness of breath, 'don't be an idiot'.

"I hope that you can help me settle in, Sally, and of course Malcolm…." Oh what a prat he was.

Her eyes laughed at him, but her lips barely flickered. Richard leapt to his feet and ordered another beer.

They settled once more, and she shepherded the conversation smoothly and they talked of their families, how long Sally and Malcolm had been in Kaduna (three years), the good things, the bad things, and the impossible. She missed good beef, English apples, and cold weather. She loved the time at the end of the rains, "her people", as she put it, and she loved her garden. They had no children nor did they want any. She hoped fervently that Malcolm would be transferred back into the mainstream, hopefully in the next eighteen months.

Richard reported on his wife of five years, the lovely Joan, and their twenty month old baby David. He also bemoaned the parlous state of Galadima Road.

Suddenly Malcolm reappeared, "Okay Richard, they're ready for us now."

"Off you go Richard, be nice to the admissions committee, just a formality."

Shit, shit, shit, panicked Richard as he followed Malcolm upstairs.

"Informal meeting with some of the chaps, nothing to get excited about." comforted Malcolm. However the sense of panic still gripped Richard's belly.

He was ushered into a room some quarter of the size of the bar, but still a large room. The room was set with the inevitable brown leather furniture, but there was a large table at one end. Around the table sat a group of five men, three white and two black. In front of the table stood one empty chair, it looked so lonely and spare.

"Gentlemen," pronounced Malcolm, "may I present Mr. Richard Smiles, lately appointed General Manager of Universal Metals in Kaduna. I can recommend him to you as an able executive. A sportsman who plays golf and rugger; and who will soon be joined by his wife and family. I commend Mr. Smiles and his family as suitable to become family members of the club."

He turned to Richard, "May I introduce you to our committee." He gestured to the tall distinguished African sitting at the centre of the table, "Doctor Sam Eli, our President," then to a handsome, bronzed man with curly grey hair, "Mr. Henry Ash, our Treasurer, Don Rawlings, Deputy Chairman, Jack Williams and our Secretary Major Ezekiel Addo" Each in turn stood and shook Richard firmly by the hand.

Richard stood rooted to the spot, his panic unrelenting. It became even worse as Malcolm quietly took his leave.

"Please sit down, Mr. Smiles." commanded the deep rich and surprisingly English cultured voice of Doctor Eli.

The interview was agreeable and pleasant and Dr Eli in particular seemed sympathetic to Richard's circumstance. He revealed after the interview that not only was he the Club President, Golf Section Captain, but also Universal's doctor and would consequently become the Smiles' family physician. The other members of the selection committee were courteous enough, but were obviously just going through the motions since it would be unthinkable that the General Manager of Universal Metals would not be a member of 'The Club'.

After some twenty minutes he returned back to the bar, where Sally was sitting with three other ladies, all wives of the selection committee. Mrs., Eli was a tall English lady; Mrs. Ash and Mrs. Rawlings were pleasant middle-aged matrons. After two further Star beers Richard quite forgot which lady was which?

The husbands joined the party and Richard wobbled into dinner supported by Sally and the elegant Mrs. Eli, Charlotte by name. Richard was not sure what the cause of his inebriation was, was it fatigue? Or was it the Star beer? In any event he tried desperately not to slur his words, but in so doing seemed to exaggerate his rapidly increasing and chronic slur.

Everyone at the table smiled politely and continued to converse, addressing him as infrequently as they could.

"Tell us about your family, Richard." an imperious command from Mrs. Rawlings.

"My Joanyzz wunerful and an lil David's a beauful boy, he's tweny."

"Surely not" cried the incredulous Mrs. Rawlings.

"Absolutely, absoluly, wadya mean?" Richard held the table tightly to prevent him falling backward.

"I think Richard meant twenty months." intervened the kindly Sally.

"Time to get you home old lad." said Malcolm, helping Richard to his feet.

There was a confused farewell and the Hetherington's gently marched their charge to the car park. Malcolm seemed quite untouched by the Star beers and Sally seemed cool perfumed and highly desirable.

As they bundled Richard into the back of the car, he rambled "You are very kind, very, very chind." he snorted, "Malcolm, ...your wife is an absolu dish, do you know that? ... Do you know that? .... An absolu dishhh"

They laughed, "Yes I do' said Malcolm, "Yes, indeed I do."

As he staggered from the car and waved farewell, he struggled to reflect on the number of bottles of the local brew that he had consumed, his inner consciousness urging caution. He was startled out of his reverie by a masked man in Arab dress sporting a bow and arrow. The drunk's first cry was a muted whimper, but he gathered himself and exclaimed :

'Bloody Hell, who are you?'

'Rank a de de' muttered the masked one, at which point Richard lurched into the bungalow hoping that the hapless Joseph was on hand. He was, he giggled at Richard's confused state and between titters explained that the masked aberration was,

"The Magardi Mastah! It is the Magardi Sah! He is a Tuareg man Sah! He keep away dee tief man Sah!"

It was all too much for Richard who made his uncertain way to bed to sleep a sleep of such depth as that normally reserved for the dead. He woke in the early hours, the room span, his stomach heaved and the evening's digest was returned uncomfortably into the toilet. As he knelt in vomitorial prayer he watched the ants scramble busily around the base of the bowl. He prayed silently for himself in his unmitigated misery.

# CHAPTER 4

The morning light pierced the cotton curtains and burned holes into his eyes. His head throbbed abominably; his mouth was dry and foul. His bed smelt of sweat and also urine, the latter not of his own making. He rose stiffly and gazed at himself in the corroded mirror and did not much like what he saw.

'Today, you silly sod,' he berated his mirror image, 'is meant to be making a grand and impressive entrance at work. Look at yourself, you hopeless turd.'

With that he staggered to the bathroom, reviewed the filth remaining from last night's upheavals and was relieved to see that the bath water was warm, but still pale brown. He bathed, shaved and dressed and appeared for breakfast, not knowing what to expect. What he got was a meal of bullet like boiled eggs, tea that must have been brewed before dawn, disgusting warm condensed milk and cold burnt toast.

Joseph appeared, happily seeking direction for the evening meal. Unsure of how to respond, Richard thrust a ten pound note into his delighted steward's hand and muttered;

"Get some steak or something, I'm not sure what I'll be doing tonight."

"Yas Sah!"

With that there was a tap on the door and Adebayo, the driver, beamed his wide smile,

"Good morning Sah. We will fetch Meesta Regan and go to the factory, Sah."

Richard climbed warily into the back of the car, already perspiring in the early morning heat. Edward Regan smartly attired, shoes polished, face scrubbed, sweat free, leapt with enthusiasm into the back of the car and beamed at Richard.

"Trust you had a pleasant evening with the Henderson's, introduced you to the club and all that, thought we'd move as fast as we could and get you sorted, hope it all went well."

"Yes, fine, lovely people, thanks for arranging it. I just hope I wasn't too tired, felt the pace a bit, to be truthful." He trailed off, could he be fired for naff social behaviour he wondered.

As they drove through Kaduna, Richard was delighted to learn that on Regan's departure, Adebayo, together with the splendid Peugeot, would be his. Kaduna continued to please the eye, the main roads were broad and they had leafy trees on either side. The sidewalks were clean and the crowds of colourful locals looked ordered and cheerful. Traffic was busy with over laden lorries. Taxis known as mammy wagons made their busy way packed with up to twenty passengers, when capacity was probably twelve. Local women carried improbable loads on their heads. Men pushed hand carts with immense effort. Everything buzzed with energy and purpose.

"It all seems very industrious and busy." remarked Richard.

"This is the high spot, the coolest part of the day. By ten o'clock things have slowed to a dead stop" responded Regan.

There remained in Richard a determination to dislike his boss and despite his hangover he glared out of the car window and stubbornly refused to believe whatever this arrogant prick had to say.

The factory was another pleasant surprise. It was modern, twenty thousand square feet and set in a clearly fenced and cared for compound. The grounds were well manicured with an array of tropical plants, shrubs, and flowers.

The office building was neat, joined to the manufacturing plant by a covered walkway. A uniformed guard stood at the entrance. He saluted smartly from his post as Adebayo swept the car through the gates. The office itself had a glazed reception area where the company's products were neatly displayed. There was a backdrop of a world map showing the spread of the Universal Metals family of companies and affiliates.

Regan marched passed several expectant African office workers to a door marked "General Manager". He stopped outside and gestured theatrically to Richard.

"Welcome Mr Richard Smiles, General Manager, United Metals Northern Nigerian Facility." With that he threw open the door and with a bow and a sweep of his arm beckoned Richard to enter.

At first Richard stood quite still in the door way "Christ its bloody freezing in here"

"You'll get used to the contrasts. Sit in your chair; let the circus commence."

"I hope it's not going to be a circus."

"I hope so too, but believe me you'll have to be a good ringmaster" quipped back Regan.

Through the louvered windows Richard could see a pretty black girl who seemed frozen over her typewriter, not daring to look back at her new boss.

Regan flipped the louvers and commanded, "Tea for me and Mr Smiles, Rhoda, chop, chop."

Regan produced all the work documents; budgets, performance to date, productivity performance graphs, revenue budgets, capital expenditure proposals, labour cost budgets. All the familiar tools of the trade and it made Richard feel comfortable.

There was a tap at the door that opened to the collective shout of "come in." Rhoda brought in the tea, all the time looking down at the floor. She laid the things on the coffee table and departed, mumbling an almost silent, "Thank you Sah."

Edward ignored her completely. It was as if she did not exist for him. Richard was astonished and barely recovered in time to shout 'thank you' as Rhoda retired silently from the room.

After an hour or so of discussions, it was Richard who ventured "Shall we go around and meet the troops?"

"No, no," responded Edward "they must come and see you here, you do not go to them."

'You silly old bastard, I can't wait for you to bugger off.' thought Richard with growing impatience. There followed a series of introductory interviews that were dominated by Regan. They were not so much interviews as inspection interrogations. Everyone came and went with heads down, with an obdurate hostility that Richard found most uncomfortable He wanted to enjoy his new-found responsibility; he wanted to make friends. He wanted to smile, to shake hands warmly, and to see people smile back. . Regan on the other hand; seemed entirely comfortable, aloof, arrogant, and in charge. Richard's discomfort grew as did his dislike for Regan.

They left for the Club at lunchtime, Richard finding it harder and harder to sustain any communications with Regan. The gulf between them grew minute by minute. The question was did Regan feel the drift? In Richard's mind he resolved that Regan was such an insensitive son of a bitch he probably was blissfully unaware of the growing antipathy.

At the Club, Regan began, "You think I'm some sort of unfeeling idiot, don't you?"

"No, of course not," lied Richard.

"Well, I arrived here a while ago and like you and everyone who starts the African experience, I wanted to live in harmony with my neighbour and my co-worker. I'm ashamed to say I failed in that goal. I'm not telling you that you won't manage differently or better, but hope you'll listen to my advice and at least give it the attention it deserves. There is no substitute for experience…believe me, believe me… I hope you do." He trailed off as if dreaming of a distant past. "In any event," he continued, rising from his reverie, "here's some advice which I know is hard to follow, but do your best, eh!"

"Don't trust anyone in the factory, not even Eke until you get to know him much better. Do not make loans or give credit to any one. Don't let housekeeping decline at all in the factory, not a millimetre, not a jot! Always personally supervise banking deposits and withdrawals. Never allow overtime unless it's your initiative. Never pay sick leave without documentary evidence. Never let the workers call you anything other than Sir, or Mr Smiles. Never visit the factory when you're expected, always visit unannounced. Only pay bonuses or special payments weekly in arrears. Never allow the factory to function without you or Eke present."

"In fact," thought Richard, "behave like a shit at all times!"

"Well, we'll visit Malcolm Hetherington at the auditors. We rely on Malcolm and his firm to oversee your financial reporting and accounts, so although you're in charge one of Malcolm's boys will come in every month and sign off on the monthly accounts. It's important you have a good relationship with Malcolm and all his colleagues, imperative in fact." There was a silence. "And then I must get the five o clock flight back to Lagos."

Richard froze. What would Hetherington report on last night's performance? Would this be the shortest career in history? How could he save face? What should he say? All too soon the car drew up outside Hetherington's office. Richard fidgeted as they waited to be shown into the boardroom.

Out swept Malcolm, sharp white shirt, neatly trimmed beard, a testimony to sobriety and business efficiency. He smiled warmly, greeted Regan like a long lost friend, and shook Richard's hand with enthusiasm. They moved to the meeting room with Richard waiting for the axe to fall. It didn't and as time wore on he concentrated on the issues so ardently and professionally debated. After an hour of focused effort it was time to break up and Richard could not avoid the subject any longer.

"It was very kind of you to look after me last night. I do hope that you'll forgive my rather odd behavior." He left the comment hanging there, he winced at his own stupidity, and surely Malcolm was now bound to expose his hapless drunkenness.

"You were jolly brave, we thought, facing the old committee on your first night here. You must have been exhausted old boy. He performed jolly well." he said as an aside for Regan's benefit.

Richard could have kissed his feet right there, but instead he responded, "You're very kind. Do thank Sally for me."

"Not at all. In fact I've made an arrangement for golf on Saturday, hope that's okay and lunch afterwards at our place."

"That would be lovely, you're too kind. I look forward to it." Richard meant it. Malcolm and Sally were two really nice people; perhaps life wasn't so bad after all.

They journeyed back to the factory for the last hour of Edward Regan's visit. They marched directly into the factory; Richard followed Regan as they approached a tall elegant bespectacled African. "Mr. Eke, come and meet Mr. Smiles." again a command not an invitation. Eke loped gracefully towards them fixing Richard with an open smile. He arrived with his hand confidently outstretched and with a warm greeting. It was Richard who spoke first; "I'm looking forward to working with you, Mr. Eke."

"You are most welcome Sir, I am sure we will work well Sir." this time a sideways glance at Regan. They toured the manufacturing facilities; again each time they reached a machine centre the African workers would look away and avoid eye contact, almost inevitably looking down at the floor. Eke ran a continuous commentary and seemed to be on top of the job.

As soon as the tour was over Richard and Regan returned to the office for tea and last minute instructions. At just after four Regan departed; "Remember my advice young man, you don't have to like it, just remember it." With that, he was gone, just a muffled "good luck" as Adebayo whisked him off to the airport.

In the silence that followed Regan's departure, Richard sat behind his grand desk, fiddled with the papers and panicked. 'What the hell do I do now?'

He tapped lightly on the partition window and beckoned to the startled Rhoda to join him in his office. She instantly appeared, tapping nervously first upon his door before she entered, still staring steadfastly downward.

"Rhoda you'll have to help me find my way around." was his opening remark and it was as if he had uttered some magic word. She broke into a broad attractive but still nervous smile and she soon produced his diary, together with all the documents that were necessary to complete the immediate chores. Some he didn't understand, so he asked her advice, some she didn't understand but she noted who she thought could. After half an hour much had been done and the next few days already assumed a purpose. He picked up the phone and called Eke to come up for a chat; they spent the next hour talking and listening to Eke's views on the strengths, weaknesses and problems that faced the factory. He looked up and was aware of Rhoda standing in her office almost trying to be seen and not seen at the same time. It was only then that he realized that the time was well passed six o'clock.

"Eke what time do we stop work?"

"Five in the office, and four thirty in the factory, Sir."

"Rhoda are you waiting for anything?"

"No, Sah, I am finished Sah" came the nervous reply.

"Thank you Rhoda, you may go home, please let me know in future when it's five and you need to leave. Good night and thank you again." She beamed a wide smile, and picked up her belongings and strutted from the office.

"Eke I'm sorry I mustn't keep you."

"It is not a problem Sir." he replied, "It is good to share with you."

"Tomorrow I'll spend time with the senior office staff and then in the afternoon we can spend more time together in the factory okay?"

They took their leave and Richard looked for Adebayo who was polishing the splendid Peugeot with much zest. It was good to have a chauffeur and Adebayo seemed such a nice guy. Life was getting better.

"Home to Galadima Road please."

"Yas, Sah."

# CHAPTER 5

Adebayo drove competently through the evening traffic, towards the soulless residence and the hapless Joseph. Richard reflected on the events of the day and the excitement of tomorrow. He looked forward to the weekend, the golf, meeting Sally again.

"Adebayo, do you know where the golf club is?"

"Dee golf claab, Sah, what is dat Sah?"

"You know… golf…. big place…. big field, with flags on greens."

"Ah, ah! Masta dee place where de white man and Doctor Eli he hit small ball with big stick."

"Absolutely, not on the horse, that is polo…yes.?"

"No horse Sah, dee man go walk Sah, hit dee ball, and walk Sah."

"Absolutely, that is the golf club. Do you know how to get there?"

"Yes Sah! I take you there now Sah?"

"No, I will go there on Saturday. Why not drive me there now, to show me the way, you're not wanting to go home yet are you?"

"No Sah, I go home when you say so Sah!"

"Okay, take me to the golf club please."

They arrived in very short time. It was nearly dark, as they drove into the car park the small club house, a circular patio to its front, laid out with tables and chairs and populated with a large number of drinkers, nearly all of whom were white. The golf course itself seemed to be laid out on very scruffy land. Richard ventured from the car and strolled to the patio, not expecting anything more than a closer recce of the place. As he stood and took in the scene he heard his name called.

"Richard Smiles, is that you?"

He looked but didn't instantly recognize the speaker.

"Henry Ash, we met last night at the club"

"Of course, how good to see you again."

"Have a beer old boy, come over and meet some of the golfing fraternity." With that Ash took Richard by the arm and led him to a table of five, well-oiled, golfers. Richard was aware of Adebayo waiting in the car and wasn't at all sure of the form. He mentioned the fact to Ash, who immediately dismissed the issue as of no consequence. Drivers and servants were expected to wait upon their Master's whim.

Ash was a senior manager at one of the larger Kaduna banks. He seemed jolly, warm and friendly. The other golfers in the party were likewise welcoming and Richard could not decide if this was their natural behavior or the result of the evening toping. They were all textile men and all from Lancashire and were keen to commiserate with Richard on his decision to come to Nigeria. They'd all escaped from the recession in the British textile business and brought their skills to Kaduna. As Richard watched, detached in his sober state, he couldn't help but wonder if all these guys could hold down such senior, well paid jobs at home. Was this the future that he was carving out for himself, he felt unsure? After a couple of beers he excused himself, bade them farewell and looked forward to meeting them again on the following Saturday. Adebayo was not at all impressed by Richard's apology and merely enquired where Richard next wanted to go. Home was the order and in a few minutes they came face to face with the strange aberration of the veiled and mysterious guardians of Galadima Road. This time Richard bade them a brave "Good evening" whilst Adebayo engaged them in a long and seemingly formal greeting.

Once inside the house, the drab loneliness of it all engulfed him. Two days had passed since his arrival in this strange country and it seemed like years. He wanted very much to talk to Joan, his love, his anchor who he took so much for granted, but now he missed her, he needed her. He went straight to the telephone, dialing the local exchange.

"Hello! Hello!"

There followed a long and frustrating dialogue with a variety of operators in the Nigerian P&T exchanges that ended an hour later with the depressing announcement;

"Okay, Sah. There is a delay Sah, perhaps four hours."

It was already gone nine, perhaps he would try again in the morning.

"Thank you very much I'll try again in the morning."

The phone went dead and Richard disconsolately turned to face the dreadful prospect of Joseph's evening offering. Joseph's under arm odor however still made Richard's eyes water and prompted an enquiry about the state of the plumbing and Joseph's ablutions during the day. There followed an incomprehensible conversation, which ended with Richard retreating to bed exhausted once more and feeling none too well.

# CHAPTER 6

The following morning, Richard woke with reluctance, the fatigue, and strain of the last two days and the strange sleeping conditions under the freezing, clattering, air conditioning were taking their toll. However his first day alone and in command was an exciting prospect and he looked forward to building new bridges with his troops. He would eradicate the old head down syndrome and build a happy team. Today would be a day that was a new beginning. Today would see change and a change for good.

His arrival in the office was greeted with broad smiles from Rhoda, but still the suspicious brooding of the others. Richard went to work with an enthusiasm and a determination to break down the barriers so obviously ingrained.

At around ten there was a tentative knock on his door and Rhoda announced;

"Excuse me Sah, there is a wacker here to see you, he is Benjamin Sah"

'A "wacker", Rhoda? What's a "wacker"?'

"From de factory Sah, a wacker."

"Oh, a worker. Okay, send him in Rhoda"

A very tall man dressed in company overalls appeared nervously at the door, "Come in old chap." called Richard. "What can I do for you?"

"Sah, my name ees Benjamin, Sah. My mother, Sah, she is dead Sah. I will have to go home to my village, Sah, to bury her and to mourn her Sah."

"Can I say how sorry I am to learn of your loss." Richard cast about in an awkward silence, then without thought blurted; "Please feel free to take a week off for compassionate leave."

There was a silence, Benjamin stood there shifting uneasily from foot to foot.

"Is there anything else I can do?" enquired the concerned, but now all-powerful and compassionate Richard.

"Sah, I cannot afford the fare to my village which is a long way off, Sah, and I need money to bury my mother Sah"

How could he refuse money to help this man bury his mother, it was a no-brainer, in one act he would show the workforce that he was generous and caring.

"Certainly," the company could certainly afford a 'dime'. "We can arrange a loan, or even a grant, how much do you think you will need?"

"Fifty pounds, Sah." was the tentative reply.

Without a moment's hesitation, basking in his magnanimity, the new boss replied, "Certainly dear fellow. Rhoda, let Benjamin have fifty pounds advance. That should cover it, Benjamin, okay?"

The startled Benjamin, the wealth of princes grasped in his sweaty palms retreated without a word.

It was close to the early close on that Friday when Rhoda requested an interview for another "wacker" named Edwin Namumba.

"Good afternoon Edwin, what can I do for you?"

"Sah, I beg you to help me Sah. My father Sah, he is very old Sah. My mother Sah, she has sent me a message Sah" There was a long pause.

Richard dreaded what was to come. Like a bolt from the blue the words of Edward Regan came back to haunt him. Surely not! Surely bloody well not! Bugger, bugger! He hid his head behind his curled and intertwined hands. No! It couldn't be, ... or could it be? Was Benjamin a crook? What if both these guys are telling the truth? What if Edwin's telling the truth and Benjamin is the liar? Shit, what could he do?

Edwin waited for help, but none came. He shuffled much as Benjamin had, then seeing no other way, he continued;

31

"Sah, I beg you that you can help me Sah. With a small loan, Sah, so that I can travel to my village and pay for the doctor. He will help my father who ees suffering much, Sah."

"How much?"

"Fifty pounds, Sah, if you please, Sah, it will help my father..."

"Rhoda" interrupted the aggravated Richard, "arrange a fifty pound loan for Edwin"

"Edwin, I hope your father gets better. I'll expect you to repay the loan, okay?"

After much groveling Edwin disappeared to a weekend of compassion or debauchery, Richard knew not what. Richard sat, much chastened by the day's happenings. He sent for Eke. He related the story of the day's events to the evident quiet amusement of his Works Manager.

"In future, I think it would be wise that all requests for welfare issues are channeled through Departmental Heads. Each one that arrives in my office will have a note of endorsement from the individual's boss, okay?"

"Of course," responded Eke. "It is just that we are not used to making that sort of decision. Your predecessor always wanted to make all the decisions." He wanted to say more, but didn't.

"Carry on, Eke, I'd really like to know what you think"

"Mr. Smiles," Eke smiled, "it will take time for you to know our ways, sir. If I can be of any assistance to you I will..." Again he trailed off, unsure of which way to continue.

Richard felt he didn't want to press further, so he let it go. He still didn't really know if he'd been conned, but he'd learned a lesson or two. The acid test would be if Benjamin and Edwin ever returned to work and repaid their loans. Fifty pounds was, after all, more than four weeks wages for these guys, no matter, he'd made good head way with the staff during the day and some had even smiled at him, ... were they smiling or laughing? He preferred to think not. He hoped upon hope that they were smiling with him.

# CHAPTER 7

Adebayo was not to work over the weekend so Richard drove himself to the golf club, to find some company and to find out the procedure for the morning. He found his way without incident and soon settled into a table with Ash's pals and was pleased to see the familiar face of Malcolm Hetherington.

Golf in Kaduna was unlike anywhere Richard had played golf in his past. There was precious little greenery, the tees were made of concrete, the greens were browns, and there were so many local rules to help manage the bizarre conditions it was all very confusing. Added to these strains was the horrendous heat, an eccentric compulsory caddie called Ephraim and borrowed clubs, since Richard's had yet to arrive. Nevertheless, a round of eighteen holes was completed with excellent company who encouraged Richard throughout. They had set off at seven forty five and arrived back at the clubhouse around four hours later. Richard was wrung out and possessed a thirst of gargantuan proportions. His arms were burned in the sun, as was his neck, but at least his head had been saved by the ridiculous hat that Malcolm had insisted he wore. He was introduced to literally dozens of golfers all of whom seemed pleased to meet him and all too many were keen to buy him a drink.

Despite the bonhomie there were some ex-pats who Richard instantly disliked. He confirmed his view that these men would never have been managers in Europe. It was not that they were 'earthy', it was because they had assumed a superiority that was entirely without foundation. Jack

33

Walker exemplified the breed, tattooed the length of his arms, arrogant and foul mouthed.

"These Black bastards", he called the Nigerians, he never seemed to mind who heard him. He ordered the staff around with never a 'Please or thank you' and never seemed to stop moaning about his lot.

"My dear fellow," responded Smiles, "if life really is so dreadful why don't you bugger of back to England."

Walker fixed him with a stare; his pale green eyes boring into the ingenuous Smiles,

"Ya know fookall mate, withart me and ma' mates there'd be no fookin' textarl industry in this God forsaken 'ole and that's a fact."

Richard felt suddenly weak, he'd only been with these guys a short while and he'd already upset Walker who looked as if he was not beyond a physical set to. Before he gathered a response, Walker pressed home his attack;

"Ya' come 'ere, fookin' public school smart arse, know 'nowt, and start tellin' us ta go 'ome. You've got a nerve lad, you wan' a watch what yer say or somebody'll ave yer."

"Come along gentlemen," broke in Henry Ash, "drink up; don't let's spoil our weekend, I dare say you both have a point,... what are you drinking.. Star?"

"Didn't mean to sound such a prat, no offence George."

Walker spat to his side; the gesture said it all. Richard shrank into himself suppressing a desire to flee the table. Malcolm babbled on as if the altercation was nothing. It was something, alright; Smiles had made an enemy.

Walker was not one of a kind. There were about six so-called Managers all from similar backgrounds, but George had two friends who shared his voracious dislike of the Nigerian population, and a macho aggressive gang-like image that set them apart.

Richard's response was foolish and short sighted; he felt he needed to show that he was the equal of Walker, so he drank Star for Star. The consequences were disastrous.

"Thou needs to be a bit better than that lad if you're goin' to make it out 'ere." Walker picked up his 'fags', spat once more and swaggered away. Smiles was left his head in his folded arms drunk as a skunk.

Richard, after a beer or three, soon confessed to his sins of the day before. There was much mirth and his leg was pulled mercilessly throughout the remainder of the evening. He joined one of the several bachelors for dinner at the club and staggered home to the chaotic ministrations of his steward.

It was only as he sank under the bath water for the third time, when he leapt in panic, vomiting the bath water and copious quantities of Star beer, did it occur to him that the local beer was an iniquitous brew that needed considerably more respect. He toweled off, feeling dreadful, hungry, and miserable. He resisted lying down because he knew he would drop off to sleep again, perhaps "pass out" would have been a more accurate description. He struggled to focus on what lay ahead, an evening with the Hetherington's; the lunch had been lost somewhere in the day. God he'd have to sober up. In his misery he reviewed his first few days in Nigeria. He'd been drunk no fewer than four times in five days, he'd eaten irregularly, the only thing he'd done properly was turn up at work and he'd made a balls of that. He resolved that he'd sort out his routine, get a decent supply of food in and work harder to get Joseph to perform reasonably. Then he needed to get a grip of redecorating and refurnishing the house for it was only five and a half weeks before his beloved Joan was to arrive.

He drank large amounts of water to detox himself and despite the lateness of the hour started on a tour of the shops in the city. The supermarket was still open and despite his alcoholic confusion he bought a vast quantity of food, with no regard to shelf life or his or Joseph's ability to cook it. He arrived home and stuffed the food into the fridge and drank more water. He tried to telephone home, for comfort rather than anything else, failed once again and slouched disconsolately back to bathe away the sweat of his latest labors and set out for an evening with the Hetherington's and the delicious Sally.

The evening passed delightfully, the food was excellent, the company engaging and Richard was able to learn much to help him on the domestic front. The whereabouts of the furniture stores, and the best manufacturing or import sources, although every one was dubious about acquiring the new furniture before Joan's arrival. Finding a decent decorator was less difficult and Bill Ewing, an architect and also a guest at the dinner, promised to line up a firm who would be able to start within a couple of weeks. Sally and Marjorie Ewing promised to help in choosing the curtains and advising on a color scheme. For the first time Richard steered clear of the beer, drank copious quantities of water to assuage his thirst, and took a little wine with his dinner. The result was, not surprisingly, that he arrived home in relatively good health, although the rigors of the afternoon and their after effects still lurked in the background.

Sunday passed with no further wayward behavior and Richard threw himself into reading works documents and customer records. To combat his occasional bouts of loneliness he attempted on several occasions to phone home, this made his loneliness all the more unbearable. He missed Joan, her quiet soft and perfumed presence. Someone to touch; someone to hold. His little boy David just eighteen months old, how would he face the heat and the strangeness of it all? Joan who'd been his wife for four years had never traveled much and he began to wonder and worry how she would settle. He dreamed of her lovely body and of the love that he missed so much, God it seemed like years.

He spent an hour with Joseph inspecting in some detail the steward's disgusting living quarters. They were disgusting, not because they were miserable by design or facility, but they were disgusting because they had not been cleaned seemingly ever. The furniture, what little there was, was all in a state of disrepair. A filthy upholstered armchair lolled with one leg missing, the table yawned where a leaf was absent and the cupboards had one door out of four. The toilet and the shower room were indescribably filthy. Rubbish and decomposing food was everywhere, largely centered on Joseph's bed. The most worrying thing of all was that the whole place reeked of stale alcohol. Richard was horrified, not only about the way that Joseph chose to live, but that this man was meant to be looking after the household. He did not talk to Joseph during the inspection for fear that he might gag, so he called him into the house some time later after having considered the problem, but without resolve. He had no idea how to address the problem; could Joseph be coached into acceptably hygienic ways? If he fired Joseph could he find someone better? Was he being fair? What could he do to move things on?

"Joseph, I must say your quarters are disgustingly dirty. You must keep them clean" was Richard's inept opening.

"Yes, Sah." was the cheerful reply. Joseph grinned without any pretence at taking the matter seriously.

"Joseph, I'm serious, you either smarten up and clean up your quarters or I shall have to make you go away and get somebody who is cleaner. This must get better."

"Mastah," began Joseph more plaintively, "the last mastah, he give me not'ing at all, no chair no t'ing. My uniform he is old Sah, my house he neva paint am. De pipes no work at all, no watta 'cept from de laundry, Sah." He began to appear as if he were going to burst into tears.

Richard's response was one of immediate sympathy. He melted quicker than a Nigerian snowflake. Richard retreating from righteous indignation to positive sympathetic support produced an immediate plan. Despite Joseph's pungency, his chaotic ways, his smile always cheered Richard. Despite his reservations Joseph was still his closest colleague in this strange land.

"Okay Joseph, this is what we will do. Firstly, go and buy two new uniforms, secondly the plumber will come soon and mend your pipes. In two weeks, when the painter comes, he will paint your house as well. When the new furniture comes you can have what is available from here."

Joseph's delight at the news was palpable, his grin spread from ear to ear, his eyes lit up and circled between the lids.

"I will be 'dee best clean man in dee place, Sah I will not fail you Sah."

He paused, not sure if he was elated or yet again caught out. He continued as if to hedge his bets. "Of course Joseph, if we do all these things, then I shall expect you to keep up the best standards. There will be no second chance."

Joseph beamed back his most engaging smile 'Yes, Sah, you can be sure, Sah.'

Richard inwardly groaned, if only he could.

# CHAPTER 8

The next days passed swiftly as Richard got to grips with the job. He made it a point to tour the factory every day and to stop and speak to every one he could. He had a plan that demanded that he had spoken to every one of the two hundred or so employees by the month end. He found it hard. Often he was met with blank indifference and often the worker would attempt to drag him into a grievance or seek an outrageous favor. He stuck to his task and soon heads began to rise when he walked into a work place. There was eye contact. There was the beginning of mutual respect.

It was not unusual for a local contractor to bring in a bag full of thirty thousand pounds since cheques were so frequently given to bouncing. Each note was counted on Richard's desk, bagged and put in the huge safe. Later, Richard would gather "his posse" as he called them and they would troop off to the bank. At the bank the money was counted again and the whole process took hours. Richard toyed with the idea of delegating the task to others but Regan's words rang persistently in his ear. There was really no alternative to these hours spent counting money, into the office and then again into the Bank.

On the Thursday morning Richard arrived bright and early at the office to find to his horror that the phones did not work. He enquired if all the bills were paid, if there were any other problems with the Posts and Telegraph Department. Rhoda responded with that enigmatic lethargy, which implied "find out if you can, do we have a surprise for you?" Eke, likewise, was very coy about the problems, and suggested that they should send a message by hand to the 'P and T'. Adebayo was dispatched with a written note beseeching the corporation to sort out the situation without delay. Hours passed. There was no sign of Adebayo, no phone and of course no car. Richard sat in his office and fumed.

It was early afternoon when Adebayo returned.

He reported "I go see P and T manager, he no be dayo."

"I'm sorry Adebayo; could you say that again, please?"

Adebayo looked confused, "Mastah, I go lookam, I go seeam, he no be deyo, he not on seat Sah."

Richard called in Rhoda who explained that Adebayo had spent much of the day waiting for the Section Manager who was absent.

"Oh, bloody wonderful." grumbled Richard, strumming his fingers on his desk. "Come on Adebayo, we'll go back together and sort this out." and with that he rose to leave.

Rhoda quietly mumbled "Excuse me Sah, the P and T Engineer he will come at three o'clock Sah."

"What Rhoda, what?" What was she saying? "How do you know that Rhoda? You can't possibly know. Has somebody called? Why wasn't I informed?" Snapped the very angry Richard.

"He always come, Sah," she almost whispered. She hurried away to her desk.

"What do you mean? They know the phone is down and they send someone? Jolly good. Pity didn't tell me before, that's very good I must say. Will he fix the phone?"

"He will talk to you Sah." Busying herself with files on the desk.

"Will he fix the phone?" Richard shouted, but to no avail.

At three o'clock on the dot Rhoda announced the arrival of the P and T Engineer.

He was smartly attired in the corporate overalls; however he arrived without transport or tools. He shook hand with some glee and welcomed "Meesta Smiles" to Kaduna and continued, "Meesta Smiles, I have come to see you after a very busy day, to welcome you."

"You could have used the telephone," spat Richard a little spitefully, "if it was working. However you may know we have no service just now."

Mr. Simon, the Engineer, feigned shock "Oh, gracious me!" he exclaimed, "Surely that line of yours is not down again."

There was a pause as Simon scratched his chin theatrically, "Mr. Smiles," he announced, "I shall see to it, immediately. I will put you on the urgent list for emergency repair."

"Oh thank God, so we'll have the phones back on today then?' snapped back Richard.

"Well, now Sah that is deeficult. All the Engineers, particularly in this district, are verrry busy. All have much work ahead. I doubt if we can get to you this week." He wrung his hands in torment. "I am very sorry Sah." he finished plaintively.

"Sorry, bloody sorry, not good enough my friend, not good enough...."

Before Richard could continue his ranting, Simon continued, "But with poor wages and no overtime allowed it is not possible to do things faster... I am very sorry Sah."

"Are you telling me that we can't get the bloody phone back for a week?" exploded Richard. "What sort of bloody company are you running?" He slammed the desk. He gathered himself a little, trying to find his way out of this black hole of frustration.

"Look, if you can't deliver, I want to speak to someone more senior who can, do I make myself clear?" He paused for breath, "I want to speak to some senior people? We simply cannot run the business without the phones"

"You cannot Sah," replied Simon emphatically, "because there is nobody who can fix things in this district without my Engineers, Sah." The "Sah" was very soto voce.

Richard did his best to contain his rage, but it was fast becoming a loosing battle, he grasped his fists into tight locks, he could hit this idiot, maybe...........

"I can see Mr. Smiles that this is most unfortunate for you. Perhaps, therefore, I could propose some extraordinary measures to help you, to extend a helping hand, as a mark of our welcome to you Sah, to Kaduna Sah." He smiled a lugubrious smile. "I will personally help you Sah. I will get my men to work overtime especially for you Sah"

Richard's anger evaporated with the relief, he was delighted. Progress because he had been firm. "When can you fix it?"

"Today Sah! This afternoon, very shortly, but I have to pay the Engineers overtime from my own pocket and it will be twenty pounds Sah." He leered at Richard and stood expectantly.

It dawned on Richard then, 'God damn it, what do I do now?' He looked at Simon, his victory complete, his smile one of calm assurance.

"Wait here" he mumbled and withdrew to the office of the Chief Clerk, Mr. Adegbulu, who had a voucher for the twenty pounds already prepared on his desk. Without a word he slipped the voucher over to Richard to countersign and handed over the twenty pounds.

And so it was every three to five weeks throughout the tenure of Richard Smiles' reign that Mr. Simon of the Posts and Telegraph Company picked up his twenty pounds. After three months he no longer bothered to cut off the phone, he simply picked up the money "for preventative maintenance".

# CHAPTER 9

The weekend was absolutely miserable. Richard was sure that he'd brought a bout of flu with him from the UK. He shivered in the air conditioning and perspired in the warmth. He had a headache of truly horrendous proportions, so he just hid himself away in his bed.

Joseph's ministrations were touchingly caring. He visited his master every hour or so throughout the weekend administering tea, cordials and other fluids. The decorators were due to arrive on the following Tuesday but Richard was confident that he would have recovered in plenty of time. On Monday morning however, Richard was aware that he was very unwell. Despite Joseph's protests, he struggled heroically out of bed and virtually fell into the back of the car. He remembered little more, until he was half carried by Adebayo and a nurse into Dr Eli's consulting room and laid on a couch. He shivered uncontrollably; at the same time he burned a fierce fire inside that caused rivers of sweat to pour out of him. His joints ached appallingly, even breathing hurt. He lapsed in and out of consciousness and later would only hazily recollect the doctor taking blood from him and then administering injections. Adebayo and the nurse escorted their burden back to the house where the nurse expertly undressed him and put him back to bed, ensuring firstly that the linen had been changed.

The next hours passed fitfully, Dr Eli visited twice that morning and Richard dreamed of Sally Hetherington mopping his sweating brow. By evening the pain returned with his consciousness. He became aware of Dr Eli, Sally and Malcolm and Eke in his bedroom. The confusion was too hard. It hurt to work it out. The thirst that gripped him was terrible and the first water was the most precious gift he'd received in a long time. He just noted that he was attached to a saline drip and dropped into an exhausted and fitful sleep.

He felt the tattooed arms of Jack Walker tighten round his throat, he saw Joan's plane fly straight past and no matter how hard he tried to stop it, David screamed, sitting on the wing of the giant jet as it disappeared and disappeared and disappeared. Joan sat helpless in the window shouting soundlessly disappearing, disappearing. Edward Regan laughed as he pulled Benjamin and Edwin on two leads; they were on all fours and snarled at Richard, more a baying mocking screech than a bark. Then there was Sally too far away, sometimes closer mopping and cooling his brow. The factory workers all looked away, 'Look at me, look at me', but they refused and walked away; no one looking back. 'Let me go home,' he was a little boy, he ran over the rooftops pulling down his short night shirt to hide his parts, and then came the giant jet with David howling on the wing, and the telephone why wouldn't the pilot answer the telephone……

It was about dawn when he woke feeling weak; but more at peace, with less pain and discomfort. He struggled to get out of bed, but in the dark a gentle hand restrained him. As light filtered into the room he recognized the nurse from Eli's team, who'd obviously taken the dogwatch. She was in her fifties, a large, round, Hausa lady who filled her white uniform amply. The thing that struck him most was her constant alertness; her focused concern, her innate kindness. She was physically strong and lifted him with apparent ease. Her name was Rebecca and Rebecca had the loveliest smile that ever made a man feel safe. From then on it was easier, he rapidly improved, Dr Eli returned and quizzed him about his malaria prophylactic regime and discovered that Richard was one of increasing numbers who needed a more effective than standard regime. He had lost an amazing amount of weight and despite feeling weak, felt almost cleansed.

He remained haunted by his dream, his doubts crowded in on him. 'Was this worth it, just to get on in the bloody company? How could he put Joan and his son at such risk? What if they succumbed to malaria or some other dreadful disease, cold he ever forgive himself?'

The dear Rebecca left in late morning. Sally arrived with home made soup and by evening Richard staggered to the kitchen to supervise Joseph's catastrophic scrambling of eggs and ritual burning of the toast. However they tasted good.

That night he slept well. He missed Joan and David and dreamt dreams of them both and traveled to another day.

His recovery was remarkably swift and although there was some residual weakness, he was soon up and about organizing the decorators to come in, getting down to the office, and generally catching up on lost time. One disadvantage was that Joseph had to be dragooned into doing the shopping with dire consequences once more, a selection of grotty and unrecognizable vegetables and fruit.

On Joseph's return from the market Richard sat dosing in his chair. Still he felt weak as a kitten, lonely and miserable. The sight of Joseph's return cheered him.

"Well Joseph how was the shopping?"

"Fit fine, Sah"

"And what delicacies await us, dear boy?"

"No delicacies, Sah, just dee food Sah."

"OK, let's see what we've got, I'm beginning to get my appetite back."

In the kitchen Joseph unpacked his purchases, from unfamiliar packaging that appeared to be old newspapers. There was a suspicious lack of lining paper, and as the miscellany of meat squirmed its way onto the draining board there rose a stench that left Richard gagging.

"Jesus Christ Joseph what is that?" He stood at arms length pointing at the putrid bloody mess, with its veins and yellow fat and green and black organs.

His enquiry was met with the most enormous smile as Joseph pointed with pride at his purchases. "This is dee rabbit Sah, and this is dee goat, dee parts will make you well Sah, I see my butcher man and dee doctor from my village Sah. This weel make you fit fine again Sah."

Richard returned to the sitting room, sat his head spinning. 'Oh shit what's the use, if the disease doesn't get me the food will. But Joseph, the bugger's doing his best, oh bugger it.' "Joseph you'd better start cooking the dinner, I think we'll try the goat."

"Yes Sah, came the enthusiastic cry from the kitchen, "Yes Sah, we make you fit fine Sah."

"If only," muttered Richard reaching for the whiskey bottle, "at least this is safe."

# CHAPTER 10

Joseph remained resolutely unable to boil an egg, but otherwise did approximately as he was bidden. He smelt less, washed more, and responded unfailingly with abroad smile and an emphatic; "Yes Sah, "or " Yes Mastah."

The relationship between the two men remained that between boss and servant, but there was a trust that operated both ways. Richard took many puzzles of local origin to Joseph for his interpretation.

"Joseph, these armed robbers, I believe they go shoot'am, and people can go and watch. What do you think of that?"

"Very good Sah, shoot dee bad men, very good Sah."

There was a pause, "Mastah it is OK if I go to see, Sah."

"To see what?"

"Dee shootin' Sah, they go shootam in dee stadium on Friday Sah, OK if I go Sah, many people go Sah."

"Jesus, are you telling me that they really do shoot these guys in public? I mean just any body can go along?."

Joseph beamed, "Yes Sah, it teach us to be good Sah, no steal from my brother with the gun."

Richard was shaken, what sort of place is this? Public executions were a nineteenth century barbarity, yet Joseph saw nothing but the literal propaganda, 'A deterrent.'

He shook his head, "OK Joseph if you want to go, go."

At about the same time much palaver was abroad at the prospect of the introduction of decimal currency. The pound, with all its colonial associations, was to be scrapped in favor of the Naira. The native population found the prospect overwhelming, and a number of superstitions sprang up, all associated with this massive change. These jujus' were numerous, some good, but most bad.

Some were too fantastic for Richard to think about, but others caught his imagination.

"Joseph, what you think of the story that the Yoruba juju will capture the pickins and use them to make the new money."

Joseph emerged from the kitchen relieved that he could stop work and talk with his Mastah;

"Tis true Sah, dey be bad men Sah, they take away our children and they keel them Sah, they cut'am," he slashed across his throat with his finger, "and dee Gods, they make him throw dee money from his gut Sah." He made a vomiting impersonation that Richard found only too graphic.

"You think this is true? Who told you this?"

"It is so Sah, eet is well known." No questioning, to Joseph this was fact. Richard knew no end of argument or attempts would persuade Joseph that this had to be superstitious nonsense. 'Or was it?'

His main struggles in life were that he still had not recovered entirely from the malaria, which still gave him sudden bouts of fever and headaches, and the new furniture for the house showed no sign of materializing. The bungalow itself had been decorated in shades of magnolia and other pastels and the furniture had been cleaned making the home appear, at least to Richard, much improved.

The garden looked much better, albeit developed in the most haphazard way under the supervision of Mussa, who spoke only the most basic "pidgin" English. Conversation were frequently confused, so that shrubs and plants were moved back and forth, the   consequent curiously accidental design emerged, to which Richard eventually surrendered.

Richard had by this time made a good many friends at the clubs and learned to respect the local beer. He looked forward with almost uncontrollable impatience to the arrival of Joan and David, which were now only days away.

He worked hard with the company clearing-agent to ensure that Joan was met and escorted through the nightmare of customs and immigration. She was due to arrive on an overnight flight from London later in the week. He was determined that he would do all he could to ensure as stress free an occasion as he could. His excitement was tempered by the fear that if this episode went badly wrong, then settling Joan and David down could be a challenge beyond him.

As the day approached Sally Hetherington and Pat Davies gave the house a once-over and gave Joseph his toughest day yet of his tenure. They arranged flowers to be delivered, checked that all the furniture was indeed clean, polished and appropriately aired. The lingering odors of former residents were disguised as best they could, though Richard doubted that they could be hidden from Joan's ferret like instinct for cleanliness very long.

# CHAPTER 11

December the second, virtually six weeks to the day after Richard's arrival. The great day dawned when Joan and little David, now twenty months old, were to arrive on the BOAC VC10 at seven in the morning.

Panalpina, the company's agents, had arranged a courier pass for Richard so that he could meet his family at the immigration desk and escort them through customs. The plane landed on time. Richard watched from the viewing gallery the passengers file off. He counted one by one, straining his eyes for a glimpse of his wife and child. He waited and waited, it seemed for a terrifying moment that all the passengers had disembarked, then, after a pause that seemed like a lifetime, there she was, framed in the aircraft doorway, clutching little David's hand, being assisted by a member of the crew. They picked their way down the stairway from the aircraft looking confused and vulnerable; David's teddy was dragged disconsolately along the tarmac. Richard waved, but in vain, they didn't respond. He could tarry no longer, with Jeremiah, the agent's man; they rushed to the immigration desk. Just as with his own arrival, the place was chaotic. The noise was deafening, the heat gathered its uncompromising oppressive weight. Joan he knew was at the end of the queue and that it would therefore take time for her to get to the desk.

And time it took. It was nearly an hour before he could wave and be recognised. Despite Joan's encouragement, David resolutely refused to recognise Daddy and was clearly overwhelmed by the clamour of events. Joan for her part looked hot and bothered. Despite the efforts she had

49

made to look good for her husband, she looked a wreck. Richard, despite his ardour, could not help feeling a tinge of disappointment. Somehow to him she looked different, had it only been six weeks since they had parted? He understood her tribulations in the heat of the strange airport and the chaos, but she still looked "different".

Their embrace was above all sticky. David burst into hysterical screams and floods of tears, but something, Richard knew not what, held them fast together. Despite this unpromising start, Joan looked with trust and reliance, giving with those blue, though weary, eyes an absolute assurance that she loved him.

Richard, for his part, wanted to cry with sadness and with joy. Most of all he wanted to hug them both, but the soap like surface of their sweating limbs and bodies made the experience less than beautiful.

David, who was blonde and sturdy, wore short pants and a neat striped shirt. His tears subsided and he eventually took his father's hand. To all the Nigerians he was a marvel and a delight. They tussled his blonde hair and ushered the family through to the front of the queue to the customs desk. Even the Customs Inspector took to David, he took no interest in the baggage and like all the others he smiled and spoke sweet things to David and waved them through like family friends.

Adebayo was equally tickled pink by the new "young mastah" and made a fuss of the bedraggled new "Madame". They drove to the Central Hotel for breakfast and for Joan and David to shower. Despite his most noble intentions, Richard could not but help hope that David would sleep and that he could make love to Joan. When they got to the room; David seemed to have lost all his fatigue and was alive with curiosity and excitement. Richard's lecherous aspirations faded and not without some petulant aggravation, but he settled and began to enjoy his son. He had really changed over the last six weeks. He was bigger and plumper, no doubt spoiled by Grandma's grub.

When they'd bathed, and in the respite of the air-conditioned room, Joan clung to him, "When you left," she whispered, "you left something with me."

"What's that, then?" he idly replied, his mind still toying with the pleasures of the flesh.

"I'm pregnant.'" and she began to cry.

Richard's thoughts swam. In the stillness he held her tight and tenderly, "How wonderful." he cooed, "God help us" he silently prayed.

The journey back to Kaduna was uneventful and boring as usual; they did not stop at Zaria as they were keen to get "home". Joan dozed fitfully and David slept the whole way.

The arrival at Galadima Road saw the steward and gardener standing bolt upright, almost to attention, Mussa, the garden boy, in his uniform of rags and Joseph, proudly sporting his number one dress uniform, a pale grey safari suit. Joseph and Mussa could hardly restrain their curiosity and delight; they were enchanted and fascinated by David's angelic blonde hair.

Richard loved his family with all the will he could muster, but it was hard to conquer Joan's bewilderment and fear of her new surroundings. From the first moment she entered the house she detected the odours and smells they had tried so hard to conceal. She hated the food, found dealing with "servants" totally alien, missed her parents at the end of the phone and after just three weeks, started morning sickness with vicious and monotonous regularity.

It was during her third unilateral declaration to return home that the furniture turned up, the day before Christmas Eve. This was a diversion that called on her homemaking skills and eased her preoccupation with her own misery.

Every thing that could go wrong did. Their personal belongings, exported by sea months ago, had apparently disappeared and cockroaches persisted in leaping out of the sugar bowl every time Joan went near it. The arrival of Joseph's wife to share the now excellently furnished "boy's quarters" brought new problems... Soon after she arrived mayhem broke out regularly, particularly after Joseph's evening or day off. Richard and Joan would sit in the house listening to crashes and screams, always anxious not to interfere into what appeared routine behavior. Joan's anxiety increased every time Richard needed to "go on tour" to visit his customers in the far-flung reaches of the North, as business grew so did the frequency of his absences. These overnight stopovers soon reached once a week.

Their friends did their best, but Joan was determined to fend off all things and people new, and engross herself in her misery. She ground away at the sacrifice she had been asked to make. Did Richard love her? Could

Richard love her?.....On bad days she wished him dead, on good days she hated his work that dragged him away from her. Through all these early days there was no hope, just a sense of loss, of alienation discomfort and fear, there seemed no end for her.

David on the other hand had settled easily after the first week or so when the heat got to him, but after that, he adored the life which consisted of playing in his paddling pool or spending much of the day in the garden with Mussa. Both Mussa and Joseph spoiled him outrageously so that he lacked for nothing.

Christmas was a trial, except of course for David. Joan was chronically homesick and found it hard to enjoy a turkey, which some claimed to be a vulture, if the taste and texture were anything to go by, they could well have been right. Richard had bought her some beguiling and sexy night attire before he left England in October. This choice went down like a lead balloon, to a wife whose belly was beginning to spread at the behest of the child within.

The heat and the insects tormented her and her bright moments remained elusive. Despite the kind ministrations of the Davies' and the Hetherington's there were few happy moments. Richard grieved for the adventure that might have been, but had turned into a marathon of patient tolerance for this girl he loved so much, but who now would not let him get near her, either in body or mind.

David became almost inseparable from Mussa. They had developed a language all of their own. It fell somewhere between Mussa's "pidgin" and David's baby talk. Try as they may, neither Richard nor Joan could discover the secrets of their mystic but happy world. Watching David play was one of the few things that gave them shared pleasure. David became in some ways the bridge between them. The snag with that was they both tended to turn to David for consolation when Joan's depression struck or when Richard's patience wore thin.

The relationship survived through pain and separate loneliness. Richard worked harder, played harder and generated a world of involvement outside the home. Joan for her part did not object, she stayed at home and waited, she waited for her new child and a new beginning. She wanted to be more outgoing, to join in social things but the black hand of her oppressor would not allow it. Since her arrival sex had been a difficult business, she'd tried to enjoy it as she had before, but it had become a chore, performed for him. He had soon received the vibes and even in his horniness he acknowledged without words that sex was off the menu.

News came in early April that Sir Ted Rawlings, Group Chairman, would be visiting Nigeria and would include a visit to Kaduna in his itinerary. Edward Regan informed Richard that the Chairman would spend a day and a night in Kaduna and that Richard was to arrange a suitably engaging day for both the Chairman and his wife. Richard was elated at the thought of such a splendid exposure to the boss of bosses and he went home that afternoon bursting with the news.

"Joan, sweetheart, guess what?" he opened brightly.

"I can't imagine." she responded dully.

"Sir Ted and Lady Rawlings are going to pay us a visit. What do you think of that, eh? They're going to spend a day and evening with us. What a break; it'll do a great deal of good you know."

"'No, I don't bloody know." she shouted. "What are you thinking about you idiot? Do you think I give a damn about Sir Ted bloody Rawlings?'" She got heavily out of her chair and walked stiffly to the kitchen. "'Shit, I hate this bloody place." she cried as another cockroach leapt athletically from the sugar basin.

After much cajoling Joan was persuaded to put on a dinner party at home for the visiting party. There would be eight sitting down to dinner, including Sir and Lady Rawlings, Edward Regan and his wife Joan plus the British Deputy High Commissioner and his wife, Peter and Anne Marshall.

The house was scrubbed and polished and new crockery was acquired. The menu was carefully put together after consultation with Sir Ted's secretary in London. Special consignments of Sokoto beef were organized and the region scoured for decent wine. Richard was determined that his Chairman would be impressed.

Joan seemed to snap out of her depression and focused on the task with enthusiasm. She not only worked hard, she seemed to thrive on the stress. The preparations were fun. Joseph was fastidiously coached. How to address the VIP's, the order of the evening, the right glasses to serve, keeping the food fresh during the preparation, right down to the towels and loo-paper. Washers-up were to be brought in the form of friends' stewards. Joan had taken command and would supervise the kitchen. All that remained to do was to pray that there would not be a disaster such as a power failure or some such from an outside agency.

Sir Ted was a big, good-looking, fifty something. He was a Yorkshire man who did nothing to disguise his roots. He was Chairman of United and held several other distinguished appointments. He'd gained a first at Cambridge in engineering and had gained a Doctorate in the USA at MIT. What surprised Richard most of all was how easy he was to get along with.

At seven o'clock precisely up rolled the car and they greeted their guests, at first rather hesitantly, but Pat and Ted Rawlings were so charming that within minutes it seemed that they were old friends. The Regan's couldn't stop trying to steer the evening, but to no avail, as Sir Ted seemed totally focused on making a fuss of the hostess. Peter and Anne Marshall arrived within minutes and proved to be affable and engaging guests. After drinks and canapés they sat for dinner on Joan's prompt. Richard, as they had rehearsed, rang the bell and awaited the appearance of Joseph. Two full and agonizing minutes passed. Richard refreshed his guests' glasses and rang the bell a second time. This time more assertively. Again there was no response from the kitchen. He raised his eyebrows to Joan who replied with a wistful and suppliant gaze towards heaven. Two more long minutes passed and he rang the bell for the third time.

Joseph appeared triumphantly sweeping confidently in from the kitchen, "Yes, Sah!" he announced with a flourish.

Fatefully Richard enquired, "Where have you been?"

To which came the loud and sure reply, "For a shit, Sah."

There was a momentary stunned silence at the table, the host mumbled, "Well good, I hope you've washed your hands." This was met with a further resounding affirmative from Joseph.

"Please serve the first course."

"Yes, Sah, right away, Sah."

From the Deputy High Commissioner came the toast, holding his glass high, "To Nigeria and its gorgeous people." They drank and laughed and had a wonderful evening.

That night, although both exhausted, they slept sweetly together. Joan cuddled comfortably in his embrace.

# CHAPTER 12

Following the visit of the Chairman, Joan seemed to have escaped her depression, the visit had been a great success, and they had made it a success together. Joan brightened up considerably even the morning sickness subsided. Her bright eyes shone her peaches and cream complexion returned, even her hair regained its auburn lustre. Best of all; that wide and open smile, her renewed interest in the home and garden. She quickly acquired the respect and affection of Joseph and Mussa, an affection she readily reciprocated. The self-consciousness of her pregnancy disappeared and she carried her burden with pride. She was much more alert and alive and interested in the things around her.

The locality was changing too, on both sides of their compound on Galadima Road they had started to build new villas, the one to the south looked to be a palace in the making.

In the garden David now had established a life with Mussa and seemed almost to be leading rather than following the garden boy. Mussa, whose work had never been prolific, seemed to be bonded so closely to David, that David dictated the rate and direction of work. Mussa for his part was delighted to have a twenty four month old assistant and their new language had assumed a degree of sophistication and extensive vocabulary, known only to them.

"Der be dayo, haba, haba,"

"Daaveed, dadoot."

"Oo,ho beeg flower haba, haba,"

It all meant little to Joan or Richard, who were happy enough to see David fit and free in the sun so far removed from the misery of an English winter.

David toddled about swinging the garden implements he could manage in comic imitation of his friend Mussa. Mussa though, seemed over protective of the boy, insisting that David stay by his side, alternatively Mussa would follow David on his gamboling runs up and down the garden.

It was Joan who complained to the master of the house that Mussa seemed to be doing "…bugger all, except playing with David. You must speak to him and make sure he does as he's meant to do. I don't know what's come over him."

On the next occasion that Richard saw Mussa in the garden on the Saturday morning, as usual David was in close attention.

"Mussa," called Richard casually.

"Yes Sah!" responded the startled gardener who was used only to conversing with David.

"Mussa, eh … you must work harder, d'ye see?"

"Yes Sir," replied the puzzled garden boy.

"David," he said pointing to his son, "You must not spend so much time with him….d'ye see?"

"Yes, Sah."

"You mustn't let him distract you from your, um, um, work,…. understand?"

"Yes, Sah." replied Mussa, now entirely lost.

"Good," said Richard, "I'm glad that's sorted. David come into the house with Daddy, now!" His voice now full of authority.

David's response was to turn on his heel and run down away from his father as fast as his little legs would carry him.

Richard rooted to the spot commanded, "David, come back here at once!"

Mussa stood confused, but after a moment trotted off after the recalcitrant boy. David accelerated toward the implement shed and compost heap.

Mussa shouted "Dandoot!" or something to that effect. David stopped and looked thoroughly dejected, even Mussa was coming out against him.

Richard, now quite cross, but also aware that Joan was watching the whole episode from the house ordered Mussa

"Mussa, get back to work. I will look after David."

Much to his surprise Mussa took no notice. He continued to walk slowly and steadily toward David, muttering in their secret language. Richard, his anger growing by the second, was not sure whether to shout at David or Mussa. He was quite determined to bollock someone.

Richard was two yards or so behind Mussa when the garden boy stopped and still facing away toward David. He raised his hand and stood quite still. Richard instinctively stopped and heard Mussa speak to David quietly and calmly. David stood as if rooted to the spot. It was then that Richard saw it. The snake was about four feet long. It was grey- scaled but browned in the latterite dust, its head was flatter than its body and there was a darker pattern on its head.

"Dandoot, stayo," whispered Mussa and David did just that.

All three watched the cobra make its leisured way past David and in front of Mussa, to the compost heap where it paused and sampled the air with its flickering tongue, and from there off into the corner of the fence, and into the compound beyond.

"Come, Daaveed." Said Mussa gently.

David taking a wide arc from the corner toddled up to Richard and exclaimed with glee, "Wiggly worm, habbah, habbah beeg wahn."

David went then to Mussa's side, who took the boy's hand and walked him to his father and said in a matter of fact kind of way, "Plenty snakes, Sah." He smiled and waving his arms indicated that the building plots on either side were disturbing their formerly content residents.

So they turned, David hand in hand with Mussa and his father, they walked back to the house. Mussa in David's eyes had become the guardian as well as gardener, and David could do a lot worse than to learn from this gentle man.

Joan took the news of the snake with less equanimity; she wailed a heart broken howl, in a split second all her recovery from depression was gone;

"Cobras and my little boy, are you crazy? All for your glorious career in this God forsaken back of beyond with snakes and ants and I don't know what else. You bastard I'm leaving now with David, I'm going now, today," she was screaming now. "Now! Today do you hear me you crazy bastard, now! If you don't want to come, fine stay here and rot, I'm not going to have my baby in this hell hole, ...Do you understand." The tears flooded down her face, sweat poured down her brow, and the peaches and cream dissolved into a blotchy reddened smudge.

She looked broken. David observed all this with curiosity, but soon decided that life was much more equitable with his friend Mussa, so he slipped away to his garden territory, despite his mother's shrieking protestations.

Insanely, Richard attempted a rebuttal;

"Sweetheart, come on darling, you know that Mussa and Joseph will keep us safe.... "

Joseph, who, as always, had been listening to the domestic drama, chose that moment to serve a tray of coffee and biscuits. As he entered the room, Joan, in floods of tears, turned to flee to the bedroom. As she turned she collided with Joseph and the coffee, crockery, biscuits and all were cast high into the air, landing on the furniture and daubing the walls with dark coffee stains.

With a wail of heart rending proportions Joan fled to the solace of the cool bedroom.

Richard and Joseph looked at each other in bewilderment, but beyond the boundaries of race and culture, they recognized the common bond of maleness. The Madame they agreed 'was upset'.

# CHAPTER 13

News of Edward Regan's visits were never received with much joy in Kaduna. Richard just did not like Regan, however hard he tried, though he had to admit he had not tried that hard,. On this occasion the news was worse than usual, Regan was going to be accompanied by a newly appointed Financial Controller. Yet more drones from Head Office, thought Richard, more dead hands trying to get their hands on the tiller. Even for Universal this was an unexpected move, but the bureaucrats were slowly but surely dragging Universal away from its entrepreneurial past towards a turgid regulated and ultimately declining future. What could this new man do? He would monitor the company staff and financial controls that were already monitored by the auditors on a monthly basis. For sure Richard would have to spend more of his already pressed time, answering silly questions posed by the new inquisitor.

The new man was about the same age as Richard. He was a Canadian of Irish descent, sported a small, and to Richard's mind, silly little beard and moustache. He was, one of those people born to be a staff man, incapable of decision-making, but very capable at nit picking other people's decisions. Not that it took Richard long to come to these decisions, it just struck him as this 'twit' walked alongside Regan from the aircraft steps. His heart sank as he watched them approach and as he licked his wounds from the recent domestic upset, he almost felt like surrendering to the pressures and returning with Joan to the land of his fathers and pack it all in.

That evening, still sulking from the snake incident, Joan declined to entertain the visitors. So after a long day, particularly for Richard, the three men were condemned to either the Club or the hotel for dinner. For some bloody minded reason Richard chose the Club, where without much ceremony he proceeded to get hopelessly drunk. He recklessly sank beer after beer almost daring Regan to challenge his behavior. After a miserable dinner Regan and Butter, the new man, made their excuses and went back to the Hamdalah Hotel.

Richard stayed on drinking destructively. He drank to hurt Joan the miserable and unforgiving wife, he drank to cock a snook at Regan and his new ridiculous crony. He drank because he was sorry for the pathetic mess he'd got into, but he drank principally because he was sorry for himself. Eventually, at some unearthly hour of the morning, he was escorted home by one of his golfing pals.

He was not received well, banished to the spare bedroom where he collapsed into an alcoholic coma. He was roused by his angry wife, despite suffering a catastrophic hangover, force fed a cold breakfast and ejected to the care of Adebayo to face a lonely day of further agonies with Regan and Butter.

"Gentlemen I feel I should apologise for my behavior last night." he began grudgingly, "It's just that things have been a bit strenuous at home, it won't happen again."

"No problem, old boy," muttered Regan, "let's forget it." he concluded with little conviction.

'One up to that bastard Butter,' but the day's discomfort did not end there. They discovered an increase in labor rates, which Richard had deliberately introduced as an incentive. This increase had been more than compensated for, by productivity and bottom line performance.

"Richard, you must inform me or Neville (Butter) of any changes in standard costs. You must have agreement before proceeding. Is that clear?" Regan was on his high horse, demonstrating to Neville Butter his authority.

"Yes, of course, quite so." responded Richard whilst ruminating to himself, 'You, you miserable bastard, wouldn't cede a wage rise as long as your arse points to the floor and you Neville, you jumped up second-rater, what the hell do you know?'

Neville Butter took copious notes during the meeting and took obvious pleasure from Richard's discomfort. Eventually the brutal day came to an end and the Lagos delegation headed home. Another battle, another day, but despite all the crap, the business was going well, sales were up, costs, not withstanding wages were down and profits were ahead of budget in absolute and ratio terms. Perhaps one at the golf club on the way home and then maybe he should go home and win a few battles there.

He loved Joan, almost so much that it hurt, but the barriers of her suffering and insecurity of the last few months made life so bloody miserable. The only time he seemed to have broken through was during the Chairman's visit, but apart from that he'd not been able to get close to her. Try as he might he didn't seem to be able to crack the ice between them. He thought he understood her problems, but still he couldn't share them.

Braced by a hair of the dog, taken at pace at the Golf Club, he arrived home expecting the worst. However he was greeted with a warm embrace.

"Have you had a bloody day?" she asked. He could see the warmth again, the bright eyes, the love without the rancor. Joan continued "I'm, sorry but the snake thing spooked me. I just can't be comfortable with the idea of David dicing with death in the garden." Richard began to interrupt, but she put her hand gently to his mouth, she continued, "David is to start in a nursery group, next week, its run by Maggie Spence and it costs very little. I know David won't like it, being torn away from Mussa, but it will only be in the mornings and at least he'll have his English reinforced."

"That's great, sweetheart, I'm sure that's a great move, but don't worry too much about the creepies, I'm told that they'll bugger off to pastures new as the neighbors develop, so it's just a temporary thing. Let's hope so anyway," They came together in a soft embrace, where each tenderly re-assured the other.

# CHAPTER 14

It was a hot Saturday morning in May. Richard was demonstrating to Joseph for the umpteenth time how to boil an egg. This process, which had been more or less continuous since Richard's arrival, had reached a point close to neurosis. On this occasion Richard had briefed Joseph the preceding evening that they would follow a set procedure. It was to go as follows; when Richard got up, he would call to Joseph in the kitchen, who was to put on a saucepan of water, which he would bring to the boil. This was clear. Then when Richard had finished his shower he would shout to Joseph the command "egg on". At this point Joseph would place the eggs into the now boiling water. Richard would dress, this would take precisely four and a half minutes and on Richard's exit from the bedroom he would shout the order; "egg off" and Joseph would retrieve the eggs from the boiling water and place the egg onto Richard's plate; Richard, if all went to plan would arrive at that precise moment.

And so, on that morning Richard arose at seven a.m., as was customary on Saturday mornings, David was anxious to greet Mussa at eight when he began his half day stint.

"Joseph." called Richard.

"Yes Sah!" came the willing reply.

Richard made his way to the shower as planned and as he toweled down he called, "Joseph."

"Yes, Sah!"

"Eggs on."

"Yes, Sah!" came the sharp reply.

Richard dressed ready for golf and as he finished putting on his long socks he shouted, "Eggs off!"

"Yes, Sah!" came the confident reply.

As Richard sat at the table, alas there was the toast, the tea, the egg cup, but no eggs.

"Joseph where are the eggs?'"

"The eggs have quenched Sah, but I will be sure Sah, when the Madame she bring 'am next week Sah."

Richard could do no more than stare at the empty eggcup in disbelief, that Joseph would complete the whole exercise without eggs was beyond him. However the day was to bring the unsuspecting Smiles other surprises which he would find harder to forget.

After his truncated breakfast Richard was about to depart to the Golf Club when there was a kafuffle at the front door. Gordon Mbamane the Works Charge Hand was there seeking the "Master".

"What's all the palaver?" enquired Richard, anxious to get away to the club.

"Master the Tief man, he has come Sah!" exclaimed the obviously excited Mbamane.

"What bloody thief man, what about the security?" responded the aggravated Richard, seeing his golfing morning dissolve before him.

"You must come Sah, the aluminium for the power station it is all gone Sah!"

"Shit, are you sure?"

"It is all gone Sah!"

"Very well, ....buggeration let's get to the factory, now, now, get in the car Gordon." Richard left a message for Joan to ring the Golf Club and set off at a reckless pace down to the factory. On the journey Mbaname chuntered on about the apparent theft and much more besides, not much of which could Richard comprehend

On arrival at the factory, Richard remembered that Eke had gone on leave and that Mbamane was the man in charge. He cursed to himself that such bad luck had befallen him without Eke's support.

As they got out of the car, Richard said, "Okay, Gordon let's take this slowly. Tell me what happened, step by step."

Mbamane responded, almost unintelligibly as he rushed the words, half in his native tongue and half in English. In any event the conversation was confused, but eventually Richard picked up the essence of the facts as reported by the overwhelmed Mbamane.

"I came dis mornin' Sah to finish BEWAC job, I open de' factory and dey no be dayo, first I no see am, but then I see they no be dayo Sah."

"Okay, how much is missing?" asked the boss as they walked towards the factory.

"All, all is gone Sah!"

"All? All three bloody tons of aluminium sheeting, you're bloody kidding me?"

He was not kidding, the place where the pristine lifts of aluminium sheeting had stood was empty. Where last evening had stood six half ton bundles of ribbed aluminium sheeting, destined to line the insulation of a new power boiler, there was nothing.

Richard at first couldn't take it in. It must be somewhere, were they sure that the customer had not come and picked up the material? Had it been shipped by mistake?

"Were the factory gates locked when you came this morning?"

"Yes, Sah." replied the plainly frightened Mbamane.

"Are you telling me that three fucking tons of twenty-gauge aluminium sheeting worth three thousand pounds has gone missing? What does that idiot on security say?"

Richard began to rant, he just couldn't get to grips with the concept that someone obviously from within his ranks had calmly driven a lorry into the factory used the crane to load the booty and drive away through the only set of gates, manned by so called security guards.

"The guard, he know nothing, Sah, he start at six o'clock dis morning, de man he take guard from he know nothing, or he say nothing," he paused, "anyway dat wot he say."

'Get hold of the night guard, now, now, I want to see the bugger pretty damn quick."

Richard paced up and down the factory drive getting angrier and frustrated by the moment. He noticed that the Saturday crew of workers stood around nervously, watching his every move. He summoned Adegbulu to check inventory, awaited the location of the security guard and thought through his options. Should he report the issue to HQ, should he wait until he was absolutely sure, should he call the police? Richard had a direct confrontation with the security guard, the one who'd allegedly started at six that morning. He was plainly frightened out of his wits. Further, he spoke very poor English and the stress of the affair made him unintelligible.

Eventually Adegbulu arrived and they examined all the files relating to inventory and orders due for dispatch. Richard still hoped that this whole episode was one administrative cock up. Armed with all the detail and dragging the alarmed Adegbulu in tow, they found Mbamane and began the tour of the factory. As they stopped to count other valuable and attractive street value items; a 'wacker' of tall and gangling gait hesitantly approached;

"Yes, …Peter isn't it, what do you have to offer? "

"Excuse me Sah," he started tentatively, "I 'tink someting Sah!"

"What is it?" responded Richard, anxious to receive help from any quarter.

"Sah, if you look above Sah," he said gesturing above his head to the top of the wall where it met the roof, some twenty feet above the floor.

There they all observed a hole some four feet high tapering over four feet width to nothing, where a cladding sheet had been bent back.

"Sah," continued Peter with more confidence, " that is where de tief man come Sah and he take de goods Sah. It is bad ju- ju Sah."

All the assembled workmen, including Mbaname and Adegbulu, all muttered their assent to this. There were oohs and aahs and general twittering in various dialects. It was as if the whole mystery had been explained away.

Richard took a moment or two to take in the concept presented to him, after a brief moment of incredulity he bellowed;

"Bollocks, I've never heard such complete bollocks. Are you guys telling me that unbeknown to the security people someone spirited away these six foot sheets through a four foot hole? Absolute bollocks, you're all bloody mad."

The assembled company looked on their boss with considered sympathy; it was obvious, was it not? That bad ju-ju was the cause, these white men would never understand.

With that and with the anxious Charge Hand in attendance, Richard set about inspecting the compound boundary fences, there were no signs of damage or forced entry. Despite this, at every opportunity the workers followed at a distance, pointing every so often at the hole in the eaves of the building, clearly they could not comprehend why "de boss" did not share their wonder about the clever "tief man" and his awesome magic.

Eventually Richard had no alternative other than to ring the police and report the theft. The phone call itself consumed half an hour. Eventually it was decided that the police would visit and that in the meantime no one was to leave the premises.

This news was received badly by the staff on site. Several suddenly had urgent reasons to leave, even Mbabane begged to be let go, but Richard, assuming that every guiltless person had nothing to fear, would have none of it and ordered everyone to stay put. Two hours lapsed and it was getting on for midday when the navy blue land rover of the Nigerian police drew up outside the office. Out loped one of the tallest Nigerians Richard had ever seen. He wore the rank of Sergeant on his smartly pressed blue short sleeved shirt, his navy blue pants were pressed to knife edge precision and his boots shone with a brilliant shine. He was festooned with attachments; including badges, handcuffs, a radio, a truncheon and a side arm. However prolific this array of kit, they were all astonishingly neatly arranged, as if they belonged. Above the model uniform there was a strong, menacing bony face with piercing blue eyes. He dripped authority, he swaggered with confidence and he frightened the gathered work force, just by his presence.

The Sergeant was accompanied by an almost as smart Corporal, and an incongruously untidy plain-clothes man who was indistinguishable from any one of the workers. Amazingly the Sergeant's name was Jones. He spoke as crisply as he was dressed and listened with a great intensity.

Sergeant Jones by way of introduction asked;

"Do you know Hendon?... Mr. Smiles" The Mister was used much as a Sergeant-Major addressed a second lieutenant.

"Not really, - North London, not my neck of the woods really."

"I was there Meester Smiles, at the Police College, some three years ago."

"Oh, really, we can expect some slick detection from a London trained Bobby then." Quipped Smiles; immediately regretting his half-witted attempt at humor.

The Sergeant remained straight faced, "I was a Commonwealth Student at the Police College, I learned a great deal there, although things in Nigeria are different as no doubt you appreciate."

Richard had no idea what to say next so he asked, "Tell me isn't Jones an unusual name,"

The Sergeant's face stiffened, the eyes for the first time left their unwavering gaze. "History, history…. You must excuse me I must get on." He rose with a clatter, he smoothed his creases and loped away to terrorize his prey.

The taking of statements was a long process, as each word was laboriously written on the prescribed forms. The process rolled inexorably onward with several visits to the factory. The boss of the security firm was eventually found and denied strenuously any knowledge of the events. Amongst all those gathered he seemed to be at ease with the menacing Sergeant Jones. Even Ardebil, the delightfully obliging Chief Clerk was interrogated. The day passed into evening, how long could this go on?

Despite Richard's anxiety not to rock the boat, he burst into a conference between the Sergeant and his team. The sun was going down.

"Sergeant, don't you think it would be a good idea" he intoned, "to circulate the description of the goods to mobile units, who could inspect heavy goods vehicles? After all there's unlikely to be a load like it, three tons of aluminium troughed sheets, six foot long, twenty gauge." he paused, then more plaintively added, "Don't you think?"

"All in good time Sir.' the blue eyes, unlike any others, bore into him. Richard shuddered. "But you'll be pleased to know that we've finished for the day, you can be assured that we shall get to the bottom of this, Meestah Smiles." His smile was more of a leer. Richard could not wait to get home. What a day it had been.

At nine thirty on the following Monday the giraffe-like specter of Sergeant Jones followed by the same entourage arrived.

"It was an inside job." confided the Sergeant, with a conspiratorial air.

"Oh, really?" The sarcasm missed its mark.

The Sergeant explained that he and his team would interview all the staff, now that a full complement had shown up for Monday. He stated, somewhat ominously, that some individuals might be taken to the Police Post for "in depth" interviews "to extract detailed information". Richard wondered how long all this was going to take. He noted that there were a few absentees from the Saturday crew and dutifully passed the information to Jones. Smiles soon realized that no work would be completed that day since the police took no care or interest in who did what, but simply dragged staff in for interview in strictly alphabetical order.

Even more alarmingly, more and more staff seemed to be shipped down to the Police Post for "in depth" interviews and only a proportion returned, many nursing minor injuries.

Jones' interrogation techniques were apparently driven by his malevolent resolve to follow tribal rather than forensic clues. It became apparent that a high proportion of those who were taken to the Police Post sustained injuries; particularly to their fingers, many of which were bruised and broken.

The consequence for the factory was dire, not only was production sorely interrupted, but staff on sick leave escalated at an alarming rate, so that by the Wednesday there was no production at all. Richard, by this time, was beside himself with frustration and confusion. He somehow felt guilty about calling the police. He felt some paternal affection for some of those who were being abused by the dreaded Jones and his cronies and he was sure that some, at least, were nothing whatever to do with the theft.

On the Thursday, deep in depression and with only forty percent of key staff now available, for such was the fear of non-Hausa staff that many had run away, never to return, Richard resolved to speak to Jones' superior.

# CHAPTER 15

He arranged to meet with Inspector Ambe that afternoon. In his confusion he neglected to plan what to say. He felt vaguely that he could clear the air in some way and that in so doing; the excesses of Jones would be curtailed.

Kaduna South Police Compound was not a cheerful place. The buildings though were vaguely familiar and made him feel more at ease. They were military in nature, as a former National Service Junior Officer he gained some comfort from this. Sure, the place was not as spick and span as regimental HQ at home, but it was nonetheless reminiscent, being an open quadrangle of single story building with a veranda running along the front. To the front, inside the open rectangle; that had been used as a parade ground in earlier days, was a large car park. Off to one side in a barbed wire compound was the detention wing; this building was modern and built of concrete blocks, in stark contrast to the painted wooden walls of the main building. In front of the car park the flags of North Central State and Nigeria fluttered lazily side by side. The whole complex was much more military than a British police station and Richard felt a curiosity as he entered, despite his familiarity with things military, nevertheless, the navy blue and silver police crest and white painted stair treads gave a sense of order.

His comfort did not last long. The reception area was a shambles. There was no one on the desk, except, fleetingly a Sergeant, who made brief visits, always avoiding the gazes of the waiting throng. There were complainants, prisoners in handcuffs, there were what Richard assumed were lawyers, but there was no one, except the pimpernel-like Sergeant in charge. He had the happy knack of disappearing each and every time a visitor approached his desk

Driven more by impatience than courage; Smiles set off through the reception area and ventured into the corridor running the length of the building. He chose to go right and walked tentatively passed offices crammed with humanity and piles of paper. It was hard to decide which took up more space, the paper or the people. He traversed the corridor until it came to an end and, now encouraged by the lack of challenge, turned left and proceeded down the corridor, where the gradual hard changes; the closed windows, the bars all conspired to send shivers down his spine.

He stopped sharply and stood quite still. There it was again, the swish and strike of the cane, the thud of the strike on flesh and the muffled cry of the gagged victim. This was the custody wing. The darkness and foreboding dissolved into the hot darkness. As his eyes became accustomed to the half-light he saw the instruments of interrogation, bamboo cane and heavy leather belts piled carelessly at the custody gate. There it was again, the cane on flesh, the cry muffled and gagged, this time followed by a curse and what sounded like a laugh. He turned and fled back the way he had come. Just as he turned back into the main corridor he almost bumped into Jones.

"Mister Smiles, I was coming to fetch you." no longer the leer, but almost a nervous deference.

"I'm sorry." responded Richard, "I couldn't seem to get any help at the desk."

"May I ask where you have been?"

"Just here, just offices, just like police stations at home." said Richard airily.

"Well, this way please." Jones led off with his giraffe-like stride.

Richard was shaken. He somehow imagined that his interview with the Inspector would be without Jones' involvement, or knowledge even, why he thought that, he had no idea.

They retraced their steps passed reception and at the other end turned into a corridor that was altogether different. It was carpeted, the walls were clean and the doors were closed. On each door there was the neatly painted name of the occupant. They stopped at a door that was anointed with 'Inspector of Detectives' J.M.Ambe.

Jones knocked politely and without waiting, opened and ushered Richard into the presence of Inspector Ambe.

He could not have been more of a surprise. Where Jones was lean and sinister; Ambe was plump and homely. Where Jones leered, Ambe smiled warmly. Ambe was short and balding with a moustache that was graying. He looked like everyone's idea of Uncle Tom, warm and cuddly.

"Welcome, welcome." smiled the rotund Ambe as he shuffled round his desk, his hand outstretched in greeting. The handshake was strong and assured and Ambe looked Richard directly in the eye.

"It is most unfortunate," he continued, "that we should meet under these circumstances." He gestured to a seat in front of the desk. Jones sat in the other free chair which made Richard's heart sink. What could he say now? With the omni-present Jones there could be no airing of even the mildest concern.

Ambe sat back in his chair and motioned to Smiles to begin. Richard was, for a split second, unable to think of anything to say. He felt a bloody fool. What on earth was he doing here? He eyed Jones who'd reverted to his cocky sure self.

"Well, Inspector, as you say, this thing has been most unfortunate and I'm sure Sergeant Jones has filled you in on the details." he blustered. "Perhaps we should discuss progress and what our strategy should be to prevent any future recurrence." He paused for breath. 'What a load of baloney, I want that bugger Jones off the case.' he thought. No one was going to help. There was a pregnant silence.

After a moment of awkwardness, Ambe came to the rescue with an enthusiastic endorsement of Richard's hapless rationale.

"Sergeant Jones, have you anything to add for Mr. Smiles?"

"Not much at the moment, Sir, but we are confident that we shall catch the perpetrators and probably recover the goods. I'm sure Mr. Smiles is aware of the thoroughness of our investigation." He raised his eyebrows quizzically.

"Of course, of course." responded Richard with a feigned enthusiasm.

"What about helping the firm prevent any future thefts?" came back the affable Inspector.

"Well, Sir, could I suggest that your employment and recruitment standards are sustained at the highest levels, Mr. Smiles?" he grinned, "And you can never be sure who is going to be a viper in your nest, unless you are rigorous in your vetting procedures."

"Thank you for that. By the way is there any news of the stolen goods?"

"Not as yet, Sir, but we think we have a good chance to recover them. As you know, we are sure that this was an inside job and it will not be long before the perpetrators are brought to book." His look with those curious blue eyes was at once dismissive and vengeful.

Richard suddenly wanted to get out of there, he had offended Jones by naively going to his superior, and God knows what the consequences would be.

"Well, there we are Mr. Smiles." The Inspector waddled round his desk with his podgy hand extended in cursory farewell.

Richard still shocked with the sounds of the caning in his ears, Jesus what a place! Not even fit for the guilty, he sat in his car and stared across the bleak car park and at the wings that extended down each side. One with the avuncular Inspector and the legions of paper pushers; and the other where God knows what was going on. Law and order, god help them if this was the way, surely no one need be delivered up to this.

# CHAPTER 16

The Security man who had been on duty on the night of the theft had disappeared. The visits from the police became fewer. However, the staff were jittery and upset and a number could not do their jobs properly because of their broken fingers, which seemed the most common consequence of police interrogation. Smiles wanted desperately to shield his workers from the hideous treatment being meted out at the Police Station, but he was powerless to do so.

Usman Jalingo, the company agent, was the man to bring the first news of a breakthrough. Usman was an independent agent who sold goods to the remoter construction sites where smaller contracts and contractors were involved. Usman Jalingo was a fine big man with the biggest smile in Africa. Richard really held him in high affection and always enjoyed his visits. Not least amongst his attributes was his appearance, which was always impressive, his beautiful robes always spotless, adorning his gargantuan frame. Crowning this was an infectious grin, the ready smile and tangible warmth. When Usman spoke, Richard listened. He was reliable in every sense, he was always a good judge of local contractors' credit worthiness, he always delivered his sales quotas and he was always punctual, something of a rarity in Kaduna. Further, he was a gentleman by any standards. He was proud yet humble, he was articulate and a patient listener, he was physically massive but a gentle fellow. He was humorous but never at the expense of others. He was above all a devout Moslem who would pray at the appointed hour no matter what other matters were at hand and share the delights of his Holy days with his family and his Christian friends.

The Smiles household received choice parts of sacrificed goats on the appropriate Holy days. They were always received with delight, though Usman expected no thanks. He was planning to make Hajj that year and so he was very focused on achieving ambitious sales and income to fund his pilgrimage.

On this particular day Usman unusually, arrived without notice. He beamed his usual smile and announced,

"I have found the aluminium Sir. It is for sale in Kano in the market."

He had then gone and reported the matter to the Kano police and now it was for Richard and Jalingo to go to the Kaduna post and report the details.

As usual, things were not as easy as they might have been. Sergeant Jones was not available, 'not on seat' as the locals would have it. Inspector Ambe was likewise unavailable. However, the Duty Sergeant assured them that he would pass on the vital message. Not trusting to fate or the Duty Sergeant, Richard had typed duplicate messages for Jones and Ambe and had Adebayo deliver them without delay.

Usman returned to Kano, a drive of some one hundred and twenty miles, to keep an eye on things. 'Thank God for Usman' thought Richard, rather; thank Allah, he corrected himself.

# CHAPTER 17

The theft of the aluminium had become an almost total preoccupation for Richard, the affair gobbled up valuable time. The goods were recovered and retained as evidence by the Police. The dreaded Jones had demanded expenses to send men and vehicles to Kano to recover "the material evidence".

For some reason, that Richard could not even begin to understand, the Kano Merchant had not been arrested. According to Usman Jalingo, he had 'good' relationships with the Kano Police.

The investigation dragged on and on and eventually arrests were made. Two former employees who Richard did not know were detained and formal court proceedings would be undertaken by the Alkhali Court.

The Court, which was near the Police Post, was a Victorian building which had seen better days. The front of the building had an arched portico along its front, which had once been quite stately, but now was covered with a peeling dirty ochre wash. When the day of the trial eventually dawned Richard ventured into the lobbies that were akin to the traditional idea of a lunatic asylum. Richard arrived at the appointed hour of ten o' clock and after fighting through a scrum of bedlam proportions, eventually found an official who directed him to Court Number One.

After struggling through even more humanity he eventually caught sight of the head of the giraffe-like Jones above the crowd. For once he was glad to see the policeman despite his distaste for the fellow.

"I'm sorry to be late." said Richard anxiously glancing at his watch, which registered seven minutes past ten.

"We have a small delay." replied Jones, "Find a seat over there."

He pointed to a wooden bench against the wall. He continued to talk to his colleagues and it was as if Richard had not been there at all. Richard dutifully sat on the very edge of the already crowded bench, balancing painfully on one buttock. He was disinclined to push for more purchase since his fellow bench tenants appeared to be a group of thieves and cut-throats, who had body odors as noxious as their appearance. After five minutes of extreme discomfort, Richard could stand it no longer. It was incredibly hot, he was perspiring profusely and his nostrils were assailed with a variety of noxious smells that began to induce nausea. He also feared that he would be physically assaulted at any moment.

Sergeant Jones had disappeared into the crowd. Richard left alone in the crazy throng had no idea what to do next. Another fifteen minutes dragged by. He strolled or shuffled back and forth, keeping the Court entrance in sight. It was now unbearably hot. Richard took off his tie and wanted desperately to get outside away from the insufferable stinking heat and clamor, but he dared not move from the spot.

"Mr. Smiles," it was Eke.

"Thank God, what the hell's going on? Its eleven fifteen and I have absolutely no idea what the hell is happening."

"The Court is behind in its business." said Eke disinterestedly, "They will tell us when they are ready."

"And when, if you please, will that be?"

"Who knows Sah? We will have to wait and see."

Twelve o'clock and Richard was beside himself with frustration and discomfort, - Twelve thirty – "Bugger this Eke!" exclaimed Richard, "Eke find that fucking policeman and tell him we're going back to the office. He can call us when he's ready."

"I beg you Sah, you must be patient." urged Eke, "I will try to find out what is going on, please wait there Sah."

With that he dashed into the crowd and was swallowed up.

Richard was left to curse and swear and to suffer from his own impatience. He wanted desperately to relieve himself and necessity being the mother of invention; he found his way to the public lavatory. The experience did nothing for his humor; he almost gagged as he straddled the Moslem toilet. The stink of a thousand bladders and the droppings of a thousand unwashed males were tough to take.

The relief was in the escape and as he moved back to the front of Number One Court, he felt that all suffering was relative. He resolved that no matter what; he would avoid those dreadful bogs, come what may. He would prepare, he wouldn't eat, he wouldn't drink and then he wouldn't need the bog. As he leant against the wall as one of the heaving mob, he closed his eyes, 'it can't get any worse than this' he inwardly prayed. But it could.

As if from nowhere, Sergeant Jones materialized at his side.

"The Court has broken for lunch." he smiled, "We must be back here at two o'clock. I'm sure you will be required shortly after that Mr. Smiles, so don't be late." and with that he slid back into the rapidly diminishing crowd.

Eke arrived a moment later with the same news. Richard drew a sigh of relief that at least they would be out of that hell hole, if only for an hour or so.

At two o'clock precisely, Richard resplendent in clean shirt and fresh pants, arrived refreshed and ready to give evidence. Eke was similarly prompt, but it was almost immediately clear that they were practically alone. Gone were the crowds of the morning. Activity seemed at a low ebb and the scarcity of policemen and Court officials did nothing to reassure them.

"Eke," snarled Richard, "I don't bloody believe this, that son of a bitch Jones is just pissing us around. There's no bugger here except us. What in the hell is he playing at?"

"Perhaps we should remain patient." replied Eke.

"Patient, you have to be bloody kidding. For Christ's sake we've wasted practically a whole day for bugger all. It's nearly a quarter past two, where the hell is every body?"

He stamped his foot petulantly, Eke looked away with embarrassment. No sooner had the words fallen from his lips than suddenly a tide of humanity flowed into the concourse and in the twinkling of an eye the bedlam of the morning was restored, albeit fifteen minutes behind schedule.

At twenty past two Sergeant Jones smirking his slimiest smile, "I'm sorry for this short delay," he said sounding pleased, "I'm assured that the preceding case has been wrapped up and that we will get underway soon."

Richard could only muster a nod, a dumb sign of assent, he was afraid to say anything, lest he should regret it.

At two forty five the case was called, Richard and Eke followed the melee into the courtroom where the Alkhali or Magistrate was dressed in an African agdaba with a scarlet fez type head gear. Richard thought the magistrate looked rather exotic. No sooner had they sat down when the Alkhali pointed at Richard and Eke and enquired of the prosecuting officer Jones as to their identities. There was some whispering at the bench, then the Alkhali asked Richard and any other witnesses to leave the court until after they had given their evidence.

Eke, followed by Richard, self consciously slid along the bench where they had perched and walked conspicuously along the wooden floor, towards the door from whence they had come not five minutes before. Eke seemed to have silent rubber shoes, whereas the sound of Richard's English leather brogues echoed, it seemed, throughout the length and breadth of Kaduna. They left the courtroom to wait in their allotted place, a filthy little room almost knee deep in rubbish, with the sign "witnesses" hanging vertically on its nail beneath the cracked frosted glass in the top half of the door.

As they sat on the bench in their new place of trial, Richard mumbled to Eke, "This has to be some sort of bad joke, how long do we have to wait? This is driving me barmy."

Eke grimaced, "Please be patient Sah, it will not be long now Sah. I beg you to be patient."

Richard took a deep breath, reined in his curses and accepted as best he could the advice of his excellent subordinate.

At three fifteen, pandemonium broke out as the court doors were flung open and the people poured out. Richard rushed to the door and couldn't believe his eyes. The only person he could see was the dreaded Jones. However, emboldened by his now long lost temper he stormed into the courtroom where the Sergeant at the prosecution desk, stood chatting to colleagues. The Alkhali and all other court officers were nowhere to be seen.

"For Christ's sake Jones, what the hell is going on?"

"Ah, Mr. Smiles, the Alkhali has decided that it is too late to start a new case today and requests, Sir" he spat the word, and continued, "that we start again at ten o'clock sharp in the morning. You will be aware that your summons to appear remains in effect and that we shall expect to see you on time."

He smiled his most threatening smile and Richard shivered. Richard said nothing as he turned on his heel and left the court building for the Golf Club and the bar. Tomorrow would be another day.

The following day, Richard was called to give evidence at ten forty five. He simply repeated what he recalled, and attested to the description, quantity and value of the stolen goods.

He was offered the Bible or the Holy Koran on which to swear his oath.

Sergeant Jones was the prosecutor in this lower court. He fixed Richard with his icy stare and lead him through his testimony all of which was factual and unexciting. Despite the simplicity of his testimony; the whole encounter was recorded in the laborious hand of the Alkhali. There were long gaps between each question and answer, Richard kept wondering off and imagined the suffering of the two wretched accused. The Clerk duplicated everything, also at a snail's pace so that it was an hour and forty-five minutes before Richard had finished.

As he prepared to leave the witness box he could not help but feel sorry for the prisoners in the dock. They seemed to have suffered multiple unpleasant injuries. He did not recognize them since they had apparently been dismissed just about the time that Richard had arrived in Kaduna. Despite all that, he could not bring himself to believe that these two lowly operatives could have masterminded the considerable logistical organization involved in the theft and movement of the aluminium.

'May I make a statement to the court, Sir?' he heard himself say.

The Alkhali, who had not finished writing the previous evidence, seemed to take no notice and continued to write. After an embarrassing interminable two minutes of absolute silence the Alkhali smiled broadly at Richard and nodded his assent.

"With respect to the court Sir, and the excellent efforts of the Prosecuting Officer, I believe justice would be best served if the receiver of the stolen goods and the security guards who were present during the removal of the goods, were called to account, Sir."

"Thank you" smiled the Alkhali, "You may go."

Richard left the building muttering his utter disbelief at the whole episode. The irrelevance of it all, the poor buggers in the dock probably had little if anything to do with the crime, but they belonged to the wrong tribe. They were just two 'wackers' one about twenty the other older, perhaps forty. It was always difficult for Richard to judge age since many lived such hard and deprived life styles. The younger looked forlorn and utterly bemused. What struck Richard most was the look of utter resignation and defeat that was etched into the young face. The older man was more belligerent, he had fight in him, but even he was dispossessed of any articulate defense. They were a sad pair miserable and probably innocent. One thing was for sure; being in Police custody seriously damaged your health.

# CHAPTER 18

As the business of the court case receded into the mysteries of the local judicial system Richard slogged his way through the ever-hotter spring, with Adebayo at his side, more accurately at the wheel as they covered thousands of miles of the North. Richard's obsession with success meant that the work rate was high, the miles almost doubled by the need to get home each night to the family.

Adebayo was a stocky round man with a slightly crippled gait. He was at least fifty and his head was close cropped with tight grey springy hair. He smiled habitually, but was seldom drawn to conversation. He was not articulate in any way and his English was poor, he swallowed his words and mumbled pidgin at a breakneck speed. He almost fell over himself to please, his devotion was without reserve. Unlike Joseph he was always clean and well turned out, he kept his uniforms cleaned and pressed; he was a smart proud and well presented driver.

Adebayo took it all, the work and the miles in his stride. Since that first moment when Richard tried but failed to make a handshake, Adebayo had been cheerful reliability itself. The car was always shining reflecting his pride and joy. He adored the Mastah's family and nothing gave him more pleasure than to take the Madame shopping or drop off Daaveed at the nursery school. Richard had developed a fondness for his driver, he was not an imp like Joseph, and he was more of a friend on whom you could absolutely depend.

Adebayo returned to the factory after yet another early morning dash from Sokoto, routine in itself, but obviously a tiring experience for Adebayo. As normal, when not on driving duties, he did odd jobs for Eke. So, having assured Richard that he was not too tired he disappeared into the factory.

Some half an hour elapsed before an agitated Eke burst into Smiles' office; half shouting, half spluttering, "Adebayo, he is dead! Sah!"

"What's the matter, dead, what do you mean dead?"

Smiles leapt and pushed Eke to turn about and get to the scene of the drama. They rushed back into the factory where they found Adebayo prone on the factory floor. The majority of the shift surrounded him at a distance. There was much "ooing and aah-ing" but no one was rendering any assistance to the poor Adebayo. Although not familiar with epilepsy, Richard had encountered it once at school. He immediately recalled the convulsions, the grinding of the jaw and the rolling eyes. At once he recalled the symptoms and felt also sadness for Adebayo, so vulnerable, so humiliated in the sight of his peers. He set down on his haunches, took Adebayo's head gently and asked Eke to get a pillow or something to make his driver more comfortable.

However nobody moved in response. Instead they mumbled concern "Master, get back," they cried, "it is the bad ju-ju."

"Get a bloody blanket, now. Eke, move your arse." He shouted angrily.

Adebayo's convulsions subsided. As blood and saliva frothed from his mouth, the workers became more agitated and again urged Smiles to get away from the "bad ju-ju". Richard mopped away the blood and saliva, cradled Adebayo gently onto the makeshift pillow and watched with sadness as dear Adebayo pissed himself and the pool of urine flowed over the factory floor. The group surrounding them gaped, he looked up, and was angry. He didn't know why, he was just sad and angry at the same time.

"Go on, bugger off back to work. Go on, bugger off."

But they stood transfixed by the drama, were they waiting for Richard to be struck down by the "ju-ju".

"Go on, bugger off.'" he said with a resigned but quieter voice, "Come on Eke, help me get the poor sod tidied up."

Reluctantly Eke stepped forward and helped Richard to get the groggy Adebayo to his feet. They helped him to the sanctuary of Eke's office, where he gradually came to. His tongue was badly damaged, but otherwise he seemed to be unharmed. Eke was sent to get clean overalls, and Richard got the still dazed and confused driver some water.

"We'd better get you to the doctor." smiled Richard, and with that he went to get the car. As soon as he pulled up at the factory door, Adebayo stood groggily and made for the driver's door.

"Not this time. It's time for the boss to drive you."

Despite his protests Adebayo was coaxed into the front seat and driven to the clinic of the ubiquitous Doctor Eli. As they drove, Richard felt for Adebayo who was immensely proud of his job as the Boss's driver, which was minutes from coming to an end.

Dr Eli confirmed, subject to further tests, that Adebayo had suffered from an epileptic fit. Indeed, Adebayo reluctantly admitted that such episodes had happened before and so it fell to Richard to tell Adebayo that he would no longer be the Boss's driver. He explained that as a consequence of the illness he would not drive for at least a year or two.

Adebayo listened, slowly comprehending as tears came to his eyes, he mumbled downcast "It is bad ju-ju, maybe it will go away and I can work for you and the Madame."

"You will go home and rest, then when you feel better you can come back to the factory and work for Mr. Eke, no problem same pay, same take home pay." Replied Richard, "This is not ju-ju this is an illness, and Doctor Eli, he will make you okay. This illness happens to white people, black people, and yellow people in fact every people. Not juju my friend, just an illness that if you do what the doctor tell you, you will be fine."

"I will be your driver Sah?" he looked imploringly at his boss.

"Well no, not for a while anyway, but I don't want you to worry about that, you make sure that you take the medicine from Doctor Eli, then you have no more fall over, okay?"

"So, so, sorry Sah."

"Don't be sorry, get well. You must take the medicine daily, every day, you understand?"

"Yes Sah."

"Off you go. Come back to start your new job, maybe tomorrow if you feel okay." he stammered, "Madame say you must be good and do what Doctor Eli say, okay?.."

Adebayo crest fallen, but reassured by the same 'take home pay', went hiding his shame as best he could, skirting the factory and slipping away to his family.

They all missed Adebayo, the reluctant search for his replacement was pursued without enthusiasm, drivers came and drivers went. There was 'Clever', tall and gangly who seemed to be permanently asleep. During his short sojourn he was seldom on time, never washed the car and was always 'somewhere else' when he was needed.

Julian fared no better, true he was more reliable, but two trips to Kano persuaded Richard that his prospects of survival were short enough. Julian should have been born a rich Brazilian, and become a grand prix driver. He was none of these things and far too dangerous to remain as the family chauffeur.

At last there came Mohamed, on the recommendation of the splendid Usman Jalingo and another family friendship was established.

As the summer advanced, so the heat oppressed the Smiles household. Young David's sojourns in the garden became less frequent and of shorter durations. Tempers became frayed at home and at work. Joan got larger by the day and the baby she carried became more boisterous.

In May, as ever on a Saturday morning, news of a fresh disaster reached the Smiles household. Richard was filling David's miniature swimming pool in the garden when the works van screamed up to the house and a hysterical driver leapt from the cab yelling;

"Mbamane Sah, he is fatally injured Sah!"

"You mean he's dying? What the hell happened?"

"No Sah! He is dragged into the roll former Sah!"

Richard was already on the move, dropping the screaming David into his half empty pool and dashing to the house for car keys. At the same time as he barked orders to Joan to ensure an ambulance was on its way to the works, he leapt into the car and was away at speed. She as ever with cool deliberation did as she thought necessary.

The scene at the factory was hellish. Workers gathered round the scene some covered with the blood of the victim, some incanting tribal spells others staring transfixed at the horror before them   The poor man was hanging by his mangled arm quite unconscious and near death. Eke, who had been absent on an errand during the critical time, was in charge of releasing the victim from the embrace of the machine.   Blood was everywhere and it was obvious that Mbamane had lost critical quantities. After steadying himself, Richard let Eke continue to work as delicately as he could to loosen the grip of the machine, whilst he organized a table from the works office to be put under Mbamane to support his torso. The blood pumped, albeit weakly, from the gaping tear in his armpit and Richard rushed to the first aid kit to try to find a dressing to staunch the flow.

The wailing continued, desperately Richard and Eke struggled;

"For Christ's sake Eke get two blokes to help support the weight."

The gangly Peter came forward and immediately he was helped by two other colleagues.

The ambulance arrived quite soon after they'd managed to release Mbamane from the machine and the paramedics were surprisingly efficient and caring in giving first aid and getting the injured man away to hospital. Richard and Eke listened to the tale of what had happened. Mbamane was finishing the alignment after a tool change when his shirtsleeve caught on a test sheet he was manually feeding into the machine. The rest was gruesome history. They set about locking the stable door, but both Eke and Richard were sorely chastened.

Richard returned home depressed and filthy with the oil of the machine and Mbamane's blood soaked into his shirt. He sank into Joan's arms and wept.

Richard visited the poor man in hospital and was somewhat shaken by what he saw. The wards were very crowded and it was hard to recognize who were patients and who were attending families. The rooms were littered with pots, pans, and all manner of household items, as the relatives provided food and victuals for their relatives.

His first problem was to find where Mbamane was. There was a sort of reception area, an open court, with the odd desk, but none of them attended. It was, he supposed, because it was Saturday. It made him feel like an interloper, wondering around aimlessly, into the suffering of these private people.

The Ahead Bello Hospital was a modern hospital and the largest in the north. The buildings spread over a large area and accommodated a large number of beds. Richard tentatively wondered around the massive buildings with its mile after mile of corridor. He asked several nurses where to find Mbamane but none offered any sensible help.

After some twenty-five minutes he was almost ready to give up the search. He was tired of hiding the ridiculous gifts of fruit and grapes. What he should have brought was bread, tins of sardines, towels and cash for supplies. What good were grapes if he was dead?

"What's a Goddamn Brit doing in a joint like this?"

The gruff Canadian drawl of Professor Keith Coker, gynaecologist extraordinary, senior voluntary service specialist and fellow Rotarian boomed. He had his usual cigar clenched between his teeth, his white coat was stained with blood and his pockets were stuffed with notebooks, pencils, stethoscope and other various bits of medical kit.

"Am I glad to see you." Richard shook hands and quickly explained his presence at the hospital.

"This your first time here?" he smiled.

"Yes it is, a bit bewildering I must say. All life is here." Richard mused.

"And death too, too goddamn much of it. So much of it, so bloody unnecessary. Anyway let's see if we can find your chum. Let's hope he's not in the morgue"

With a huge puff of smoke from his cigar he set off at pace. They traveled at speed through the corridors that seemed more like a railway station than a hospital. People were everywhere; bags and baggage were strewn willy-nilly. The variety of possession was amazing. Pots and pans, blankets, tins of food, packets of fresh vegetables and fruit, clothes of all sizes and shapes, shoes, kettles, primus stoves, gourds and bottles.

Coker, his white coat billowing after him, his cigar occasionally blasting off a plume of exhaust, cursed and swore violently as he swept on; Richard scurried almost running, in his efforts to stay in touch.

"It's like this every god damn weekend. Security will kick these characters out into the car park tomorrow, but they or their successors will be back in next Saturday the moment the god damn Security Department scales down for the weekend. It's God damn chaos and bloody unsanitary, you've no god damn idea." He stopped, without warning, Richard almost running into his back. "We gotta build these people a shelter so they can rest. Now you've seen the god damn mess you can support the idea as a local project in Rotary, okay?"

"Sure, absolutely." replied the bemused Richard.

"See, these people have come from miles around, the patients rely on their relatives to bring them food and all sorts of support. This is not like Canada or England, these are rural peasant people in the main, obviously some local townies, but they ain't sophisticated and the hospital can't afford to feed and nurse like you and I would expect. No sooner have I operated on some poor broad, than she contracts an infection, which keeps the mortality rate so high here. God damn it, it's all so bloody avoidable. It's not doctoring skills they need; they've got some good guys going through. Its nursing and hygiene skills that could save thousands of lives. Shit, I'm sorry I'm preaching again. Let's go and find your buddy."

"There's only one person I know who'll be able to track him down and that's Mighty Mouse. She's a god damn marvel you'll see."

Mighty Mouse turned out to be the Assistant Matron Maidaribi, a petite attractive forty something. She positively sparkled in her sharp blue starched uniform. From her headdress to her shoes every item of her dress was perfect. She had an elegant and attractive head, her teeth shone, not a hair was out of place. Her hands were beautifully manicured.

Coker crashed into her imperfect office, which by contrast to the Assistant Matron's personal appearance certainly showed signs of mortal stress. Her desk was covered with pieces of paper and files, they were stacked in some sort of order but the sheer number was overwhelming.

"Mighty One, I bring you a suppliant." cracked the smoke enveloped Coker.

"Out with that foul cigar, Professor, or you'll get no help here!" she shooed him with mock waving one of her many files.

Richard stood back, not knowing what to make of it all.

Maidaribi saw him, put down her mock weapon and smiled a dazzling smile, "Oh, I'm sorry, please don't mind the Professor, he's a dear really, please how can I help?"

Coker didn't wait for Richard to speak, he just waded in with the facts as he saw them. They were largely inaccurate, but Richard felt unable to interrupt. When the Professor had finished Maidaribi patiently took the details again, this time from Richard. She consulted one of the many documents on her desk and selected one without hesitation and nodded.

"Your man has come out of surgery. He was very ill, but at the last report he seemed to be holding his own. I don't think he'll be fit to receive visitors yet, but we'll go and see and I'll show you the lie of the land."

"Another one of God's dramas solved by Mighty Mouse" cracked Crocker, "I'd better get cleaned up and go and enjoy the rest of my weekend." He slapped Richard heartily on the back and exited, magically re-igniting his cigar by a vigorous inhalation.

Mighty Mouse took a moment to adjust some papers on her desk and led Richard away after locking her office. On their walk down to the High Dependency Unit she explained the strengths and weaknesses of the hospital as she saw them. She had been trained in London and had returned to Kaduna after fifteen years working in St Mary's. She'd ended up as a Senior Sister (Theatre) and had come back as Assistant Matron on the invitation of her Grandfather who was by all accounts a heavy mover in northern Nigerian politics. She didn't comment as to whether she was glad she'd returned other than to say 'these are my people and they need us.' Richard assumed that "us" meant those who'd had the benefit of education and training.

Richard was not allowed to see Mbamane. Mighty Mouse went into the HDU after gowning up and returned after about five minutes. Mbamane was indeed holding his own, the surgery to put his arm and shoulder together had been arduous and long, but the surgeon had been reasonably satisfied. She was clear, however, that he would for evermore be crippled and be, effectively, one armed. It was too early to say how long the convalescence would be or if he would continue to mend.

"This is not England Mr. Smiles. There will be no follow up surgical procedures, there will be some rudimentary physiotherapy if Mbamane can make the appointments, but he probably won't. The only person who's going to be able to make a difference in a constructive way is his employer," she turned and looked right into his eyes, "you, Mr. Smiles, you can make a difference."

"Anyway come back tomorrow. If all is well Mbamane will be in surgical ward six." She turned, took his hand in her perfectly manicured gentle hand, and shook it with surprising firmness, "If there's anything else I can do, please let me know." She smiled her brilliant smile and walked smartly away.

Richard made his way back through the maze of corridors towards the exit, still clutching his pathetic gifts. He stopped and saw a small child in a ragged nightie leaning at a ward entrance. She sucked her thumb and mucous ran from her nose. Her skin was grey and her eyes dull. Richard thrust the food at her, she was startled and began to wail, so Richard put the packets of fruit and grapes on the floor and made a hasty escape.

The following day, Sunday, Richard accompanied by Joan, made their way back to the hospital armed this time with more appropriate food and supplies. They arrived at the hospital and fought their way through the hawkers into the main building and towards surgical ward six.

The chaos took Joan by surprise, more for the contrast against the Mission Hospital where she was to have her baby than anything else. After several false starts they eventually found the surgical ward where the unfortunate Mbamane lay; enclosed behind screens, in amongst the shambles that passed for the male surgical ward.

It was not the ward that was so chaotic; it was the attendant relatives who outnumbered the patients by around six to one. These relatives, furthermore, did not seem to be behaving as if they were visitors. It was obvious that they were there to stay. They had their household goods and chattels to prove it. The smell in the ward was appalling; there was rottenness, a stink, of urine, excreta, and disinfectant. It was all they could do to contain their nausea.

Mbamane was obviously extremely ill; his color had that paleness that implies a close brush with the Grim Reaper. His lips were caked dry, he had several tubes running from his good arm and he was wrapped in graying sheets.

Mbabane barely acknowledged their presence. Richard made small talk and comforting noises about the firm not forgetting its own. Joan quietly made him more comfortable; both tried to avert their eyes from the blood soaked plaster of Paris that encased half his body.

Joan went off in search of the ward sister who eventually emerged from another patient in dire straights behind another screen. She was large and jolly, seemed quite efficient and was happy to advise them as to what the support requirements would be. She confided that she was concerned that the bleeding in side the plaster continued and that it might be necessary to strip the plaster and stop it directly. This procedure would be 'hard, very hard for Mbabane'.

They took their leave after about half an hour and Mbabamane seemed relieved to see them go. They would revisit in the afternoon and from Monday Richard would ensure that a support group would be set up at work.

Mbabane survived through the Sunday and the bleeding stopped and when Richard made his third visit of the day the patient seemed to be substantially improved.

On the Monday morning first thing, Richard sent for Eke and they settled on two items, prevention and how to look after Mbabamane.

Eke was curiously disinterested in the Mbabane's care programme.

"I cannot go and see him," he stated with finality, "he is not of my people."

"Eke, for Christ's sake don't talk bollocks. He's one of our people, he works here, and if it wasn't for our corporate negligence the poor bugger wouldn't be in the awful bloody mess he's in now!"

Eke remained obdurate, "You do not understand our ways Mr. Smiles, his people will look after him."

"He hasn't got any people; they're all in his village God knows where, now bloody well sort it out. I want him visited by somebody responsible once, preferably twice, a day, and I want to see that all his needs are met. Am I being clear?"

"I will send Gabriel, Sah," replied Eke, "he is one of Mbamane's people."

"Are you fucking deaf, Mr. Eke? I said someone responsible, which means you, Adegbulu, or me. Don't give me all this tribal ju-ju shit, I've had all I can take. This lad works for me and you. We are responsible. I don't give a fuck if he's a Martian, do I make myself clear? We, me, you, we look after him. Do you understand?"

Richard's voice had now reached screaming pitch and the whole office sat in shocked silence.

Eke shifted uneasily, "It is not our way, but I understand you Mr. Smiles. I will do as you say and see that all is carried out." with that he walked head bowed from the office.

# CHAPTER 19

As May passed oppressively into June, Joan and Richard looked forward with eagerness to the birth of their second child. They both involved David by encouraging him to listen and feel the ever more boisterous goings on in his Mummy's tummy.

The heat bore down on them, but despite this hostile environment Joan, in her eighth month of pregnancy, seemed to bear up best. Richard as ever was going through the trials and tribulations at the factory and continued putting more pressure on himself by ensuring that he never stayed away from home overnight. Thus he spent long days with Mohamed driving huge distances to Kano and beyond, returning always to Galadima Road. Despite Joan's protests and assurances of support from the Hetherington's he insisted on this arduous regime, come what may.

The heat seemed to affect the natives just as much as the expats. Things at the factory became fractious and in the city the instances of sectarian violence increased. There had been an announcement that Emperor Haille Sallassie was to visit northern Nigeria. There was to be a great Durbar, when the warriors of the Fula and Hausa nations would show their prowess as fighting men and their noble traditions of horsemanship. This news reaffirmed the Moslem consciousness; southerners approached the city with caution. The Hausa and their allies were on the march to glory again.

During early May an unwary Yoruba businessman strayed from the commercial centre. He walked into a mainly Hausa residential area, parallel to the main road, Amador Bello Way, it was about the middle of the day.

On the street corner a group of young Hausa children playing under the supervision of their aged Grandma. In the oppressive heat she dosed in her chair, and from time to time checked on the little ones. It was hot and her dose wafted into sleep. It was some minutes later and then she woke with a start as her head fell to her ample chest. She looked around and to her dismay the children were no longer there.

What was there, was the Yoruba man. She knew how wicked these men could be and that they sometimes spirited children away for evil juju. She checked momentarily and could not see the children anywhere. She found it hard at her age to rise from her chair, so she shouted for help. The Yoruba man heard her and crossed the street towards her, presumably to lend the old lady assistance.

Her reaction to the approaching menace was to scream more hysterically, this time attracting the attention of some young bloods who were till then standing idly by. She shouted to the effect that the Yoruba man had stolen the children.

The Yoruba turned and ran hurriedly away, only to be caught and punched and kicked to the ground by the young thugs.

Now a mob quickly assembled and the hysteria grew. The Yoruba now lay defensively curled in the foetal position on the dusty road. The growing mob rained blows with their feet, with sticks, with anything they could lay their hands on. Bloodstains began to well through the once smart blue robes and the smart leather briefcase was trampled in the dust.

A passing T.V. camera crew pulled up and began to film the horrors; the gluttony of violence increased in frenzy, until someone poured gasoline over the barely conscious Yoruba and with glee set the defenseless man on fire.

The victim seemed to come frantically alive as he danced his way to death which, was all too slow in coming.

The mob became quiet. The dead torso stank in the midday sun. People began to slide away from the fringes of the mob. The screaming had halted. There was an uncanny silence. Still the T.V. crew filmed on.

More people now came to look and to talk over the dreadful scene; the old Grandma gathered her grandchildren about her and warned them of the dangers of bad ju-ju from people of other tribes. She tut-tutted and shepherded her charges into the safety of her house.

It was an hour or more before the police arrived from the nearest police station a good quarter of a mile away.

That night the whole grizzly affair was shown on the local T.V. news. There was no editing; the event was shown in every gory detail.

The Smiles', like many others, were horrified. Joan broke down, overwhelmed by both horror and terror, few could hide their distress.

Joseph though was more philosophical, "He was probably a bad man Sah!" was his only comment as he went on serving David's evening meal, as if nothing of any importance had happened at all.

Joan rushed from the living room, sweeping David up in her arms. They disappeared to the bedroom, David bemused by the happenings, demanding the remains of his evening meal. Richard followed and found Joan weeping uncontrollably and being consoled by her two-year-old son.

"How could they, how could they?" she wailed, "How could these people, so kind to David and their children turn so easily to slaughter. Let's go home." she implored.

She got up from the bed and started throwing down cases and throwing clothes in any order anywhere. Richard watched silently and waited for the emotional storm to subside.

He said nothing for there was nothing to say. They would never, could never, understand.

How could Eke decline to help his subordinates? 'Because they are not of my people.' the words came echoing back, 'Because they are not of my people.'

Despite Joan's protests the evening's program was brought back to order. The cases were put back, the clothes carefully re-stored. David was allowed to finish his supper and he was put to bed. They dressed and departed at the appointed hour for dinner with friends at the Club.

There may have been murders and mayhem but the Club was unchanged. The usual crowd was assembled at the bar. The talk was of the horror of the day;

"Bloody poor show!"

"What do you expect?" Whined Jack Walker, "bloody savages."

"It makes you think."

"We've seen it all before."

"Who cares, as long as it's amongst them, eh?"

Joan was visibly upset; Richard held her hand under the table, communicating silently a prayer for restraint. Sally Hetherington seemed likewise threatened and soon collected Joan and they fled to the shelter of the ladies room. They returned; some pact in place and sat down again, both demanding a double gin and tonic.

There seemed to be a two-tier group, those aware and those not. Those who were here to achieve; and those who were here to sponge; those who were here to learn; and those who were here to order people about because no one would listen to them at home in England. It was depressing. Both Richard and Joan felt the draught of discomfort blow through their hearts.

At home later they lay side-by-side, stroking and comforting each other.

"What the hell are we doing here?" muttered Richard.

"Right now," replied Joan, "I'm having a baby and that's all that matters"

"What do you want my love? It'll be better for you after the baby's here, stay on here for a couple of years?" There was a silence, just the buzzing of the air conditioner. "You know, I love the job, I like my people, and I really enjoy it."

"'What do you mean? 'Your people', they're not your people, you sound like those idiots down at the Club"

"Oh come on, Joanie, you know what I mean, I think we're doing a good job. We've created ten more jobs since I started, wages and bonuses are up and I think people trust each other more."

"God's gift to Africa's development, smarty pants." Quipped Joan.

"I'm buggered if I know what to think"

"I know what I don't like." said Joan, emphasizing the 'don't', "I don't like some of those sneering half witted ex-patriots. You can't blame the locals from branding us all prats."

"Some of our chums are okay." he replied defensively.

"Yes, some; Malcolm and Sally, the Marshall's, one or two others, but you can have the rest." she said with determination. "It's time for us two to go to sleep" she said turning slowly from his embrace. "Good night. I love you. I hope you didn't drink too much beer and disturb us all night" and with that she was asleep.

Richard listened to her gently snoring, and loved her very much. "God bless you both and God bless this crazy bloody country." He slid into the depths of a deep sleep where bodies burned in the streets.

# CHAPTER 20

The days that followed were patient, waiting days; the baby was due on the 21st of the month. Joan retained her bloom though and seemed to enjoy her daily visits to the Kikuri Mission Hospital and the gentle, but practical ministrations of the Nursing Sisters of Mercy.

The hospital was run and managed firmly and efficiently by Sister Theresa, a large bony woman who, despite her gargantuan gait, had the kindest humor, a lovely Irish lilt to her voice and twinkling blue eyes. She was obviously in charge. Her staff responded instantly to her directives but always with good humor.

The place had two large public wards, one female the other male and fifteen private wards, either double or single occupancy. The place was a great contrast to the Amhado Bello Hospital, since visitors were strictly controlled, there were no hawkers or traders, no litter; and there prevailed a general air of cleanliness and order.

Primarily two further Irish nursing sisters, one Sister Bee, a midwife, and Sister Ruth, a theatre specialist, assisted Sister Theresa. There were a number of locally trained nurses who seemed to compare well with their colleagues at the main hospital.

The senior medical staff was drawn from the local medical fraternity who gave of their time freely to the public ward patients but reaped a fair return for attending the private patients.

Doctor Hamdi, an Egyptian of quiet calm, efficient manner and sexy blue eyes had medically supervised Joan through the latter days of her pregnancy. Dr. Eli had kept a fatherly eye on developments and all assured the Smiles' that the delivery in Kaduna would be secure.

Sister Beatrice, or Bee as she was known, was short stocky and bright. She always made light of any problem, constantly made little jokes in the face of adversity and ended every consultation with the expression; 'Everything is fine, God is looking after us, surely he is.' Always followed by a laugh, of almost intoxicated merriment. It was impossible to leave a session with Bee without feeling better and more confident than before.

As the heavy leaden days of June passed, Richard and David seemed much more stressed than the mother-to-be. The 21st was to be a Friday and as the day drew near Richard could not help but ask at ridiculously close intervals; 'Any sign yet?' He fussed, Joseph fussed and David became cross and vexatious. He was fed up. He declined to take his seat at lunch and marched in protest to play with his pal Mussa in the garden, at least there, he'd get some attention.

Joan ensured that he had his sun hat on and smiled an indulgent smile and cuddled her first born. She wished secretly that Richard would go and play somewhere else too, if only he would stop fussing.

The 21st came and went, the 22nd dawned hot and oppressive, again only Joan seemed relaxed and in control. The sun climbed and as each lazy leaden stepping hour passed Richard fidgeted and David whined, since he knew it was Saturday and Mussa would go home at lunchtime.

After lunch, Richard suddenly announced "Bugger this darling. How about going to the Polo Club? It'll keep David amused. I think there's a match on today. I can have a beer and all those guys jogging up and down on horse back might inspire our second born to make an appearance."

"Good idea," said Joan, "let's get organized and go."

On arrival at the Polo Club there was much hullabaloo, policemen and soldiers everywhere. They drove to the members' entrance; where, much to Richard's annoyance, a police asked to see his non-existent members' entry pass. Fortunately Eduardo Cerrutti, an acquaintance from the business and also Captain of the Club, was at hand to facilitate entry.

Richard shepherded Joan to a corner of the veranda and ordered drinks for them all. As he sat he began to realize that there was an event out of the ordinary happening that accounted for all the unusual security.

It was not just the State Governor who was visiting; it was none other than General Gowon the Head of State of the Nigerian Federation.

As the Smiles family settled into their corner with their drinks, the official party came out of the dining area and walked toward them. There was a body of at least ten people including the State Governor and several hangers-on. To the huge consternation of the Smiles', General Gowon broke ranks and walked directly to them. He was a handsome dapper man, smartly dressed in civilian clothes of exquisite cut.

He nodded to Richard who bolted to attention with indecent haste. The General smiled and turned to Joan and David, who was unimpressed and chose that moment to spill his lemon drink all over the chair.

"Dear Lady, when can Nigeria expect another brother or sister?" he asked politely, "Please don't get up."

"Today, actually." beamed back Joan.

"Oh my goodness!" the General almost, but not quite, took a step back, "Good luck to you."

He turned to Richard, at the same time ruffling David's blonde hair, "Look after her my friend. I hope you feel at home here in Nigeria."

"Thank you, Sir." stammered Richard.

With that the General and his entourage swept on to the grand stand.

They sat in silence for a short while, "Well, he seemed a nice bloke." whispered Richard.

'He's gorgeous, you're lucky I'm in this state, you silly sod, or you never know, he's absolutely gorgeous. Come on let's go and watch some polo.'

The polo was so-so. Richard never really understood the game. Some players seemed wonderfully skilled and their ponies magnificent, whilst others seemed rather hopeless. It looked a dangerous and tough business, but to Richard it mattered not a jot.

As if from nowhere Sally Henderson cruised into view "You cunning little harlot." she crooned, "How'd you manage an audience with gorgeous Gowon?"

"My husband's influence, of course." quipped back Joan. "I'm knackered. Number two child here is taking his time, or her time. Whoever, I would like an appearance sooner than later." She patted her tummy, "Come on you, we're all waiting."

They chatted some more. Richard and Malcolm made for the bar and another beer or two, the girls chatted in the shade of the veranda. David soon lost interest in the polo and it was time to return home.

As they entered the house it was beginning to cool down, but even the short outing had exhausted them. They looked forward to some refreshment, a bath and the comfort of their air-conditioned bedrooms. However, on entering the house there was no sign of Joseph but there was a ruckus coming from the rear of the house. There was much crashing and banging.

Richard unlocked the rear door, "What's up now for Christ's sake?" and strode towards the noise.

"Back! Master, back!" cried Joseph, wielding an unmanageable line post some fifteen feet long. He waved the unwieldy weapon with almost total lack of control, almost knocking Richard on the head.

"Steady up, Joseph you mad bugger, what are you about man?"

Then he saw it; the snake was only about two and a half feet long, it had a broad head, and moved sideways, well within the range of Joseph's manic lunging. The snake had already received a blow to its head that exhibited a tear in the skin.

At this point he felt a tug at his trousers and found David keen to join the fun.

"It is the snake of no tomorrow!" gasped the breathless Joseph.

Without further ado Richard picked David up by the scruff of his neck and bundled the screaming boy into the house. From his golfing bag Richard withdrew a three iron. He shouted to Joan that they should all stay indoors and returned to the fray.

Joseph had miraculously scored another direct hit upon the unfortunate, but deadly, reptile and it lay still on the dusty floor. Richard filled with bravado advanced and smashed the three iron as the coup de grace.

"Nothing to it, old boy." He said with savoir-faire.

At this point the snake slithered once more. Richard leapt into the air, smashed down the three iron once more, this time missing the quarry by several inches. Worse, the golf club hit the bone hard ground so hard, that it bounced and jarred from his grip and flew several yards beyond the injured carpet viper.

He froze, not three feet from the snake, when Joseph's pole crashed down once more, this time scoring a vicious direct hit to the snakes head, which split under the assault. This time the snake was still. Joseph advanced with caution. This time his machete in hand, he set about the prone viper with a frenzy, cutting it into several pieces.

When he was done, he stood there, sweating and breathless gazing down at the now pathetic remains.

"Well done, Joseph old bean, that'll teach the buggers." Said Richard warily stepping over the dismembered form and retrieving his badly damaged three iron. He withdrew to the house. Once inside he reached for a cold beer, drank deeply and sat without a word.

Only later at dinner did he remark quietly "Good job Joseph and I killed that snake, nothing for you to worry about." he added casually. He prayed fervently that this would be his last encounter with the local creepy crawlers.

After dinner the humidity reached unbearable levels. Even David was happy to be put to bed in the cool haven of his bedroom. Soon after there was a loud clap of thunder and then the beat of the first rain, huge hammering drops, that soon became a deafening torrent of noise and water. The rain rained as they had never seen before, they stood hand in hand at their door looking out, the intensity was incredible. Within a minute or so they were joined by David who clung to his mother's skirt in wonder and fear at the raging storm. It was a moment they would never forget as the family of nearly four felt the lifting of the clawing humidity and the cooling and refreshment of those first rains.

Thunder and lightening of huge proportions clattered down, it seemed almost on their heads. David was at first alarmed and began to cry, but after a short time was put back to bed as the thunder abated.

As suddenly as it had started the rain stropped, but the air was fresher and cooler. They were thankful the rains had come. As usual, Richard went to lock up and as he did so he reached down to fix the patio door fret that acted as a lock. As his hand grasped the handle of the fret lock, he froze: Not more than twelve inches from his hand a Black Mamba slid quietly past over the patio, now about an inch deep in water. The serpent slithered past and disappeared through a drain hole. Richard stayed stock still, until the snake had disappeared. He shut the door and stared into the blackness of the patio garden. Please God he prayed, keep us safe.

He turned and saw Joan waiting for him, "Any news from our new born to be?"

"Still rehearsing her entry. Come on let's go to bed."

As he lay awake Richard thought of snakes and babies. He preferred babies.

Sunday dawned bright and clear. The rain had brought a new freshness to the day, though it was still hot. Joan arose without complaint. Richard rushed to ensure that David stayed out of the garden because of the snake activity and checked that Joseph would keep an eye open. Joseph was at first amused by Richard's tale of his late night encounter but was obviously rattled when Richard described the intruder.

"It was a Mamba, Sah. Veeerrrrry bad snake, he keel you, he chop you." he waved his arms making chopping motions.

Richard needed a coffee. He decided not to share this latest news with Joan.

Just before noon the balloon went up, or rather the waters came down. The household burst into a well-rehearsed routine: Sister Bee and the Hetherington's were phoned, one a warning order and the other to fetch David. The pre-packed case was hurled into the back of the car and within minutes Joan was carefully strapped in and was whisked off by an excited Richard to Kikuri.

Sister Bee and Sister Theresa were waiting for them and they were ushered into the clean and air-conditioned ward. It was plainly furnished and opposite the bed a simple crucifix was the central focus.

Richard was hustled out for Sister Bee to examine her charge, "Every thing is fine. God is looking after mother and child. It's going to be a wonderful day, even for fathers." quipped the Sister as she emerged, "You can go and be loving to your wife, for a while anyway, we've a bit to wait." and scuttled off to other duties.

Nothing did happen for a while, an hour then two passed slowly, contractions started then stopped; a seemingly endless series of "this is it", get Sister Bee, but then anti-climax. The serial stresses began to take their toll on Joan who began to look grey and tired and for the first time ill. The bloom she'd carried all these months suddenly faded, in minutes she became vulnerable and sick.

Richard became increasingly alarmed and his anxiety increased Joan's discomfort. Then at six o'clock, the nurse who was charged to look after Joan, breezed into the ward to bid her farewell since her shift was over. She picked up her stethoscope, blood pressure measure and trumpet for listening to baby, and unceremoniously departed.

They were alone; suddenly the script had gone dreadfully wrong. No sign of Sister Bee, no sign of anyone. They held hands and looked to each other for comfort, but in each other's eyes they saw the fear. They said little but prayed that help of some sort was at hand.

Five minutes, five long minutes of silence dripped past second by second, to ten minutes then fifteen. There was still no sign of staff or help of any kind. They had long since stopped trying to ring the bell that did not work. Joan's contractions started once more, this time stronger, still no sign of help.

At six thirty the strongest contraction yet, Joan sweated and muttered, "The baby wants to come, the baby wants to come." She was moaning an exasperated and weary cry.

Richard smoothed her brow, not knowing what to say or what to do, afraid to leave to look for help, afraid to stay perchance the baby came. Another contraction then another, Richard could bear it no more.

"I won't be a minute." he fled from the room in panic and in search for help. To his immense relief after two minutes of sprinting into empty X-ray departments, and various other empty rooms he bumped literally into Sister Bee hurrying to Joan.

"You've no need to worry," she assured as she broke into a trot, "I'm sure Joan will be fine."

At the door she pushed Richard and commanded him to wait outside, as if by magic two further local nurses arrived with a trolley and almost immediately Joan was whisked to the delivery room. Richard trotted behind and waited tentatively outside the delivery room. The door opened and a shy nurse masked up offered him a surgical gown, mask and hat. At first he looked bemused but then hastily put on the sterile garments and gingerly pushed through the doors of the delivery room. Joan was on the trolley with an oxygen mask clamped to her grey sweating face.

"Give Joan a bit of comfort, will you" commanded Bee, "we've a little way to go but with God and Doctor Hamdi at our side all will be fine" She giggled with a hint of nervousness.

He mopped Joan's brow, stroked her hair, and held her sweating hand with all the tenderness and love he could muster. The time passed, but oh so slowly, then through a commotion of clattering doors and the hasty gowning up, it was Doctor Hamdi.

After quickly assessing the patient he almost immediately administered a number of injections that seemed to dissolve Joan's pain. There was still much huffing and puffing and pushing and heaving. Around an hour after the good doctor's arrival; another miracle, another birth.

At eight twenty p.m. Emma Smiles made a cacophonous entry into the world. She was small at six pound and ten ounces but she was beautiful and she was well.

As soon as they were settled into the ward with tiny Emma in bed cradled in her mother's arms, in came Sister Bee. "Everything is fine. God is looking after us, surely He is." she laughed. She then took Joan's free hand and said, "Joanie you're a brave girl, so you are, will we say a prayer of 'tanks together now?"

And so they did, the three adults, two of them very tearful, held hands and thanked God for his goodness.

The following day, mother and child were greeted like the celebrities Richard thought they were. David greeted his new sister with gentle wonder and snuggled under his mother's free arm and seemed quite content.

By the afternoon a steady string of visitors arrived bearing an astonishing array of gifts. Richard took time to visit the factory where news of the birth was genuinely greeted with joy and celebration. Richard received a number of delegations all bringing their salutations and good wishes. The most touching of these was lead by the delightful Usman Jalingo who, after his midday prayers, presented Richard with a beautifully worked "pickin" dress and a leg of goat.

# CHAPTER 21

Eke came separately, and offered his congratulations in his usual gentle and diffident way.

"I wish you and your family, all that I would wish for my own," he intoned.

"Sit down Eke. Thank you for your greetings. I know Mrs. Smiles will value them. We get on pretty well don't we?" he mused, and then after a pause, he continued, "I'm still a bit unhappy about the Mbaname affair." he paused again, Eke looked steadfastly down to the carpet "There's obviously something I don't understand,"................ again a silence, "Do you get what I'm saying?"

Eke, blinked behind his horn-rimmed glasses but he did not answer. More seconds dragged by and Richard began to regret raising the issue. Then, just when he was about to move on Eke looked up and smiled a wistful smile and said

"Today for you is a happy day, you must enjoy it. It is not a day to talk of unhappy things."

"It is a good day for me to listen, even to unhappy things if it makes things better between you and me. It's not a day to talk about factory schedules I agree, but I'd like to take this time to understand a bit more, okay?"

"You do not understand Sir. You have not seen what the Hausa man has done to my people." His voice was calm but quiet.

"Go on, I'm listening."

"This war Sir, it was not like your wars, ....... it was not fought with guns and bombs, soldier against soldier. It was fought with bayonet and club, ...........it was soldier against us all, women and children included." He paused clenching his hands before him as he swayed in the chair. He continued staring into the middle distance. "We were not well lead in retrospect, but we believed that we had a right to the wealth that was under our land, I don't think even Ojukwu thought it would come to all out war, but soon, too soon, we were at war with those who had been our brothers."

Again he trailed to a silence.

"If you fight your brother, you fight the devil. Yes, they beat our soldiers, such as they were, but they didn't beat our people, they murdered them." There were tears in his eyes. "They murdered our children, they raped our women, and they maimed the old and defenseless. These were our brothers, our fellow Nigerians." he stopped to wipe his eyes, and then again staring at the floor, "They raped with bayonets, they cut the children's heads from off their mothers backs as they chased them for sport. They shot, burned or hung any male that got in their way" he fell silent and then, as if counting and remembering with a metronome like beat, "My brother, my sisters, and one of my sons. He was nine years old." Then after another silence that echoed round the stillness of the office, "You see, Mr. Smiles you can never understand."

They joy of Emma's birth lay forgotten in Richard's profound sadness. He looked at Eke and wanted to hold him, to some how share his pain. He sat immobile, staring at Eke, his mind in numb panic behind his fixed glazed eyes. He had no idea what to say.

It was Eke who stood, put out his hand and said, "You must forgive me, I do not mean to spoil your day of joy"

Richard rose to take his hand, "Oh, no trouble, old boy, no trouble at all." he muttered uselessly. He then looked down at the floor. Eke quietly left his boss's office.

As Richard left for the hospital a little later, he acknowledged for the first time that Eke was right, he did not understand, and he doubted if he ever would.

Mohamed; now a firm family favourite, knew none of the agonies of Eke, the war had barely touched him or his family. His faith was true and strong and it gave him an air of innocence and quiet strength. He was wonderful with David and very protective of Joan during the latter days of her pregnancy.

On the morning that Joan and Emma were to be brought home the car was cleaned with extra vigour. Mohamed was excited, as was Joseph, they gossiped like two old women as Richard prepared to depart to bring home his precious cargo of mother and new "Missy".

When their good-byes were complete and Joan was shepherded to the car, cradling the tiny Emma in her arms, Mohamed was absolutely transfixed by the tiny white baby; he was rooted to the spot. Eventually he put the case in the boot and hurried to open the car door, his face wreathed in the broadest of smiles.

"Master, you very lucky man, Missy beautiful, little Missy very very beautiful - you are blessed, Sah"

"You're right, Mohamed, you're so right." Sighed the proud father.

With that, before closing the door, hovering over mother and child, he muttered something, which none of the Smiles understood.

"What was that?" enquired Joan.

"A small prayer for little Missy and Madame, Madame." and he drove off back to Galadima Road and a new life for the four Smiles'.

# CHAPTER 22

The arrival of Nigel Butter always aggravated Richard who loathed his mincing ways, his inept and unhelpful sarcasm. As far as Richard was concerned Butter was a typically useless Head Office Wally. A knit picker, a pain in the arse and not even having the saving grace of being a good drinking companion. His Irish Canadian drawl, his complete disinterest in sport and his sneering sarcasm for anyone or anything local all got under Richard's skin.

Joan likewise did not take to him. So, after three visits Joan avoided making dinner at home with the excuse that the new baby demanded all her time, which meant Richard was condemned to keeping company with Butter, not only during the working days but also in the evenings at dinner.

On the evening of his latest visit Richard left reluctantly (and late) to meet Butter for Dinner at the Hamdalah Hotel. He left Joan and the children feeling fairly sorry for himself and drove the short distance round the racecourse perimeter to the Hamdalah Hotel.

On arrival at the Hotel Richard was waylaid by Henry Ash who babbled about the latest scandals at the Club and how awful the food had become at the Hamdalah.

Eventually Richard arrived in the Lounge Bar some fifteen minutes late and at first couldn't pick out Butter. So he ordered a drink from the bar and it was then that he saw the Head Office nerd deeply engrossed in conversation with a smartly and traditionally dressed Nigerian in the corner of the room.

Richard walked over "Good evening, Nigel." he announced.

Butter turned, startled, and replied with an overly hearty "Well, hello, Richard." and turned to the tall willowy Nigerian in the elaborate and expensive traditional dress, "Excuse me, this is my business connection - see you later."

With that the tall stranger walked briskly away.

"Who's that?" enquired Richard.

"Just another Hotel guest."

"Unlike you to fraternize with the natives, old boy." cracked Richard and thought no more about it.

Despite all the excitement of Emma's arrival, Richard returned to the routine at work where things, Butter apart, were generally going well. He looked forward to leaving for Lagos and the approaching annual conference of the African region, albeit with some reservations about his appraisal where the dreaded Nigel Butter would do all he could to make things uncomfortable. He had the knack of picking up minute incidental issues and making a big deal of them. Regan for some reason always fell for the gambit and appeared always to take Butter's point.

He looked forward to meeting colleagues from the other regional centers; they would come from Port Harcourt, Dahomey, Kinshasa, and Nairobi. There was to be a one-day conference at the Ikoyi Hotel, followed by a corporate dinner when no doubt some corporate big wig from UK would preside.

The appraisal sessions would take place on the days before and after the conference. Richard was scheduled late on the day after, due to the relatively closeness of his office to Lagos. Edward Regan would chair the conference, which would guarantee for Richard a high degree of boredom, since he only grudgingly respected the man and found him humorless and insensitive.

Richard knew only one other delegate, Geoff Dyke, who ran the Port Harcourt operation. Richard liked him. He was a tall, gangly, West Countryman with a broad Bristolian drawl. He was single and, in the parlance of the "boys", would shag anything, young or old, black or white. Richard mused that if the stories of Geoff's prolific sexual adventures

108

were half true, then he must assuredly have contracted a number of diseases; however, Geoff always laughed the subject off. Amongst his other endearing qualities was his ability to sink ten Star beers at a sitting, further, he constantly riled against Head Office interference and thought Nigel Butter was a complete nerd. All in all, for Richard he was a thoroughly good chap.

As far as Regan was concerned Geoff was a constant pain. He had been summoned to Lagos on a number of occasions to answer charges ranging from spending capital without proper authorisation, introducing innovative but non standard products, extending credit to native contractors, going missing for days on end and inappropriate relationships with local females, including on one occasion being caught in flagrante with the wife of the local Bank Manager.

The reason why he survived at all was not easy to assess, however, his operation did make profits and it was almost impossible to get anyone to work in Port Harcourt under horrible climatic conditions and even worse infrastructural chaos.

Geoff always looked slightly untidy and Richard thought that he had a marked squint in his left eye, which completed the picture of eccentricity. For all that, women were attracted to him. Even Joan, who had met him briefly twice, confessed that he was "cute" and that he stirred her mothering instincts.

The other delegates were fun too, all with the exception of one in their early thirties, all fairly bright and all hopeful that their apprenticeship in Africa would pave the way for bigger and better things in the great global empire that was Universal Metals.

The older man was Bill Havill, a huge man of some six feet six inches. He looked after the Kenyan company, was divorced and it was rumored was going "bush". He'd been in a number of locations within the African region over the past twelve years and had got to the point that he seldom bothered to return to the UK for annual leave. He preferred instead to roam the Far East, no one knew in what pursuit, but many guessed.

Driscoll and Lamb, two of the other General Managers, were fun, but more intense and ambition dripped from their every move. They drank at about a third the pace of Richard, Geoff and Hayden. Neither did they join in the merry jesting at the expense of Regan and Butter.

After a drunken dinner, Richard found himself sandwiched between Dyke and Hayden in a Lagos taxi bound for a notorious establishment called the Kit-Kat Club. When they arrived, Richard had no idea where, the 'Club' turned out to be a steel-sheeted warehouse and throbbed to an ear-numbing beat. They entered through a noisy throng, Bill Hayden using his bulk to drive a way through to the box office. It was dark, almost pitch black. Richard just followed and eventually they found themselves amongst a rhythmically swaying multitude of several hundred. As Richard's eyes adjusted to the dark he began to realise that they were the only white guys there, that is to say three ex-patriots and around a thousand locals.

The air was thick with the smell of rancid sweat sweetened by a fug of marijuana. The lights were low but their shirts glowed in the ultraviolet light. Richard had the uncomfortable thought that they were gazelles in Lion country, but Hayden's bulk gave some comfort. Geoff shepherded them to the bar, bought a round of beers and before you could say "knife" was off gyrating and writhing with a pretty black girl. Soon he disappeared into the crowd.

Bill and Richard continued to drink until Bill had to make his way to relieve his bladder. Richard was charged to watch the drinks and hold the small table they'd managed to secure. Richard stood self consciously avoiding the variety of fluttering eyes and smirking threats of some of the men. When Bill returned he was arm in arm with two beautiful ebony girls. Bill and his partner disappeared in a trice leaving Richard standing by his delicious new girl friend. In desperation he led her to the dance floor. She pressed against his sweat sodden body and purred incomprehensively into his ear. Her perfume was sweet; almost sickly sweet, which mingled with her musty scent. Despite his fear and his drunkenness the animal in him began to rise. They writhed, swayed in a sensual embrace, Richard lead by his inflamed desire.

The music stopped. He led the girl by her hand back to the bar. There was no sign of Geoff or Bill. He offered the girl another drink, she smiled a lurid assent. She hung off his arm as if that was where she belonged, her perfume smoking off her like a fetid candle.

At the bar there was a mighty scrum and he found it impossible to be heard amongst the din and jostle. After a while he saw the girl watch him, this spurred him on to be more aggressive. Suddenly he felt a sharp pain as a large Nigerian elbowed him viciously in the small of his back. The man smirked down at him daring him to respond.

'Oh Lord', he thought, 'I don't want to be here'. He retreated from the bar, swept past his new belle, "Going to the john, won't be a tick!"

He fled, through the mass of gyrating bodies and out onto the cooler street. It started to rain. He looked for a taxi, there wasn't one. The street was heaving with life, mainly low life, Richard felt lonely, exposed and vulnerable.

"You want nice girl mistah? You come with me."

He strode away.

"You want live fuck show?"

He turned and almost ran. He tucked his wallet down his shirt front and took off down the road, to he knew not where. He was soaked through as the rain poured down. He walked blindly on, desperately seeking a taxi. He rebuffed a hundred beggars; then from a darkened doorway one leapt out and bound him in a stinking embrace,

'Money boss, or I keel you!'

His breath was so startlingly disgusting that Richard leapt with almost superhuman strength, bursting from the beggar's embrace and at the same time kneeing the unfortunate destitute in the balls. He crumpled and sank to his knees. Richard sprinted off again in no particular direction and was almost hysterical when he came upon a rusting taxi depositing at least half a dozen occupants at a tumbled down apartment block.

He was wet through and scared witless, "Ikoyi Hotel, please." he pleaded, taking his seat in the back of the ramshackle taxi.

"No, Sah!" came the obdurate reply.

"Look, please, I'm desperate." pleaded Richard.

The fat Yoruba man bedecked in his curious floppy head dress sucked his podgy fingers, peered at Richard and started to argue that the Ikoyi was not on his beat and that there was no way that he could do it. It would cost too much and he would loose all his Apapa customers.

Richard sat firm, finally he said, "Okay, how much?"

"Forty pounds."

'You bloody thief.' thought the relieved Richard. "Okay, forty pounds. Let's go."

The first problem that Richard encountered when they arrived back at the hotel was that he didn't have forty pounds. He only had thirty-two pounds and some change, enough money under normal conditions to pay for five return trips from Apapa to Ikoyi. He thrust all the available money into the taxi driver's podgy hand. There followed much abuse and shouting. The hotel night porter was no help at all. He looked disdainfully at Richard's shambling attire and seemed to enjoy the palaver. After several minutes of this Richard marched into the hotel foyer,

"Bollocks." he railed. "Thirty two quid is a bloody rip off."

The taxi driver followed him in and grabbed him by his arm with strong fat fingers. Suddenly he looked tough, he was hard.

It was two thirty in the morning and all this ruckus led to the intervention of the security officer. He was as tall as the taxi driver was fat and looked even meaner. He checked that Richard was indeed a resident at the hotel, despite his impression of being a street beggar. The night manager, a dapper little Nigerian then joined the fray. One thing led to another, the taxi driver pushed Richard, who consequently fell backwards over an armchair, the receptionist half pushed, half restrained the taxi driver who in turn had a swipe at the security officer.

The big man was not amused, and Richard, from his supine position behind the chair, winced as a truncheon, produced as if by magic, bounced with a "clonk" off the taxi driver's head. Before the driver could recover he was bundled out the doors to his cab.

Richard suddenly sober stood shaking, all at once the object of obsequious service from the receptionist. They were soon joined by the guard who caressed his truncheon with a loving stroke, having enjoyed its deployment, as well as the profuse thanks of Mr Smiles, a most valued guest.

Richard retired, overwhelmed once more by his own stupidity, riven with guilt and addled with alcohol. He collapsed into the haze that enveloped him and before he could finish his prayer to Joan for forgiveness, he passed out.

The conference was predictably boring, with statistical drivel from Nigel Butter being followed by what Richard thought was gibberish and facile nonsense delivered by the visiting Vice President Human Relations. However this man, it was rumored, carried weight at Head Office, so there was a noticeable increase in enthusiasm from the small audience. The best part by far was the forum that discussed issues of common interest to the General Managers. Richard delivered a paper on marketing planning, with particular emphasis on international prospect tracking. It was a great success and generated a genuine and spirited debate.

During the lunch hour they all returned to the Regional Office on the Marina to look at the new communications system installed at great expense, and there for the express reason, as Bill Hayden saw it, to police the individual companies.

It was during this interval that they became marooned in the office as security advised it would be unsafe to leave the building. They were aware that the day had been declared a bank holiday, since there was to be a public execution of six armed robbers.

What they now witnessed was the return of the spectators from the grim spectacle, which had been enacted at Bar Beach. Some one hundred and twenty thousand people had been present at the event.

The Universal Metals delegates watched from their high vantage point, as thousand after thousands poured down the Marina returning from the event. The excitement and hysteria was tangible, as they watched silently from on high, they were afraid.

After that, the events of the conference ran late, but eventually they broke up before dinner. It was rumored that more spectators than criminals had lost their lives. The count of other fatalities included three trampled to death in the rush, two knifings and one shooting. There was some speculation that the shooting was not a shooting at all, rather a stray bullet from the firing squad.

"Geoff, where the hell did you get to last night?"

"Oh, I got myself fixed up," was the sheepish reply.

"You'll end up with the pox or something worse."

"It's alright for you married blokes," responded Geoff by way of explanation.

"And what about you, Bill, you bugger, you left me in the middle of I don't know where. I was scared out of my mind."

"Come on brother, what about that pretty little girl I left you with?" smirked Bill.

"I skid addled as soon as I could, ended up with a fight with a taxi driver, ruined a pair of slacks, Christ knows how I'm going to explain it to Joan."

"Skid addled from a lovely piece of stuff like that? You don't expect us to believe that, do you?" Giggled Bill.

Edward Regan intervened with the schedule for the morrow's meetings. They made their way into dinner and Richard was distraught to be placed next to the dreaded Nigel Butter.

The almost predictable consequence was a ferocious attack on the wine. By the time came for dessert Richard was high as a kite and loudly goaded the miserable Butter. He ranted on about the ratios of cost to the uselessness of Head Office personnel.

"Let's face it Nigel, you're just a bloody paper pusher, no use to man or beast." slurred Geoff, "'No harm meant, I'm sure, but if I were you I'd get a proper job." With that he giggled at his own humor.

"Must be bloody wonderful flying round an' round, just nit-picking' - just runnin' back and forth telling tales to the boss." joined in Bill nastily.

Butter was very uncomfortable and when Bill and Geoff saw this they joined in like sharks in a feeding frenzy.

Regan, at the other end of the table tried to keep the VP in conversation, but he was furious. As soon as dinner was over he took Bill to one side and dressed him down.

Hayden returned to the corner where Richard and Geoff were sitting, "Consider your wrists slapped." he said, slapping his own hand. "Edward thinks we're rude, immature twits and he wants us to stop taunting his precious controller."

"Oh bollocks, if he can't fend for himself he shouldn't have the job."

"Do you think he's queer?" muttered Geoff.

"Who? Edward? Never." said Bill.

"No you daft bugger, Nigel."

"Wouldn't be surprised, never seen him with a bird, certainly my Joanie thinks he's odd - who cares?"

"Who indeed, just wish he'd lighten up a bit and stop going round like a sneak - I'm going to bed."

With that they all retired, dreading their reviews the following day.

Richard's review went well. The session was chaired by Edward Regan, aided and abetted, but not smoothed, by Nigel Butter. The HR big-wig, whose name was Tony Pritchard, was apparently very interested in Richard and they talked at length about prospects and training. For once Richard was obliged to acknowledge that this Head Office person was a useful and pleasant man.

Richard was in good humor as he left the Lagos office in a hired limo, with plenty of time to get to Ikeja airport for his flight back to Kaduna. The traffic was, as usual, chaotic and mightily congested. The Lagos traffic jams were legendary and this afternoon was no exception.

The Government had tried to ease the traffic problems by introducing a law that allowed cars to travel only on alternate days, according to their registration numbers. This meant that cars with even numbers as their last registration digit could go out on Mondays Wednesdays and Fridays, and cars with registrations ending in odd digits could travel on the alternate days. Unfortunately, the Government had not reckoned on the ingenuity of the general populace who simply went out and bought fake number plates, which they used to circumvent the difficulty. The police could not possibly manage the implementation of the law but they did find it a useful angle for increasing their personal cash flow, since practically every other car was found to be at odds with the law.

The journey, though long and tiresome, ended with Richard being deposited outside the domestic air terminal with plenty of time to catch his Nigerian Airways flight to Kaduna.

Usually Johnson, the company chauffeur, would have taken his ticket and waited in line and got his boarding pass but today, because of the number of visitors, Richard had been assigned a hire limo and thus he would have to fend for himself.

The terminal was bedlam as usual and Richard looked with dismay at the scrum, which was as only an African queue could be. Everyone in the melee seemed in a panic that bordered on hysteria. Patience or impatience had no place here, everyone raced against the demon time, nobody ever won and everything took longer, or at least seemed to.

Richard gamely maneuvered his way towards the front and eventually, after twenty-five stressful minutes, he found himself at the check-in desk.

He smiled, presented his ticket to the agent, who after a cursory glance handed it straight back to him,

"Sorry, flight full." she said it matter-of-factly, as if all the flights were always full. What she said sounded more like "flight fool". She beckoned to the big Nigerian behind him, who without ceremony pushed Richard to one side.

Richard made a grab for his bag but in so doing lost his possession of the position at the desk. He was jostled by other passengers in the adjoining desk and soon found himself isolated, angry and helpless, some way away from his objective.

As if by magic a tall, rather scruffy Nigerian appeared at his side. The man however sported an identification badge that re-assured Richard.

"Can I help you, Sah?" he politely enquired.

Richard, relieved that help was at hand, launched into his story of the last traumatic minutes.

"I can help you Sah," beamed the man, "ten pounds, Sah, and I can arrange your seat and everything Sah." Immediately he snatched the ticket from Richard's one hand and the bag from the other and was off like a gazelle with a sure-footed litheness, into the crowd.

Richard stood aghast, wondering if he would ever see his ticket or boarding pass ever again. It was hopeless, he was hopeless, he decided to do nothing and wait. Minutes passed agonizingly slowly. The time of the flight departure became ever nearer and he felt so lonely standing in the heaving crowd. His nerves stretched, his headache thumped, what would he do next, all was obviously lost. Then, as if the gene had come from the bottle, his scruffy friend was at his side. He waved the boarding card with baggage tag affixed as a small celebration of his triumph.

"Bless you. How on earth did you manage that?" Beamed the ecstatic traveler.

"I'm afraid Sah that the ticket manager is not a good man. He takes dash and I had to promise to pay him fifteen pounds because many people want to get on the plane Sah."

Richard relieved, but still shaking, took fifteen pounds from his wallet and gave it to his rescuer.

"Excuse me Sah, will you reward me?" he wailed "I have worked so hard for you, this fifteen pounds will all go to the ticket manager, I shall

116

get nothing," he looked expectantly at his benefactor, his face collapsed in disappointment as if he were about to cry.

Without hesitation Richard thrust another fiver into the man's hand, but then, as the tears gave way to a knowing smile of a thief, "Bugger off!" said Richard. "The next time I come to Lagos I'll look for you first, but just a tenner, eh!"

The man disappeared to find new prey.

Richard boarded the F20 and waited for the aircraft to fill up. It never did. They left with eight to ten empty seats. Richard reflected upon the ingenuity of the natives and mused to himself how much better things would be if that ingenuity were turned to legitimate pursuits, rather than the endless conspiracies to cheat.

He arrived home tired, but with the secrets of his night on the tiles made safe through the good offices of the Ikoyi Hotel's emergency laundry service. He crept guiltily into bed beside Joan, yawned and mumbled how boring the whole trip had been.

# CHAPTER 23

Emma did not seem to retain her feeds very well and her weight gain was well below that which was normal. Both Drs Eli and Hamdi agreed that Emma should be presented to specialist pediatricians as soon as possible. Richard communicated these concerns to company head quarters and the establishment swung into action, arranging travel for Joan, David and Emma. Universal could be slick and when employee support was the issue they were tops. Within two days of the request to arrange the medical support, tickets were issued, transport from London Heathrow and appointments with pediatric consultants were arranged.

Joan was unhappy that she would have to travel with the children alone, but relieved that Emma's problems were being attended to. It meant that Joan and the children would be on their way on the Friday.

All this was a rush, to say the least. So Edward Regan's call that Richard should attend a meeting in Lagos on that very day reduced the family to a state of chronic neurosis. Joan was beside herself with anger that Richard would be unable to go to Kano to assist and to say his goodbyes. Richard at first resisted Edward's call to Lagos, but he had insisted, acknowledging that it was difficult, but still insisting that Richard attended.

Even more distressing, Edward refused to divulge over the phone what this so urgent business was.

And so it was that they parted tearful company at Kaduna Airport, Richard southbound for Lagos and his family in the care of Mohamed, bound north for Kano and home.

Richard arrived at the Regional Office in Lagos just before midday. He was still angry at being torn from his family in a time of their own crisis and had contemplated telling Edward to stick his job, but here he was tapping on the boss's door, feeling a betrayer and betrayed.

"Sit down, old lad." a suspiciously affable greeting. "Firstly, please understand that I fully appreciate that you've had to make a substantial effort to come here, and…" he mumbled, obviously finding it difficult to say the right thing, "please let Joan know that I'm personally indebted to her for these um, um, series of events, very grateful."

Richard wished he'd get to the point, 'I hope this is all for a bloody good reason you old fart.' mused Richard and then, as if Edward had read his thoughts;

"To get to the point, I'd like you to listen to me, without interruption," he paused, "and then I shall seek your views. I might add that this is a very sensitive matter and I've chosen you to share in its deliberation because I trust you to keep mum and I think you'll give sensible advice and support. You must, I repeat, must, give me your considered and honest view." He continued, almost afraid to get to the point, 'I must say there is no right or wrong answer.'

Richard was now on the edge of his seat with anticipation. What could it be? Had Edward blotted his copybook? Had the company foundered on the rocks of fortune or fraud?

Coffee was brought in and there was an awkward silence. Richard decided that Edward had been fired, or he himself was to be posted.

"It's Nigel Butter." he began hesitantly. "As you know he's got dual nationality, Canadian and Irish. Well, the night before last he apparently went to a reception at the Canadian High Commission and on the way home he was attacked or hijacked. Evidently, Nigel was made to drive home at knife point and give his cash to the assailant."

"Bloody hell." responded Richard, "That's awful. Was he hurt in any way, poor sod?"

"Yes, he's okay, but sadly that's not the end of it. Apparently the police came to Nigel's flat. They said they'd received a complaint from this local, who said Nigel had picked him up, invited him home and made sexual advances to him. According to this guy, who didn't want any of this, said that Nigel gave him money to shut him up." Edward stared at his desk. There was a long silence.

"Oh dear, oh deary me." muttered Richard. His mind flashed back to the incident at the Hamdalah Hotel.

"The police have asked Nigel to present himself to the police station tomorrow with, with his passport."

"Oh, shit, not good, not good at all." Richard shook his head, he wished fervently that this was one confidence that Edward had shared with someone else.

Strangely, he didn't judge Butter. His first thought was how to help Nigel escape the ignominy and sheer horror of being thrown into a Nigerian prison, particularly under these circumstances.

"Look, go and chat to Nigel, he's expecting you. Hear for yourself what he's got to say, we'll then have another chat and decide what, if anything, we're going to do." Edward ushered Richard to Butter's office and withdrew.

Nigel Butter looked haggard and drawn. His eyes were bloodshot with heavy bags under them. He looked like a man at bay. Gone was the flip sarcasm, no cleverness now, he looked weak and vulnerable.

"Sorry to hear your troubles." opened Richard, "Edward's suggested we talk things through if that's okay with you." He spoke quietly, as gently as he could, as if Butter was so fragile he might break at the sound of his voice.

"Sure, sure" responded Nigel weakly, he smiled a shadowy grin, and looked away.

"Talk me through what happened, then."

Nigel then related what Richard, rightly or wrongly, adjudged to be a curious tale, full of inconsistencies, and nervous asides. When he'd finished Nigel had tears in his eyes.

"You do believe me?" he begged, "Don't you?"

"Doesn't matter a bugger if I do or don't believe you, Nigel. Will the Nigerian police believe you? That's the point." then relenting, "Of course I believe you Nigel,...... but sadly that's not the point."

Back in Edward's office all three sat over coffee and sandwiches, which Richard consumed alone.

"Richard, what's your view on the next step?" asked Edward, almost staring at his subordinate.

"No question, no bloody question at all. Nigel has to be out of the country before his appointment at the police station tomorrow. No bloody question at all.'" He stated it flatly, without expression, except a determined 'that's my last word' emphasis. Richard sat back and looked at Nigel who, gripping his hands together until the knuckles were white, stared disconsolately at the floor.

"No point in approaching the Canadian High Commission I suppose?" muttered Edward, "No point." he answered his own question.

At this point Nigel got to his feet and rushed from the room, "Excuse me." he gagged. He was shaking and about to burst into tears.

Left alone, Richard and Edward looked silently at each other. Edward lit his foul smelling pipe as if to signify the gravity of the situation.

"I concur," Edward announced, "'we've got to get him out, tonight or first thing in the morning. I believe he's due to report at the police station at midday. I hope it's not a cause celebre yet and that there won't be any watch on airports." He tapped his pipe and a body of disgusting tar and ash was disgorged into the ashtray. "We've already asked our travel agent to enquire about flights out today but they're all full. KLM has a flight tomorrow at around ten a.m. and that's our last hope. I'm waiting for a reply from Pat Graham, the General Manager, who, if there are any seats left, will make out a ticket after the office is closed, just in case there are any notices to airlines which the staff might see."

Richard was impressed. Edward was ahead of the game and had taken some risks in helping Nigel out. "If we're implicated in getting him out," he went on, "we'll stick to the line that he came to us with a family problem and left on compassionate leave. Understood?" Richard nodded.

"That story is important, because if you're willing I'd like you to go with Nigel in the morning and see he's checked through all right, if that's okay?" Richard nodded once more without thought.

The phone rang. Edward answered and talked in hushed tones to Pat Graham of KLM and fellow Rotarian. There was much muttering that Richard could not hear. Eventually the plot was hatched and Edward put down the phone.

"We've got a seat booked in the name of Van de Merwe, You and Nigel are to report to the first class check-in no later than eight fifteen. Ask for the Station Manager. Now don't get this wrong for God's sake." he read from his scribbled notes "The Station Manager, a Mr. Andres, remember it must be Andres, no one else, announce yourself as Mr. Van de Merwe and say you are not sure you will travel today. You've got that, you 're Mr. Van de Mewe and you not sure you can travel today." he repeated. "He will reply either; 'That's okay, Mr Butter can travel in your stead' which is all systems go, or... God forbid, 'I'm afraid I can't change the ticket at this late stage.' This will mean a no go situation."

There was another silence, "What then? I mean in a no go situation?" asked the increasingly anxious Richard.

"You go straight to the domestic terminal and fly back to Kaduna as per your ticket. Nigel will have a stand by plan. I've already asked too much of you really, so you must promise that you will stick to the plan".

Richard nodded his assent once more.

Nigel returned, "Any news?" he asked tentatively.

"Yes Nigel. You'll be glad to know that all being well we have a seat for you to fly home via Amsterdam. I hope you get home safely and in time to visit your sick Aunt. It is your Aunt who's mortally ill, isn't it?"

"Um, yes I see, yes of course, Aunt Moira. Thanks for your help." he looked down, anywhere, not to look Richard or Edward in the face. His hands shook, his chin quivered and tears ran down his sad and frightened face.

"Richard is travelling to the airport on his way back to Kaduna so he'll come along with you in the morning, if that's alright? Anyway, Johnson can do the one trip which will be convenient." Edward clenched his pipe tightly, determined to sustain an outwardly normal exterior. He continued, "Perhaps you should go home and pack. Johnson will take you and no doubt Richard will dine you out tonight, eh Richard?"

"Absolutely, my pleasure Nigel." lied Richard.

The evening passed tensely. Richard was once more put up at the Ikoyi where through the usual system of dash they had deprived some unsuspecting visitor from their reserved accommodation.

To Edward's everlasting credit he relented on his command that Nigel and Richard should dine out and invited them instead to his home, which relieved the insufferable problem for Richard of having to nurse Nigel Butter through a nerve-racked evening. As it was, Nigel was a twitching wreck and even in Edward's house nervously watched every movement of all those who came and went, certain that the doorbell would ring and they would come and take him away to jail.

Edward had not shared the current problem with his wife that made for a more than usually curious evening. The conversation was stunted and as the evening went on the already worn out Butter was obliged to elaborate on the condition and history of his Aunt Moira. Mrs Regan, a nosy lady, would not stop pursuing the subject;

"How old is your Aunt?" – " How old is she?" – "How long has she been ill?" -

until Edward eventually intervened, seeking respite for the sad Butter who was obviously distressed by this sad affair, and who was in danger of contradicting himself.

Mrs Regan retired after dinner, her natural curiosity ill at ease with the goings on, but equally sure that she would needle out the truth from her husband in the days that were to follow.

They did their best to encourage Nigel to drink, but he would not. Richard as usual had no problem in filling the gap and unusually Edward Regan, followed suit. As a consequence, Robert and Edward became quite drunk, whilst Nigel Butter cringed in their company, but sadly was afraid to go home alone lest either the police or his "assailant" would be lying in wait.

Richard and Butter set off from Regan's house after ten, Smiles relaxed by the wine but exhausted. Butter still shook with fright, hunted and haunted, his red eyes surmounting his grey baggy eyed and haggard face. He was in the true sense pathetic, lost and alone with his secrets, his guilt and his fears. Was he a rat in a trap? What ever he had or had not done his agony was plain to see and Richard could feel nothing but sorrow for this sad little man.

The car drew up at Butter's apartment block, all was inky black, the palm trees swayed and the bushes hid a hundred demons. Butter stuttered a good night, but didn't move to get out of the car.

"Come on old lad," encouraged Smiles, "time for bed, we've got an early start in the morning."

"Sure, sure," Butter shifted uneasily, "I know this is foolish …but after what happened last night I wonder if, if you'd mind coming to the door? I know it's kinda' silly."

In the dark Richard could almost touch the fear. "No problem, old boy, no problem at all."

They walked tentatively through the pools of light and the caverns of dark to the bottom of the stairs,

"OK, bum boy, where you been? From the shadows there emerged a tall black man he was tall and dressed in jeans and tee-shirt, on his head flopped a Yoruba hat, his features were hard to see in the light. Richard's heart jumped, time stopped, his mind blank with fear. Worse was to come, there emerged from the shadows another assailant, all they could see of him was his outline smaller than the man in front of them but more menacing in his cloak of darkness. There flashed the glint of a knife, the two paralyzed ex-patriots stood in icy silent fear.

"Jonah? Is that you?" Butter spoke, his voice strangely firm. "Jonah, what do you want, I gave you all the money I had last night. Please leave me alone."

"Is this another bum-boy friend?"

"This is a colleague, from my office; he's just picking up some documents for work." The voice was still firm, confident even.

Smiles, his mouth dry as dust, his jaw locked tried to say something but failed, he made a guttural sound rather like a cat coughing.

"You get me some more money Bum-boy, or I'll feed you to dee river."

"Sir, what eyes dee problem, I go fetch police, now, now." It was Johnson, who'd emerged from the car, still some distance away, but close enough to the car to make a getaway.

Jonah turned to mutter to his accomplice, he stepped back into the shadow, his confidence shaken.

"Run, fucking run," Smiles was off, he reached the car, turned and searched for Butter who was close on his heels. They both scrambled into the car,

"Go Johnson, Go!"

"Whereto Sah?"

"Any-bloody –where, just go."

The car sped away, they saw the two bandits chase a few futile yards behind them and then they were safe the terror left behind in the darkness.

"To the Ikoyi Hotel, Johnson, make sure there's no one following us." In the car there was silence. Richard was suddenly aware of the smell of the Canadian, he had never smelt fear before but it was unmistakable, something primeval.

"Nigel, do you have your passport?"

"Yes, yes I do,… why?"

"Not to put too fine a point on it, Old boy, I don't think you can go back to your flat, we'll have to fix something at the Hotel, and from there straight to the airport."

"What about my things? …… Need to pack."

"Tomorrow I'm afraid you're going to be traveling light. Don't worry about your things the company will send them on."

At the Hotel the two made strenuous efforts to get a room for Butter, but to no avail, no amount of bribery and dash could conjure up a room, the hotel was full. Richard felt uncomfortable about sharing his room with Butter, but what the hell, he'd come this far, if he did turn out to be 'funny' Richard would whack him with a bottle or something.

They showered, both gingerly stepping round the other, each aware of the others' contagion. Eventually they went to bed Richard in the single bed and Butter wrapped in a spare sheet on the floor. Butter lapsed into an exhausted sleep, and snored mightily. Richard lay awake, cursing his fate, 'I don't even like this pen-pusher, I hope someone, somewhere is aware of my efforts, no body cares,….. I wonder how Joan and the kids got on; he hoped they were home safe and sound.' He dosed fitfully; resisted the onslaught of Butter's snoring. Morning couldn't come soon enough.

It was at six thirty on the following morning that Richard checked out of the Ikoyi Hotel. Johnson arrived, Butter, now looking absolutely dreadful joined Richard as they bundled him into the back of the company car. Despite his almighty snoring Butter had obviously had spent another sleepless night and was now fleeing the demons of his past or future, Richard did not speculate which. Despite his own wretched state he still could not help feeling sorry for this sad young man by his side. The Saturday morning traffic was light and they made it to Ikeja without problems and with plenty of time to spare. They drove to the International Terminal and Richard could see the tail fin of the KLM DC10 over the fence, Butter's salvation.

They entered the building and went to the first class check-in and asked for the Station Manager, as per brief. They were alarmed to learn that the Station Manager was not "on seat". At first they didn't know what to do, so they retreated to the entrance for a "team talk".

"Oh Jesus, what do we do now?" Begged the shaking Butter.

"First, don't fucking panic!" Richard moved from one leg to the other thinking furiously. After a moment he looked at his watch, "It's not eight fifteen yet. As I remember, they were very precise about that, so we've got a half hour yet to wait. This guy probably doesn't turn up till the first class brigade start to check in, so back to the car and the air-conditioner, okay?"

Butter dropped his baggage and ran to a toilet leaving Richard standing self consciously alone. As he stood there, every other body seemed to be a policeman; however they seemed to wonder about with no particular purpose. Butter was an age in the lavatory and when he eventually emerged his jacket was soiled. He'd obviously been sick. 'Shit.' thought Richard, 'he's going to come apart.'

"Nigel, it's going to be okay. Just hang on. There's a fella." he encouraged. 'Please God let him hold it together.' he prayed. The half hour was largely taken up finding Johnson who had found an obscure parking spot, so no sooner had they arrived, they nervously departed again.

They approached the KLM desk, where there was already a first class passenger with the largest collection of luggage that either had ever seen. They waited patiently whist the fat Dutchman and his vast array of bags were checked in. Richard approached the desk.

"My name is Van de Merwe, could I speak to the Station Manager please?" he smiled at the attendant.

"Are you traveling with us today enquired the attendant?" grinning his "first class" receiving smile.

"I'm not sure yet." was Richard's absurd reply, "I'd like to see the Station Manager, he's expecting me."

"May I have your ticket, Sah?" responded the attendant.

"Please could you get the Station Manager. Its company business, you understand?" he winked at the attendant, who God bless him did understand and he dashed from his station to much tut-tutting from the line of passengers now formed behind.

Butter stood, as if turned to stone. His greyness was indeed stone grey; however the sweat pouring down his face belied his pretensions to statuehood. Eventually the Station Manager appeared, clutching a ticket. He waved at Richard and called him to a vacant desk.

"My name is Van de…"

"It's okay; I've got Mr. Butter's ticket. All okay. Okay, Mr. Butter?" Nigel sidled up.

"Yes." he whispered cautiously.

"Let me check you in Sir. It's nice to know you are not a celebrity." he grinned at Nigel.

When the formalities were done Nigel looked as if he had shed years, his color had returned and he looked almost as he had always looked. He shook Richard's hand with his sweat-soaked palm and it was with difficulty that Richard evaded a farewell embrace.

Then he was gone. Thank God for that, thought a relieved Richard as he slouched back to the car with his hangover returned.

# CHAPTER 24

Richard fell into a miserable depression when he arrived home to the empty house. It was astonishing how different the house was without the family; the home had become a house. The quietness hung in the air, the echoes of David and Emma were ever harder to recall, company at the table was the hapless television programme or a lonely silence…He slipped into a heavy weekend of drinking at his usual haunts. Despite the exhausting business in Lagos, Sunday saw him join the bachelor boys on two rounds of golf and umpteen rounds of Star beers. He arrived home catastrophically drunk and barely noticed that the steward, Joseph, was in a similar state.

The working week was little better, a series of hard days at work and hard nights at the club. After a week of absolute chaos in Galadima Road, Richard awoke on the next Saturday morning to a household reduced to a complete shambles. Joseph was nowhere to be found, his quarters were empty and Richard noted; reverting to their former disgusting state.

Richard set about the housework with a vengeance and after the whole of Saturday devoted to cleaning, washing and shopping he restored the home to something approaching normality. However, there was still no sign of Joseph; he'd been missing since the middle of the previous week, so Richard simply waited to see what would happen. Strangely, he missed Joseph's company. It made the temptation to dally in the club with his drinking cronies the more difficult to resist. Advice from the Club varied from "fire the bugger" to "wait and see, he'd be back when he runs out of money".

Richard didn't have to wait long. On the next Sunday evening he returned sober from a luncheon with the Hetherington's.

There was a great hullabaloo from the boy's quarters, so much so that even the normally somnombulant Magardi were moved to investigate. Richard found the two guards, bows and arrows at ease, idly peering at the source of the din; Joseph's quarters.

Richard bravely walked straight into the building and was immediately assailed by the overpowering stink of sweat, alcohol, vomit and urine. He retreated as if by reflex; nevertheless he was able to register that the furniture had been smashed to bits; that Joseph was wielding a leg of a broken chair; and under the pile of debris he thought he saw a body.

Once outside he shouted with his best and most authoritative parade ground voice "Joseph, what the hell are you doing?"

There was a silence and then a clattering as Joseph fell over the chaos and emerged swaying at the door. A minute passed. Silence. Joseph sniggered a drunken grin; he leant on the doorpost for support, but still managed to sway, his shoulder acting as a hinge.

"Massa." he mumbled, "Ma woman she no good at all."

"Joseph, you drunken bugger where have you been?"' he was making conversation, he didn't know what to say, his mind still dwelt upon the body he thought he'd seen. Had he seen it? What had he seen?

"'Been to ma villajjj," he slurred, "'to get ma woman. She no good, no good no good at all."

Then he heard it, a soft whimpering from inside the building. At this point Joseph slid untidily down the door post and was out for the count, snorting and grunting like a pig.

Richard stepped over the reclined drunk and ventured once more into his servant's quarters. He signalled to the guards to follow and with handkerchief clamped over his nose and mouth, he gingerly tiptoed over the pile of debris and into the living room. There was indeed a body, but at least it was alive. The poor woman had been badly beaten. Her mouth was bleeding and swollen, as was one of her eyes. She clutched her abdomen where she seemed to have sustained a severe blow. Her legs were bruised, as were her arms, which looked as if they'd been her only defence against the flailing chair leg. The horror of it all was a shock to Richard. This wasn't from a passing car, nor on the television, this was right here, he could touch the pain, feel the misery, smell the piss, and watch the flesh swell and bleed.

He tentatively reached out to the prone woman, his hand extended, "Come, my dear." he said as gently as he could, but she curled into a foetal ball and wailed. Richard stood back and once again was lost.

The guards stood haplessly by the door looking on with little apparent concern. It occurred to Richard that maybe if they helped bring her out she may be more relaxed, so he beckoned them to come and help lift and carry her outside. Their response was immediate and unhelpful. They picked up the unconscious steward and carried him away and left Richard with the injured and possibly hysterical woman. Richard tried to approach the woman again, this time she just whimpered softly and tightened her gait.

She was lying on the collapsed bed. At least she was on a mattress, albeit a filthy one. He withdrew to the house, drew a glass of water and returned to the wounded woman. He placed the water near her and withdrew again and decided to send for reinforcements.

He rang the Hetherington's and Sally answered the phone. Malcolm was on his way to Lagos for a Monday meeting, but yes, she'd bring her steward and his wife. She thought they were from the same people as Joseph. He put down the phone, relieved that help was on the way. He ventured outside to the guards' station in the car port and there he found Joseph still in a deep alcoholic sleep. He gestured to the guards to keep him at that location. They grinned a reply and Richard made his way round to the injured woman, not at all confident that the Magardi had understood his message.

The woman was now sitting up, her bruised legs uncomfortably folded underneath her; he now saw how vicious Joseph's attack had been. She had her front teeth knocked out and her finger stamped upon, or broken in some other unimaginably brutal way. Again he approached as gently as he could, this time the woman barely flinched, as if resigned to more punishment. He held the glass of water for her and she drank a little, but obviously her lips and broken teeth made it difficult. He tried to stroke her matted hair but failed to make contact, through revulsion, or fear, he knew not what. He hesitated and withdrew his hand.

"Mamma coming, she help you.'" is all he could say, and then he added "Joseph he no come back. I send him away." He touched her fleetingly on her arm and left to greet the arriving car, which he hoped to God, was Sally and the rescue column.

"Sally, thank God. Thank you for coming." he hugged her. "Thank you Paul and Missy Paul for coming too. Please, this way." and he lead them to where the woman lay.

Sally was plainly shocked by the extent of the woman's injuries, but soon recovered and organized Missy Paul to comfort the injured and translate her questions related to the extent of her injuries. She ordered Richard and Paul to organize hot water and first aid kit and then set about cleaning up Mrs. Joseph, who's name was Ruth.

Some half an hour later Sally washed up in the kitchen.

"Your Joseph seems to be a vicious psychopath from the looks of things. The little bastard has beaten the daylights out of poor Ruth."

"I'd never have guessed he could be so cruel. He's been great with the kids and he worships Joan. I'm damned if I can understand it."

"Anyway, she'll have to go to hospital she keeps passing out. I reckon your brave steward landed a few bits of furniture on her napper."

"I'll get Paul and his wife to drive her to the hospital, we'd better ring and warn them.'"

Richard rang the hospital, spoke to casualty who were, or sounded, quite efficient. Ruth was half carried, half walked to the car and Paul and Missy Paul drove gingerly off to the hospital not ten minutes away.

"Fancy a drink? Gin and' tonic okay?"

"I'd love one. Then you must take me home, I was just out the bath and ready for an early night when you called, you bugger." she smiled, relaxing back onto the sofa.

"Sorry Sally, with all the palaver I'd just forgotten that Malcolm had pushed off for Lagos. Anyway, I'd have called you because you're the only pals we've got."

He placed two large gin and tonics on the coffee table and sat down beside her, he looked at her long legs, her raven hair and her smiling brown eyes. 'Joan, Joan, where are you?' Her perfume filled his nostrils. He felt his desire for her rise, and despite his reservations he wanted to sin, to have, to enjoy her to be comforted by her.

They drank their gins and talked small talk, not least what was to be done with Joseph and who would assume responsibility for Ruth. Where would or could she go if she was discharged? They decided that Joseph would have to go, if only for trashing the furniture that had been given to him only six or so months ago. Sally promised that Paul would contact Ruth's people who would assume responsibility.

At that point, just as Sally was standing to go, there was a crashing at the door and there the ashamed and much bedraggled Joseph stood, stinking, bloodshot eyes appealing to his Mastah for understanding.

Perhaps because Sally was there, he remained unmoved and with solid resolution dismissed his steward with immediate effect.

"Joseph you are a bad man. You are a goat who beats women and smashes furniture. You are a hopeless clown."

"Zorry Mas'ah" Joseph still swayed, his bloodshot eyes failing to focus.

"I cannot trust you any more you must go." Even now Richard was reticent to dismiss this crazy little man, who'd been such a companion, whose eggs would forever be bullet like. However with Sally standing behind him he had to be firm.

"Go away; now you must go away, ten minutes, I do not want you at all."

"Mash's, I'm going Ash, I am goin' I am a bad man."

He shuffled off, still staggering, he made a sad figure as he weaved his way one last time to the boy's quarters. Richard felt dejected.

He shouted after his disconsolate steward:

"Clear your belongings, tomorrow go to the factory and collect one month's wages. If you do anything outside these clear instructions you will be reported to the police for assault and destruction of property."

"Do you understand, Joseph, am I clear? You are a bad bugger and I don't want to see you after tomorrow ever again, do you understand?"

"Yes, Sah." replied Joseph, turning, looking down with tears filling his eyes. "'I understand Sah, I am a bad man." He turned and shuffled off to pick up his night's belongings.

Richard turned and sighed, despite himself he felt remorse at breaking with Joseph, he turned to Sally.

"I can't help but be sorry for the silly sod. I know that this has been a dreadful do, but he's never been much trouble before and he was so good with the kids and Joan." He stuck his hands deeply into his pockets and turned.

Sally walked straight to him held him softly by the shoulders and kissed him on his mouth. He was too surprised to respond, she backed off a little and said in her warm Lancashire lilt "You poor lost little Welsh boy." She looked him directly in the eye. He put out his arms and drew her to him and in an instant they kissed.

Their kiss moved from innocence to lust in a flash. Their tongues stroked and teased, pushed and tempted. His hand was on her breast, stroking, feeling. He fumbled and opened her top and felt her small sweet breast and tugged at her brassiere so that one nipple was pushed, naked upward. He thrust down on it with his mouth and Sally sweetly encouraged him with her soft cool hand on the back of his neck.

She drew him to the sofa, made him sit, she stood before him and removed her brassiere, and then she pushed him back so that he lay looking up at her. She smiled calmly down at him, slipping from beneath her dress her panties.

He tried to rise and pull her but she stood aloof, her fingers to her lips gesturing "quiet".

Then as he lay back, still standing above him still in her dress, she reached down, undid his belt, unzipped his fly, and bared his cock. He was entranced, scared, but most of all beside himself with desire.

She again pushed him back and as if mounting a pony, straddled him on the sofa. She sat bolt upright, the heel of her hand bearing down on his chest. She guided him into the warm lushness of her vagina with practiced ease. He wanted to buck and thrust, but she smiled down on him, her hands still pressing hard onto his chest.

"'Easy, boy, easy does it lad," she crooned, "let Aunty Sally spoil you."

He tried desperately to relax, to make it last. She moved with a sinuous writhing that worked him in wondrous unknown ways. The space between them meant his arms were outstretched to hold her breasts. The distance between their faces gave the moment a voyeuristic dimension that heightened his pleasure. Here was lust, for once unmasked and uncomplicated, they both knew it.

Try as he might he knew his control was almost lost.

"I'm going to come." he moaned through clenched teeth.

"Don't you dare." she stopped all movement. "Wait you sod. Wait for me." She reached down and he felt her stroke herself, "Now! Now!'" and they bucked and heaved as they drew the juices from each other as if they would never shag ever again.

Then quiet. Sally arose with the modest dignity she could muster and made off to the bathroom without a word. Richard, after a minute of blank silence and equally blank mind, reached for tissues cleaned and tidied himself as best he could.

Sally returned looking as though nothing untoward had happened.

"Right Richard, you naughty boy, you can take me home."

"Right, I'll just wash and we can go."

In the car there was a silence, broken after a moment but seemed to him an hour.

"Well, that was lovely, but that was it." said Sally almost casually. "You won't believe me I know, but I'm going to say it any way. I've never been unfaithful to Malcolm before, and as of now I'm not going to again."

"I... I..."

"Shut up and listen. I love Malcolm. I wouldn't do anything to jeopardize our relationship or hurt him, so if you tell a soul I'll see to it that you have your dick cut off in public, do you get that Richard? I am deadly serious."

He felt her stare at him. "Yes, I quite understand." He answered obediently.

He dropped her at the Hetherington household, still in darkness. Paul and Missy had not made it back from the hospital yet. He got out of the car and opened the door for Sally.

"Wait there" she ordered "while I put the lights on. Magardi!" she shouted and from the shadows emerged her guards. "Okay Richard you must go now.'" she pecked him on the cheek. "'I expect Malcolm will ring from Lagos soon, I'll tell him all the news," she hesitated, "about Joseph, ... good night."

Richard returned to his empty house, empty that was except for his elation, his guilt and his loneliness. He had another sleepless night.

# CHAPTER 25

"CANADIAN BUMBOY FLEES JUSTICE" trumpeted the Lagos Weekend. The Lagos Weekend newspaper brought much amusement to the expatriate population, as well as the locals. The report regarding Butter was detailed and graphically described by the "victim" of this apparently dreadful assault.

Other stories that week detailed how police in a hair-raising episode had pursued an armed robber and was headlined "ROBBER TURNS INTO GOAT TO ESCAPE POLICE". According to the report, the heroic Lagos police had cornered the armed robber, a dangerous fugitive from justice. However, they were unable to arrest the felon since, by the use of powerful ju-ju, he had turned himself into a goat. A black goat which, it transpired was a good deal more athletic than the police and had consequently escaped.

The police, however, were not to be easily evaded and they had later found and killed a black goat, which had subsequently been butchered and eaten.

A tail piece noted that the goat's owner had protested the goat's innocence. However the police were, adamant that they had got the right goat.

Later that month the paper excelled itself with the headline "PRICE OF A F**K GOES TO £5". Trade Unions had claimed that these rises were far in excess of Government guidelines. The workingman was again the victim of unseen taxes on his everyday pleasures.

These and other fables added to the fascination of living in such an enigmatic country. Love, hate, startling ingenuity, kindness, cruelty, plenty and poverty, all lived hand in hand. Together they weaved an intricate pattern, society always teetering on the brink of disaster or salvation.

Richard longed to be together with his wife and children. The remaining few weeks before he could join them seemed like years. The Club life with the "boys" had become tiresome and the absence of a steward added to his woes.

Since his adventure with Sally Hetherington he had avoided the family and not a day went by when he didn't feel the guilt gnawing at his soul. If no one ever found out he would still know and how could he face Joan and look her in the eye? What would happen when they returned from leave? He cursed himself and bemoaned his fate.

His housekeeping was as close to hopeless as had been Joseph's, but doing it himself made him regret the absence of the chaotic old steward.

He'd grabbed a few precious telephone conversations with Joan who'd urged him to get a new steward organized, but so far he'd been stubbornly indolent and done nothing.

On such a day, when his loneliness was at its highest, he returned home from work to find there was nothing to eat, so reluctantly dragged himself to the Club to find company and food.

Jack and Jill Walker, Lancastrians who'd been in Kaduna for twelve years, were the only people in the bar. The Walkers' were the sort of ex-patriots that both Richard and Joan disliked most. Jack Walker was a big coarse man who held down a middle management post, a level that he could sustain here, but not in the UK, or so Richard surmised. Richard had never forgotten his run in with Walker, neither had Jack. They disliked each other with an intensity that was almost tangible. Richard remained entrenched in his view that their length of service in Kaduna attested to their inability to generate a like standard of living elsewhere.

Jack smoked and drank heavily. He spent virtually all his leisure time in the Club, consuming vast quantities of Star beer. His bovine wife, who matched his drink consumption, usually accompanied him. Her tipple was 'gin and anything'. Richard had never heard her say anything other than 'Yes, love.' or 'that's reet Love.' in her broad Lancastrian accent. What aggravated Richard most was their obvious belief that they were in some way superior to any Nigerian and Walker always addressed them with that attitude entirely evident.

Richard received an invitation to sit with them with a sinking feeling. he sat and must have shown his reluctance.

"Eh, Lad, you do look fed oop. Have a Star. Daniel!" he ordered, "Bring Mister Smiles a beer," and then unnecessarily, "and be quick about it."

"What's up lad, missing a cuddle from Joan, eh?"

"Well, yes, that and other things. I'm without a steward as well, so things are hardly going smoothly at home, that's why I've come out for supper, no bloody food at home." He poured his beer and downed a cooling draught.

There followed a conversation that Richard did not enjoy. He was tempted into describing the circumstances of Joseph's departure that was meat and drink to Walker.

"All the bloody same, can't trust the bastards." He made no attempt to speak quietly so that Richard became acutely aware of Daniel the barman who could hardly do other than overhear.

"Whatever," intervened Richard, "I'm not doing very well without Joseph despite his exotic behavior."

The conversation continued to slice into Richards sensibilities and he was close to telling Walker where to stick his ideas when Sally and Malcolm entered the bar. Sally walked straight over and pecked him on the cheek, acknowledged the Walkers, and thrust three letters into his hand. Malcolm stood smiling just behind her.

"Didn't expect Sally to let you down, did you?"

Richard stood uncertain, clutching the letters and wondering what on earth they were.

"There we are, three references for stewards who are either immediately available or becoming available in the next few weeks," beamed Sally, "courtesy of Paul our steward and his peoples association."

Richard looked at the letters in his trembling hands and saw that they were indeed the particulars of domestic staff available, complete with employee references.

"I can't thank you enough. You know Sally was very kind during the fracas a couple of weeks ago. Hope you weren't put out Malcolm?"

"Why should I be put out, just the emergency for my Sally. ... Where have you been since?"

"Busy with work and trying to keep house actually." He relaxed slightly, but still could not bear to look at Sally.

"Anyway, join us for dinner. I've got some boring old business to talk about. I hope Jack won't mind if I drag you away."

There was no escape. He stood, excused himself from the Walkers' and trouped obediently to the dining room, behind the swinging chassis of the delicious Sally Hetherington. Dinner was a difficult hour. Richard kept stumbling and loosing the conversation.

Sally put her hand over his smiled at her husband and said, "Poor dear he's missing Joan and not looking after himself properly. Sooner you get the new steward, the better." She smiled, turning to Richard, "You can't go on leave without a steward fixed up, so you must crack on and see these chaps and soon. If you want any help, Malcolm and I will see them as well if you want a second opinion."

"You're very sweet but I'll muster my man management skills and hopefully choose the right man, but any doubt and I'll give you a ring." he drank his beer, "Thanks for rescuing me from the Walkers', you're both very kind." He excused himself, shook hands with Malcolm and kissed Sally lightly on her cheek. Her perfume almost overwhelmed him, not from its strength but the evocation of their coupling. He stood, gathered himself and walked away, not daring to look back.

As Richard counted down to his leave he faced up to the responsibility of hiring the new steward. The references were all very encouraging but at the same time all very different.

They varied from; David is honest and hardworking, to a lengthy description of the excellent casserole of pork, which another applicant cooked. Only two intimated that the candidate was good with children, which Richard and Joan had agreed was the prime quality they were looking for. From the variety of the references that the Hetherington's had gathered and a large number that were simply pushed through the gate, Richard decided to meet three of the hopefuls to start the ball rolling.

The first interview was with Peter, a tall, willowy man who presented himself punctually and was well turned out in his 'whites'. He was understandably nervous and quietly spoken. Richard liked him.

"Do you have a wife, Peter?"

"Yes Sah."

"Does she live with you?"

"No Sah, she lives in our village, it is not too far away."

"How often do you see her?"

"Once a month Sah, on leave days, Sah."

"Do you have children?"

"Yes Sah, two Sah, one boy and one girl Sah."  He smiled engagingly.

"Unfortunately we only have accommodation, one room, so room only for your wife if she visits."

"My wife she stays at home, I send money to keep them well.  She lives with my mother Sah." he explained.

"What do you cook?"

"Many things.  Chicken, rabbit, breakfast, meat and jelly." he beamed.

"Did your last Master like the food you cooked or did the Mistress cook?"

"Yes Sah, when the cook was off, he like my food plenty fine, Sah."

Richard's heart sank.  However, he continued to talk about children and other issues and Peter became more relaxed and engaging.  He smiled more and talked volubly about his own children and what the future held for them.  It struck Richard that he was at least a loving father and probably a decent housekeeper, but certainly a lousy cook.

He continued his search with ever diminishing returns.  Each candidate that followed, all gave Richard grounds for reserve.  None seemed as clean as Peter and none seemed as genuinely interested in children.  When he thought about it, cooking was not that important since Joan, supervised or cooked most meals of substance herself.

After a number of conversations with Joan grabbed over snatches of available and infrequent telephone connections, Peter got the vote.

He was to start the following week, since his existing employer was already packed up and ready to leave.  Richard was able to contact the man, a Mr. Mahaffey, who he'd met only once, but who confirmed that Peter was reliable and honest.  "Bloody awful cook, mind you, but an obliging and loyal lad."  Peter arrived three weeks before Richard was due to depart on leave. The whole business of boiling eggs and preparing toast again became a major area of focus, but Peter learned faster than his predecessor.

Geoff Dyke arrived from Port Harcourt when there was but a week to go. He was to supervise Universal Kaduna during Richard's six-week leave. Dyke's propensity for the consumption of Star beer was already a legend in Universal, so Richard vowed that during Geoff's stay, he drink moderately and avoid any benders with Geoff. All went well until the night before the departure for home. He and Geoff dined at the Hamdalah Hotel and fatefully decided to go to the Club for a night-cap.

The consequences were dire. It was midnight when Geoff, assisted by Mohamed, piled Richard into the back of his car. Mohamed raised Peter from his slumbers and they both manhandled their boss from the car into the house. Peter was somewhat taken aback, but soon relaxed as he and Mohamed fell into hysterical giggles as the paralytic Richard mumbled nonsense.

"Peter, you're're, a good man, a good man." he mumbled, not to anyone in particular. "Tomorrow, I'll, I'll, I'll, be home with my, my, my, beloved. Isn't that splendid?" He closed his eyes for a minute or a moment, and continued, "You'll, you'll, like the Madame, she very, vewey pretty. I love her to pieces, isn't that splendid? You, you…. mus, you must…." his eyelids dropped, followed by his chin.

Peter gently prodded his Master, "Sah, it would be good if you went to bed Sah." he whispered imploringly.

"Where was I? Ah, yes, you must be sure the house is in splendid order for Madame's return. You're a .."At which point eyelids and chin collapsed in unison.

The morning was not kind. Richard woke fully clothed on his bed with a mighty hangover which, even after showering, showed no sign of improving. He felt ghastly and cursed the jolly Dyke and his infectious drinking habits.

Peter was up and preparing breakfast; paw-paw, boiled eggs toast and tea. The noise of the crunching toast gave him cause to wince.

With difficulty, he toured the house with Peter and Mohamed writing down the maintenance chores that needed to be done during his leave and making sure that Peter knew where to get hold of Dyke or Eke during his absence. Matters of leave pay and comings and goings were confirmed and by eleven o'clock Richard loaded his luggage and climbed in beside Mohamed for the journey to Kano and then on to six long weeks leave in dear old Blighty.

News from England was good. Joan and children had settled in with Joan's parents in north London. Universal had organized all the logistics related to Emma's medical needs. Consultations at the Great Ormond Street Hospital had been arranged and chauffeurs were on hand to take Joan and Emma as necessary. The baby's condition responded well to the regime the medics imposed and soon she was putting on weight and catching up with lost ground.

# CHAPTER 26

Love was new, fresh, and fun. They'd missed each other. Joan was transformed back to her slim, attractive and sexy self. If anything, she was more attractive now than before her second pregnancy.

Emma, in the few short weeks, had transformed from a seven pound vulnerable baby to a twelve pound bouncing bundle, intent on passing the stone barrier. His Grandparents had spoilt David hopelessly. Grandma and Grandpa Page were in their mid sixties. They lived in north London in a three bed-roomed house that belonged to the local council. It was a far cry from their bungalow in Nigeria; here there were tiny front gardens and row after row of anonymous Victorian semidetached or terraced houses. The roads were jammed with parked cars, most of which were fairly ancient; many were in a state of dis-assembly, standing like cripples on jacks or bricks. Litter floated on the wind and danced a dervish dance in the corners of the buildings. The trains clattered by, rattling the terraced windows as they passed.

Richard tried his best to like his in-laws, but with his father-in-law, George, he found it difficult. George, a bony, mean looking man, had received scant education, was barely literate and a habitual gambler. He constantly smoked his foul smelling, roll your own cigarettes, coughed continuously as a consequence and complained about the variety of illnesses that had kept him from working as long as Richard could remember. George sat in his chair in the kitchen, always apparently unable to move due to his bad back. "Oh, oh, oh," was his constant moan, every time it was necessary for him to move, unless he was invited by Richard or other relative to visit the local pub, in which case his ability to move, miraculously and consistently improved.

Despite his illiteracy he studied the 'Racing Post' in finest detail and was able to squander large proportions of the meager family income at the bookies. He seldom won; at least that was what he led other people to believe, though Richard held the suspicion that he hoarded his winnings. When he did admit to a win he was off to the "George", his local pub. He never, as far as Richard knew, ever shared his booty with his long-suffering wife.

Emily the matriarch was by contrast one of the most generous and kind persons that Richard had ever met. She had been married to George for thirty-six years and she had borne him three daughters and three sons. All three daughters had inherited their mother's pretty face and her generosity of spirit. So too had Donny the eldest boy who was good looking, bright and quite an entrepreneur. The other two boys, however, inherited much of their father's qualities; to wit, indolence and a scarcity of grey matter.

All the children had left the parental home and there was but one other occupier beside George and Emily and that was Uncle Arthur.

Uncle Arthur was short, broad and ungainly. His age was hard to guess, though Joan believed him to be her mother's younger brother. He worked as a dustman for the Tottenham Council and was one of the last un-mechanized refuse collectors in the district. He pushed his cart shovels and brushes around the neighborhood, meticulously cleaning the pavements and gutters. He was happy in his work.

Arthur, unlike George, was a generous soul and showered his nieces' children with gifts and goodies. He was interested in listening to tales of life in Nigeria and beneath his shy and inarticulate exterior there lay an inquisitive and intelligent mind.

Arthur alas, was occasionally given to going on wild benders, particularly on the nights following payday. After the house had fallen asleep they would be awoken by Arthur's calamitous and supposedly quiet early morning home comings. Emily would always leave the door unlocked for him. Arthur would ignore this fact, despite the absolute certainty. He would struggle to get his key in the lock, mumbling all the while in a confused cockney chunter, scraping his key hither and thither, sounding like an army of rodents trying to gnaw their way in. This din would wake everyone within. They would hold their breath and wait for the inevitable aftermath. This consisted of Arthur falling through the door, which would open unexpectedly, at least for him. He would then pick himself up and slam the door behind him. He would make his way down the hall and up the stairs, bouncing from wall to wall, frequently displacing ornaments and flowerpots as he went. He would pause from time to time, balancing on a stair tread. Again the household would hold its collective breath lest he should collapse backward, which he sometimes did. He balanced precariously there, laughing a deep throaty laugh and then would continue to bungle his way to the tiny back bedroom, which was his modest castle. The final part of Arthur's nocturnal ritual was dropping his hobnailed boots one by one. There were always three and then there was a cacophonous snoring that reverberated down the street.

The little house accommodated the Smiles, but at a price. The children slept peacefully in the bedroom betwixt Uncle Arthur and George and Emily. Richard and Joan slept fitfully on the put-you-up in the tobacco stained sitting room. The novelty of their physical union in the first week sustained them, Joan released from the confines of pregnancy rejoiced in lovemaking which had nothing to do with making babies. Richard was first astonished by Joan's passion but found it easy and exciting to enjoy and encourage their new discovery of each other. Each night they waited hungrily for the rest of the family to retire so that they could get on with their night games. The risk of waking the house with cries and yelps of delight faded as they relaxed in the familiarity of the close little room and the assurance that George and Emily heard only what they wanted.

Despite the luxury of built-in baby sitters and London's theatres within a stone's throw, the claustrophobic nature of the arrangement soon began to pray on Richard's nerves. They had to endure three weeks in Tottenham before moving on to South Wales to do the rounds of Richard's family and three weeks seemed a long time. Joan, who had already spent a month with her parents, held on patiently, largely out of loyalty to her parents, but even she became ragged as the days ticked slowly by.

The two children were paraded passed the ranks of the Page family, tea parties, weekend lunches, all of which were torture to them both. Joan grinned and bore them; Richard did his best, but often took to groaning and complaining.

The first half of their leave passed as a patchwork of eroticism, theatre, family aggravation, impatience, treats and tribulations.

When the time came to pack up their family belongings and take the caravan on to the Smiles' home in deepest Wales, it was a mixture of pleasant relief and, for Joan at least, tinged with a little sadness.

Emma now with a clean bill of health, David strangely tetchy and grumpy, were packed like so many of the other bundles, firmly into the back of the car for the long journey west.

Joan dallied sad that she would not see her parents for another year, Richard relieved to be escaping the crowded house. They gathered on the front steps of the terraced house on the Saturday morning to bid their farewells. George complete with flat cap, waistcoat, and fag dangling from his unshaven lips, Emily weeping quietly, yet managing to smile for the children, and dear Uncle Arthur, not quite recovered from the excesses of his Friday night, gently rocking on his booted heels.

Arthur slipped his last ten pounds into Richard's hand, "For the little 'uns." he mumbled and turning, disappeared back into the house, leaving, as minor players do, to the principals' final curtain.

Richard embraced Emily with warmth and a hint of regret. He shook hands with George, and sat in the driving seat whilst Joan had one last hug from her Mum and Dad.

They were on their way to the land of his fathers, to Wales.

Wales was a place where they'd lived together before, so they looked forward to friends and family. Richard's parents, Muriel and Percy Smiles were in their sixties and had been married some thirty two years. Life had been hard, but they seemed to have been good for each other, although Richard was not naïve enough to believe that their relationship had been other than imperfect. One thing was certain, they'd loved Joan as their own since the moment they'd met her.

Percy was now unwell, he'd suffered a number of cerebral strokes that had greatly impaired his mobility and his speech, he walked with the aid of a stick, but his intellect (despite the more cumbersome speech mechanism) and humor seemed unimpaired. His excitement at the prospect of meeting his new granddaughter was at such a level that Muriel feared that he would become ill again. As a consequence of Percy's illness their business had failed so that they now lived in a modest house near the sea, outside the industrial town of their upbringing.

Muriel was a mercurial diminutive and pretty woman who, despite the trials of their latter years sustained a bright and quick humor which was never subdued, even in the toughest of times.

On their arrival late that Saturday afternoon, Percy's excitement bordered on the dangerous as he caught his first sight of Emma. He laughed and cried at the same time. His joy was unconfined. His inability to say what he wanted to say did not seem to matter. He had lived to hold his second grandchild was a gift beyond his measure. As he cuddled Emma, David and Joan in turn, the tears of thanksgiving poured down his face, Joan joined in sympathy, love and understanding.

Muriel, although she didn't join the emotional collapse, smiled wryly and understood, there in the midst of her family, that Percy's journey on this earth was all but complete.

The leave home was to be a terraced house in the town, which Muriel had arranged to rent for the three weeks of their stay. It was a short car ride from the Grandparents.

The town itself had changed since they had lived there. Much of the local industry of steel making and coal mining had closed. The town itself looked down at heel, empty shops scarred the main thoroughfare and knots of unemployed men, old and not so old, punctuated the street corners. The coast was scarred by the empty shells of old steel works, the whole town had an aura of a place that 'had been' something but now was lost.

It drizzled as they drove to their new temporary home and as they did their hearts sank at the prospect of staying here for another three weeks. The euphoria of the homecoming gave way to dread. Industrial South Wales in October hardly seemed exciting. The house itself was comfortable enough, though dark and damp on first impression. Joan, as always, accepted the positive side of everything, so soon the fire was alight, familiar toys unpacked and an air of comfortable togetherness prevailed.

The one event, which dominated the local scene, was the imminent visit of the New Zealand All Blacks rugby team that was to play the Scarlets, the town's pride and joy. The Welsh, as only the Welsh can, generated a tense sense of anticipation, this game of rugby football transcended all in importance. Even the obituary column in the local paper was cut back to accommodate stories, however remotely linked to the big match. Nothing else mattered, politics, disasters of national or international dimension deserved no mention; only the match. This match would put the town onto the world map, every man, woman and child in the borough was affected, their lives depended upon it, The Scarlets would win and add to their historic scalps of Australia and South Africa the biggest and the best, the All Blacks.

Hope reigned supreme, this time the mighty would fall, brought to earth by the heroes of this small town. Small boys and girls believed it would happen, old ladies with shopping trolleys believed it might happen, old men with short memories believed it could happen, drunks in pubs predicted it would happen. Richard wanted a ticket, then and only then he would be part of anything that was going to happen.

His search for this Holy Grail took him that first night, with Joan's reluctant permission, to his old rugby club, one of several in the town. He was received warmly, but casually, for people who left Wales were after all of limited importance. His old friends greeted him as if he had never been away. They showed complete indifference to his African exploits and expressed mild surprise that anyone could be away from home when the match tickets for next Tuesday's match went on sale. Such behavior clearly brought into question his sanity.

"Well, Smiley," they said nodding their sorrowful brows, "we'll do our best, but tickets at this stage are rarer than rocking horse shit, sit here bach, and have a pint. We'll put out the word, but we can't promise."

Relatives were equally incredulous. Richard had always been an eccentric boy, first he'd married an English girl, nice mind you, but there were plenty of nice girls here in Wales. Then going off around the world; to Africa, if you please. Richard had callings beyond his station - no doubt about it. Now, however, his eccentric behavior was confirmed, coming home at the last minute and expecting to get a ticket for the big match, a ticket as prized as a Bardic crown, the boy was, without doubt odd.

Joan took all this curious tribal behavior with equanimity. This part of Wales was no place for an English girl with no idea about rugby football. She felt like a Buddhist at a Welsh non-conformist convention. She paraded her children to aunts and uncles, but was more content to spend time with Percy and Muriel with whom she was comfortable and with whom she shared real love and affection.

David, now getting on for thirty months old, got along with Percy almost as well as he did with Mussa. The two spent ages in the garden and walking down by the sea side. David still gabbled pidgin' mixed with a dash of Hausa, much to Percy's huge amusement and his mother's annoyance. Percy responded from instinct and it mattered not a jot to David that his Granddad talked a hesitant gobbledegook. They played happily hour after hour, the old invalid and the sprightly toddler. Muriel doted over Emma and became Joan's firmest friend.

A day to go, and still he had no ticket for the big match. Richard abandoned his family and embarked on a continuous crawl of the pubs and clubs. Joan put up with his anxieties and impatience, but objected to his intemperance. He eventually struck lucky when an old Irish Welsh friend by the name of Shanahan presented him a ticket. They celebrated the event with much vigour at the bar. Richard felt duty bound to reward his new life long friend for the great favour that he had bestowed. They drank prodigiously and enthusiastically as they analysed and postulated on the results of the great day that was to follow. Hope lifted the Welsh hearts although Richard had a tiny reservation that perhaps there was some whistling in the dark.

He arrived at the temporary home in the early hours and, due to the relative unfamiliarity with the place, made a somewhat uncoordinated entry, falling over the umbrella stand in the finest traditions of Uncle Arthur.

Breakfast was not a happy event.

"I'm fed up with your Welsh antics. Since we've been down here you've ignored us entirely and dumped us on your parents." she announced stiffly, as she served the children their fruit, "'Today is the last day, do you hear, you selfish sod,"

"Sorry sweetheart." replied Richard staring into his cereal bowl, "I'm going to the game." he waved his ticket in triumph, unable to suppress a wide and stupid grin.

"Hooray, hoo-bloody-ray." responded Joan, just as Emma slid her bowl of porridge onto the flagged floor. "Who cares about your bloody ticket?" She said, as she mopped up the mess.

David gurgled, "Grandpa Percy, hah, he does playa, Rank a de de."

Joan packed the children up, ready to take the children to Percy's without another word. Just before she was to leave she relented, she turned and kissed Richard on the forehead. "I hope your boys have a good day. Behave yourself and get home safe and sober, that isn't too much to ask, is it?"

"Celebrate if we win and drown our sorrows if we lose." he kissed her back, "I'll try to be good."

They started at the rugby club at eleven thirty. At two thirty the ground was full to overflowing, by four fifteen, God had kissed the little town. Scarlet's; nine, New Zealand; three.

Joy was unconfined. The town became a cauldron of hubris, pride and swagger. Not that there was any malice or condescension to the visitors, there was only togetherness, a sharing and a common delight. Here amidst the industrial decline there was still a reason for it all. Here, despite the depression, was fame and character and heroism. Our boys, had triumphed where few dare to hope. Our boys were a team of skill and guts that made you proud.

The pubs and clubs were filled to and beyond capacity, laughter was in the air, myths were borne, heroes were exalted. The team coach was declared a genius, which confirmed a view already widely held.

"Did you see, did you ever see such a thing before?"

"What a kick!"

"Wasn't it wonderful?"

"Bloody wonderful."

"Smiley, you don't see things like that in bloody Africa."

"Lend me a quid."

"Have a pint."

"I'll owe you one."

"Have another."

And so it went on. The great wonder was that amongst that heaving, drunken mass, there was not an atom of ill temper, no fights, few arguments, nothing but warmth, camaraderie and hospitality. The Welsh, they call it "hiraeth".

Many people reached their capacity and could drink no more, if they bent over at their waist neat beer would be decanted from their saturated torsos.

Others fled to their houses in time to pass out, some were driven by hunger. They went home to eat, determined to return to the festivities. If anything was underdone that day it was food. The pubs and clubs never dreamt that fifteen thousand spectators would produce a party of twenty five thousand. Fathers, brothers, sisters and mothers gathered in the streets, poured into their locals and joined the celebrations.

At seven thirty things started going badly wrong, the first pub ran out of bitter beer and soon the crisis spread, until at ten o'clock those dedicated to drinking the night away converged in masses into the town centre. Here the Mardi gras, Coronation night, Victory in Europe all rolled into one.

Richard Smiles, a relatively well-trained drunk had stayed the pace. As well as a Welshman who could drink, he was also a Welshman who, by all the laws of music, could not sing. But on that night he sang his heart out. The whole town sang, and the flat basso profundo of Richard Smiles mingled with a thousand sharp Welsh tenors, an equal number of slightly off key baritones, a lesser number of delicious sopranos, and low and behold - beauty!

The darkened sky was filled with music and Smiles was part of it all. He belonged.

In time, stomachs and heads could take no more, so the town slowly quietened down until at midnight only the hardiest were still on their feet.

As he crawled into bed alongside his beloved, he nuzzled under her outstretched arm and filled with Welsh melancholy descended into a dream filled sleep.

He did not belong, that was the issue. He would in all probability never return to live in Wales. He was an adventurer by nature. In his dream he sailed forever from Galadima Road, passed Stradey Park, via Tottenham and strange lands he didn't know. The strange thing was he could never get off the boat, but to his dismay, Joan, David and Emma stood on the shore waving, waving... he had to stop...

The party went on for days. The pubs were replenished; the legend was massaged, polished and nurtured. Even visitors like Joan could not help but be caught up in the euphoria. She resigned to looking after the children and visiting Pa and Ma Smiles. Richard was having his week of weeks, something she knew he would live on for years, something that was dear to him, almost as his family, his tribe.

Percy too, although unable to join in the extremes of merriment, had been taken out by Richard to share in the creation of the new legend, to meet some of his old mates. Some barely remembered him and he had difficulty in placing who was who. But it didn't matter; they were comrades who'd been heroes in their day, albeit on minor fields.

For the men of the Smiles family these were golden days together. Percy, Richard and the girls and children were one. Percy was overwhelmed by the gifts of his grandchildren, wakened from his invalidity to share briefly with his son the boisterous joys of maleness and comradeship.

All too soon though it was time to go. Percy was beside himself with grief. He knew, they all knew that this would be his last farewell.

As they all settled into the car, Percy let out a dumb wail - he said "I love you, Goodbye, I'll watch over you from heaven."

Richard could hardly see through his tears as he steered the car into the traffic. In the mirror, Percy shrank clutching his walking stick, but supported by his rock - Muriel. She stood, her arm around him, waving, her eyes quite dry, her heart resolved.

# CHAPTER 27

Their return to Nigeria was as uneventful as a return to Nigeria can be. They travelled for the first time as a family, their collective experience having in some part prepared them for what was to come. Even the rigours of Kano airport immigration and customs were taken with aplomb. The parents unashamedly used their children as decoys for grumpy officials, all of whom fell for the gambit and waved them through.

Mohamed greeted them with his beaming smile, with warmth that reflected his genuine affection for the family. He reported on the way to Kaduna that Peter, the new steward, had been working hard preparing the house for their return.

"Sah, Peter is a good man. He is afraid that Madame will not like him. That she will throw him away."

"Don't be silly," Joan responded, "'you sound sillier than the Master's tribe in Wales. If Peter is a good man as you say, I'm sure we'll be happy working together."

After the tedious journey from Kano, the car swept into Galadima Road. Mussa, the garden boy, stood to attention; rake in hand straight, as a soldier's rifle. He peered into the car with unconcealed delight at the prospect of being reunited with David.

Despite the parents' decision to limit David's time with Mussa, this resolution was an attempt to rescue David's chaotic grasp of English, it seemed churlish to spoil their reunion. David was home and he was happy, Mussa took David's hand gingerly, but David embraced his friend exuberantly before dashing into the garden.

Standing at the front door, taller than Richard remembered, was Peter. He was immaculately turned out in a sparkling white uniform.

"Darling, this is Peter our new Steward. Peter this is Madame. She is the boss." He made the introductions lightly, but Peter remained taught and strained.

"Welcome Madame, welcome Sah." Said Peter bowing stiffly from the waist.

"It's good to meet you. This is Emma and David is the noise in the garden."

They entered the house and stood, as if rooted to the spot. The house shone from the floor to the ceiling everything was as clean as a pin. The woodwork was highly polished the curtains and soft furnishings were bright as new. There were flowers freshly cut on the table. The bright, clean regime extended throughout the house and included Peter's own quarters.

Joan pinching her husband's bottom, "You've got something right, smarty." she whispered.

Not only was the house as spick and span as Joan herself would have delivered, all the bills for cleaning the curtains and maintenance repair were laid out in order, all countersigned by Geoff. The kitchen was well stocked and the fridge was full, although some of the products were not the usual. In particular there was a large quantity of yam and in the fridge some very strange looking meat, which looked as if it had been cut with a very blunt instrument.

Joan prepared the childrens' supper early and got them to bed early. Peter laid the table immaculately for dinner. Joan casually enquired about the dinner menu and they both grimaced at the prospect. They had mumbled and cogitated over the prospect of the rabbit and yam. As far as they both knew there were no rabbits in Nigeria. A series of casual questions to Peter elicited few enlightening answers.

"Where did you get the rabbit?"

"From dee market."

"Do you often get rabbit?"

"Yes, Mam."

The odor from the kitchen was rich and overpowering with the smell of cooking palm oil and the meal was proudly presented at seven thirty.

The yam was fibrous and bland, but not too unpleasant, however the meat was the toughest either had ever experienced and even Richard's carnivorous instincts were blunted. They thanked Peter who was clearly disappointed; he stood at the kitchen door.

'Excuse me Madame,' he enquired, 'what shall I do with the rabbit, there is plenty?'

'Well Peter, we're very tired after our journey and not really hungry. Why don't you take it for your supper?' replied Joan. 'Tomorrow we'll go and get some chicken and things, okay?'

Peter seemed pleased and retreated.

After a dessert of fruit and custard, sourced from the safety of tins, they bade their new Steward goodnight and retired exhausted to begin another tour.

They showered, retreated to the balm of their air-conditioned bedroom and lay naked side-by-side, reminiscing and speculating. They mingled their thoughts, their hands and then their bodies in lazy love, which was abruptly interrupted by the screams of the over-heating Emma.

It was good, was it, to be back?

Peter's ability and keenness to keep house was not contested, however his culinary skills left much to be desired. Echoes of past disasters persuaded Joan to assert herself in the kitchen, taking a firmer and firmer hand in the cookery department. Soon Peter was settled in the role of assistant chef. Peace, cleanliness, harmony and good food reigned in the Smiles household.

# CHAPTER 28

Eke was genuinely pleased to welcome Richard back. Although everything seemed well, Geoff Dykes' role and rule over the preceding six weeks had tried Eke's patience. Eke liked order and to be left alone to get things done. It emerged that Geoff, though friendly enough, was erratic and unpredictable.

Mbamane had returned a cripple, his right arm a useless disfigured appendage. Eke had found him a job as Works Planner and he had applied himself with studied application, learning to use his left arm for everything, including writing. Mbamane greeted Richard with a respect that he, Richard, did not think he deserved, but for all his misfortune he seemed content and determined to succeed.

Adebayo the former chauffeur was happily employed in the stores and Eke reported that there had been one further epileptic attack and that had been nowhere near as severe as the first that they had witnessed.

Sales and customer relations had not apparently suffered under Geoff's reign, but there was a long list of customer visits throughout the North that needed his early attention. This would mean at least two days away from home each week for the foreseeable future.

Socially, change was more dramatic. On their first week back, the Hetherington's threw a dinner party and Joan had been an instant hit. The belle of the ball. The attitude of the males present was enthusiasm with barely concealed lecherous undertones. The females who'd been so friendly during Joan's pregnancy could hardly conceal their astonishment at her transformation. Even Sally Hetherington, usually the centre of attention, behaved differently, taking Joan confidentially aside and later making eyes at Richard. Those eyes carried an unmistakable message – "come and get me".

When they got home that night Joan was flushed with her own success.

"Isn't it lovely to be normal again." she purred.

"You're just gorgeous and everyone knew it."

"Don't be silly."

"All the guys, including Malcolm Hetherington, wanted to have you, and all the ladies, including Sally were jealous as hell."

"And what about you, my Richard, my Dick, would you like to have me?"

They made frantic lustful love. Joan was more passionate than he could remember. Many of her inhibitions had melted away, her sex was something central; a powerful core, an essential part of her he had not seen before. She was renewed, liberated and loved it.

In their lustful murmurings they opened the box of their secret dreams, their fantastic visions, they fed on each other until they lay exhausted, it was as if a veil had been removed from between them, revealing a beautiful, exciting but dangerous promise.

The first Saturday was the monthly dinner dance at the Club. They joined the Hetherington's, whose other guests included Major and Mrs. Sandhu, seconded from the Indian Army to the Nigerian Defense Academy, Donald and Sue Rawlings and the new General Manager of the Bank, John Gombe, a Nigerian, and Anna his wife, a beautiful Singaporean.

The Gombe's were interesting. They had met at university in the UK and John, though still in his thirties, was obviously marked for the big time. Anna his wife was charming but reserved.

After dinner they all danced to the dissonant strains of the NDA band. Richard and Joan smooched, despite the heat and he whispered in her ear.

"I'm the luckiest man in the room."

"Only in the room?" she giggled, "Don't tell lies, I've seen the way you look at Anna. By the way, her husband's not bad either."

"Into black fellas are we?" quipped Richard.

"I don't know about you, I can only speak for myself." she licked his ear.

Later in the evening two young Nigerian Officers came over to the table ostensibly to present their compliments to Major Sandhu. Then one spoke to Malcolm and one to Richard and asked permission to dance with their wives.

"Sir, may I have the honor to dance with your wife?" they intoned nervously, but in unison.

"Please, ask the lady," replied Richard.

"Certainly." responded the urbane Malcolm.

Sally and Joan smiled, accepted with alacrity and were swept away by the young gallants. John Gombe was quite taken aback, he whispered to Richard in his best British "I say old boy, that wouldn't do for me at all."

"Would you mind if I danced with Anna?" was the only response Richard could think of.

"Not at all"

"Anna, a dance?" Richard stood his hand outstretched. Anna's reserve showed no sign of weakening. They danced stiffly; he was reminded of a china doll, fragile, vulnerable and quite unbending. In a few short moments the number came mercifully to an end.

Joan and Sally were escorted back to the table by their beaus, who bowed politely and expressed their thanks with solemnity. After they left Sally whispered conspiratorially to Joan just within Richard's earshot, "I wonder what he had in his pocket?" They shrieked with laughter and downed their cocktails.

Suddenly, Richard became angry, jealousy and lust, stirred by alcohol, changed his good humor into something altogether uglier. Without a word he made his excuses and ushered Joan away to the car. They travelled the short distance home in stony silence.

They slept back to back, neither sure if they knew the cause of the fracture.

# CHAPTER 29

Domestically, life was a lot easier. Their daily routine started at sun up. Richard showered, breakfasted, while Joan got the children started for the day.

Peter's only shortcoming was his complete lack of sympathy with cooking and food. If left to his own devices in the kitchen the results turned out to be bizarre. However, his other attributes far outshone this shortfall. The house was always clean, the laundry sparkled and was crisply ironed and there was never a time when the parents had to fret about the safety or welfare of their children.

David had joined junior school a step up from nursery and his English was gradually improving to that of a nought year old. He tended still to spend time with Mussa in the garden after school and so he reverted to their secret but incomprehensible language.

Emma had settled down well, was the apple of her mother's eye and all her health problems seemed to be solved. Joan divided her time between the children, supervising the kitchen and socializing with the ladies, frequently with Sally Hetherington, who seemed to become her bosom friend. This last issue caused Richard some anxiety, he didn't know why. Perhaps it was fear of his dalliance with Sally being revealed, perhaps it was because he had not forgotten "the eye" that Sally had so purposefully given him, and perhaps he was afraid that the devil that was in Sally could get to Joan too.

Despite all this domestic bliss Richard was not faring well at breakfast, where Peter just like Joseph before him, found it impossible to boil an egg. After yet another catastrophic result of Peter's attempts to serve boiled eggs and toast, which resulted in a minor fire and the welding of an aluminium saucepan to the cooker, Richard was determined to set up a systematic training programme focused solely on the preparation of boiled eggs.

"Peter, tomorrow I want you, for breakfast - no I don't want you for breakfast - I want you to boil de water for de eggs when I tell you, okay? I will tell you from de shower- okay?"

"Yes Sah."

"I will shout 'put on de water. You put on de water to boil, okay?"

"Yes Sah."

"When de water boils you shout to me 'water boil', okay?"

"Yes Sah." responded Peter, accepting these absurd proposals with equanimity.

"You get de eggs on the side ready, okay? Then when I say to you 'egg on', you put the eggs in de boiling water, okay?"

"When I shout 'egg off', you take the eggs from de water, okay?"

"Yes, Sah." Peter was taking attentive note.

"Okay, that's what we do for breakfast tomorrow, okay?"

'Yes Sah.' Peter withdrew looking confident.

The next morning Richard awoke as usual at sun up. From the bathroom, after finishing shaving and before stepping into the shower he shouted "Peter!"

"Yes, sah."

"Boil de water."

"Yes Sah."

After showering the shouted commands continued "Peter, eggs on!"

"Yes, Sah"

Richard slipped into his pants trousers and shirt in the four minutes that intervened.

"Peter!"

"Yes Sah."

"Eggs off."

"Yes sah." came the confident reply.

Richard marched brusquely into the dining room where the table was, as usual, neatly laid. The toast was in the rack, the paw-paw in its bowl, his tea cup, saucer and tea pot in their precise place, as was his egg cup, and at last after two years of frantic efforts there were two perfectly boiled eggs.

"Peter!"

"These are perfect – well done."

Peter beamed and Richard, could hardly contain his delight, such a small thing but at last, - at last - success

The quality of boiled eggs remained erratic, largely because Richard failed to sustain his training programme and because Peter had no feeling for food of any sort. However breakfast did improve but only when Richard remembered to shout his 'Egg on' instructions. This parade ground nonsense aggravated Joan beyond measure. David though went to school each day shouting "egg on, egg off" much to the bewilderment of his teacher.

Peter for his part remained obdurately kack- handed as far as food was concerned. He would eat absolutely anything, from raw eggs to dead rat, all seemed to be food to him, the process of eating, a necessity to be endured. Far better that he spend his time polishing, folding or carving wood, which he did in his spare time and did it rather well.

# CHAPTER 30

Three weeks had passed since their return.. Richard was at the Central Hotel in Kano when he received a phone call that he had dreaded, but that he knew would come.. Percy had had a stroke that Muriel feared would be his last.

"Darling your bag is packed, I've asked Rhoda to arrange any available seat for you tonight on Nigerian Airways, it leaves in about two and a half hours. Malcolm's driver is on his way with your packed bag, he should be at the airport in about an hour from now."

For a moment Richard couldn't take it all in, "Aren't you coming?" he stammered; suddenly lost.

"I'd never get the kids organised love. I've spoken to Muriel and she doesn't expect me and the children. It's you she really wants and I don't think there's much time...."

"Okay, I suppose so....Well done my lovely, you've done a marvelous job." his mind began to pick up the pace, "I'll ring you when I've got a seat confirmed and if I can't get through I'll send a message back with Mohamed or Malcolm's driver. Shit, where's Mohamed? He's got the night off. Never mind let me worry about that. Look after the brood, I'll be back as soon as I can, I love you."

The Nigerian Airways desk was amazingly helpful, yes his agent had made a reservation, and yes the flight was on time, and yes they would make arrangements for him to check in late, up to half an hour before take off.

He phoned back Joan and amazingly again got through at first try. She had already made the support arrangements through Regan.

A hasty and tearful farewell; "Don't worry about us, love." sobbed Joan tenderly, "I hope you get home before - you know – dear, dear old Percy..." she trailed off.

"I'll tell him you love him. Goodbye my love"

He swallowed and quietly put down the telephone and was off to the airport. He left a note for Mohamed with the car keys and left, now only to receive his travel bag and passport, which duly arrived earlier than he expected.

The journey to London was comfortable and the eight hours to London Heathrow passed half in a doze and half in a reverie about him and his father, Percy, Percy who would give his son his last penny. Percy who loved Joan almost more than Richard himself, Percy who loved Emma and David as much as anyone in the world, Percy who'd been Muriel's charge for the last ten years - Muriel without Percy - a life without a smile.

.Universal had sent a chauffeur from Head Office to be at his disposal and certainly to drive him to Wales. The Chauffeur was George by name.

The journey to Wales was a blur of sleep and confusion. He woke at the outskirts of his home town and gave George directions to Percy's little house. It was not yet eleven in the morning.

The door opened, Muriel threw her arms about him,

"Richard, my darling boy. I never dreamt that you'd get home so fast - who's this?" she enquired, seeing George standing respectfully behind her son.

"This is George, who's kindly driven me down from London. George, this is my mother, Muriel Smiles."

"You must both be tired. Come in and have a cup of tea." said Muriel turning and darting into the house.

"How's Dad?"

"Not well I'm afraid, he's in the 'Bryn'. You know, the geriatric hospital. Doctor Tom didn't think there was any point in sending him to the General or Morriston. Your Dad had a very bad stroke yesterday morning as he was getting up. Tom, that's our Doctor," she explained for George's benefit, "came right away. Percy was on the floor and I couldn't lift him. He called an ambulance right away. I don't think your father knew anything really."

She poured the tea.

"How's Joan and the children? Percy really fell for Joan you know."

"Joan fell for Percy." Richard responded to no one in particular.

"Excuse me, Sir." said George, "You are to ring this number Sir; a Miss Elliot will want to help you with anything that you may need. Here is a package for you. Could you sign for me here Sir?" He handed over a large envelope. Richard had no idea of the contents.

"Do you have a 'phone, Mrs. Smiles?"

"May I Sir?"

"Sure"

George dialed the number, explained the story so far to the ubiquitous Miss Elliot and handed the phone to Richard.

"Good morning Mr. Smiles," she sounded efficient, "how is your father?"

"Hanging on, thank you, and oh, thank you for all you've done so quickly."

"No problem. It's group standard practice if issues of a compassionate nature arise for our ex-patriot senior managers. Do you mind if I run through a check list?"

"Not at all." Replied Richard suddenly very weary.

"You've received the envelope from Mr. Gilchrist?"

"Gilchrist?"

George politely coughed in the corner from behind his tea cup.

"Oh, George, yes thank you."

She went on and on about the hire car that would be delivered to his parents address and the details of his passport and Nigerian visa. Her efficiency somehow grated on his weariness and the urgency to be with his father. She went through the details of the contents of the envelope that consisted of cash and contact numbers. He was relieved when she eventually put down the phone. She was gone. Miss Elliot, he imagined, flapped her starched angel's wings and got things done by white ju-ju.

"I shall be leaving now, Sir." said George, "Can I drop you anywhere on the way Sir?"

"Yes please George, you can drop me off at the hospital it's on you way – okay mum?"

"You go. I'll come after lunch. Evan next door will give me a lift."

Percy lay in a single side ward. He was waxen white, in a sparkling white hospital gown. A tube ran from his nose and another to his arm. He looked, for all the world, that he was asleep.

Richard stood stock still, a male nurse at his side, "Is he asleep?" he whispered.

"Not exactly, he's in a coma really." replied the nurse with a sigh.

"What's the prognosis?"

"You'd really have to ask the doctor, but well you know he could improve, but then again he might not." He shuffled and looked at the floor and then he walked neatly round the bed and tidied the already tidy pillows. "Come far, have you? You look tired."

"Only three thousand six hundred miles-ish, from Nigeria actually." Richard replied, trying to sound matter-of-fact and low key.

"Good gracious, do sit down Mr. Smiles." The nurse was impressed.

Richard sat, the nurse left on tiptoe. He took his father's hand in his.

"Chwmae Bach, how goes the battle?" he whispered. He was not sure if there was a response or flicker, perhaps the tiniest reflex.

"Dad, I'm here. Joan sends her love…" he drifted .."We all send our love."

Percy's breathing was irregular, but in a constant sort of way, but he realized that those hopeful signs of recognition were a figment of his imagination.

He sat there fretting whether he should be with Percy or Muriel. He didn't know how to behave; fatigue swept over him and his whole world lay with his father's hand in his. In the moment he did knew that Percy had been his best friend. He knew that Percy would willingly give his last breath to his son. He knew that whatever love was, he loved his father. Tears welled up and he sobbed a farewell to Percy. After a few minutes he stopped crying. He resisted sleep, but in vain.

Richard blinked awake, it was gone two o'clock. Muriel appeared "How's your Dad?"

"Just the same I think."

The nurse returned and shooed them out of the room while he attended to Percy.

Muriel and Richard sat together with the comatose Percy.

"It's not always been perfect with your father, but I wouldn't have changed any of it,…..for the world."

"He has always been my best pal, especially in the last ten years, I shall miss him."

"We will all miss him,"

Richard started to cry again, "Don't be a silly boy, come here." and his mother hugged him. He detached himself gently and looked down on his dear dying father. His breathing became shallower and bubbly. They sat and waited. At five o'clock Richard stretched;

"Come on mum, let me take you home. You can make me a quick meal. I'm starving. I'll come back later."

They drove home in silence. Richard, bathed, changed and devoured bacon and eggs. They watched TV for a while and Richard stood and paced the room.

"Okay mum, I'll just slip up to the hospital to see how Dad is doing."

"I'll come too."

"No, bach you stay here and rest."

He arrived back at the hospital at around eight p.m. Percy was as they had left him, his breathing was still uncertain. Richard sat and took his father's hand once more and settled to the long watch. His first impression was how cold Percy's hands and fingers were. He felt for his feet and these too were freezing.

For no reason at all Richard began talking, about Joan, the children, the experiences in Nigeria. He talked about the Scarlets and the All Blacks, he talked about Percy's business, his own childhood and the things they had loved to do together.

Percy slipped away some time late that night, around midnight. His breathing stuttered for some time and then stopped.

In the perfect silence, Richard held his dead Dad's hand, said a prayer of thanks and commended his beloved father to God. He sat, released his father's hand, wrapped his arms about himself and wept. After ten minutes or so, he walked to the nurse's station and said quietly "Mr. Smiles has slipped peacefully away."

The nurse leapt up and began to dash to Percy's side, Richard gently restrained him and said "No, no, leave him be at peace."

The nurse, more sedately now, checked Percy's pulses and nodded.

"Would you like to stay a while?"

"No, it's okay. Thank you for your kindness to my father. You've looked after him beautifully." He shook the nurse's hand, patted him on the shoulder and left for home.

He quietly opened the front door and tiptoed into the house. Muriel was asleep in the chair. He kissed her lightly on the forehead, "Come on mum, it's passed your bed time."

He helped her up the stairs.

"How's your Dad?" she asked sleepily.

"Asleep." He whispered, "Asleep"

In the morning Muriel was at first angry with him, but soon she regained her humor. They both leant one upon the other in their grief. After an hour or so they set about the "arrangements".

By noon, news of Percy's death spread and a stream of visitors began to arrive at the house. Muriel's sister arrived that afternoon and assured Richard that she would stay as long as it takes to help Muriel recover from her loss.

The funeral was as funerals are. Friends, relations and lots of people that Richard did not know turned up in droves. The Welsh have a way with funerals, the older women particularly, assumed a oneness with the widow, almost like a supportive maul of rugby forwards, all those closed round the injured one, helping her carry her grief.

The men, however, seem to behave more like rugby three quarters, enjoying of their privileged closeness with the deceased. Showing off, claiming intimacies that were much exaggerated.

The service in the small house was moving, not least because of the proximity of the mourners to the coffin. As was customary, only the males accompanied Percy to the crematorium.

The men sang 'Bread of Heaven' to a tape-recorded accompaniment, as Percy's remains slid away into the furnace. The returning cortege stopped at the 'Island House' where Richard bought forty-two pints of Bass bitter to toast Percy's memory. Close members of the family then went on to join the ladies back at the house for ham salad, cake and afternoon tea. There were also huge helpings of family gossip.

Muriel was remarkably strong throughout the events of those five days that led to the funeral. They had been married nearly forty years and she had obviously prepared herself. This preparation had not lessened her grief but it had strengthened her resolve to manage her future, which would be largely alone.

Two days after the funeral Richard held his mother in a fond, sad, farewell embrace. Only then did she weaken and show her vulnerability, it was Richard's turn to be strong. He failed. They both stood weeping violently in a hug neither could bear to end.

There were promises of visits to Nigeria, how time would soon pass, and once more Richard pulled away and with a choking lump in his throat set out for London and Nigeria.

# CHAPTER 31

At Kano he had a palaver with immigration because the Nigerian Embassy in London had made a technical mistake in renewing his re-entry visa that led to a delay of over an hour and stretched Richard's patience to its limit.

"Where have you been?" demanded the large intimidating Immigration Officer.

"Home for my father's funeral." responded the exhausted Richard, deadpan.

"You should have had your re-entry permit regularised before you left the country." responded the official.

"I didn't have time, my father was dying."

"I thought you said you went to his funeral?"

"He died when, rather the day after, I got home."

"So you did not go to his funeral, you went to see him. You should have had your visa stamped before you left the country."

Richard felt a strong urge to punch his lights out, but patience prevailed.

"I'm sorry officer. I went home as a matter of urgency. I thought your embassy in London had regularised the visa situation. If they have not I can only apologise, but here we are. Now, what do you suggest?"

The objectionable fellow insisted "I do not know if we can let you back into the country Mr. Smiles. The embassy is only appropriate for people with residential permits, not work permits or dependents' permits. It is…" he spread his arms for emphasis, "a most unfortunate and irregular business." He continued staring at Richard's passport "Please take a seat. I'll talk to my senior boss. He may or may not be able to help you. I will do what I can, but it will be difficult for me."

'Bollocks' thought Richard, 'if I have to sit here all day I am not, not, not going to give this bastard a dash.'

Another hour went by. Richard became anxious that Mohamed might assume that he had not made the flight and depart. He knocked on the door marked "Immigration Officials Only".

"Please wait." The unmistakeable nasal tones of the oppressor bade him stay outside. A further ten minutes, Richard knocked on the door of the immigration department again. This time the rotund official emerged, clearly chewing the remnants of his breakfast.

"Mr. Smiles." he leered, "I have been unable to reach my superior officer, I am sorry." he sneered, "You'll have to wait a bit longer."

"How much longer?"

"Not too much - it depends when I can reach him."

"Look," said the surrendering Richard, "it's important I get to Kaduna. Is there anything I can do to help get your senior officer back here?"

"Well Sah," he beamed, "I will have to telephone his home and since this is not his shift I will have to get a taxi to bring him back, Sah!"

"Would twenty five pounds cover your expenses?"

"'More like fifty Sah." he replied, staring straight into Richard's eyes.

Richard put the fifty pounds down.

The fat man exited, pocketing the money as he went, five minutes later he returned.

"All is okay, Mr. Smiles. Welcome to Nigeria." He stamped Richard's passport and handed it to him with a flourish.

With only hand baggage, Richard scooted through the empty customs hall and found Mohamed anxiously pacing the arrivals concourse.

He had never been so glad to get home. It was as if all the grief, the exhaustion, the frustration all fell away as Joan held him in her arms and David tugged at his trousers and Emma cooed from her cot. Yes he was so glad to be home.

# CHAPTER 32

On Monday he was glad to be back in the old routine, work, the factory, things to decide, things to do. Daniel Oki, one of Malcolm's audit clerks, was doing the monthly trial balance and was as usual seen concentrating hard on his job in the outside office. He tapped tentatively on Richard's door.

"Good morning, Meester Smiles." he smiled nervously.

"What can I do for you Daniel? Sit down old boy, have a coffee."

Daniel sat shuffling his papers, even more nervously than usual

"I think we have a... a... problem, Sah." he almost whispered the last words.

"Don't call me Sir, Daniel, I've told you before. What sort of problem?"

"I cannot balance the month end; I am two thousand pounds adrift."

"How can that be, are you sure?" He asked the question, but he knew the answer, of course he was sure. "Oh, shit. Any ideas how or who?"

Daniel shuffled on his seat, adjusted his spectacles, coughed, shuffled again, but said nothing.

"Come on Daniel, you must have some idea?"

Again more shuffling and little grunts, "It's definitely a cash shortfall, not a stock problem."

Just then Rhoda tapped on the door and peered into the office.

"Not now, Rhoda love."

"But Sah, it is the Sergeant of Police!'"

"The Sergeant of Police?" He looked at Daniel quizzically. Daniel shook his head vigorously in the negative.

"Tell the Sergeant I shall see him in a moment."

Rhoda retreated as ordered.

"I say, Daniel." he said as soon as Rhoda departed, "You don't think the police are on to something, do you?"

"No, Reechaard, it is impossible. I only found out my first suspicions this morning."

"Okay, could you wait outside till I find out what this bugger wants?"

Daniel gathered his papers and shuffled out as fast as he could.

His place was taken by the familiar figure of Jones. Jones assumed his usual smarmy arrogant posture.

"Good morning Sergeant Jones, how nice to see you," lied Richard. "What can I do for you?"

"You will be glad to know that, Sah, that the business of the stolen aluminium is soon to be concluded"

"Of course, of course. The matter is quite finished as far as we are concerned; we just look forward to the return of the stolen goods. Mind you, our insurers only paid seventy per cent. But nevertheless the aluminium is very valuable so we shall have to find a suitable use for it."

Richard rambled and Sergeant Jones peered down his nose at the rambler. "So I'm reasonably happy, Sergeant." He looked up, avoiding the predatory eyes, "I hope you are?"

Jones smiled his leering smile, "Sah, the case still has some way to go. You will recall that the case was referred to the High Court. As a matter of fact I have come to serve your subpoena to give evidence on Tuesday."

"Co're Blimey Sergeant, I thought we were through with that sort of thing. That's not good news, I'm due in Sokoto, very important,..... could Eke stand in for me?"

There was a heavy silence; Jones leaned forward and as he did he slid the subpoena across the desk.

"I'm sorry," he said sneering, "but I can do nothing,... however if you do not appear," he paused, "you will be in Contempt." He left 'contempt' hanging in the air.

"No, no, duty calls and all that." Richard mumbled absently, "I do hope we wont be kept hanging around like last time."

"Oh no," replied the Sergeant "The High Court is quite formal, and you must be prepared to give evidence and be cross examined by the defence." He rubbed his massive hands together, spread open palm to open palm, "It would be helpful, Mr. Smiles, if we could show in court that the two prisoners had been disgruntled employees,... been trouble,....and that you found them to be bad men.   Would be grateful if you would search your records that will surely attest to these issues."   He stared across the desk into Richard's eyes, Jones let his eyes dwell on their target an eternity, and then looked away his face wreathed in smiles. "I think you will be helpful in resolving this case."

Richard swallowed hard, sat up in his chair and looked straight back at Sergeant Jones. At first only a pathetic whistle emerged from his choked throat, but he gathered his resolve;

"Sergeant Jones, I didn't know these buggers you arrested, you know I find it hard to believe that these two could conspire to steal a sandwich from a street trader, let alone arrange all this. I will not testify to anything I have not witnessed, or to anything that I cannot affirm from my direct experience." There, he felt better, at last he'd stood up to this bully. There was an awkward silence.   Richard's nerves were still very much in a flap, he gabbled a follow up; "By the way have you arrested the Kano merchant or for that matter anyone from the security company?"

Jones said nothing.   He cradled his hands under his chin. Once more he glared his fearful glare; "Are you implying that,".... A silence... "Are you implying that this investigation is not being effectively conducted, or that a person in my department is not doing his job properly?"

His eyes pierced Richard like ice shafts. Transfixed; Richard couldn't move or speak, like a scared rabbit in the headlights. Eventually he broke contact, stared down at his desk and nervously shuffled some papers. Another eternal silence, at last he looked up at Jones who leered back.

"Certainly not, certainly not," again the curious squeaking voice, "just seemed strange that's all, - I'm sorry that I can't help you further with my testimony, but I really did not know the -um –um –suspects... I look forward to seeing you in Court,"

"The culprits I am sure," Responded the Sergeant, "you may be contacted by the defence, and then again you may not."

Jones rose to his full height, he looked down at the shaken Smiles, extended his huge bony hand. Richard shook it, shivered at its latent strength, but did not get up. Jones was gone. He put his head in his hands, stared down at his desk, -'Jones was one evil son of a bitch – one thing he could not afford to do was to cross him. Was it too late?

In his fright, he had quite forgotten about Daniel and the latest drama, a tap on the door and it was back to the present, no more pleasing than the past. Another theft, the solicitous Daniel sat down and continued with the details of his findings. Richard lost concentration and drifted away consumed by the sole purpose of avoiding any further contact with the police.

After a while it was obvious to Daniel that Richard had not followed a word, he stopped;

"Is that so Richard?" he enquired, the question hung in the air,

"I'm sorry Daniel I've lost you, I was miles away,...... what do you think of Sergeant Jones?"

"What about Sergeant Jones, for that matter who is Sergeant Jones?" replied the bemused audit clerk.

Richard launched into a detailed tale of the 'aluminium theft' as he saw it explaining as he went expressions such as 'sent down'(sent to prison) and bent (corrupt).

"Is there any difference where you come from?" asked the phlegmatic Daniel.

"Well we do have bent- sorry – corrupt policemen, but they are the exception rather than the rule, and even they have to produce credible evidence against suspects. Here, it seems to me that the police pick who they like, largely on the evidence of what tribe they belong to, and its game set and match-sorry- then it's all over for the poor sods they pick on."

"This is often the way," Agreed Daniel without surprise or hesitation.

"Anyway, what about our new problem? – I'll tell you one thing before we start, - we are not going to involve the police, - not that bugger Sergeant Jones and his cronies, - I couldn't bear it."

There was a stony silence, then Daniel, obviously ill at ease, shuffled and mumbled apologetically, "you can't do that, Sir."

"Daniel for God's sake don't call me Sir, - can't do what?"

"You can't tell people that you are not going to call the police, you see, it is the fear of the police that keeps many people honest. If your employees here, heard that you will not fetch the police, - I tell you that the factory will be dismantled by the morning." He grinned sheepishly. "It is the way here Richard, you cannot go outside the system."

Richard groaned inwardly, another brush with the law seemed inevitable. Images of Jones torturing the admin staff floated by. They must be sure, they must be sure themselves and then the police would only have to 'process' the proven thief.

Daniel explained with comforting assurance how the theft had worked; it was by a complex piece of misadministration of credit notes and material returns. The process, if Daniel was right, could only involve two people one of whom had to be the second book keeper, a large Yoruba man named Francis Ayala.

"Can we prove this?" asked Richard, hoping against hope for an affirmative answer.

"Yes, I believe so, I think we can."

"What a bugger, I like old Francis he's been with us I don't know how long – what a bloody shame. Look Daniel it's not that I doubt your findings, or trust you other than absolutely, but we must be absolutely certain about the facts, - so if it's OK by you I'd like to run your findings past Malcolm and we'll check the conclusions and proofs together. I know they'll be validated, but deep down old lad, I hope you're wrong. Would you like to ring Malcolm and make an appointment as soon as we can; - in the meantime, we say nothing O.K?"

Daniel rose, adjusted his already immaculate tie, smiled nervously; "Yes I must validate my findings with a partner and client, you are quite right and I will ring Mr. Hetherington now now, we'll try and get together today, or latest first thing tomorrow, O.K with you?"

"Sooner the better, - before you go, - is this a one off thing or has it been going on for some time?"

"I don't know for sure, if they squared off between audits it would have been difficult to spot, just reflected in lower margins, - we'll have to see, - but we've got this event absolutely exposed. I shall be interested to see if there are any changes to the books in an attempt to cover up, see you later, Sir."

Richard threw a notebook at Daniel, "Any more, 'Sir' and it'll be you that's in trouble." Daniel ducked and made his way out. "Cheers!" shouted Richard after him, but without conviction, he sat still and miserable, disappointed and with aching haemorrhoids..

# CHAPTER 33

On the journey home that evening he exchanged chitchat with Mohamed as he often did. The police remained his uneasy obsession, the spectre of Jones pervaded every thing.

"These policemen are they bad men?"

"Many of them, Yes, Sah." Replied Mohamed, "but it is sometimes good, Sah, that they are bad...." He trailed off, hesitantly, perhaps recognising the absurdity of his statement.

"What do you mean?"

"Well Sah, people are afraid of them, - they are careful not to be caught up with them, - sometime people get caught up with them, they never come back again, at all, at all."

"You mean they disappear?"

"They are in jail - sometimes - sometimes they run away, anyway sometime we never see'am again Sah!"

Richard thought of the two so called culprits, who would in all probability languish in jail for years, for something that at worst they were minor participants. Those who could had bought their way out, the merchant and the security boss,

Richard sighed; "What a way to run a country!"

As they rounded the next corner, a woman walked determinedly down the road carrying a full size wardrobe, precariously balanced on her head. This was no light load, it was a full six foot high and double width, it must have weighed a huge amount. Her brown mahogany muscles rippled under the strain in the evening sun light, and as they passed Richard glimpsed the sweat and the pain on her face.

"Mohamed, - why that lady carry that huge thing?"

"She, poor lady - she carry load for money - maybe she move whole house for somebody."

"How far will she carry the load?"

"Maybe, plenty far, Sah."

Richard reflected on the poverty, the injustice, the miserable lot of the majority, - he felt depressed.

At the start of the main road into the city they witnessed an accident right out or the fantasy world of the 'keystone cops.' A mammy wagon crammed as usual with twelve occupants in its eight seats, attempted to turn right. The driver misjudged the speed of the on coming lorry also laden to precarious levels, and so collided a glancing blow across the front of the brakeless juggernaught. The mammy wagon capsized and slid across the highway, snaking its crazy way into a petrol station and slicing a petrol pump at ground level. The conveyance eventually came to a halt and the twelve passengers scrambled out followed by lucky thirteen; the driver. The lorry in the meantime ghosted to a brakeless halt at a right angle to the traffic flow.

Mohamed pulled up some fifty yards behind, the third vehicle in line from the incident. A crowd materialised in an instant, and surrounded the dazed and bleeding taxi driver. They joined the driver of the lorry and the manager of the petrol station in a general hysterical haranguing. The lorry driver looked something of a desperado and held in his hand a machete.

"Mohamed, lets get out of here - now!"

Mohamed needed no extra urging, but already the road was filled with vehicles of all descriptions. The hubbub and noise from the petrol station reached a new crescendo, the protagonists massaging their hysteria to new heights. Richard anticipating an explosion from the gasoline, which miraculously had not yet ignited;

"Mohamed, please get the hell out 'a here, that fuels going to go up any moment."

"Yas, Sah,"

Mohamed, much to Richard's alarm, got out of the car, not to join the spectators but to figure a way out, which he did. He leapt back into the driving seat, and slickly and skillfully backed the car into a side alley; they turned and accelerated away, horn blaring.

Behind them perhaps half a mile away there was a tremendous explosion, a black plume of smoke floated above the petrol station.

Richard arrived home shaken; Joan looked bright and came to greet him;

"Your son is a hero!" beamed Joan.

"What do you mean he's only two and a half."

"At school today, apparently a snake of some sort appeared at the back of the play area, Norma that's the supervisor went to pieces."

"Don't tell me, David wrestled with the snake and subdued it." He sniggered.

"No, - he did something much braver, - he held the teacher's hand, stood quite still, while all the children were shepherded back into the house, - he never took his eyes off the snake until it was time for him to go in too. When he got home he couldn't wait to tell Mussa, - isn't that fantastic?"

"God bless him, he'll grow up speaking gibberish and charming snakes, - Oh! I'm sorry, brave little fella' - where's he now."

As if on cue David burst into the room, Richard picked him up and hugged him tightly,

"Who's a clever fella' eh? How was school today?"

"Saw a snake, - a beeg snake, - Mussa teach me, - never take eyes off snake - I watch heem, - beeg snake." He laughed heartily, chuckled really as only three year olds can.

"Never take your eyes off Dee snake, David, - Good boy." Peter was more pleased than the parents, " Sah, I weel geev David ice cream Sah?"

"Certainly not - proper tea first then ice cream."

"O.K. Sah," Peter retreated to the mysteries of his kitchen.

After the children were in bed Richard and Joan sat on the patio. Richard poured out his troubles of the day. Joan countered that his luck was in and they'd been fortunate not to be injured in the petrol station explosion, which had featured on the evening news.

The telephone rang, "It is Mr. Ash Sah!" announced Peter.

"Hello Henry, what can I do for you?"

"Won't keep you long old boy, just wanted to know who the guest speaker is for Rotary dinner on Wednesday?"

"Wednesday? - Rotary? - What? - Oh Shit! - Henry I'm terribly sorry I forgot, - I haven't got a speaker."

"Sorry, dear boy, you have to produce somebody or perform yourself, - remember the Secretary of State for Education is our principal guest, - leave it with you." The phone went dead.

"Shit, - shit - shit - I don't believe it - what the hell am I going to do? - I've got to find a speaker for Rotary for the day after tomorrow, - Can you think of anybody Love?"

"Yes, your son on snake management." She laughed.

He was cross, "Don't make bloody jokes, this is serious!" They spent the rest of the night ringing every one who could remotely fill the bill, but came up in the end with nothing. Eventually they trudged to bed, Richard unhappy in the knowledge that that added to his other burdens, he must deliver an engaging speech to his Rotary pals on Wednesday evening.

The following days proved difficult; it was confirmed at Malcolm's office that there was definitely a deficiency that could only be the result of deliberate theft and as Richard had expected Daniel's conclusions were confirmed.

Richard and Malcolm with detailed advice from Daniel discussed at length the best course of action. Company standard practice dictated that Richard was bound to report any irregularities to his Regional Director, Edward Regan. Regan though would insist that the perpetrators were prosecuted and the police brought in. This Richard wanted to avoid at all costs. Malcolm as the company's auditor also had an obligation to record and pass on his findings in a 'timely' manner, although he acknowledged that the extent of the known theft was below the level of materiality. However he cautioned that further investigation could reveal more and substantial levels of losses.

"O.K." said Richard, "I've heard all the arguments, - one; we know that two thousand pounds have been misappropriated during the last three months, - two; we know pretty conclusively who that perpetrator is, i.e. Francis Ayala, with the connivance of one other.

If we kick them out - and investigate no further - then we know the extent of our reportable loss and we are as certain as we can be that it won't recur. I can report to Edward that this was a one off and has been dealt with. I do not, emphasize not, ask you our auditors to investigate further, because I see no reason to do so, margins after all are within budgeted expectations. So what, if Francis has been ripping us off for years, we're not going to get our dough back, I don't think there's an insurance issue here." He paused and hoped he sounded convincing, Malcolm was pointedly looking out of the window and avoiding eye contact. He continued, "The alternative is too glum to contemplate, the police, court, God knows how much management time and auditors time taken up, legal and professional fees will make the two thousand look like chicken feed, - all for what?"

Malcolm remained silent still avoiding Richard's look. Richard continued desperately;

" We can also be sure after the event, if we keep a sharp eye on this, and close the loophole that this will never happen again, margins after the event will also reveal any anomaly if this business has really been material, but it will only show up as a positive. The downside is that we have to get a new book keeper in and keep this business quiet."

The silence continued, Richard got the distinct impression he was talking himself into a hole. Accountants and particularly auditors are not in the habit of taking risks however small. Although Malcolm was probably Richard's closest friend, he would exercise his professional judgment without that issue influencing him at all. After what seemed an age Malcolm swung round in his chair and faced his client:

"I agree that the issue is not one of materiality in your overall annual divisional performance, but this is an irregularity which we are unable to define without further investigation, we have to report the facts in our quarterly report, otherwise we serve no purpose other than to pick up our fees. So we will report the facts as we find them."

Richard's heart sank, the prospect of criminal proceedings and all that that entailed engulfed him in a cloud of depression, he stared into his empty coffee cup, he felt the black residue reflected his mood.

"Not only that, I agree with Daniel," continued Malcolm in a 'holier than thou' accountant like sermon, "You will have to be seen prosecuting the thieves or your place will be a shambles by this time next week."

A grown man does not easily weep, but Richard was close to it. "Couldn't we just fire Ayala and report it's under control?" he almost begged in desperation.

"You and Edward Regan can do what you like with Francis whatzisname, but there is no way round us reporting to full extent," he softened, "look, you and Regan are the Managers of the business you can do what you like, but just be aware that if this thing turns out to be ten or twenty times bigger than we think, unlikely, but possible, then we have to be seen to do things by the book."

The phone call to Edward Regan was surprisingly calm, Edward asked for time to think things through, and half an hour later rang back, and told Richard that the auditors must define the total loss as far as they could, he would leave the matter of the handling of the perpetrators to Richard, he 'would like to see them off the site by the end of the day'.

The scene in the office later that day was a sad one,

"Francis, you know Daniel, from the auditors…I'm afraid that we've discovered a discrepancy in the last quarter's accounts… Can you help us explain it?"

At first Ayala denied any wrongdoing, his eyes widened, his large hand gestured that he knew nothing, and indeed he was at a loss to know what the conversation was about.

"Sah, everything is fine Sah, are you unhappy with my work?"

"You are not aware that the accounts are two thousand pounds short, a shortfall we know that could have only occurred through Credit notes and returns, both your area of responsibility?"

His massive head swayed back and forth, his smile collapsed, his fists tightened.

"What do you know? You know … I have taught you all you know, you know narthing." Suddenly his huge hand crashed down onto the desk, Smiles and Daniel both leapt involuntarily. "You know nartheeng" he snarled now leaning; both hands on the desk, his powerful frame ominously towering over his accusers. His prominent white teeth with a gap in the middle of the top row snarled. "And you," he glared at Daniel, "are a heathen, ungodly bastard who sides with the bosses, you have no faith in your brartha' I weel keel you, you bastard."

Richard felt slightly out of the immediate firing line, but remained scared out of his skin, 'Are you in charge?' he asked himself, he got no answer.

"Uhg- uhm, Francis, steady down, there's a good chap." It was a feeble command, but much to Smiles' relief and surprise, Ayala took his hands off the desk, blinked holding back his tears and looked at the ceiling. "Do sit down Francis, we're anxious to hear what you have to say, but we must be calm, O.K.?"

At last he settled down and there followed a futile discussion about the findings of the auditors, which Francis denied at every point, and countered with a myriad explanations all of which were untenable.

After nearly an hour, Richard, anxious not to raise Ayala's violent ire, cajoled and persuaded as best he could the strength of the case. Eventually the accused capitulated, this he did, like a beaten dog, head down hands clasped before him staring at the floor.

"Francis, it boils down to this, we have sure proof that you have taken money from the company; you are therefore dismissed with immediate effect. You will go and clear your desk now, Daniel and I will come with you. You will either submit a letter of resignation which will take immediate effect and free the company of all its obligations of pay, pension etc., or I shall suspend you, again with immediate effect, and inform the police of our findings."

The staff in the outer offices usually moved like light at five o clock, but tonight because they knew something was up, they stayed all pretending to be working diligently at their desks.

"Adegbulu" shouted Richard, " tell every body to bugger off will you we have work to finish here."

"Yes, Sah." Responded Adegbulu; pocketing his pen, standing and signaling all at once. The office emptied in a trice.

Richard pushed over the resignation letter that they had drafted earlier, Francis snarled as he read it, and then started to rant and rave once more. He screamed about his years of service, about his efforts, the failure of the company to recognize his talents, about his miserable rewards, and then he transcended into curse after curse on the company and Richard in particular. At one point he brandished a heavy ashtray engraved with the Eiffel Tower; this brought an immediate response from Daniel who attempted to dive under the side of the desk bumping his head in the process. Richard flinched but at least remained above desk level.

In a tremulous voice Richard tried to reassert some authority; "Francis, sign the goddamn letter or I ring the police - now, now."

He signed, stormed to his office, followed at a safe distance by Richard and Daniel, he ransacked his desk throwing its contents any and every where, he pocketed what he wanted, actually kicked the waste bucket across the office narrowly missing a bemused cleaning lady. He slammed the door and was gone.

They returned to Richard's office there was a nervous silence, and then a 'phew! Thank God that's over' chat. Richard enquired if Daniel understood the local language that Francis had used. Daniel looked grave, shook his head and said.

"He has cursed you, Richard, he has cast a bad ju-ju on you."

"Oh, bollocks," said Richard, "lets go and have a drink."

# CHAPTER 34

The following morning after an early start at the factory, Richard presented himself at the High Court. Mercifully things here seemed much more orderly than at the Alkhali Court.

In the corridor he met a gaggle of other witnesses including Usman Jalingo, Mr Eke. They had not long been engaged in small talk, when the fully uniformed Sergeant Jones emerged to seek out his witnesses. His smile reminded Richard of the head of a cobra he'd once seen in the garden.

"Good day, Gentlemen." He smarmed, "Mister Smiles I assume that your jacket is in your car Sir?"

"Jacket, what jacket?"

"You must wear a jacket out of respect to the Court Sir."

"Why didn't some bugger tell me?" Once more the initiative was with Jones. He turned, ran to the car and dispatched Mohamed to fetch an appropriate jacket. The jacket was eventually returned in time for Richard to join the others in the witness room. The witness room was much like any other, benches down each wall, those he knew of course, but other people too. He assumed that some were witnesses for the defense, they looked cowed and scared. No jackets for them but they were nevertheless in their finest traditional robes, despite their obvious poverty they clung together in their tribal unity. There were others more well- to- do; Richard had no idea who these people were.

He sat next to Usman Jailing and enquired as to the identity of those present. Busman knew them all. Richard was surprised to see that the opulent Altai at the end of the bench was none other than the receiving merchant from Kano. Busman said that the merchant had been charged with receiving, but that in turn for turning state's evidence he would say he was duped; and bought the goods from the accused.

Once more Richard felt upset to learn that Jones was manipulating the system. Jailing however brightened his mood with an affirmation that:

"Mister Justice Bello, is a fine man and he will find the truth."

A half hour passed, the room became uncomfortably hot, the ceiling fan for some reason ceased to work. Richard's bladder urged him to take relief, but he felt the moment he went to the bathroom he'd be called. Eventually he gave in to nature, a policeman escorted him to a toilet which was nearby and clean. True to form he couldn't pee, however hard he tried he couldn't, then after what seemed an age relief came, to him and the policeman shuffling his feet and waiting his turn. On his return to the witness room the Court Usher was waiting for him;

"Meestah Smiles - you are late Sah - the Court is waiting, follow me."

Her black cloak swished and billowed as she led Richard into the Courtroom. It was an imposing room. The judge sat high above the multitude, the Defense and Prosecution teams sat in their respective pew desks. There was no jury.

The judge was a rotund, bespectacled gentleman who looked as though his grey wig had grown naturally onto his fine African head. His voice was clear and he spoke impeccable English. Above his head was the court of arms of the federal state of Nigeria, flanked by the North Central State insignia.

The court was not crowded but those who were there, clearly divide into Northerners and Southerners, the latter being supporters of the accused. There were two journalists who appeared to be sleeping in the back row at ground level. The spectators were elevated in pews reminiscent of a Welsh chapel.

The judge was first to speak, "Mr. Smiles," in a voice as clear as a bell, "you are welcome in this court as a valuable witness. Your evidence will be vital in our deliberations and I want you to consider your responses carefully. If there is any doubt in your mind about the clarity or precision of any of the questions you are to express it. Do you understand?"

"Yes, Sir, I quite understand." Responded the nervous Smiles.

Richard chose to take the Christian oath.

"Proceed" ordered the judge.

After the formalities the Prosecuting Lead, who despite his local accent was easy for Richard to understand, began to question the witness. He was a big sturdy fellow with a handsome moustache and glistening white teeth, he obviously enjoyed his job and his confidence Richard felt, knew no bounds.

"Mr. Smiles how long have you known the accused?"

"I don't know them at all - they left our employment shortly after I took up my post last year."

"Why did they leave Universal?"

"I don't know precisely, - I understand from staff reports that they were encouraged to leave by the works Supervisor, as they didn't settle aptly into their training. They had been with us a short time and were not permanent members of staff."

The judge intervened; "What do you mean by permanent staff?"

"Well Sir, everyone who starts undergoes a three months probationary period, to see if they settle and adjust to the work, skills requirements and training. If their Supervisor deems them to have satisfied these criteria they are given permanent status. If not, as in this case, then permanent status is not offered, and they are asked to leave."

"They were not satisfactory?" was it a question or a statement, Richard wasn't sure.

"That's so, perhaps ill fitted would be a better description"

"Quite, they were, for what ever reason, not satisfactory."

"That's so."

"They were upset and angry?"

"I don't know."

There was a pause whilst the plump prosecutor shuffled his papers.

"Apart from being unsatisfactory, - they were trouble makers, - were they not?"

"Not as far as I am aware."

A withering stare from the prosecutor, who was obviously playing the Jones line, either innocently or otherwise. Richard was not going to be bullied, whatever the prosecution's plan.

"As far are you are aware," the prosecutor bore in, "they were asked to leave?"

"Yes they were."

There was much more tiresome and barely relevant questioning about procedures and labor relations at the plant; it seemed to go on for ever. Richard became more comfortable and confident as time went on and answered with a straight bat, he avoided being drawn into implied criticism of the accused. They adjourned for lunch at the end of the prosecutor's examination of Richard.

At quarter to two Richard returned to the courtroom as always anxious about being on time. In the room there was only one person the counsel for the defense. He was the antithesis of his adversary, small, wizen, and though dressed in the uniform of counsel, it was threadbare from his wig to the shining gown and stained waistcoat.

His cheekbones stood out over luminescent skin and his sunken eyes betrayed a hundred lost causes. He studiously avoided Richard's gaze and continued to read his notes. Soon the Court filled up and precisely at two o clock Mr. Justice Bello resumed his seat on the bench.

"Mr. Smiles please resume the witness stand, I need not remind you that you are still on oath."

"No Sir," replied Richard as he took his place in the witness stand.

"Mr. Watami, for the defense, you may proceed."

"Thank you your honor," Watami whinnied in a high strained voice, but his accent was surprisingly British.

"Mr. Smiles," he opened, "how long have you been in Nigeria?"

"Some fifteen, sixteen months, - this is my second year tour."

"Before you came here, what was your job?"

"I was a training and development manager in the U.K."

"So this is your first General Management appointment?"

"Yes."

"Are you qualified for the role?"

"In the judgment of my employer, yes, and things have gone well over the last year."

"Gone well for whom? - Mr. Smiles, - for you? - gone well for your employer? - gone well for my clients, the accused?"

"The company has performed well, we are profitable, and we have a good record as a stable and progressive employer."

"A stable and progressive employer," he raised his eyebrows and his arms in a hyperbolic gesture, "A stable and progressive employer? - When Mr. Nimbi and Mr. Ota were dismissed without cause, were you being a stable and progressive employer?"

Richard, his discomfort increasing looked hopefully to the Judge, who seemed intent upon his notes. - A silence.

"Were you the General Manager at the time that these gentlemen were dismissed from 'Universal'?"

"Yes, I arrived on the 23rd of October and the records show that these gentlemen were - let go - at the end of October."

"You said you did not know them?"

"That is correct, - it was my first week here, it was impossible to get to know everyone of the one hundred and twelve staff in that first week."

"Can we assume, Mister Smile, newly appointed, some would say inexperienced and unqualified," -

"Come, come, Mr. Watami," interrupted the Judge, "No more 'some would say' if you please, you know better."

Watami bowed, an almost nod in the direction of the Judge, never taking his eyes off Richard, he continued;

"Can we assume, Mr. Smiles,- that in the list of your priorities, - the dismissal of two lowly, BLACK" - he almost shouted the word 'black' - "Was not high on your agenda."

Richard's discomfort increased, what was this guy about? Was he really trying to play the race card? Did they really think that this was a white versus black thing?

"Mr. Smiles will you answer."

"All staff matters are important, but since I had just arrived I deferred the decision to the works manager, Mr. Eke," - an afterthought, - "Who is a - Nigerian national."

Watami shuffled his papers, made a curious clicking noise with his teeth, - eventually he looked up and stared at Richard for several seconds, he flicked imaginary dirt from his stained waistcoat, and then he resumed;

"How is it Mr. Smiles, that after six months after the dismissal of my clients from Universal Metals, that they are named to the police as suspects?"

"I have absolutely no idea." Replied Richard flatly. What was this guy thinking about he thought, what is it he's trying to prove here.

"Is it not true Mr. Smiles that you gave the police the names of the defendants as a malicious act, to hide your own incompetence, to cover up your mistakes in the loss of these goods? - A silence, Richard could hardly believe his ears, - "And is not also true that you couldn't care less about Nigerian employees and that you stood by whilst these confidential employment records were handed over to the police?"

Despite a strong desire to reply with a resounding 'Bollocks' Richard kept quiet, he was mildly confused by these whimsical accusations and lost track of the multiple questions, he could feel the perspiration roll down his chest,- he looked round for help;- there was none,- The Judge seemed to be disinterested and disinclined to intervene. Eventually he gripped the rail of the witness box, cleared his throat, and in his best Richard Burton imitation;

"Absolute nonsense."

"Mr. Watami," intervened the Judge," where is this line of questioning taking us?"

"If you please your honor I believe we can show that my clients have been the victims of a conspiracy, and that the management of Universal Metals were involved in that conspiracy."

"Is this a main focus for the defense?" asked the Judge.

"It is one of a number of strands we shall bring together, Your Honor." Whined Watami.

"You may proceed but you must not let this degenerate too far into unsupported innuendo, do you take my point Mr. Watami? - Proceed."

More shuffling of Watami's papers, - Richard was now thoroughly unnerved, he'd always been instinctively sympathetic to the poor sods in the dock, and here was their defense trying to prove him the villain of the piece, it was all disorienting from a logical point of view, he was sure that whatever came next would be unexpected, his confidence already battered, began to drift away.

"Mr. Smiles, we have established that you have not much interest in the lives of your employees, and my clients in particular, and we've established that under your management Universal Metals put forward my clients' names, and confidential details of their employment records, have we not."

Enough was enough, "We have not Sir, - further you need to know that the police subpoenaed the employment records, it was not, I repeat not, a company initiative, - I resent the implications of your arguments, which are specious and unfounded."

"Mr. Smiles!" intervened the Judge, "you've made your point, please confine yourself to answering Counsel's questions, you are not here to argue - do you understand?"

"Yes, Sir." Richard shook with nerves and some anger.

"Mr. Watami", continued the Judge, "will you stick to the evidence, I have given you ample leeway."

"Thank you, Your Honor." Watami bowed this time from the waist.

"Mr. Smiles on the morning when the theft was discovered," Watami continued, "were there any signs of a break in at the premises of Universal?"

"None that was relevant to the execution of the theft."

"None, - are you sure?"

"If you are referring to the holes in the eaves cladding, I do not consider these to be pertinent to the removal of two point six tons of eight foot by three foot aluminium building sheets, - no Sir, - none."

"The police report refers to this damage - it states and I quote; -'there was evidence of damage to the walls of the factory, some wall cladding had been prized open' - unquote."

"There was damage at around fifteen feet above ground level; the total aperture was not more than four feet by two feet. It would have been impossible to remove the missing goods through that gap, particularly fifteen feet up, off the ground."

"Did any of the staff allude to this damage at the time?"

"They did."

"And what was your response, Mr. Smiles, Mr. General Manager of six months in Nigeria?"

" my response was the same as it is now - this damage had no direct connection with the removal of the goods from the factory, although I conceded that it could have something to do with effecting entry into the factory."

"Are you saying that this damage may have something to do with the theft, - are you now changing your story?"

"No, I am not." Richard replied flatly.

"Are you saying that this damage to the wall of the factory which was not there before the theft, was or was not, an issue related to the theft."

"I'm saying that I don't think this issue is key to the removal of the goods, but could in some way have been a diversion, or a minor incident in the crime."

"You don't know, nor are you certain?"

"That is correct."

"Thank you Mr. Smiles that will be all."

"You are excused Mr. Smiles, please see to it that you do not contact any other witnesses, or discuss this case with anyone in any way involved until after the case is over, do you understand?"

Richard made his way from the witness stand in a state of turmoil trembling through confusion, disbelief, or ridicule. He left the courtroom dizzily; outside he sat with head in his hands trying to make sense of it all. He couldn't.

Richard was entirely perplexed by the Court's proceedings. The whole thing had become a grotesque episode of error and deliberate disinformation. As far as Richard could see on the one hand the police were determined to pin the crime on these unfortunate ex-employees, and the defense was determined to pin the blame on Richard or the company. It was all so crazy and all based on what tribe each participant belonged to; white man, Benue plateau, or Hausa. The Hausas had it; a win situation.

He'd been sympathetic to the cause of the accused, but now he felt injured and slandered by the defense that'd implied he was an incompetent racist half-wit. By the time he arrived home he'd almost persuaded himself that they were right.

# CHAPTER 35

After a few drinks at the club, Richard had been persuaded by Malcolm to go home. He was taxed and stressed, all the pressures and strains on top of his father's recent death weighed heavily upon him. He dreaded another farcical performance in court and then there was this silly bloody speech he would have to deliver to Rotary. The last thing he needed was to spend the rest of the evening writing the wretched speech. At home at least all was well, even Peter showed some progress in the kitchen under Joan's patient guiding hand. David had almost dragged the whole family into 'pidgin' but now they had hopes that he had drawn back from the brink of irreversible linguistic disablement at his new school. Joan seemed happy enough, although he'd seen hardly anything of her over the last three weeks. Richard had been surprised by the depth of her grief over Percy; she had been quiet and withdrawn on his return.

Her intimacy with him had also changed it was intense as ever, perhaps even more so, but some times the violence of her lust almost frightened him. She spent a lot of her time with Sally, they seemed very close almost too close, and he felt excluded in some way that he didn't understand.

That night after the children were put to bed he turned to the preparation of his Rotary speech.

"What the hell am I going to talk about?" he asked no one in particular as he supped his post-prandial scotch.

"What about 'Scarlets - nine, New Zealand - three,?' volunteered Joan.

"My dear girl, one tribe will never understand another, the majority of the club is Nigerian or Indian, all nice blokes, but trying to explain rugby - I'd do better on brain surgery."

He idly scanned the bookcase, and fell upon a dusty narrowly bound volume. He pulled it out and noted the title 'Le Petomane'. The cover showed a sepia print of a moustachioed Frenchman of Victorian vintage in silk knickerbockers.

"I say old love," he enquired, "Where'd this book come from?"

"I don't know, we acquired them with the house."

Richard began to skim through the odd little volume.

"Bugger me, - it's about a bloke who farted for a living."

"You can't be serious."

"Honestly I can't believe it," he continued to scan the little volume; "Apparently this chap could fart the Marseilles's all through his bottom, - Manna from heaven, - what subject for Rotary."

"You can't," protested Joan, "Didn't you say there was some sort of dignitary attending, Richard you really can't."

"Bugger it; it's all I've got."

With that he sat at the dining room table and began to write a speech, which would be long remembered in the Rotary Club of Kaduna.

He felt profoundly depressed and not in the least looking forward to delivering his idiotic speech to the Rotary Club. His reception the next day at home did little to comfort him, as Joan was preoccupied with two children with upset tummies, the last thing she wanted was a third, with a bruised ego. Things were not made any easier when Richard announced that he was leaving at the crack of dawn the following morning to visit Kano and Sokoto. He would have to be away two nights. He'd vainly hoped that emphasizing the rigors of his day he would receive a warm reception.

"You're a silly, self centered sod, pushing off and leaving me with two sick children, - not only that you're going out tonight to get stoned with your pompous Rotary buddies,- go on push off, I'll be glad to see the back of you," - she fumed towards an explosive climax, -" As far as you're concerned everything, bloody everything, comes before me and the kids, work, golf, Rotary, anything, - absolutely anything - just push off."

Richard retreated, feeling injured and at odds with the world at large. Today would surely go down as one of the great disasters. His speech would no doubt compound the embarrassments of the day, - should he do something else? - what? - No time, - sod it.

He departed for the Hamdalah Hotel at seven; he'd kissed the kids good night, - they'd howled their disapproval of Daddy deserting them. His attempt to peck Joan on the cheek met with an avoiding jink worthy of a Welsh outside half.

"Wish me luck."

"Bugger off."

He sank into the back of the car; at least Mohamed smiled a welcome.

Home was so hostile he'd left earlier than need be, and found himself in the hotel bar, with a good half hour's drinking time before the dinner was due to start. Brian Legge the drunk whose fame as a sleeping dinner guest was legend was already propping up the bar.

"Fancy a beer old boy?"

"No thanks, I'll have a scotch and water, - family size if you don't mind." Richard pressed the self destruct button.

"You're the speaker tonight, - are you not? - don't get too pissed old fruit, - never do, - don't you know."

"Oh, fuck off, Brian, I've had the most ghastly bloody day, - and the rest of the week doesn't look much better either, not least tonight's debacle."

"Bottoms up!" responded Brian, sinking his pink gin with alacrity.

Minutes and drinks passed speedily, when the Club President Prof. Coker arrived, chewing his perpetual cigar. Richard was well on his way to an unseemly and catastrophic end to the night. Coker though knew Richard well.

"Richard don't be a dick all your life, that's your last drink, O.K.? Remember the Alhaji does not drink, and if he sees you in a pickle it will confirm his view that all white men are piss artists." He stood back, looked Richard in the eye and commanded in a paternal but firm way; "Please be a good boy." With that he patted Legge on the shoulder and with a puff from his foul cigar was off to greet the guest of honor, His Excellency, as ministers liked to be called; Altai Isla, Secretary of State for Education for the North Central State of the Federal Republic of Nigeria.

Brian Legge dutifully plied Richard with iced water. They discussed the day's proceedings in Court, perhaps Legge could throw some light on the mysteries of the day.

"How did the defense counsel get selected, do you think, Brian?"

"He will have been hired by the BP tribal association in Kaduna" replied Brian now on his fifth pink gin.

"Why did he have to have a go at me like that, the so and so?"

"Elementary, dear boy, there's tribes and tribes and tribes, and you are a safe one to have a go at. They can't have a go at the police, - they can't have a go at the Hausa boys from Kano, - they're the heavy mob - so; q.e.d.-have a go at the colonial twits in charge, namely dear old Richard Smiles."

There was a pause, Richard's worst fears confirmed, he desperately wanted another scotch but Brian dutifully restrained him.

"In fact, old boy, if they can persuade the Judge, that all the facts are confused because of your perceived incompetence, and your man Eke, - Ibo isn't he?" Richard nodded. "Perfect, - bloody perfect, - they don't offend the police, they attack a Brit and an Ibo, - they'll chuck in an alibi, true or false, and hope for the best."

The gong sounded for dinner: There was a full turn out for Rotary that night, the Alhaji was due to give a short address, Richard as a consequence of his speaking duties noted with some discomfort that he was to be seated next to the Minister. A cloud of smoke from Coker's cigar enveloped Richard, the ebullient doctor introduced Richard to the Secretary of State.

"Alhaji, a great pleasure to meet you." Opened Richard.

The Minister was large and portly; he was a good deal taller than Richard and positively dwarfed the diminutive Coker. He had a huge head, a dazzling smile which displayed his splendid array of gold teeth. His robes were elaborate and on his head he sported a gold and crimson Hausa cap.

"Mr. Smiles is entertaining us after you've given us your views of education priorities in the state, - maybe we can identify a project on which Rotary can give support" he spoke addressing both men.

"Quite so, Professor," smiled the Alhaji.

They sat as directed, Keith Coker on the Alhaji's left, Richard on his right. Coker chatted on holding the Minister's attention, Richard, relieved continued small talk with the Brian and other Officers on the top table.

"What's the subject of your speech Richard?" enquired Henry Ash politely.

"You wouldn't believe it so you'll have to wait and bloody well see." responded the still half inebriated Richard.

"Meestah Smiles," it was the Education Secretary, obviously trying to escape Coker's incessant chatter, "what do you think of the Americans being on the moon?"

"Splendid Sir, a quite splendid feat of modern technology."

"You do not think it is propaganda?"

"I'm sorry, Sir, propaganda?"

"Yes," the Alhaji shook his head slowly, "yezzz, I have thought about these, surely it is propaganda."

Richard was stumped, what was this gentleman talking about? Yes of course the landing of men on the moon was a splendid coup for the Americans, but he didn't see where the 'propaganda' came in. He chewed a mouthful of the better than usual chicken, 'change the subject' came to mind.

"Propaganda," repeated the Minister, "I tell you, propaganda, if the Americans are on the moon, I'm sure we could see them, at least with a telescope, don't you think so Meestah Smiles?"

"Well Sir, you'd expect a fair amount of publicity, - men on the moon and all that, -rather splendid, - don't you think?"

The Alhaji a large and impressive figure, folded his hands dramatically in front of him, paused, shook his head and looked Richard straight in the eye.

"I see you are pro American."

"Don't think so, not particularly Alhaji." Richard felt panic welling up, - 'Please God doesn't let me cause another palaver' he prayed silently.

"You see, Meestah Smiles, - or rather you don't see, that is the point, - I believe its propaganda, - American Propaganda."

Richard remained mystified and bemused. He was unsure even what the conversation was about. God, he wished he hadn't drunk so much.

This senior State Government Minister was rambling about American propaganda, - men on the moon, - what were they talking about? Richard held his breath, looked politely at his important guest and could think of nothing to say except;

"Quite so, quite so."

"Ah! Ah!" responded the Altai, "you know Mesta Smiles I have been looking every night, even with my nephew's telescope, - I can tell you - I cannot see them, - at all, at all."

The penny dropped.

"Gracious me," responded Richard avoiding coughing a mouthful of dinner over the distinguished guest, "I hadn't thought of that Sir, perhaps they landed on the other side Sir, - I'm sure its very technical, but you may well have a point Sir, - you may well be right."

Richard, relieved, tucked into the remains of his dinner. His nerves started to jangle, his desperate gamble to address the audience about a Frenchman who farted for a living, seemed unwise to say the least. However there was no way out, unless he feigned a seizure or faint. His nerves stirred the whiskey, prawn cocktail and chicken into a nauseous brew, perhaps he would be ill after all.

The dinner finished, the toasts were drunk and Coker introduced the first speaker; Altai Isla, North Central State, Minister for Education.

The Minister rose to his feet, resplendent in his traditional robes, which were of a most magnificent ivory material, woven with silver embroidery. He spoke with authority and delivered his message, if message there was, in a turgid and deliberate way, he went on and on and on.

Richard half listened fidgeted and tried to calm his rumbling nerves. He wanted to go to the bathroom, but of coarse he could not. The Alhaji droned on and on. He reconsidered the strategies, perhaps slumping over the table, feigning a heart attack; God knows his heart was beating fast enough. He could just walk out, never to return, pretend he had an attack of amnesia. He fancied the heart attack ploy best, at least that would stop the Alhaji, or would it? Perhaps on the other hand if the Altai went on long enough as he showed every sign of doing, Richard might be excused altogether.

After an excruciating forty minutes the Minister sat down to polite applause. The Professor delivered a short speech of thanks, promised that Smiles would make them happy after a short comfort break.

Richard dashed to the toilet in absolute panic, fearing at the very least that he was going to have an embarrassing accident on the way. In the toilet all the Rotarians unloaded their not inconsiderable cargo of drink. Like horses in a stable they whinnied from their stalls, greeting each other. Richard was assailed with their well meant but often inept greetings.

"Looking forward to your speech old boy."

"Knock 'me dead Smiley."

"Must be a first rate subject," noted one, "or he would have asked a guest speaker."

"Smiles tell a good tale." quipped another.

Smiles groaned a groan to accompany the other noises emanating from his nether end in the isolation of his cubicle. Then having done what had to be done he returned to the table, he was alarmed and astonished to find that the Minister had remained in his seat and was set to listen to Richard's offering. He had assumed that the guest would have left once the spotlight had fallen from his Ministerial being. His mind raced, what was the Muslim view to this sort of humor? Would his offering result in humiliation and disgrace not only for him but also the Rotary Club as a whole? He shook with nervous apprehension.

His mouth was dry, his first attempt to speak to the Minister failed completely. His tongue had somehow adhered to the top of his mouth. There was no water in sight; the waiters with unaccustomed efficiency had cleared the tables completely. Desperately, despite the re-assembly of the members, he left the table and found the Head Waiter.

"Water" he croaked, "water, now, now."

When he returned to the main dining room armed with a glass and pitcher of water, he was received with a good-humored cheer from his closer pals. As he took his place again at the table his hand shook uncontrollably, his efforts to fill his water glass resulted in half the water in the glass and the other half on the table. He nodded a sickly grin to Coker that he was ready, - this was going to be a trial.

The Club Chairman rose, and announced;

"It is rare distinguished guests and fellow Rotarians, that we are addressed by one of our own. Tonight however, such is the case. Mr. Smiles has been a member for just over a year now and I know that his humor holds a promise to entertain us well, I for one look forward eagerly to hear what he has to say." With a sweep of his arm towards Richard, "Distinguished guests, fellow Rotarians - Mister Richard Smiles."

Richard stood, he took another gulp of water, he fumbled with his notes, and placed them on the lectern before him. There was some encouraging applause, then silence.

He looked down and the first thing he saw was the last page, the end of his speech staring up at him. His spastic fingers fumbled miserably until at last page one came to the top, - God only knew what order lay beneath.

He started, his voice amazingly strong and steady, after his formal greeting he launched steadily into his subject, making light innuendo lead towards the first punch line. It was delivered as well as he could have hoped. He paused, - silence......, the pause hung in the silent air, the confidence began to drain away. He pressed on another lead, another amusing aside, another punch line, another silence. Another gulp of water, he pressed on with his tale, the silence was clawing, his mouth was drying again, - should he sit down? Then from the corner of the room there was a commotion, then another from the left, then another, then screams of uncontrolled laughter, hysteria gripped the room. Laughter rose to a crescendo that filled the room, the Alhaji joined the merriment, - every line drew a laugh and when Richard sat down some fifteen minutes later, it was to a hilarious and standing ovation.

Keith Coker in his closing remarks thanked the Alhaji for an illuminating address and Mr. Smiles for the most unusual and entertaining speech he had ever heard at Rotary.

Richard sat slumped and exhausted in his seat. It had been a long day, - he should go home, - but he didn't, he stayed to drink and enjoy the adulation.

# CHAPTER 36

He left for Sokoto at five a.m. His head thumped, his throat and nose were powder dry, his stomach rumbled. He climbed into the back of the car feeling very sorry for himself. Joan had obstinately refused to make peace, so he had left the house without a word, angst hanging sourly in the grey dawn air. Mohamed reliably as ever, un-phased by the pre-dawn start, smiled his welcoming smile and drove with his usual sureness and speed towards the distant Sokoto some seven hours to the north. They were to meet the engineers and specifies for the new hospital, which were Lebanese, and were briefly on site on a one week visit from their head quarters in Beirut. The plan was to meet in the afternoon, stay over in the Government Rest House and return via Kano the next day.

The journey was long; mile after mile of scrubby bush eventually gave way to mile after mile of semi desert. They swept past native villages with their round huts of mud and straw, small stockades of woven bush sticks, their packs of dogs and herds of goats. The overwhelming impression was of dryness, scarcity, and poverty. Despite that at each small village the locals waved at the speeding car and smiled their bright smiles.

The roads north of Kano were twin single tracks, sometime of tarmac sometimes of dirt. Vehicles hurtled up and down, north to south and south to north at breakneck speed. One could see approaching vehicles miles away over the huge flat horizon, the dust clouds spearing like will o' the wisp suspended in a mirage of the shining blistering heat. Distance lost its meaning as the vehicles careered towards each other, frequently closing with unexpected alacrity. These closures became life threatening as dual tracks suddenly and without warning became single, or tarmac gave way to rutted dirt.

It was after such a near miss that Richard asked Mohamed to stop and rest while Richard took over the driving for a while. They were five hours into their journey, and had only taken brief pee stops. Richard ploughed on with a heavy foot on the accelerator, and soon was making great progress as the Peugeot cruised at close to a hundred miles an hour. They came to a rise and as they sped to the crown of the hill, Richard was horrified to see a herdsman with his large herd of goats meandering down the hill some three hundred yards to his front. At the same time the road became a single track of tarmac, the speedometer read ninety-eight miles per hour.

Hand on horn, - foot on brake,- slide,- dust envelopes them,- goats scatter,- herdsman leaps,- smash,- Mohamed wakes and thrusts his arms against the dashboard,- crash, once twice , - crash, crash, crash, the bodies of goats and kids fly over the bonnet, thumping into the windscreen, - crack!

Suddenly they were through the herd, several were dead and dying, Richard still had the car on four wheels, still doing seventy miles an hour, he braked again,

"Do not stop Sah!" insists Mohamed, "Go! Go! Do not stop Sah, they will keel us."

In those moments Richard took the instant decision not to stop, he accelerated away, in his mirror he saw the herdsman waving his arms in fury and distress, Richard felt shaken and ashamed. Amazingly the car had not sustained other than superficial damage; there were no leaks from the radiator or even a flat tyre. They stopped to inspect the damage a few miles up the road, all seemed to be well except a severely dented front and cracked windscreen.

They argued about going back and making reparations to the herdsman but Mohamed was very animated and firm about the folly of such a move. He intimated that the whole village would be out looking for the culprit, and rational dialogue would be out of the question. Allah had preordained the whole incident and anyway the herdsman should know better than to drive his goats down the road. Richard was again reluctantly persuaded to acquiesce to local counsel, and so they set off again, Mohamed restored to the driving seat.

They arrived in Sokoto on schedule at twelve thirty, Richard was exhausted after the rigors of the journey and his previous night's excesses, he felt he could kill for a bottle of beer. However getting a bottle of anything alcoholic in the seat of the Fulha Sultan, and the most devoutly Muslim area of the country was easier said than done. Here the Shia Moslems reigned with a strictness and absolute respect for their faith.

They drove directly to the Government Guest House, where Richard was relieved to find that his room was booked, so he secured his base, dumped his luggage and set out to find the dining room and satisfy his ravenous appetite. The dining room was a plain affair, a thatched room with concrete floor and around twelve tables all set with linoleum tablecloths and adorned with steel cutlery and plastic salt and pepper pots. Only one table was vacant so Richard took it and gazed out onto a view, which immediately did much to take the edge off his hunger. Outside a vulture picked his way over the seeping cesspit, finding morsels for its fetid meal. The smell was appalling, but there was no time to move since the waiter was already poised with order pad. The menu common to most of the guest houses was the usual; 'Brown Windsor Soup, Fried chicken or Pork chops with boiled potatoes and vegetables.' The waiter solemnly informed him that that the chicken was 'quenched', namely had run out. Richard waited without enthusiasm for the food, averting his eyes and olfactory organs as best he could from his unsavory neighbor, the vulture. Whilst waiting impatiently for the main course, a Nigerian neighbor, rose from his table, gagged and spat a globule of phlegm, with expert accuracy over Richard's table setting and into the offending lugubrious seeping cesspit.

He could stand it no more, he rose and fled from the room; outside the hapless waiter pursued him with his pork, potatoes and vegetables. Richard persuaded the fellow to deliver the food to his room, which would have been more accurately described as a hut.

He consumed his miserable lunch in the isolation of his hut, a roundel with bathroom attached. Cold water only, but the cold water was very warm even hot since it was stored in a metal tank raised above the compound.

As soon as was practical Mohamed and Richard set out to the site which was at the very early stages of development and some distance from the centre of the City. There were management huts in the process of being erected, as were the hoardings proclaiming the project, its designers, engineers and contractors. The Architects and Engineers were a Lebanese firm; Dar al Hadassah, a company of international repute based in Beirut. This was the biggest contract up for grabs in Northern Nigeria. The main contractor was a British household name. The value of the total contract was several tens of millions of pounds sterling, and the potential for Richard's Universal share could be as big as one million pounds plus.

He was to meet a Mr. Bashir, of the engineers, who was visiting from Dar's Beirut office. Richard's aim was to persuade the engineers to adopt systems and designs of roofing and ductwork, which Universal could manufacture and service from their Nigerian base. Bashir was expecting Richard and had already experienced one day delay due to Richard's wretched court appearances.

Bashir was on site but not available for the appointed hour, so Richard and Mohamed kicked their heels in the searing heat. Eventually at close to four o clock, Richard was ushered into a surprisingly well-appointed site office. Bashir was tall, an olive skinned handsome fellow. He was balding, but what hair he had, retained a glossy life echoed by his voluminous moustache. His eyes were sharp and clear and addressed Richard with an openness and directness which was both welcoming and slightly intimidating. On first impressions Richard liked him, he hoped this was mutual; he needed to make this work. They spent an hour together, Bashir with an intense and focused competence put Richard through the mill, whilst he listened intently to Richard's responses, there was no doubt who was the mover and shaker here. The good thing was that Richard felt comfortable, and even was able to admit to some shortfalls and gaps in his knowledge with candor, but with firm assurances that these problems could be answered.

Just after five, they brought their meeting to a close. It had gone well and Bashir was certainly interested in the local supply angle from a subsidiary of a well-known international player: Imports to the extreme north of Nigeria were going to be a huge headache. The snag was that Richard's proposal would necessitate a radical change in some parts of the design. This was also attractive because of a consequent substantial cost saving potential; however decisions would have to be deferred to Beirut. Could Richard visit? It was an exciting invitation. Bashir would give Richard schematics and let him work up a technical feasibility study to be presented in the Beirut office within the next six weeks.

To Richard's delight Bashir invited him to join his expatriate colleagues that evening in their quarters. Luxuriant they weren't, but compared to the Guest House however they were heaven. There was beer, excellent food and good company. The evening passed easily and Richard bade farewell promising to make arrangements to visit Beirut within the next six weeks.

In Kano Richard could hardly contain himself; the prospect of a visit to Beirut was too exciting for words. He made a beeline for his Lebanese customers and enquired about everything from airline schedules, hotels, places to see, things to do, what sort of money and in what quantities.

Michel Chigoury one of Richard's most constant customers, his polished head shining, sat in his crowded office. As usual there were four diverse groups all talking in different languages, Hausa, French, Arabic and English. Chagoury promised through the smoke laden Babel, that if Smiles travelled as planned then Chicory himself would be home on leave, - Oh! What sights he would show him, what food they would eat, the Lebanon was indeed the promised land; of sea, sun and alps, of French wine and food, of middle eastern magic, of history and romance.

Richard could hardly wait; he didn't even consider what Joan, not to mention Edward Regan would have to say. He would go, he would get the contract and it would be fun.

As he left Kano later than planned, the hot Saharan sun, set in scarlet hew, burning the old city walls, making the brown mud but noble buildings and city wall glow a golden ochre, and as if to add magic to the moment a caravan of camels cruised from the darkening horizon towards its destination in the old city.

On arrival home, Joan had mellowed from her stormy mood of the days preceding his departure; the children had recovered well in the short time of his absence. They put the kids to bed and settled to a quiet dinner for two. Despite his extreme fatigue he was anxious to break the news of his impending trip to Beirut with casual but considerate aplomb. 'Take your time' he said to himself, 'be good and listen to the news from the home front.'

Joan was full of the children's recoveries that seemed miraculous. She mentioned that they'd been well enough to leave with Peter the night before and that she'd had dinner at the Hetherington's, who'd had a guest from overseas. She'd been picked up from and dropped back at home, and although rather late, had had a pleasant evening. They'd also received an invitation to Mr Solomon's house warming which was to be on the following Saturday, Mr Solomon was the man who had built the palatial dwelling down the road. She'd accepted, O.K.?

Of course it was O.K. Solomon was Lebanese wasn't he? Quite coincidentally he explained that he might, just might have to travel to Beirut on business and try to win the biggest contract ever for Universal.

"That would be nice, a feather in your cap," remarked Joan, "how long would you have to away?"

"Don't know love," he responded casually, "depends on airline schedules, at least three or four days I suppose."

The next day Friday he worked feverishly on the Sokoto documents and tried to contact Edward Regan, who it transpired had gone to the U.K. because of a health problem that had suddenly arisen. What to do? Richard pondered whether to go ahead and start arranging the trip, or seek the permission of Regan's boss in the U.K. He decided that a combination of the two; sending a written assurance to Dar al Handassah that Universal was committed and asking them to reply formally and propose precise dates. Then he sent a message to Universal in UK intimating that the prospect was a hot one and that the visit was both vital and as close to a guarantee of success as could be imagined. MEA it transpired flew once a week Kano to Beirut, a visit of less than seven days seemed impracticable.

Despite his conspiracy, he was able to contain himself and the weekend got under way with a comfortable equanimity. They spent the morning playing with the children in a prefabricated swimming pool. During the afternoon Joan as ever was preoccupied with what she was to wear at the Solomon party.

"By the way who else is going?" asked Richard idly.

"Malcolm and Sally, because of Malcolm's business, but not many others we know, the Lebanese community, and some of the CFAO people,

Les Français!" she curtsied in a mock gesture, "it will be good to meet some new people, other than those idiots at the Club."

"Oh! Come on old love, they're not all bad, at least a few are good fun."

"We'll have to see, wont we, I'm going to wear my best frock and knock them dead, and you my handsome, better get out your best bib and tucker."

They arrived just after the prescribed hour, they'd watched the Mercedes, and BMW's purring up to the Solomon palace, and so walked down the road, to be met at the gates by a sparkling steward who escorted them to the entrance. There through double doors, Solomon and his wife stood receiving his guests before a champagne fountain as big as either Smiles had ever dreamed of, never mind seen. Hosi Solomon was handsome fifty some year old, dressed in an immaculate off white linen suit, silk shirt open at the neck, and expensive but to Richard's mind vulgar white shoes. His wife was shorter, dumpier and seemed quite void of the sleek style of her husband.

Solomon shook hands with Richard, "How delightful to meet my excellent neighbour and his lovely wife." He took Joan's hand and brought it smoothly to his lips, "How beautiful you English ladies are," he crooned. Richard felt mildly embarrassed, but Joan beamed and blushed the tiniest blush. Mrs Solomon, whispered or muttered and barely shook hands, the timidity of her almost could be felt to the touch.

"Champagne, please enjoy." entreated Solomon, turning to greet other arrivals.

Opulent was the word, every thing was just so, perhaps a little ostentatious, perhaps a little too extravagant, but definitely opulent. Through the circular entrance hall with the stairway of marble and lush red carpet, was a huge reception room, already full of Solomon's guests. The chicque, the wealthy, people they did not know. They stood there not quite sure what to do, champagne in hand. Evidently Joan's silk calf length gown was up to standard as a majority of the men turned and looked appreciatively in their direction.

"Come on," grimaced Richard "lets meet our new public."

A series of, 'good evenings' were exchanged, receiving the occasional 'bon soir' response, a familiar face here and there, but no one absolutely no one, they could relax with. Then much to their relief the Hetherington's emerged behind them, Sally as ever gorgeous and Malcolm as ever the ideal Auditor. Malcolm knew more of the guests than the others; so he introduced them to as many as he could. Richard as ever guzzled the champagne that seemed to be in limitless supply. They met Traders, Travel Agents, Diplomats, Fixers, Frenchmen, Nigerians, Lebanese, Indians but very few other Brits.

Soon the music started which varied between Swing and Middle Eastern music of a strangely hypnotic strain. Sally and Joan marvelled at the house and soon persuaded the detached Mrs Solomon to show them round the whole estate. The girls returned after their tour and found their husbands admiring the pool and garden and some of the more exotic lady guests, who were decorously seated around the fantastic water garden. It was late when the dining room, banqueting hall, was flung open to reveal a magnificent buffet of mesa, imported meats, crustateans and other delicacies. The tables groaned with food of such quality and rarity that it was almost beyond belief. They dined sumptuously and drank copiously, champagne, Lebanese wine, surprisingly delicious, and fine wines from France. All served perfectly in beautiful glasses, accompanying the glorious food, served on exotic china.

The reception room now became the dance floor; the lights were low and the music easy.

Joan and Richard smooched and joked about the riches of their surroundings and the wealth of their new neighbour, both were quite tipsy and enjoyed making sly jokes about the appeal or otherwise of their fellow guests. Still the champagne flowed and Richard was getting the worse for wear, Joan began to get cross, so Sally came to the rescue,

"Come on you drunken bum, dance with me." She led him to the dance floor and they swayed out of Joan's fiery stare. Sally whispered, her breath caressing his ear, "Now be a good boy, or I'll have to have you taken home," she kissed him gently but with languorous lips which made him tingle.

"Joan was a hit at our dinner party on Wednesday, pity you couldn't come. Harry Morgan was very taken with her, it did her ego no harm at all."

"Harry Morgan, who's Harry Morgan?"

"Malcolm's visiting senior partner, dishy actually, hope you didn't mind him taking her home?"

"Taking her home?"

"Well I was a bit tiddly, we all were, but Harry had to get back to the Hamdalah, so we thought it would be O.K. if he dropped her off on the way."

"Oh! No problem." Muttered Richard, sobering in a trice. Sally started once more to nibble his ear seductively, and pressed close hip to hip, her lips and breath promising the fruits they'd vowed to forgo.

"Come on Sally, have a heart, don't be a bitch."

"It's just nice to play some times." She purred in his ear. "Don't we all?"

The music stopped and they gathered again at the bar, "Water for Richard he's promised to be a good boy." She kissed him full on the mouth, "there's a good boy, that's your reward." Joan and Sally laughed in unison, Richard felt shaken and isolated.

Hosi Solomon loomed, his white suite shining in the half-light. Alongside him was another tall handsome man equally spectacularly dressed in pale blue cottons from Saville Row.

"My dears, how are you enjoying my new home?" he smiled smoothly his bejewelled hand smoothing over Richard's shoulder, "This is my younger brother Freddie,"

Freddie shook hands with Malcolm and Richard and he theatrically kissed each lady on the hand. Freddie's expression when he took Sally's hand was plain for everyone to see, did Malcolm? He spoke with an immaculate English accent, no hint of his Lebanese roots, well perhaps just an inflexion here and there, if anything more French than Middle Eastern.

"Freddie went to school in Shrewsbury," interjected Hosi, "whereas I studied in more humble places, Beirut and later in America." The small talk drifted on and they were joined by Freddie's willowy French girl friend that just reeked of sexuality. She was tall blonde, had a sensuous face with full lips and wide big startling green eyes. Her figure was slim but not thin, her curves full but no hint of fat. Her skin was olive brown, more suited to Cape d'Antibe than Northern Nigeria. She hardly said a word and Freddie seemed to ignore her completely. Mrs Solomon was nowhere to be seen.

Hosi led Joan onto the dance floor, Freddie swept away with Sally, Malcolm excused himself with a look of hopelessness, so Richard had little option other than to ask the French vision of beauty to dance.

They danced uncertainly, "I' sorry I didn't catch your name?" said Richard conscious of his stale champagne breath and trying not to be too close.

"Gabby, I am Gabby," she replied, and then she held Richard at arms' length and almost shouted above the music, "I am 'ere because of zat son of zee beetch, Fghreddie, Ee ees u Bastar', he bring me ear to zis 'orreeble, Oh quelle horreure!"

"Oh! I see, come, come, its not as bad as that is it?"

"Oh. Piece off you English dolt." She disengaged and marched away, leaving Richard standing dancing with an invisible partner. He gathered himself and followed, he found Malcolm at the bar getting into a serious state of drunkenness.

"That French piece, she may be gorgeous, but she's wild, just called me a dolt, and told me to piss off." He reaches for another champagne,

"Women, bloody women, old boy," slurred Malcolm, "all the bloody same." Malcolm guzzled his umpteenth glass of fizz. The French glamour girl was now draped over the shoulder of a tall man of Middle Eastern origin, there was no sign of the girls and the Solomon brothers.

"Come on old by, lets go and rescue the birds, from the clutches of the Arab Valentino's and hope we're in time to save their virtue."

"Bit late for that." Responded Malcolm; sliding uncertainly off his stool.

Freddie was dancing with Sally, outside the reception room on the patio and Hosi and Joan were sitting in a garden swing chair. Hosi got up a little too quickly when he saw Richard approach, straitening his jacket.

"I was telling your lovely wife that I can help you with contacts when you visit Beirut."

"How kind," - 'you lecherous son of a bitch'- Richard smiled through clenched teeth.

"Freddie's been telling me how wonderful it is to live in Monte Carlo," Sally beamed breathlessly.

"Gabby was just telling me how much she loves it here," smiled Richard, 'are all you bastard's lechers or just you two?' "We must go, its getting late, come my dear, I'm sure we'll be able to reciprocate Hosi's hospitality,- thank you Hosi its been great. "

There was a thump in the back ground, they turned as Malcolm picked himself up having obviously fallen over his own feet.

"Yes," said Sally, "We must go." She marched Malcolm unceremoniously toward the door, Freddie rushed to lend a hand but she shrugged him off, she radiated anger, it did not bode well for Malcolm when she got him home.

Richard and Joan walked the short way home in silence. Richard seethed with jealousy, who was Harry, what was Hosi the slimy one up to, what was Sally up to.

Joan said nothing just hummed a little tune to herself, volunteered some enthusiastic sex and went to sleep. Richard lay tired, drunk, but afraid, 'His love,- could she betray him?, could she let other men make love to her?- he'd erred, why shouldn't she,- what was Sally's kiss all about ?'- the Iago in his soul turned the knife of jealous hating lust.

# CHAPTER 37

The time to visit Beirut arrived; Richard could hardly conceal his excitement. In Kano he had met and teamed up with Peter Goddard. Peter, an Englishman of around his own age, was married to a Lebanese girl, and the family had extensive business interests in Kano and the Lebanon. He was going to join his wife on leave in their family home, near, though some way out of Beirut. Although Smiles knew Goddard only slightly, he knew him to be 'one of the boys', a man who enjoyed a beer or two. He would be an ideal source of information on the delights of Beirut.... Beirut where Richard was going to conquer new fields for Universal, where Smiles would make his name, Beirut... he could hardly wait. The fleshpots of the Middle East beckoned; every young man's dream. So travelling with Peter was an ideal opportunity for Richard to map out his Beirut plans.

The Sokoto project would be just the start, Richard Smiles would turn Universal's African business on its head, and this would be the start of his stellar international future.

Both the men, in the spirit of 'end of term', enjoyed their time in the bar. The 707 was almost empty so they sat together for the five-hour flight. The hostesses were glamorous and attentive. They graduated to champagne once on board and continued to celebrate as the plane made its way northeast across the Sahara, Egypt and onwards towards Beirut.

The hostesses' were charming. They were full of chat, and since the plane was so sparsely populated, they were able to spend a good deal of their time in flirtatious banter with Richard and his new found pal. As the party atmosphere on board grew more intimate they were soon talking of a getting together as a group on the Saturday. It was agreed; noon on Saturday at the St. Paul Hotel, in the terrace cocktail bar.

It occurred to Richard, albeit through a very pleasant haze of champagne, that Peter was about to join his in-laws and that dating air stewardesses was not quite a smart thing to do.

"I say, I do hope you're going to make it on Saturday,"

"No, problem, old stick, I'll be there." Mumbled the inebriated Peter, "not a word at the airport, the wife will be there to meet me, what?"

"Absolutely, mum's the word." Smiles giggled.

It was night time and the lights of Beirut, shone with a promise so different from the candlepower of Kano. His hotel; 'The Palm' was just across the road from the sumptuous 'St Paul' but was none the less very comfortable and quiet, protected from the din of traffic by the long gardens that ran in front down to the shore road.

Richard was ferried from the airport by a plump mustachioed Palestinian taxi driver whose name was Abdul. Abdul engaged in continuous chatter from the airport to the hotel. He seemed to know a great deal about the local scene and offered to be Richard's guide throughout his visit. Abdul was such a friendly guy it was impossible to refuse, so after showering and changing it was Abdul who whisked Richard into the City proper to a Restaurant called 'The Captain's Table.' There; Richard dined on his favorite things delicacies entirely out of reach in Nigeria; he washed it all down with generous quantities of local wine. This was the life; this was what he wanted to do; see the world, the headiness of it all swept the thoughts of Joan, David and Emma into a distant corner of his mind. What a great day, and tomorrow, tomorrow promised more adventure, yes, this was the life.

The following morning, Richard was somewhat surprised to find Abdul sitting waiting in his splendid Mercedes outside the hotel.

"I will show you Beirut, I will be your guide," he swung his worry beads back and forth in his chubby hands, "I will make for you to remember," he gushed, "for ever this garden of Eden, this country of your Bible and of the Romans," and waving his arms almost embracing the slightly alarmed

Richard, he continued; "Abdul will be your guide and friend, there is nowhere in Beirut that I am not known, you will see, you will see."

They drove around the breathtaking Cornice stopped to gaze on Pigeon rocks, marvel at the blue Mediterranean Sea, and watch the beautiful people at the sidewalk cafes. The sun shone brilliantly, but whilst it was warm, it was fanned by a light sea breeze that was a million miles from the burning summer sun of the plains of West Africa. They drove past the palm-lined boulevards, the American University; they stopped at the port where Abdul led the way round a variety of traders and dealers in every imaginable commodity from Hashish to magnificent Persian carpets.

Sign posts to Tyre and Sidon, to Tripoli and Baalbeck, to Damascus and the places of biblical history. It was heady stuff, snow-capped mountains to the east and the inviting warm and balmy sea to the west. Lunch was taken early in the warm sun soaked walled garden restaurant of Abdul's choosing. He sampled Lebanese mezza that was a delicious assortment of meats, olives, vegetables and couscous. He washed it all down with a couple of beers, resisting the offers of arak mindful of the afternoon's business.

That afternoon the now faithful Abdul delivered him at the appointed hour to the offices of Dar al Handassah, there he was given the most courteous reception and whisked to a plushly furnished conference room. This room was a little different, since the furnishings whilst of the highest quality reflected the purpose of the business, with a central drawing board which could be swung in a full circle and form the centre piece of any discussion.

Pictures of completed projects adorned the walls, interspersed with concept drawings for prospective clients. This was it, Richard needed to succeed, he was confidant he would. Through the window there was a wonderful view down to the sea over the top of a city of a thousand years and a thousand cultures.

Bashir breezed in full of smiles and warmth; Said Buzzi head of engineering followed him and Sami Khoury, the project Manager brought up the rear. After prolonged greetings and a little small talk the plans that Richard had forwarded from Kaduna were spread onto the centre drawing board, and each man in turn fired questions at Richard.

Khoury was the one who demurred, he obviously was against such a radical change and he raised every kind of objection. When Richard responded to his objections he became short and turned to his colleagues and spoke in what Richard took to be Arabic. There was an animated discussion that Richard watched rather than heard; since the language meant nothing to him. Eventually they came back to English; Khoury turned to Richard, extended his hand rather stiffly and explained that he would have to leave.

The three men Bashir, Buzzi and Richard were left in the silence that Khoury left behind. After a short pause it was Buzzi who broke the silence;

"Mr. Khoury, is the man ultimately responsible for the project, and at the moment he, um, um," he fiddled with the drawings, "he doesn't think that the State government will accept the architectural amendments necessitated by your proposals."

Richard's heart sank, he'd come all this way, spent God knows how much money and these buggers were not going to go through with his proposal, Universal were going to get nothing. The specter of Edward Regan brandishing his expense report flashed before him, it was not a pleasant thought. At the first fence his aspirations were thrown in the dust. 'Why hadn't Bashir warned him? For God's sake he'd look a fool' Regan would crucify him.

Bashir was more supportive, "Khoury has agreed to put the savings proposition to the client, in fact I will be doing that and then, if they agree, and I think there is a good chance that they will, then I believe we will look at this proposition again."

There was a silence everyone knew that the exercise had been a disaster, Richard was as embarrassed as could be, what the hell was he going to do, fiddling around in Beirut until next Wednesday on an expense account which, as of now had dwindled to miserable proportions.

Buzzi by way of rescuing suggested that he was involved in a number of other projects, which might interest Universal. He left the conference room, and it was Bashir who put his hand on Richard's shoulder, and apologized for the disappointment,

"Richard, may I call you that?"

"Of coarse, old boy," responded Richard rallying.

"In a small way to compensate you for the problem, perhaps you will be good enough to be our guest for dinner tonight?"

"How kind, thanks a lot I look forward to it."

Buzzi barged back through the door, clutching a bundle of drawings which he spread on the centre board.

"These are the outlines of another hospital project in Nigeria, this time for North Eastern State to be at Maidugari, it is at a much earlier stage and we are just finalizing for concept approval. It is smaller than Sokoto, but not much!"

Bashir broke into a broad smile, "Of course Said, of course, Richard we can work here, it is not yet my business, but will be after the concept and tender estimates, now you work with Said,"

They gathered round the drawings and began work, and by six o clock as a brilliant sun set over the Mediterranean they adjourned from the conference room, Richard's gloom replaced with a glow now, that his expense account, not to mention his reputation had been snatched from the jaws of ignominy.

That night was a most pleasant experience, they dined late in an expensive and distinguished Lebanese restaurant, where Bashir and Richard ate well and demolished a number of beers and copious quantities of arak. Buzzi a staunch Moslem drank nothing but was nevertheless great company and a fund of priceless information about the emerging force of Moslem politics. The growing power of the Gulf States and the desire to extend and preserve the Moslem way of life was leading to a much greater influence of the Middle East and firms such as theirs. They targeted Moslem Africa as well as Saudi and the Gulf States. Interstate aid was no more a matter of left or right but increasingly Moslem or Christian or Communist or whatever, the problems of Israel and Iran and Iraq were all in the melting pot, but the Lebanon they assured him would always remain the crossroads of all these worlds. To Richard, this was a revelation, a glimpse of the world where he wanted to be a player, but for now; one more arak.

Buzzi bade them a good night, and Bashir and Richard set off in search of further entertainment. They moved from night club to night club, Richard now in the middle stages of an alcoholic hubris had never seen such things; there were belly dancers as lush and exotic as any man from

South Wales had ever seen, there were dancers of such bewildering sexual spell as to transfix him to the place for ever, he was mesmerized, knocked out, amazed, bedazzled. Yes, this was for him!

The following morning dawned in the bright Beirut sun, Richard's first experience of arak was not a good one, his head throbbed and everything gastronomic reeked of aniseed. Nonetheless he rose with an air of enthusiasm; he tried in vain to phone Kaduna, had a hearty breakfast of delicious crusty bread and violently thick coffee. Abdul the faithful was on hand outside the hotel; worry beads encircling his fingers, his smile as constant as the Beirut sun.

"Show me the sights, my friend, show me what a visitor must see before he leaves, maybe for ever."

"Inch Allah, I shall do my best we shall go to Baalbeck, and to the hills above the city we shall look into Israel, and eat a good lunch in my village."

"Sounds good to me Abdul, be kind to an innocent abroad!" joked Richard as he settled into the Mercedes.

They set off first skirting the south of the city, past the racecourse and Richard was astounded to see the extent of the refugee camps, Chattily and Sabra meant nothing to him except that all those in the dreadful camps were victims, it was not clear to him who was the victim of what conflict, this was a view into something disturbingly different from the prospects of prosperity and trade of last night's jollity. Abdul had another view of life altogether different from the prosperous businessmen of Dar al Handassah.

He was a Palestinian, who had lived in the Lebanon for many years, his family had come as refugees in the fifties, whilst he was light and humorous he also bore a bitter edge, hardly perceptible but there nevertheless. As they journeyed on at a leisurely pace, it transpired that Abdul like most of the Moslem population felt excluded from power, despite having parity of numbers with the Christian population, he resented the United States for their intervention in nineteen fifty two, when his family newly arrived were embroiled in a violent and unhappy situation which cost them the life of his younger brother and many of their possessions. Here was a glimpse of a conflict so complex that Richard could only listen and recognize with some shame his own ignorance.

The words PLO and Golan heights so distant were now in seeing and touching distance and amidst the splendor of the Lebanon there was a fear of the future, anger at the past and distrust of the present.

They drove on through Alayh, Shtawrah climbing the steep limestone hillside until they looked down on the Beqaa Valley, they could see into Syria and off to the south toward the troubled border with Israel. Abdul cast off the gravitas of their political discussions and extolled the beauties of his adopted homeland. He really was a delightful man, who, like most people of this part of the world spoke English, French and Arabic with equal facility.

His assiduous consideration to Richard was almost disconcerting, never before had Richard encountered such devotion to client service. They had agreed the rates in Lebanese pounds, and Abdul had stuck to the hand shaken agreement with absolute commitment. He was at Richard's service day and night; he expected nothing and accepted a meal with Richard only when cajoled to keep Richard company. He regaled Richard with tales of family hardship and joy, of his childhood in Palestine and the family's forced exile into Lebanon. Yes there was an edge, but there was an almost complete lack of vengefulness, more a bitter fatalism leavened with humor.

They stopped at Zahlah at a riverside restaurant and drank the fierce coffee of these parts and then on to Baalbeck. Nothing could have prepared Richard for the splendors of the Roman Temples of Baalbeck; they were magnificent. Huge columns rose into the azure sky, the temples were all magic; perfect in line and proportion, their huge scale at once dominating and defining the locale. It was breathtaking; Abdul as always was an extraordinarily informed guide, he poured out dates and facts, pointed to details in the architecture and translated inscriptions.

The sun burned Richard's head, but the fascination with the beauties of Baalbeck kept them there, Abdul, beads revolving constantly in his clean soft hands, poured out detail after detail, every question lead to another discourse and another question. It was a day like no other that Richard had ever experienced. He felt elated and humbled at once, the world was a wonderful place, diverse, beautiful, cruel and generous, seeing it; that was the thing,..... that was the thing to do. That was the thing he would do.

Saturday; Richard was at leisure, he remembered the 'date' he and
Peter had made with the airhostesses, but had heard nothing from Peter
whose bravado, no doubt had been cut down by his wife. Nor did he
believe that the girls would turn up, but at the back of his mind there was
a mischievous hope.

He spent the morning at preparing the documents and reports that
had to be submitted to Buzzi and Bashir before he left next Wednesday,
when the phone went it was Chagoury from his mountain home inviting
Richard for a day out on Sunday, 'could Richard make it to Tripoli?' where
Chagoury would meet him. That was no problem, 'what was he doing
today?' Ha! Ha! No girl was safe, eh! Absolutely, no girl was safe.

He worked on and at mid-day he put on his smartest slacks and shirt
and walked over to the Terrace Bar at the St Paul, in case, in case.....He
sat at a table and ordered a gin and tonic, a gentle breeze drifted in from
the sea, and waiters hovered,

"Would Sir, be taking lunch? Was Sir a resident? Did Sir have a
reservation?"

"Richard, Richard we're sorry to be late."

He looked up, startled! There in front of him were two of the loveliest
girls he had ever seen. Who were they? Oh, God! It's the airhostesses,
bugger, what are their names? He leapt to his feet, spilling his now nearly
empty gin,

"How lovely to see you both again, you look absolutely lovely, do
sit down and have a drink." He held out his hand but each girl leaned
forward and kissed him politely on both cheeks. The perfume intoxicated
him at once, not the perfume they had applied but the perfume of their
whole beautiful bodies, their breath their skin, their hair, and their lovely
hands.

They sat, they were quite different, now in their short skirts and
contrasting clothes,

"Vodka screwdriver." said one.

"Dry White," said the other her brilliant smile almost blinding him.

"Peter, where is Peter?" demanded the one with the lovely red auburns
hair.

"Alas I know not, I've not heard from him since we arrived, I expect he's a bit late." God he hoped so. They waited and they waited, the drinks at astonishing prices punctuated the awkward passing minutes.

The girls looked at each other, "Ah the English." Dismissed the blonde.

"Oh, I know you're disappointed, I'm so sorry I would quite understand if you would like to call the day off, I should of course be very disappointed."

The two girls looked at each other once more, then the blonde said, "OK' three's a crowd, Richard you must choose; Leila or Sam?"

God he couldn't remember which was which, if he said the wrong thing now they would both go, maybe that would be the best thing. His nerves jangled, his self assurance ebbed, this was a dream come true or a disaster of epic proportions.

"My dears I couldn't begin to choose, Sam......," he paused looking deliberately between them, "Leila, please both stay and have lunch and then if one of you must, make up your mind then" He hoped he'd got it right Leila was the one with the auburn hair, Sam the gorgeous blonde.

After another round of drinks they ordered a mind bogglingly expensive lunch, with a nineteen sixty-six burgundy to wash down the most heavenly filet of beef that Richard could remember. The food and the wine suffused with the location into the headiest of atmospheres. He began to relax, they'd talked easily; both girls being charming and at ease. They'd both travelled to Jordan and Athens respectively since their last meeting and were on leave until the following Tuesday. Richard began to fantasize about each girl in turn, Sam blonde and thicker set but vivacious and full of wit. Leila languorous, smoldering and more intense, both were very sexy ladies. He had to leave the room, when he returned, Sam was gone.

"Where's Sam?"

"Richard," she put her hand over his, "both of us wanted to stay, so, I hope you will not be offended, we tossed a coin," she paused, she stroked his hand and smiled, "I won. I hope you are pleased"

His hand closed round hers, he took it to his lips and rather smarmingly, "My dear no man could ask for more." How smarmy could he get? He winced at his own corniness.

"Are you staying here?" she asked their hands still entwined.

His palms began to sweat….. What now? He had no idea what to do or say;

"No I'm afraid not, at a rather humbler establishment across the road, The Palm."

"Does it have a pool?"

"Yes it does, quite a nice one in a walled garden, no view of the sea I'm afraid."

"Shall we go there and take a little sun?" Her finger lightly stroked the palm of his hand, electricity shot through him.

He cleared his suddenly blocked throat, "Why not, nice idea."

They rose, the waiter brought a bill that nearly ruined his already frail composure, however he rallied even tipped generously and left, ushering the languidly swaying Leila in front of him, trying at the same time to stop his riotous imagination from taking flight.

The Palm Hotel garden was a beautiful place with a modestly sized pool shaded in the lea of some lovely trees. The patio and surround was deserted, through the door a waiter snoozed in the deserted bar, there seemed no one else around.

"If you'd like to swim, I'll get my key and I'll go and change, I think I have a spare robe in the room."

"Richard, do not leave me here" she intoned, "after all I too have to change." She pouted.

His room was not big but it was pleasant; with a large double bed, French windows overlooking the garden, the bathroom had only a shower but was light and clean. Two bathrobes hung behind the door.

Leila swung her large shoulder bag onto the bed, withdrew from it a dress that she hanged in the wardrobe, "For tonight."

Tonight! What tonight? Richard felt the panic rise. This woman was leading him by his nose, or more accurately by his dick. What was he getting into here?

She unpacked a miniscule garment that Richard took to be a swimsuit and began to slip out of her cloths.

Richard rummaged at length in his drawers, looking for his swimming trunks all the time watching in the mirror this lovely creature revealing herself. Then without any warning and without a stitch on she turned to him, looked at him standing helplessly in his shirt tails.

"Richard we should shower before we go down, no?"

"S- s- sure. Oh sure, why not," his erection pointing the way to the bathroom.

She walked over to him unbuttoned his shirt and lead him like a shorn white lamb to the shower. She was olive tan, lithe and luscious, he felt white, skinny and overwhelmingly horny. He looked down passed the one eyed devil and was alarmed to see his socks. Socks, God help him; every one new that socks were about as sexy and sophisticated as unwashed dishes. He removed the offending garments with as much dignity as he could muster.

By now the spell had been broken, despite this gorgeous creature and her obvious easiness with him; he did not feel easy with her. In the mirror he was white and pale with sunburn tidemarks around his neck, arms and knees. This might have been his lifelong fantasy, but its enactment frightened him almost, though not quite, to sexual paralysis.

In the shower they explored each other, Leila with a slow and practiced sureness, Richard with an unbridled and bungling enthusiasm that had to be contained. Somehow they came out of the shower without having consummated the moment. She dried him off gently with the soft towels pushed him onto the bed and caressed him from foot to head, stopping at the crucial point in the traverse to pay him the ultimate sexual compliment. Again she knew when to ease; she drew up beside him her olive breasts heaving with excitement. Richard wanted to respond to give this heavenly woman something back, but she would have none of it, not at least then, she restrained him and he gave in easily to her. He wanted to howl with the pent up ecstasy, this was unlike anything he'd ever known. He was pleased with her, but beneath it all he could hardly contain how pleased he was with himself.

She lay quietly kissing him on his head and shoulders; almost inducing a hypnotic trance, then when she judged the time right she mounted him and rode him with an impossible sensuous power. They came together in a thunderous climax.

They lay there whilst the sex and the alcohol wore off, sleep encroached but not for long, it was Leila who leapt from the bed, flicked him playfully with a towel,

"Come on you, lazy Englishman, let's shower and swim."

"Welsh man if you don't mind." He laughed back.

He felt he'd graduated, passed the test, although she was the master he the pupil. At last he began to relax.

She pranced into the shower, Richard lay on the bed watching mesmerized as the naked Leila soaped herself down, 'Oh what a bum, what a perfect bottom, what a figure, what a luscious bird she is, down boy!'

They spent the next couple of hours at the pool but the walls and trees soon deprived them of the sun. They ordered tea, which was of the sticky sweet variety oddly accompanied by British digestive biscuits. They talked easily; she of her favorite places in the world, and her family who were Palestinian but now lived in America. He talked of Nigeria and his more interesting experiences there. He told her about Wales its traditions and his romantic view of it all. She laughed at his jokes and they enjoyed the quiet of silences. "Don't make tomorrow too hard." She said more than once, reminding them both of the fleeting nature of their meeting. "My life as a flying waitress is hard, sometimes I meet someone like you who is a nice gentle man, but more often it is fighting off air crew or filling in time in strange hotel rooms. Do not think of me as a whore? Because I am not. I am lonely but I make of my life what I choose, and today I have enjoyed, I hope you too."

"Oh Leila, Oh my dear, you make me sad."

"Why be sad, tonight we shall go to the Casino du Liban, I have tickets from the airline, it is a fantastic show, you will love it."

"Casino, I'm afraid I don't gamble,"

"No, you don't have to gamble, we shall go to the show, it is like the Lido in Paris, you'll love it, and afterwards I will take you to my place near Juniyah, and then we shall watch the stars and then you shall fly away as free as a bird and I shall remember Richard and enjoy."

"Oh, Jesus, you make me sad again," He grabbed her and kissed her tenderly, she did not resist, but neither did she respond.

"If you mention that word again, I'm gone, Richard please do you understand?"

"Yes, I understand."

They retreated to his room to shower once more, they soaped each other and soon their passions were aroused once more. This time though Leila was more passive, more compliant, and more self centered, Richard did everything he knew to please her, and please her he did, at least he thought he did.

They dressed, she made the simplest shift look marvelous, he clambered into his best slacks, and was directed to wear a jacket and tie. A pleasant hour passed before they set off in Leila's cute little Citroen 2cv motor for the delights of the Casino du Libyan. She drove through the old city passed the Serail Citadel, through Martyr's Square and passed the souks; Ayyas, Tawileh and Al Jamail, passed St George's Cathedral and the Place d'Etoile and then out of the city on the coastal road towards Juniyah.

As she drove she pointed to all the contrasting cultures, the fine buildings each with an ancient history of its own. She loved Beirut and although her parents and siblings now lived in Cleveland, Ohio, and despite her possession of a US passport, she felt at heart a Palestinian whose roots would always be in the Middle East.

The coastal road was spectacular and the little Citroen put-putted its way towards the Casino. The building was huge with a fantastic array of neon lights advertising the delights of the gambling and 'a Show Without Compare'; it was called 'Flame' and was more glamorous, more sophisticated, more seductive than any show on earth, or so it claimed.

Leila's airline VIP tickets allowed them access to the 'diamond cocktail and dining suite' where there was the most incredible buffet, stupendously stocked with lobster, caviar, shell fish, fine cuts of meat, incredible mezzas and a flaming grill where one could order whatever your stomach desired. Richard's appetite almost made him forget his companion, but she prevailed upon him to sit and sample the Crystal Champagne.

"Have only hors d'oeuvres" she implored him, "I will cook you a supper later."

He could think of no reply, to resist these mountains of delicious food was a trial. He tried to ignore his rumbling tummy, he took her hand and kissed it. He looked around him and saw for the first time in his life the really rich and glamorous, the smooth men, the thousand dollar dresses, the million dollar diamonds, was that Hosi in the corner, was that Joan in that sensational dress?

The show! What a show; he had seen nothing like it, its scale, its glamour, the dancing girls, ice rinks and waterfalls appeared and disappeared, dancers danced and skated in a bewildering riot of color and light. After two and a half hours the show came to an end with a wall of fire and a waterfall cascading onto the massive set. Bravo, it was incredible.

"Come" said Leila, "come see the real Lebanon."

They drove not many miles, turning off the main road. The little Citroen laboring up the gravely track that led after half a mile or so to a small village, at the end of the very short main street stood an unimpressive three story building with a flat roof. Leila parked the car, and led him by the hand to the back of the property and through an unkempt but fragrant garden and from there up an outside staircase to the roof. The view was stunning down over the glitzy lights of the Casino to shimmering moonlit sea. Small fishing smacks with their lights illuminated the seascape and fluffy clouds shone silver edged in the midnight blue sky.

As Richard took in the roof, he noticed that it was a much used roof garden, with a swing seat, other chairs, a large number of flower pots and in the corner a stove come griddle with earthenware pots already simmering. They had not said a word since their arrival here, she touched him gently on the shoulder and slipped his jacket off, and she slipped away down the stairs. He started to follow but she put her hand up to signal that he should stay put, and so Richard Smiles sat on the swing seat and contemplated a heaven that he had never glimpsed or imagined.

The rigors of the long day began to urge him to slumber; in the corner Joan straddled Hosi Solomon as she made lazy languorous love. Hosi leered at him, his hands cupping around his errant wife's buttocks encouraging their rhythmic coupling.

"Some wine, some wine?"

He woke with a start, Leila stood above him holding a glass of red wine,

"You were sleeping."

"Just dozing. It's been the most marvelous day, how can I thank you?"

"You can enjoy some 'kebbe,' which Sam has kindly prepared for us."

"Sam?"

"Yes Sam, we share this or part of this building with six others, all with MEA, I was afraid they may have been up here, but it's just us."

She walked over to the stove and with expert dexterity served two bowls of 'Kebbe' mutton pounded and cooked with wheat and served with wonderful vegetables. They ate in silence, swigging the carafe of wine, and watching the moon on the tranquil sea. They were silent because neither wanted to break the spell, the silence went on and on.

"Tomorrow I must report early for a flight to Paris," Leila said to no one in particular.

"You want me to go?"

"No I want you to stay, but it can't be."

She put down her bowl came and sat on his lap, and kissed him gently, "but it can't be."

They rang for Abdul, who turned up as directed by Leila, they kissed a sad stranger's kiss of farewell, and the Mercedes moved off, he did not look back.

After a brief and disturbed sleep; more a nightmare than a sleep, filled with remorse, guilt and uncertainty. A sleep, grotesque with the visions of his own lechery and the panic of loosing the things he knew he loved. A sleep where his children cried for him, where his wife left him for a fat rich merchant and where Leila sat naked at his mother's table, telling Muriel that Richard was a useless lover.

He woke addled with the remains of his yesterday, of satiated lust, a full belly and just a hint of something lost forever. Despite his remorse there remained a sense of pleasure, he had been lead into temptation and he loved every minute of it. It was still early so he showered and shaved and sat, supping coffee from his room tray. He stared out over a quiet Beirut, a few bells called the faithful Christians to prayer, but otherwise it was still. On his tiny balcony he could see the St Paul Hotel and the sea beyond. Nothing stirred.

Then there was a noise, at first like a roaring tide and then ever louder the scream of Israeli Mirage jets, they howled past the St Paul, not much higher than the roof and perhaps a mile out to sea. They were gone in a second. But then they screamed back, this time between the St Paul and the little Palm Hotel, he could almost see the pilots at their controls. The scream became an instant thunder that clapped all around him, as the jets discharged canons, round after round into the refugee camps not a mile away to the south west. The shells tore without mercy into those sleepy

Sunday morning camps where children and mothers awoke to another cheerless day, where Palestinian revolutionaries were about to conspire an Israeli downfall, but the shells ripped and exploded without discrimination. The noise was the sound of murder, obscene, beyond the imagination of Richard the naïve, Richard the unfaithful, Richard the innocent.

The noise ceased and the air was quiet. As Richard craned his neck he saw the smoke rise from untold misery and pain. Soon the air was filled with the sirens of ambulances and the lamentations of the victims.

He closed the door, paced about his room, frightened and disconcerted, eventually he lay on his bed and wondered about the contrasts of this wonderful but dangerous place. Where did Bashir's hopes lie, where did Abdul or Leila see their future? The quiet engulfed him and it was as if those violent minutes had never happened. He went down to breakfast where the staff were largely absent, but the management served their splendid breakfast, emphasising the Phoenician credo that nothing should interfere with trade and service, not even a war.

Abdul appeared at the appointed hour, nine thirty, and wailed a sad tale of the deaths of several of his countrymen, women and children. He cursed the Israelis, but seemed equally angry with the Christian led Lebanese government, who he implied were in cahoots with the Israelis.

They drove north through Juniyah, the scene of his previous night's bliss, past the Casino du Liban, past the road that led to Leila's hideaway, on through Jubayl, Al Batrun, Shikka and into Tripoli. They went to a café in the port where Chagoury was to meet them.

He was already there, his bald head shining, his dimpled face wreathed in smiles. Yes he'd heard of the Israeli attack of the morning but seemed not unduly perturbed. He was holding court with a number of other middle aged to old men, as ever talking in a bewildering mix of languages, including French and a number of Arabic dialects. On Richard's arrival he moved smoothly into English and the gathered company did likewise, with a seamless ease.

Abdul left without ceremony and agreed to return to meet Richard at eight that night. What was apparent was that Chagoury, his imp-like polished head, his Punch hooked nose was the leading light and was holding court. His pals were not Moslem, but Christian and it was clear that there was a tangible distrust between them and their Moslem countrymen. The "Christian" view was wholly uncharitable to the plight of the refugee Palestinians, who they blamed for dragging Lebanon into the Middle East conflict, which they assured Richard would be the downfall of their homeland.

After yet another lesson in the politics of the Middle East, Chagoury drove off with Richard into one of the most scenic routes in the world. The stately old car climbed through the foothills to Bshharri, passed the Cedars and on to Dunar, the summer residence of the Mennonite Patriarch, through the village of Hasroun on the edge of the Qannobin Valley and up to Bquorgacha, the highest village in the Lebanon.

There Richard was introduced to the whole family and after a walk around the village with its captivating views; Richard was the guest of honour at a sumptuous lunch. Chagoury presided over a long dining table set under the trees in the garden. His mother was the first person Richard had met in the Lebanon who did not speak a multitude of languages. She half whispered to her son in what sounded like Arabic, but never addressed Richard directly. She appeared to be very ancient indeed. The younger female cousins, who were both at University in Beirut, chatted happily and were keen to learn about England. Wales was a fairly unknown quantity for them, so Richard eulogised at length and amused them with tales of Welsh folklore, much of which he made up as he went along.

They drank and ate with a gusto late into the afternoon, Chagoury beamed his delight and loved playing the host, it was a most comfortable and memorable afternoon, which reminded Richard of how important families are and how wonderful. In all too short a time it was time to leave and Chagoury, despite his considerable consumption of arak and wine, took his seat behind the wheel of the old car for the precipitous descent back to Tripoli. As they made their way back the sunset was spectacular over the Mediterranean Sea and a mist shrouded the valleys below. Richard was again smitten by the diversity, colour and variety of this small, but beautiful country, surely there are few such beautiful places on God's earth.

Once he transferred to Abdul's car the journey back to Beirut took on a more sinister mantle. There was quite a heavy presence of militia and police patrols and they were stopped twice on the journey, when soldiers with guns poked their heads officiously into Abdul's motorcar. The militia were sharp and officious to Abdul but more respectful when they learned that Richard was British. In the space of an hour or two yet another face of the Lebanon revealed itself.

Exhausted Richard fell into bed, not sure how he would fill the following day. There only remained a wrap-up meeting with Dar al Handassah on Tuesday, but filling in time in lovely Lebanon should not prove a problem, he slept like a rock.

He rose for a late and leisurely breakfast; his only engagement that day was to go with Abdul to shop for mementoes to take home for Joan and the family. As he mused over the weekend he was suddenly seized with the fear that he might take home a memento that he had not bargained for, namely a consequence of his dalliance with Leila. The more he thought of the affair, the more convinced he became that he was now the carrier of a sexually transmitted disease. At the same time he fought the idea with the recall of Leila, a sweet young woman, though, he could not deny; an enthusiastic sexual athlete. The dual within him continued until he was shaken from his reverie by a phone call from Dar al Handassah.

The message was from Khoury's secretary. Would Richard attend the office if possible that morning? Yes, of course he would. So he summoned Abdul and they left; Richard full of foreboding that Khoury had had the Universal propositions thrown out altogether.

He was ushered into Khoury's office where the man himself, small, spiky-haired and mustached, rose from his chair with a sprightliness that took Richard by surprise. From his sullen performance of the earlier meeting he was quite transformed, he smiled broadly and ushered Richard to chair at his conference table.

"I hope that you did not think I was against your ideas, last week? Will you have coffee or tea?"

"Of course. Tea please." countered Richard, relaxing at a pace.

"I have seen your proposals for the Maiduguri job and I understand your preliminaries are ready today?"

"Well, actually tomorrow. They are being typed up by the hotel's secretarial staff, they'll be ready for Mr. Buzzi, as promised."

"Fine, fine." mused Khoury looking distractedly out of the window. "I think that our Sokoto project and the Maiduguri project should share certain commonalities, the donors are the same you see and they will want to see the same benefits, particularly the financial factors. Buzzi and Bashir, particularly Bashir has supported the idea of a local based international supplier for this vital part of the contracts, the contractors too are in favour at Soot, so…" he spread his hands on the table, paused, picked up his tea cup, drank, put down his tea cup, "so… I have agreed to put forward your amended proposals to the client in Nigeria and if they are accepted then I shall also support the Maiduguri proposal."

Richard could hardly restrain himself from kissing the little man. "Mr. Khoury you can rest assured that Universal will perform well as a contributor to both projects, anything I or my company can do, and you only have to ask."

"Please, please…"Khoury held up his hand, "Please Mr. Smiles, you must not, as it were, how you say, count your fowl. The north east State Government and the central Government will need to approve these amended proposals, we will or may need your assistance in helping to make the case, so please… don't count the…"

"Chickens." interrupted Richard. "Yes I quite understand, but I'm sure we can work successfully together."

Khoury rose, the meeting was over. "I look forward to hearing of the results of tomorrow's meeting which I 'm afraid I will be unable to attend. Thank you for coming to Beirut, no doubt we shall meet in the future."

On the pavement, Richard stood; astonished at his good fortune His first thought was to rush to the St. Paul Hotel and buy himself a slap up lunch, but his second thought got the better of him. So they returned to the Palm, where Richard chivvied the secretarial service and spent the afternoon checking and rechecking the contract details.

That evening he spent alone with his guilt and spent hours trying to phone Kaduna, almost against his wishes, he got through at eleven o'clock local, eight o' clock in Kaduna. Peter answered the 'phone, Joan had apparently just left to have dinner with a "neighbor". Peter was not sure who. Everyone was well and the children were in bed, Madame had only just left.

Richard put down the phone and turned in, but he found it hard to sleep, torn between his own sins of lechery and the jealousy consuming his evermore, active imagination. He dreamed of Joan and Leila, of Hosi and himself in any variety or combinations. He woke sweating. Again the fears of disease and of his family finding out his sins crawled over and through him.

The next day he woke wearily after his shallow, nightmare-ridden sleep. His meeting with Bashir and Buzzi went well and they shared a light pavement café lunch. Richard invited them both to be his guests for dinner and Bashir politely refused, but Buzzi the inappropriately named Moslem, accepted. They arranged to meet that evening at six; Buzzi would pick up Richard from his Hotel.

The restaurant was pure Lebanese. The food was splendid with a spectacular mezzas buffet and a huge menu that meant little to Richard. At first it was a little awkward with the cheerful Buzzi drinking soda water, but he encouraged Richard to drink his choice and soon Richard was faced with a whole bottle of extremely strong red wine of the land.

It was an altogether delightful evening. Buzzi chatted away about his own past and aspirations for the future. He also had family in the United States and had done his training there. He was a committed member of the Moslem faith, but he was in no way narrow, recognizing the virtue and values of other religions, particularly Christianity. Richard lapsed in his attempts to respond sensibly and sensitively as the red wine took its hold. Buzzi, without being patronizing, recognized the decline in conversation quality and called the night politely to a close at nine o'clock. They bade each other a fond farewell, Richard, rather haplessly extolling the virtues and delights of Beirut and her people.

Richard driven by the ever-faithful Abdul was taken to the airport for the long journey home to Kaduna. They passed the refugee camps on the way to the airport and it was hard to see what damage the Israeli air attacks had done. The refugees had put back together again whatever small estate they had. They had no choice, but to grind on to another day, nursing an ever more virulent hatred towards those who had swooped upon the defenseless and killed their women and children. Terror fed on their hate and terrorism became their 'jihad' or holy war.

At the airport Abdul was true to his word and collected exactly the sum agreed when Richard had arrived. They bade each other a comradely farewell and soon Richard was dozing in his journey back across the Sahara to Kano.

His arrival home was a jolly affair. Joan and especially the children were pleased to see him and delighted with the gifts that he had brought. He was in truth very tired. .

That night, after the children had been settled down, was something of a cat and mouse game, each probing the other in relation to their activities during their week of separation.

It transpired that Joan had indeed gone out to dinner twice during the week, once with David's junior school Parents Association and once with the Hetherington's who had company from Malcolm's Lagos office. She reported that although they were all right, they were not 'her sort' and indeed the dinner had been boring, although Joan conceded that they were 'nice' enough.

"What did you get up to in the mysterious Lebanon, I hope you behaved yourself?"

"Darling, you wouldn't believe the horrors of that bombing business. It was scary as hell and I feel so sorry for those refugees, the noise the violence of it all was unbelievable, I guess it's the start of another hundred years' war. But Lebanon, Lebanon was fantastic, trust the human race to bugger it up."

"You look tired, shall we go to bed?"

"You're right, I'm pooped, I've worked hard. Actually, I think I've got us the biggest couple of contracts ever, at least here in Nigeria. Just as well really, Edward Regan will go spare when he sees my expense account. The miserable sod wasn't around when I got permission to go so he'll be full of righteous indignation and other harassing bullshit. Anyway tomorrow's another day...I did have a lovely weekend. Chagoury took me to their home in the mountains, right up passed The Cedars... fantastic."

In bed he gave his wife a warm embrace, but feigned fatigue when she appeared to want sex. She seemed slightly put out, but relented and kissed him gently goodnight.

"Thanks for the presents," she said, "the kids really missed you."

He curled up shut his eyes tight, but Leila insisted on pushing into his dream.

He returned to the factory and summoned Eke to tell him the good news of the Hospital projects. It would still be at least nine months before the work would be scheduled but nevertheless it was great news, although

Richard cautioned that they were not home and dry until the contract was signed and orders placed.

He rang Edward Regan whose response was extremely guarded. He took a dim view of Richard rushing off out of the country without proper planning and then spent the rest of the half hour phone call cross-examining Richard. Apparently he harbored the view that Richard had waited for Regan to go on sick leave before initiating the request to travel.

"Edward, my dear fellow we've been terribly lucky that the opportunity arose as it did, I had no idea of the scale of it, and anyway it's going to mean a huge difference to our turnover and profitability over the next two years. When will we see a firm commitment in writing?"

"Three weeks to a couple of months on Sokoto, and three to four months on Maiduguri"

"Are you sure you're up to the technical detail on this one, should we not hand this over to Head Office?"

"Are you kidding?"

"Of course I'm not kidding. I think I shall have to come up to Kaduna and go through the contract and review if it ought to be handled by the UK."

'You son of a bitch, you want to muscle in and get the credit and ingratiate yourself at Head Office,' seethed Richard, he took a deep breath.

"I am quite confident that we can handle this here and if I need any technical support I shall ask for it. You needn't worry about me screwing it up."

"Well, we'll fix a meeting next week and see. How about next Thursday, can you get your report ready for me by then?"

"Yes, sure." You miserable bastard, you could at least say 'well done'. He put down the phone.

Immediately he set to work. He drafted a report for Edward and attached the entire technical blurb, isolating those critical areas of design and sent a copy by air messenger to the Technical HQ in the UK. He addressed it to the Division Technical Director and made it clear that he, Richard, would remain the man in charge of the customer contact and have overall control of the projects. He told them that Regan had been fully informed of the situation.

Regan's reaction to learning, via the UK, that Richard had already outflanked him, was predictable. There was nothing he could blame Richard for, because in the literal sense Richard had done what he had been told. However, they both knew that Richard had grabbed headlines and the initiative. Now Regan had two choices; be supportive but responsibly so, or, withdraw support and see this young whippersnapper come to grief.

The problem was he couldn't find the generosity to do the former and he couldn't take the risk of doing the latter, so he nit-picked and whinged looked for technical flaws and generally gave Richard a hard time. At the end of his visit to Kaduna, he reluctantly conceded that Richard had done a good job.

"I believe though," he concluded, "that we know each other well enough for there to be closer team work."

"Quite so." responded the smug Smiles, slipping his gargantuan expense account into the back of the report just before Regan packed it away in his brief case. Richard wondered if Regan would ever look at the report again, having flogged through it ad nauseam during his visit. Perhaps the matter of his expenses might never be brought to book.

How wrong can a man be? The next day the phone wires burned hot with Regan's threats and cross-examination.

"For God's sake Richard, who did you take to lunch or dinner on the Saturday, it cost a fortune?"

"You'll notice it was for three, some of the 'high ups' from Dar al Handassah. But think of it, Edward, you don't get contract leads like this every day, the next two year's budgets in the bag."

"They bloody ought to be!" responded the irate Regan.

"Goodbye!" Richard put the phone down and chuckled, got you, got you, you miserable shit!

# CHAPTER 38

The great Durbar was at hand. It was to be in honor of Emperor Haille Sallassie of Ethiopia, President of the OAU. He was to visit Kaduna on the following Saturday. The city was transformed as swarms of troops and workers painted the curbs, freshened the flowerbeds and draped a thousand flags of both Nigeria and Ethiopia.

Below each flag there were joint portraits of General Yakabu Gowon and The Emperor. The racecourse became off limits, roads were cordoned off and policemen suddenly looked a lot smarter. Thousands poured from all over the north, from the land of the Fulani, from Katsina, Maiduguri, Kano and all the ancient communities of northern Nigeria.

There were camels by the hundred, horses by the thousand; great supply trains, huge lorry loads of feed, tents, uniforms and all manner of finery. The north was going to show the world and its most honored guest that this was a land of ancient, noble and rich culture like no other.

To the crowd at the Club, it was all an inconvenience.

"What a bloody palaver, old boy!"

"Expect it'll be a shambles."

"Damn fuss if you ask me."

The road to the Club itself was difficult to navigate. The way to work was at least twice as long. The main road down from Kano was blocked with massive traffic congestion and all the airlines were booked.

Even the Smiles' household was put out by all the goings on. Friday was declared a half day holiday, so that they all lost a day's production, the population in general got very excited and there was much revelry, which caused a higher than normal rate of absenteeism from work. Peter sought permission for three days leave to go and get his woman and be at the great occasion. All in all it was a time of great excitement and the suspension of normal standards.

When Saturday came Richard, Joan and the two children set out on foot to the racecourse, where they'd arranged to meet their usual friends. Immediately at the end of Galadima Road there was a different world. A battalion of camels loped up the road, each camel ridden by a warrior in green and white uniform; each man carried a lance with a flag at its end. The children were both excited and frightened by these strange, huge animals that loped along issuing an unpleasant odor and some very curious sounds, they were right in amongst them on the road, as the camel mounted cavalry made their way to their assembly point.

At the next intersection there were foot soldiers in scarlet, attendants to the Emir of Kano, beyond them horsemen in rich and beautiful costumes and soldiers in dress uniform and polished Land Rovers with important looking standards flying from their bonnets. The color, the vigor, the noise and excitement were beyond anything they had seen. Great black smiling faces shone down from the horses and camels as the riders wrapped in white desert silk scarves hailed the children, so vulnerable, Emma in her pram and David in his sweating father's arms.

Eventually they made it to the enclosure, having battled their way through an extraordinary variety of participants; they presented their tickets and were ushered to the open paddock in front of the stands. It was already very hot and although the Durbar was not due to start for another hour it was wonderful being there, part of something unique and surely memorable. Emma's pram resembled a supply wagon, apart from Emma who was turned loose in the enclosure - there were umbrellas, drinks, a cool box with food and sweets for the kids, the camera and spare film, towels and even a first aid kit.

Fortunately Henry Ash's residence was very near by on Racecourse Road and he generously offered open house with all its conveniences to the assembled group.

The wonder of it all convinced the most cynical. The sheer brilliance of the colors and the nobility of the scale of the thing was mind-boggling.

The parade stretched for miles around the racecourse and as they organized into their contingents, the blocks of changing color and sparkling weaponry and tack was spectacular.

Now the leaders came, these were no ordinary men, but Princes of ancient nations and tribes, whose attire, bearing and attendants, attested to their noble and proud lineage. They were magnificent, on fine horses, in brilliant silk robes and turbans, under jeweled umbrellas held by immaculately and brilliantly uniformed attendants. Each troop was more splendid than the last. The Emirs of Katsina, that ancient seat of learning north of Kano which has welcomed travelers from across the Sahara for well over a thousand years. And the Sultan of Sokoto, spiritual Leader and ancient ruler of the Fulani people in pure white silk, with white and gold umbrellas seated on a jeweled saddle and a mighty thoroughbred. Then the camel mounted trumpeters and the foot attendants and the cohorts of mounted horsemen, each contingent in the color of his tribe. On and on, each group bursting with pride, this was their hour.

And then there was a great shout, a huge roar and almost too far away for the Smiles' to see, the diminutive Emperor with his host General Gowon, mounted the dais. From the gathered multitudes there came a cry of welcome as lances and swords were raised to the sky. It was a moment of history, and for all the strangers like the Smiles a fleeting insight into the splendor of a civilization they could never really know. It was a humbling moment, it was too much to take in, it was a moment of a lifetime and they were happy and grateful to share it.

But that was not all, after the greeting there were speeches and ceremonial gifts exchanged with the great chiefs, some anthems and military salutes, and then, perhaps the greatest moment of all, the Durbar. Ten thousand horsemen in waves of five hundred raced to the dais waving their weapons in salute, wave after wave, the dust enveloping and creating a dream like shroud. Each wave stopped abruptly in front of the Emperor, their leader's horse gene flexing and then a salute of blood curdling yodeling, and then each wave retired. Each wave tried to outdo the other by the speed of their approach and the sharpness of their stop, it was wonder upon wonder.

And still it was not over. The whole parade marched past, the principal leaders now on the dais. It added to the fascination of an extraordinary day. At the end, much was still going on, but the children were tired and fractious and so they set out once more on foot for the short journey home.

The horsemen had particularly impressed David. They were so glamorous and dashing in their splendid robes, much more exciting than any cowboy his father had seen.

The whole scene thrilled Joan. Her naturally sympathetic nature had received the scenes of the day as signs, as a confirmation of her view that these were elegant civilized and noble people. The memories of the barbarism was at once washed away, here was her fairy tale Africa, complete with handsome Emperor and spectacular horsemen.

Richard wondered as to how such a pageant had come into being with all the complexities and inter-tribal factionism. Surely some great hand had been brought to bear to transform these various tribes and peoples into such a glorious whole. If traditions could yield such results the modernists had surely fouled up. The British Colonial Office of the fifties had created an unnatural enclosure of so many opposed nations and the succeeding politicians had all failed to deliver unity from that impossible base. The Durbar was a reminder of what might have been, if only. But credit where it was due, some great organizing hand still lived, oh that it should be used again to the glory of these wonderful people.

Here was the lineage that made Usman Jalingo such a proud and fine man; here was the character that Mbamane exemplified. Here too was the fierce tribal force that Eke had fought against and lost.

The white Tribe at the club whose elders seemed anything but noble, 'the old farts' criticism was quelled at least for the present.

Joan could not resist trumpeting her delight and wonder at the recent Durbar.

"Wasn't it splendid, weren't all the representative groups fabulous? Wasn't it wonderfully organized? Weren't they the most handsome groups and horses you ever saw? Wasn't the whole thing quite splendid? Weren't we lucky to be there?"

"Quite so."

"Very enjoyable day out."

"I must say it was exceptional."

She dragged the small compliments from them, it was a bit like drawing teeth, but when Joan was determined she could stick to the task with a vengeance. Eventually Richard became bored and nudged her to let it go, but she persisted. This caused some angst between them, he accusing her of deliberately alienating those they needed and she fighting back that "they" needed to be made to feel uncomfortable. Whether it was the weather, or just "the time in the month", this led to an unholy row at home and for the first time they slept in separate rooms.

# CHAPTER 39

Richard's next day hardly improved; with a major customer playing up over supplies made to a Nigerian Defense Academy contract. There were threats and counter-threats as the Alhaji in question took the dispute as an excuse, as ever, not to pay his bills.

Eventually they arranged a site meeting at two-thirty. It was a very hot day. Richard arrived on the site and made some preliminary measurements and looked at the job so far completed. He had to admit that the job looked a mess. The barrel vault roof supplied by Universal, together with the suspension system, looked a shambles and despite Richard's persistent efforts he could see nothing wrong with the Alhaji's work, so inevitably the suspicion had to be that the responsibility lay with Universal.

At two forty five, the Alhaji had still not arrived so Richard and the assistant, Mbamane, measured the Universal components not yet installed and discovered that it was all in perfect tolerance.

At this point the large Mercedes of the Alhaji swept onto site and out of the car came Alhaji wrapped in his spectacular and expensive agdaba. His Hausa hat was at a jaunty angle, his eyes were shaded by the latest thing in sunglasses and his fingers positively bristled with gold and diamonds. His entrance was as always dramatic, his tall figure tip toeing on his Gucci shoes, his first announcement, imperiously delivered in his curiously Anglo- Franco- Hausa accent.

"I apologies, you weal parghhdon' me, but I 'ave been with Zee Govenore."

"My dear Alhaji, don't worry about it." greeted the defensive Richard, "Seems we have a spot of bother here."

"Sbote of bother, my friend, this eez a beeg bother, I can tell you that I ammmm in problem with the General, no!"

"No," interjected Richard fighting hard to follow the crazy Alhaji, "we shall fix the problem, once of course we know what the problem is."

"The proleem, eez obvious Sah, it ees your prodwcts, your prodwcts do not feet."

"Mbamane, do we have a square with us?"

"No Sah. But I can make one, now, now."

With a three, four, five right angle quickly knocked up by Mbamane, Richard, heart in mouth, climbed into the roof of the building. There he tested his hunch; and yes, there it was, the whole building was out of square.

"Alhaji, would you like to come up here and see this?"

"See, See? See what? Your prodwcts do not meesure, Sah, they do not feet."

"Alhaji, I'm sorry to tell you that it's your building that does not 'feet', it does not 'feet' at all, it is substantially out of square."

"Square, what is these? Square, what are you sayeeng? I cannot theenk so."

Richard visually surveyed the long building and what was now easily obvious was that the building was out of square in two directions, having wandered first in parallel to the right and then having been haplessly corrected to the left. It was immediately obvious that the building would have to come down. This of course would be of dire consequence to the Alhaji and his company, for not had only the shell been erected out of square the rest of the support structure had been gerrymandered to follow suit.

Richard was immediately mindful that his own company stood to loose a substantial sum if the Alhaji went to the wall and much of the product on site would be forfeit, probably forever.

There now grew a great conversation about what was to be done, the Alhaji summoned his on-site boss who was a shifty individual if ever Richard had seen one. He was tall, scruffy, lean, with bloodshot eyes; he smelt of stale palm wine and obviously had not been near a bath in years.

He rejoiced in the name of "Topman". Richard could not imagine how he aspired to such a handle other than by his height, but even that was not remarkable.

The Alhaji and Topman had an extended and frenzied conversation in what sounded a Hausa French patois that Richard could not follow at all. After five minutes or so they became more and more animated with Topman becoming extremely agitated, suddenly the conversation fell silent.

The Alhaji gathered his robes, he beamed his most charming smile, he was all teeth and sunglasses.

"'Meestere Smailes, my 'elper and myself we agree, no!"

"I see." responded Richard neutrally, not seeing at all.

"Zee Arghmee, as put us on bad ground and so zee foundatiogn 'ave sunk, cosing mush bother. The problem is as as u' consequence of zis, you see, no?"

"Well Alhaji, what to do? That's the question. How do we finish and how do I, forgive me for worrying about my own company first, get paid? You know Alhaji, cash, money, for my hand."

"We," he emphasized, "We must go to zem no? We ask for money to correct zis problem, no?"

"Alhaji are you asking me to support your claim that to unforeseen ground conditions the building has shifted and become out of square, are you serious?"

"Mais, but of course, Meesta Smails you 'ave eet exactly, I think you know ziz prghoblem, no?"

"Alhaji, no I don't know this problem, it is your problem." Richard got that sinking feeling that here was another impossible Nigerian cock up where he would be caught in the middle.

"Ah! No no no, eet is our problem. I cannot pay if zee armee does not pay, no?"

Alhaji Jaiman was originally from Niger, he'd been active in the north for many years and had been a good customer of Universal and despite his record of late payments, he always eventually delivered. This job was worth around 51,000 Naira and would certainly hurt if the money were entirely lost. Unfortunately, on the type of system that was to be employed on this project, there would be no way to cover up the Alhaji and Topman's shoddy work. However, if the building (some 120 feet long and 37 feet wide) had to come down and be rebuilt; then the costs would have to be borne by someone. Alternatively the contract could be cancelled and another contractor appointed.

Richard considered the dilemma. His optimal strategy was to get the Universal product off site and back into his possession. Assuming the Army would still complete the project then his products would be ready and available and at the same price. In short a small loss, that would be made up in time. If his materials were not recovered then he would not be paid, they'd be kept on site whilst the dispute raged, which would be forever. He would lose title and become a non-preferred creditor; it would be 'goodbye 51,000 Naira.'

"Alhaji, what if we could take the materials back and alter them to fit the building? I can't promise that it will be perfect, but perhaps it will be okay?" he lied and hated doing so. He went on to add veracity, "Of course there will be a charge associated with the remedial work and we shall have to tell the Army that we've hit a snag, you can say what you like, except that its Universal's fault, okay?"

The Alhaji went for it, he smiled his toothy smile, "How long weel it take to fix okay?"

"I don't know, maybe two weeks, perhaps we can get stuff back here sooner, but we'll need written permission to get the material off site?"

And so they agreed. Richard left the site relieved, yet troubled, this was a cock up not of his making but the consequences, both for his reputation and cash exposure, were substantial. He would take advice from a friendly civil engineer, who would survey the building in detail, if indeed it was beyond repair, and then he would have to inform the Alhaji and the Army and their supervising staff. One thing though he would stick to, that the removal of material from site was done in good faith and with everyone's best intentions at heart. If they'd believe that, they'd believe anything.

The following Tuesday morning Alhaji Jaiman's Mercedes swept into the factory. Richard had already, with the Alhaji's permission, dismantled the materials and collected everything and returned it all to the factory. The plan as far as the Alhaji was concerned was to alter the structural units to fit the "out of square" building and somehow to gerrymander a solution.

Richard had arranged for the Alhaji to pay up what he owed and accept a charge for any alteration costs.

Over the weekend Richard had organised a local civil engineer to survey the work done and to report back. The report didn't say anything that surprised Richard. It stated quite simply that the building would have to be razed and started again. There was no way that there could be any remedial solution.

Richard's situation was, now that he had secured payment he needed to extricate his company from any suggestion that they had conspired against the interests of the client, namely the Nigerian Defense Academy. Indeed, he was clear that he had not. However, what he had done was to remove materials from the site which, strictly according to the terms of contract, belonged to the client, who no doubt had paid Alhaji Jaime handsomely in advance.

The Altai was accompanied by the unpleasant Top man who Richard directed to Eke. Jaiman seated himself and with his normal flourish, smiled his usual, flashing smile and peered from behind his ever-present sunshades.

"Alors," he began, "how ees it, good no?"

"Well Alhaji, it's proving very difficult. As you know, I made no promises... it looks very tricky, ... actually."

"Tricky? What is tricky? You can fix for me, no?"

"Well, probably no. I'm afraid it looks unlikely...' then a moment of weakness, to offer the hopeless, hope. 'But we shall continue to try, but I cannot promise and as I say, it looks tricky."

There was a long silence. The Alhaji's smile had disappeared and had been replaced by a fixed grimace.

"Meesta, Meesta, you fix orgh I shall get somboudy who weel."

"Alhaji, let's not get difficult here. We're in a hole, or rather you are in a hole."

"Yes, zee ground is zee 'ole, zee bueelding s inzee 'ole, you must 'elp. Anyway, it is your fault your prodwct does not fit. It should fit, should it not, for inside the tolerawnce? You fix... or..."

"Or? Or what?"

"I shall take zee prodwcts and I shall 'ave them made to fit and I shall sue. Yes, I shall sue you for bad prodwct."

"Alhaji, before we go any further I'm obliged to inform the NDA that we've removed product from the site for requested remedial work which has since been found to be inappropriate, as the product is well within specification. Further, I shall notify him that, as under the terms of the contract, as a nominated supplier I am in dispute with you and that I would advise a site survey and an arbitration hearing with you and the client's representative." There was a further, long silence. The Alhaji's sandaled foot tapped nervously under the desk. "Shall I do that now?" Richard reached for the phone.

"What shall we do? I know you are a respected gentleman and I know maybe zis is a problem for you, but eef you say you agree wiz zee problem of zee 'ole in the ground, maybe it will be good, no?"

"No, Alhaji. You need to get your own surveyors in. It wouldn't have been so bad if Topman had not made such a half-arsed effort to correct the alignment, but now I think the solution will have to be radical - probably pull it down and start again."

There was another long silence. The Alhaji, stared at the desk and shuffled in the sleeves of his robes. "Per'aps we can see the prodwct wiz Topman and your man. Maybe there is a way?"

To humour the Alhaji, Richard escorted him down to the factory where they found Topman and Eke deep in conversation. It was obvious to Richard that Eke had been under pressure. He seemed uncertain and agitated as Richard approached.

"What oh! Eke, I hope Topman hasn't been too demanding." said Richard as an opener. "The Alhaji and I have discussed the options and I've explained that remedials won't work."

The Alhaji flapped his robes and waved his hands. "Per'aps eet can be done, no?"

"It might be possible," said Eke stroking his chin, "it just might be possible, Sir."

Richard was stunned, they'd been through this whole thing and agreed that they would under no circumstances be dragged into a botched up job. What the hell was Eke up to? Had Topman threatened him? Had Topman bribed him?

"So, alors, we can do eet." the Alhaji smiled triumphantly.

"Hang on Alhaji, I am not at all sure that this is feasible." Richard was almost beside himself with anger, but he could hardly show dissent to Eke in front of the Alhaji and his sidekick. He turned and glared at Eke, who studiously avoided his eyes. "Okay Mister Eke,' he emphasized the "Mister", 'tell us how we're going to fix the unfixable?"

Eke pushed the bridge of his glasses up his nose, coughed and pointed to one of the big curved barrel-vault sections. "We could parallel trim the vaults. They would expose a saw tooth eaves, but that could be masked by a deep gutter. The internal ducting and straps could be made to accommodate the variations. It would mean that we would have to make adjustments on site."

"'Bollocks Eke. What happens when you get to the famous 'Topman adjustment', where the building supposedly corrects its line, what then?"

"We could fabricate an expansion joint to accommodate the alignment, Sah." He looked down at the floor, he knew that he and Richard had discussed this very option and had rejected it because it was likely to look like a dog's dinner and probably leak like hell.

Something had happened between Eke and Topman that had caused this outrageous change of direction. Now it was a matter of restoring some semblance of control. He did not want to be dragged into some dreadful scandal by this odious and corrupt Alhaji.

"Well, we'll evaluate Mr Eke's suggestion Altai, but I must again warn you that we can make no promises." He watched Eke as he spoke and thought he saw a flicker of relief register briefly on his face.

The Altai once more wreathed in smiles, put his arm round Richard and almost lead him out of the factory.

"How you say, there eel a weal and a way, no?"

"No, Alhaji, that is not what we're saying here. Eke may believe this idea is a flyer, but I do not. I need to be convinced and I must tell you that I do not think I will be."

They returned to the office to pick up the Alhaji's briefcase and as Richard was about to bid the Alhaji farewell he opened his briefcase and threw a bundle of used banknotes onto the desk.

"Per'aps zis will convince you, no?"

The bundle was 'perhaps' a thousand, Richard stared at it, put his hands firmly in his pockets, stared at the Alhaji, his blood boiling.

"'You ever do anything like this again I'll have you thrown out on your arse and if I find you have got that son of a bitch Topman to get at Eke I'll personally see to it that you are reported to the police and the client. Do you understand? Now fuck off and don't ever come back in here unless I ask for you."

The Alhaji was frozen to the spot, his black face paled, he turned to go.

"Haven't you forgotten something?" Richard pointed to the bundle of banknotes. "Your filthy lucre." he added with theatrical emphasis.

The Alhaji picked up the money and shuffled away and was gone.

He called for Eke who arrived hurrying nervously up the steps and into the office. Richard stood to meet him.

"Sit!" he settled behind his desk. No one spoke, time passed. Then Richard felt surprisingly unsure, but he began, despite his confusion. "Eke, do you have anything to tell me that I should or ought to know about?"

Eke shifted uneasily, "I think they are clever men Sah."

"How so?"

"Because that man Topman, he tell me that his boss will agree with you to do the job, he implied Sah, that you had an arrangement." He looked at the floor.

"Eke, you fucking believed him. You thought I would take a bribe and sell our reputation to that son of a bitch. Oh Eke, you must think a lot of me." He buried his head in his hands, " Did that ghastly Topman give you anything?"

"No Sir, he promised he would see me right when the job was done Sir. Sir, Mister Smiles Sir, I am deeply sorry, Sir, that I listened to them. What shall I do, Sir?"

Richard sighed a huge sigh. "Lighten up you silly bugger, just remember I may not be good enough to be an Ibo man, but I still want the best for the company, okay? We do not, you do not and I do not get anywhere near dash. Is that understood? Lets put these doubts behind us, we have to trust each other, even if we can't trust any other bugger." There was a pause, they both relaxed and Eke looked his boss in the eye once more. "Put all the work for the NDA job on hold. I shall write to the Clerk of Works and the Engineers and explain what's happened from our point of view. As long as the "prodwct" is paid for and I suppose the Alhaji can do with it what he will. We want it known that we won't compromise and that we keep quiet the bribery attempt. If the army want to botch up the job then they'll have to get someone else to do it. I have no doubt that Jaiman will find someone else to dash."

"Mr. Smiles, I am happy that we are what we think we are." smiled Eke.

"Whatever the hell that means, sounds good to me." He slapped Eke lightly on the back and they got on with their day.

Two days later Universal received a letter from the Clerk of Works from the NDA. The letter stated that there would be a Summons brought against Universal for illegally removing materials from site and causing delays to the project and a claim for consequential damages. This came as something of a surprise since Richard had had a long and amicable conversation with the CO of the NDA outlining all the issues and submitting an independent report from the Engineers, supporting his arguments.

Somewhere, somebody had been getting at somebody, in that old-fashioned Nigerian way, namely, a dash had been paid. A phone call to the Colonel resulted in yet another meeting called for the following day.

Richard arrived full of righteous indignation, to be confronted by a Ministry of Defense Officer who'd sent the offensive letter. The Alhaji was there, all sunglasses and teeth, with Topman at his side. In addition there was the Clerk of Works who'd never been seen by Richard before, as well as a Clerk who was there to take notes. The Ministry of Defense man chaired the meeting. Richard felt suddenly very alone. He'd naively expected the CO to turn up, and fewer forces ranged against him. He'd been stitched up and he quickly recognized the fact.

The meeting started with Richard being accused of delaying the site progress and, incidentally, illegally removing materials from the contract site.

Richard replied with as much equanimity as he could muster that he had withdrawn the materials from the site at the request and with the approval and co-operation of the main contractor.

"Did you have the Clerk of Work's permission?"

"No I did not. I was acting for and on behalf of the main contractor; Alhaji Jaiman and I assumed that he had been given permission by the relevant authorities."

"Is this so, Alhaji?"Asked the weasely MoD man.

"Mais, surely no, no" responded Jaiman.

"I have a letter," responded Richard with a calm smile, "a copy of which is with me. You may see it if you wish."

"The fact remains," continued the obdurate civil servant, ignoring the letter altogether.

"Look at the damn letter, will you?" Richard pushed it across the table insistently at the Chairman. Still he ignored it. "For Christ's sake read the bloody letter. I was at pains to regularize the removal of the goods for the sole purpose of seeing if it was possible to amend the products to fit this shambles of a building that the Alhaji is in the process of cobbling together."

"Aha! So your products were unable to be used on the project, so you removed them."

"Yes, and no. There was and is nothing wrong with the products and equipment supplied by Universal."

"Then why were they removed?" interjected the Clerk of Works.

"I've just told you and it's clearly explained in the letter. Are you bloody deaf? The barrel vault roofs and the service ducting that are suspended from them have to be positioned square. The building is not bloody square, therefore they will not work. Simple, even to an idiot."

"I have seen no evidence of the building being out of specification." said the Clerk, rather more tentatively.

"Right Chairman, let's all go out on site and I will demonstrate with the greatest of ease the problem I have just described."

"But you removed materials from the site, did you not?" The officious Civil Servant paused whilst the scribe wrote down for the fourth time "illegally removed material from the site".

Richard knew that he was close to losing his composure and doing or saying something he should not. "Gentlemen I think we should have a five minute break."

The Nigerian contingent nodded their assent and Richard left the room to pace uneasily in the hot sun. When he returned, the Alhaji and the Civil Servant were in deep conversation. Richard sat down and prepared to open on another tack when the Chairman held up his hand and addressed them with his best Civil Service manner.

"I have heard all the evidence and I am sure that Mr. Smiles' company has transgressed in that they removed material from the site without proper consent. However, I have been able to persuade the main contractor to consent to a settlement that will require Universal Metals to correct their products and materials so that they conform to the building requirements. Universal will do this at their own expense. They will complete this work within fourteen days and will be subject to a claim for consequential damages should the site be handed over to the NDA behind schedule. The Clerk of Works will ensure that Universal complies with this order. Thank you gentlemen that will be all."

"Hang on, this isn't arbitration, this is a site progress meeting, you won't…"

"Mr. Smiles, this has been a fair hearing and as an Officer of the Ministry it is my responsibility to resolve these disputes. That is what I have just done. That will be all."

"I shall write to the GOC General Bissala. I play golf with him. I'm buggered if I'll be rail-roaded by you guys." He barely knew the General at all. He rallied on, "Furthermore, I shall make direct contact with the Military Governor Colonel Obada who is known personally to me and I shall have your balls. This is a bloody disgrace and you are not going to get away with it."

He slammed his briefcase shut, knew he'd made probably empty threats and stormed back to the car. Mohamed tutt-tutted as his boss swore and cursed all the way back to the factory.

Once there, he charged to his office and put a call into the CO at the Defense Academy.

"Who's calling? Sorry, the Colonel is not available."

Right, bugger it. He put a call into General Bissalla. Yes, the General was in, but what was it about? A contractual matter? No, sorry the General is busy.'

Right, shit or bust, get me the Military Governor.

"The Governor will speak to you."

The Governor was kindness and patience itself. "How is your lovely wife? How is business?"

"Well Your Excellency, that's a problem and I wonder if I might seek your advice?"

There followed a lengthy discussion, more a conversation. Eventually the Governor dismissed him, "I'll talk to Bissala, I'm sure he'll see you are fairly treated."

Days went by, the weekend passed. Eventually Richard was told to report to the CO of the Defense Academy, thus necessitating the cancellation of a trip to Maiduguri and cocking up a whole week's arrangements.

The Colonel was less than cordial, though not entirely without sympathy. He advised Richard to do as he was told and fix the job, it didn't matter if the building leaked, they all leaked. "Don't make waves, old man. If you lose money on the job, I will ensure you will be favorably treated for a Grandstand project at the army sports ground."

And as usual the corrupt prevailed, the Alhaji Jaiman, got his botched up roof and services which did not leak, at least for the present and two months later Richard was invited to tender for the cladding of the new Army sports ground. Here ended another lesson.

# CHAPTER 40

Back at home the axe had not been buried, Joan was still angry about his remonstrations at the Club and now she chose, for some reason he could not understand, to raise the whole matter again.

"You're a damned hypocrite, you say you are a genuine worker here, but you support those indescribable white supremacists at the Club. What's more, you're a coward. You stand up for what you say you believe in. All your interested in is being a smart arse at work. You make me sick at times, do you know that?"

"Joan, I've had enough of your noble savage theory for the day, thank you. I do my best here and if you think it's not good enough, just bugger off and leave me to it."

"So you'd send me and the children out would you, you bastard?"

"No, of course I wouldn't, but I think you're taking this thing too far. Today I've been trying to extricate us from the follies of a crooked useless local, actually he's not a local, he's from Niger, anyway it's all a bloody mess and I'm sorry if you think I'm an arse-hole, because I really do care what you think and I love you."

He moved forward to cuddle her but she backed away, her arms folded tightly about her, she was cross, maybe about something else?

They spent the rest of the evening in morose silence. Eventually Joan announced that they had a dinner party to attend on the weekend at the home of the Gombe's. Richard recalled Gombe and his Singaporean wife,

251

she was attractive but incredibly reserved he remembered, not much to look forward to there.

"Anyone else going?"

"Sally and Malcolm, I don't know who else." she replied diffidently.

That night there was no consolation in their intimacy, there was none.

Saturday eased somewhat. They took the children on a run into the bush, some 25 miles from the city. They'd been told that there was a colony of monkeys in this place so they thought it would be fun for the kids. They packed a cold box and set off as early as they could muster. They drove off the Zaria road and drove as far as they could down a rough track. The bush on either side was thick and they could see very little from side to side. They continued, despite doubts expressed by Joan, but encouragement from David, until they could go no further. They saw what they thought was the rocks where the colony was in residence and settled down in the car to wait and see.

Minutes passed and almost immediately the temperature in the car began to rise. They thought they saw a movement 200 yards away and then another, still the temperature rose.

Eventually they could stand it no longer and Joan wound down the window. They came in clouds, biting flies by the thousand. The shrieks of horror from within the car would have scared off monkeys or any other wild beasts. Richard started the engine, rammed the car into reverse and accelerated away. The air-conditioning took time to generate any cold, but in the meantime both children were severely bitten. The car howled, reversing up the narrow track, until eventually he could turn the vehicle and they sped out to the open road. Now the air was cold so they opened the windows and miraculously the flies exited to the warmer air.

They stopped at Zaria club, where the staff was most helpful in bathing their bites. They were assured that the inflammation would not last long and that the bites should not be infected. Both children, particularly Emma, were badly bitten, but once her initial shock had subsided she seemed calm and not in too great a discomfort. David seemed prepared to laugh the whole episode off, whilst Joan made it clear that she thought that they had been recklessly exposed to danger. The adults had not escaped bites either and Joan had a particularly nasty one on her cheek just below the eye. She rushed off to the bathroom to examine the damage to her pulchritude.

They were home before lunch and made the best of it, with a picnic in the garden and the children's pool inflated and filled. Apart from the odd scratching, which had to be restrained, the children seemed unscathed by the morning's mishap.

"So much for Nigerian wild life"

"Pretty spectacularly wild flies." retorted Richard.

"Silly sod." but she laughed, "Look at my face I look a wreck."

"Darling you could never look a wreck to me. You look fine, beautiful indeed."

"Do you notice any more?" she asked, winsomely.

"Of course I notice, you chump. You're still my gorgeous, in fact more gorgeous now than you've ever been." He meant it too, she was. Since the birth of Emma and her return to Nigeria she'd slimmed in all the right places. No wonder other men fawned on her.

After much debate it was decided that the children could be left with a babysitter, Sally's steward's wife, since Peter had a weekend leave. She was instructed that if there was any sign of fever or real discomfort she was to ring the Gombe's place.

"Yes, missy everything fine." the children knew her well and seemed comfortable.

Gombe's house was a large multi storey house, not far from the racecourse. It was a mighty house, one of the biggest outside government circles. The Hetherington's, who had also dropped off the babysitter, gave them a lift.

At the Gombe's Richard was taken aback at the formality of the evening. John Gombe wore a flattering white linen jacket and lovely Hermes tie. Anna looked wonderful in a pink, silk, long dress that hugged her slim figure. The other guests in the background also seemed to be wearing jackets, which left Richard and Malcolm somewhat embarrassed in shirt and tie only. However, Gombe was charm itself.

"Don't worry old boy we shall be removing our jackets, it's pretty hot tonight. Jolly sensible to avoid all this get-up." he lied with practiced ease.

Malcolm and Richard eyed each other and after ushering their ladies in, properly dressed, of course, they headed for the general assembly and the source of drinks. It soon became apparent that the cause for the formality was the presence of the State Governor and his remarkably handsome wife. The Governor was jacketed like most others but seemed relaxed and not in any way pompous. In fact, he approached Malcolm and Richard as he came to refill his glass. He was a Colonel and had been Governor of the North Central State for two years. He was a Hausa, handsome tall and assured. He had an astoundingly big head; close shaven and graying at the temples and an open countenance that would make you instinctively trust him. He was not slim nor was he overweight, he was fit and clear in the eye. He was everything one would expect from a senior serving officer.

"Good evening gentlemen, I don't believe I've had the pleasure, at least in the flesh, we spoke last week Mr. Smiles I hope things were resolved comfortably, I'm John Obada, the Governor here."

They responded with small talk about business and the Governor listened with apparent interest. He asked about their companies' fortunes in Nigeria and what damage had been done to either of them during the recent war. Having introduced the subject, he then went on at length about the validity of Gowon's vision of an undivided federal Nigeria. They listened patiently and were careful to respond sensibly and sympathetically, after all this was the man who ordered executions, public ones, at that.

They sat at a long and rather splendid dining table. Richard could think of absolutely no reason why he should be there. Malcolm perhaps, but he was just a small guy doing a fairly small job. He had no favors to offer, he'd met Gombe a couple of times and here he was with no jacket.

It was the Governor, who smiling at Malcolm, suggested to the host that perhaps it might be permitted that the gentlemen be allowed to remove their jackets. The assembled company duly obliged.

Richard found himself sitting next to Sally on one side and a young Nigerian lady on the other. She, it transpired, was the wife of the Governor's ADC, a tall and handsome man seated next to Joan, on her other side was Malcolm. Apart from the Governor, his wife the Gombe's, there was the visiting Director from the Bank from the UK and none other than Sir Justice Bello and his merry and jolly wife, Lady Bello, otherwise known as Puffy.

Puffy turned out to be the life and soul of the party. She found Richard engaging, as much for his youth as anything and worked and worked throughout the night to ensure that he and Joan were included in the conversation. Richard studiously avoided any reference to the recent Court case heard in the Judge's Court and enjoyed Puffy's tales of marrying Amhado when he became one of the first black barristers in London in the early fifties. She shrieked with laughter when she told tales of their obviously tough times in London, the snubs and hardships, but she was at pains to talk of the kindnesses too.

The Judge, at least it seemed to Richard, appeared wary of the Governor, but put up with his wife's banter with good humor. The Governor's wife had also spent time in England studying for a medical degree in Leeds, so in the end everyone around the table had a strong connection to the UK. Perhaps that was why the Smiles' were here. The conversation was easy as each told tales, the Governor of Sandhurst, the Judge of Lincoln's Inn and the others too, the Gombe's of University. The wine was surprisingly good as it was usually extremely hard to come by in any sort of condition at all. Sir, "whatever his name was" from the Bank made a great fuss over all the women, particularly Sally and Joan. They judged him to be a boring dirty old man, which he probably was. The dinner was most splendidly done in every respect, fine food, wonderful tableware, glittering chandelier over the table and wonderfully unobtrusive service.

At ten thirty the Governor and his wife departed, followed in quick succession by the Bello's and Sir 'whateverhisnamewas'. As the Smiles' and Hetherington's' tried to follow suit Gombe was insistent that they stay for a nightcap. Anna offered to show the girls round the house, whilst Malcolm and Richard followed John to his den. There he produced two huge, but magnificent, cognacs and showed the men some of his treasures.

Richard was most interested in his temperature-controlled cellar which was liberally stocked with some very decent wine.

They ambled out into the garden and there was the most delightful swimming pool, illuminated most attractively amongst the trees. It must have been the biggest pool in private hands in the north.

"Fancy a swim chaps?" offered Gombe.

"No gear, old boy." replied Malcolm.

"Dozens of costumes for boys and girls in the cabanas. Showers, towels, the whole nine yards."

"Why not." said Richard, beginning to float on the cognac.

"Okay." followed Malcolm and in a moment all three men were in the pool. It was wonderful, so refreshing and cool.

Gombe was extremely well put together, his black torso rippled with lithe muscling. Obviously he was extremely fit. They splashed around, Gombe sweeping from one end of the pool to the other, Malcolm and Richard performing more modestly and giggling a lot.

The patio doors opened and Anna and the girls appeared. They stood back surprised to see their men fooling around in the pool. John Gombe leapt from the pool and in so doing showed off his physique to the assembled company. Malcolm and Richard took no notice.

"Come on in girls, it's fab," shouted Malcolm.

"Yes love, it's great, come on in, John has all the gear, changing rooms, everything."

Anna said nothing; she simply held out her porcelain doll hand and intimated her desire to go along with whatever the majority wanted.

Gombe sent his steward to bring the bar trolley and with a rather affected bow, offered the ladies a liqueur, which they both accepted. He also generously filled the men's' cognac glasses.

After much tittering and giggling the ladies were led to the cabana where they disappeared to change, there arose much hysteria from within the cabana as the girls went through the choice of swimming costumes. Eventually they emerged, Sally in a yellow two-piece and Joan in a lovely blue one-piece, Anna followed demurely and looked striking in a floral bikini.

Richard, having downed his second large cognac since dinner, leered at the women, nudging Malcolm who, in a similar state, uncharacteristically called out.

"Cor! John what a harem." he laughed and fell back into the pool.

Richard stayed, his elbows on the poolside, he watched Gombe operate. He smile, he charmed, he guided and stroked. He postured and he fawned over them, but he seemed to Richard like a man with a mission and that mission could be Joan.

Anna stepped ladylike into the pool and swam with a powerful grace, completing four lengths of the pool at pace.

Sally and Joan got in like two women who had been drinking most of the night. They hooted and they laughed and most of all they doted on the powerful and handsome Gombe.

Richard, his defenses alerted, swam away, suddenly sober. He watched and he furiously tried to recall what he knew of John Gombe. When they met at the Club he'd protested that the wives were allowed and enjoyed dancing with those young Officers. Did he think that they were loose because of this? After all he'd been so damn prissy on that night. As Richard watched, he saw a bizarre competition between Sally and Joan for the attention of this mysterious man, it made him mad. He looked around to find Anna, who still mechanically swam to and fro.

Malcolm was on the fringe of the trio, being ignored by all three especially, Sally.

Richard swam over to them. "Time to go I'm afraid. Come on love, the children weren't all that well; we ought to be getting home."

"It's not even twelve." protested Sally.

"Too bloody early." mumbled Malcolm.

"My dear boy, have another drink." offered John.

"Perhaps you should go if the children aren't too well." offered Anna.

'Come on,' said Richard, lifting himself out of the pool, 'thank you both for a wonderful evening, we've really enjoyed it.'

John Gombe surrendered, lifting Sally unnecessarily up the steps by her waist. They trooped grudgingly to the splendidly equipped cabana with its individual showers, showered and changed and assembled for a quick farewell. Gombe was insistent that they return the following Sunday, bring the children and make a day of it. All, except Richard, agreed with alacrity.

Anna asked Joan if she would join her out shopping one morning. Joan was delighted to accept. They drove home, three of them animated about the splendor of the hospitality.

At Galadima Road, Sally kissed Richard goodnight, whispering conspiratorially.

"Rules for hens as well as cocks."

The children had slept with minimum problems, so Richard and Joan retired and made hectic love (had sex would be more apt) and slept.

On the next afternoon, in the garden while the children played, they talked of the Gombe's amazing apparent wealth, surely the Bank, even if he was destined to be their man in Nigeria, could not be that generous.

Joan described the house as sumptuously decorated and equipped - there was even a gymnasium in the basement. The house had six bedrooms and four upstairs bathrooms, two en-suite. The bedrooms were odd, she didn't say how.

Richard pressed her, "Odd, how?"

"Oh I don't know…odd, that's all, dark; it was as if Anna didn't want to show us the guest rooms that's all."

"Funny bugger if you ask me. Anna's so charming and delicate and he's such a ladies man and so macho. An odd pair wouldn't you say?"

"Oh I found him very charming too."

"Really, I wouldn't have noticed. I couldn't decide who he was trying to seduce, you or Sally." As soon as he had said it he regretted it. He was right to do so.

"I am fed up with your petty jealousy. I thought you were in a strange mood last night, for goodness sake grow up." She leapt from the chair and walked smartly into the house.

Richard followed, but to no avail, she was cross and that was another afternoon spoiled.

Later in the week Joan and Anna spent the morning together, having coffee, doing the shopping and whatever. Joan was strangely troubled when she came home and during the evening revealed some of her conversation to Richard. Anna was apparently from a noble, even princely family in Malaysia. She had been in University in the UK and had met John there. They had fallen madly in love and she had taken him as her betrothed. Her family, however, cast her out since they would have nothing to do with having black blood in the family line. She had no option, other than to marry John and come to Nigeria. She claimed that "John in the UK" and "John in Nigeria" were very different. Although John too was descended from a distinguished family, it was a traditional chiefdom, which although carrying substantial wealth, also clung to traditional views. When they visited the traditional home for example, Anna was allowed to do very little, not to speak unless spoken to and always to defer to John's mother who was still a youngish woman.

At home in Kaduna they would have to move out of the marital bedroom and make way for the chief (John's father) and his wife. Even worse, when Anna had her period she was forced to sleep outside the house in Gombe and to sleep in another room in Kaduna. John apparently, she had implied, was not above knocking her about and behaving in other unspecified unsavory manners.

"I don't know why she told me all this. She swore me to secrecy, so please don't tell a soul."

"Darling, it's safe with me. Why do you think she told you?"

"I don't know, just girl to girl, I suppose."

"A warning, perhaps?"

"Oh come on love, we're not starting all that again are we?"

"Well my sweet, I may be a jealous idiot, but I do love you and I may not be on this occasion wrong. Give me the benefit of the doubt, okay?"

"Oh, you're a silly man." she pecked him on the head and went on to something else.

Despite these forebodings, they assembled at the Gombe's residence, complete with children, swimming costumes and other paraphernalia. At the Gombe's they were greeted by their closest friends, Sally already stretched decorously on a sun bed. Malcolm predictably was sitting in the shade consuming Pimms. Also there were the Coopers, people they knew only by sight. William "Billy" Cooper was son of the founder of the great textile business that bears the name. He was an accountant by profession, but not typical of that breed. He had a reputation as a gambler and womanizer and was also one of the top ten polo players in West Africa. He was lean and tanned, some six foot three with black hair swept slickly back. He spoke with a pronounced Harrovian twang and smoked "passing cloud" cigarettes continuously. Richard took an instant dislike to him.

Mrs. Cooper though was a different kettle of fish altogether. She too was tall and willowy, but a very attractive woman. It was hard to see where the appeal lay. Her figure was too lean for Richard's taste and her hair was neither lustrous nor striking in color. Her eyes were hazel and her mouth was too big, but for all this she was still very attractive, she had sex appeal. She also had a great and instantly struck humor. She looked Richard straight in the eye, and chanced a risky greeting.

'Welcome to the lotus eaters." She said holding his hand, her mouth smiling. Her eyes focused on his. It almost made him go weak at the knees.

The children, far from being a burden, proved to be a joy, particularly to Anna who played with them ceaselessly all afternoon. Again the level of hospitality was excellent and Richard may well have scorched asleep in the sun after lunch, had he not been woken by the delicious stroking of his cooking chest by the practiced hands of Mrs. Cooper.

He woke and smiled in his torpor, 'Ooh, that's nice, very nice.' He instinctively held her hand to his chest. Then as if waking with a start he looked round for Joan, who was oblivious to anything other than the charms of John and Billy who, with Sally, were prone on a group of sun beds a few yards away.

"I'm saving you from burning my sweet Smiles." crooned Mrs. Cooper as she sensuously continued to massage sun cream into his chest and onto his stomach. She stared straight into his eyes and smiled, her tongue seductively moistening her lips as her hand slipped close to the top of his swimming trunks.

Richard said nothing, but if only to avoid the embarrassment of the rising lump in his tight swimming costume, he bolted upright.

"Oh you are a bad sport." purred Mrs. Cooper transferring her ministrations with the sun cream to his legs. "My, aren't you fair skinned and such lovely blonde hair, um, um,"'

The children were having a wonderful time with Anna, assisted by Malcolm. Their screams of delight in sharp contrast to the subdued grownup games beginning to take shape around the pool. The spell was broken; Mrs. Cooper was already swinging her way back to the grownups. Richard leapt into the pool and swam to the children and joined in the swimming lesson. Emma was very tentative and ladylike. David, characteristically, didn't seem to mind how many times he slid under the water, each time he came up laughing. Anna was totally absorbed by the kids, she adored being with them, she read their every mood and was there, protecting Emma at every instant.

Richard, his sense returning, kept a wary eye on the group at poolside. Mrs. Cooper had joined them and had downed the top of her costume and was seeking a volunteer to cream her back. Strangely it was Sally who offered, whilst the other three carried on with their cocktails and chatter.

The steward announced tea and a cart were wheeled out, with yet another mountain of food, including a huge amount of goodies for the children. As the food arrived, John, Sally, Billy (who had drunk amazing amounts of pink gins during the afternoon) and Mrs. Cooper all jumped into the pool, professing no desire to eat. Joan, despite their protestations joined the children at the tea party. She surrendered Emma to Anna and attempted to control David's assault on the tea trolley, not wholly successfully.

Malcolm and Richard retired to the lengthening shadows for a cup of tea.

"This chap seems to have it made." said Malcolm, stirring his tea deliberately, his accounting brain deep in calculation.

"Very rich family, apparently augmented by the Bank's generosity."

"Well, if anyone can live in comfort in this place it's got to be this guy." opined Malcolm. "Can't say I like him much though, don't quite know what to make of him."

"Dear boy, there are a great many differences between us and him in the sense that he's from an absolutely alien culture. I mean, that despite the veneer of the UK University and the fine pseudo diction, here is a tribal chief in waiting. What do we know about that? ....Bugger all, old boy bugger all."

"Perhaps so, maybe you're right Richard, but there's still something I don't like about him."

Despite the offer of 'sundowners', the Smiles and their weary brood packed up for home. David gave a creditable little "thank you" speech. Billy and Mrs. Cooper eagerly filled their glasses once more. They left making wild promises of reciprocating the hospitality. They laughed at the prospect on the way home, but Joan insisted that at least Anna deserved the chance to come to an ordinary home with a blow up-swimming pool. They laughed some more.

# CHAPTER 41

The end of a tough week for Richard led to the monthly scouring of the meat market, a responsibility that Richard had grown to loathe. However, if he wanted meat other than the frozen chicken from the supermarket, then this was an inescapable chore.

Joan had long since declined to do the meat shopping, even accompanied by Peter. She could not abide the swarms of flies and other sights which offended her genteel sensibilities. Richard often brought back chilled Sokoto beef or Maiduguri beef from his trips north. He could never understand how the beef from those parts was more beeflike than any other. After all, those northern extremes on the edge of the Sahara were semi-desert and it was hard to imagine what they fed the cattle on. Nevertheless he always tracked down these reputedly finer cuts and Joan dutifully marinated them in precious red wine, but they were nevertheless tough and tasteless, though less tough and tastier than the local stuff.

When all else failed Richard was dispatched to the Kaduna meat market. It were not for his compulsive appetite he would have refused, however, his stomach was always a driving force and each month he set off in the optimistic hope of finding some delicious surprise. This Saturday morning was no exception, although he was later than usual setting out.

The meat market itself was set aside from the general food and textile market, which covered at least ten acres. Here, in the general market, it was said you could buy anything, even human beings if you so desired. Here market women ruled in an incredibly competitive and sharp marketplace.

Here, where there were a hundred millionaires and a thousand beggars and many thousands trading in anything from matches to Mercedes motor cars. Here, there was color and noise, red tomatoes, scarlet pomegranates, green watermelon and golden paw- paw. The market traders in their multi-colored dresses and headgear, carrying extraordinary loads balanced finely on their heads. Here were sweets and spices, cloths of gold, live goats, pigs, chickens and all manner of small animals tethered or caged. Here were drinks, potions and medicines. Here were spells, scribes and soothsayers, here was mystery and illusion. Here was money and lots of it. Here was a power base that few politicians outside the country ever understood. In this market there were skills of mathematics and logistics of a blindingly high degree. There were traders who could neither read nor write, but who managed fortunes to a thousand different customers and who never mistook a creditor, or forgot a penny debt.

Richard liked to venture here, never completely confident, but fascinated by the lure of this most African of places. He walked and walked, but only so far, for the little alleys between the stalls ran on and on. The further you walked the greater the sense of strangeness became. Here tribal witch doctors plied their trade, animal sacrifices were consummated, children were bought and sold and evil and good traded side by side. Down these alleys a stranger could disappear. Down these alleys there was magic - magic that would be dangerous to discover.

This vast market was without borders, but there were precise territorial precincts, where northerners and southerners carried out their businesses. There were areas where they came together, for nothing could stop the rights of commerce. But down those alleys a Welshman, a Yoruba, a Hausa or a Fulani could be just as much a stranger; friend or foe.

Having taken in the sights and sounds that so fascinated him, it was time to retreat and do battle in the meat market. This was set some three or four hundred yards away and fronted the municipal slaughterhouse which was itself divided very deliberately into the Moslem and "other" sheds. Along the front of the slaughterhouse were two rows of single storey buildings, each divided into ten stalls or shops, leased to licensed meat traders.

Each trader received the meat direct from the slaughterhouse and butchered the slaughtered beasts in his own shop. Each shop had a large gauze covered window through which the customers directed the butcher to cut the appropriate joint of meat. The meat on sale was beef, goat, sheep and occasionally camel. (At Christmas time these excellent traders were known to sell vultures which when shorn and beheaded, resembled lean turkeys.)

The problem that was always present was how to tell what meat you were getting. Joan was convinced that earlier that year they'd eaten some very old horse. Her unsureness was borne not only because of the anonymous heaps of dead animals, but also because of the blanket of flies that covered everything and everyone. The flies were very non-discriminatory and settled equally easily on the customers, the butchers, or of course the piles of meat.

Over the last year or so Richard had forged something of an arrangement with the butcher in shop B6. Richard never got to know his name, but by the universally clever system of dash or bribe or tip, B6 had once produced a piece of beef which tasted like beef. On each visit Richard would stand close to B6 until the butcher with no teeth grinned his gummy grin and Richard sidled to the window, slipping his five Naira note with slight of hand under the serving slide. B6 would then recommend, 'dee beef, dee sheep, or dee goat.'

Richard would always respond, 'De best, best beef.' which meant filet or other best cuts and sometimes, 'Dee sheep.' pointing to his own rib or leg, or very occasionally 'Dee goat.' where he always pointed at his own leg. The consequence of all these codes between the toothless occupant of B6 and Richard was that "Toothless" would retreat to the fly buried piles of meat and flail away with a sort of machete. He would weigh and wrap the meat joints into newspaper and present his finished work through a mist of flies. Richard would pay and make a quick dash to the car and race home where Joan would wash the surface of the meat and then put in into the freezer.

Although they avoided the goat, it was often the tastiest and tenderest, although none was as tender as that given to them by Usman Jalingo at the great festivals of the Moslem calendar. It took them a while to learn this as Usman's offerings were often delivered still quivering after the ritual sacrifice. The joint had to be hung in a cool place for at least a day before freezing.

With the proceeds of last week's market sortie, Joan announced that she felt they should invite the Gombes', Solomon's' and Coopers' for dinner.

"What no Hetherington's'?"

"No, Sally and Malcolm are away in Lagos."

"Shit, can we come up to snuff with the Gombes and that other prick, Cooper. I thought he was a complete dick and why do we have to have that smoothie from down the road? I can't bear him."

"That's your problem, you can't bear anybody, you're such a self righteous little prick."

"Steady, my sweet, your sweetness is slipping.'"

"Well we owe a return to the Gombes and it would be nice and courteous to invite one of their friends and like him or not, Hosi Solomon was very kind at his house warming."

"Spent all night trying to rummage in your drawers, as I remember," snarled Richard, knowing that this was a red rag to a bull.

"I'm not going to listen to your childish, jealous nonsense. Richard, please be good and let me choose who I like, just for once.'"

"Okay." he relented. He rather fancied playing footsie with Mrs. Cooper.

The invitations were dispatched, emphasizing the informality of the 'supper' evening. In the intervening period, however, Joan scoured the highways and byways for the appropriate (as she saw it) cutlery, crockery, glassware and table decorations. The menu was prepared with a meticulous care, not seen since the visit of Sir Ted and Lady Rawlings. Flowers were ordered, furniture was polished and even Peter was hard pressed to meet the exacting standards that Joan insisted on.

Two days before the dinner itself, the wardrobes were emptied as Joan fretted which dress to wear. She even selected Richard's pants and shirt and checked that they were spotless and bore none of the usual beer or food stains, of which he took no notice at all.

The children's program was planned so that they had early supper and Peter had time for one last clean around. Nothing was to be left to chance. Joan drove herself to a neurotic peak that exhausted her almost to the limit. Richard; not all that enchanted with the prospect of these moneyed and unsavory guests; did little to help. At least he had the sense to stay out of the way.

On the Friday, Richard arrived home in plenty of time and complimented Joan and Peter on the state of the house. It looked absolutely lovely, sparkling and swathed with fresh blooms whose fragrance was delicious. The children were brought in for tea and Joan retired to get showered and dressed. Richard stayed to serve the brats and help see no dirt or damage was done to the household. All seemed to be in order, so he made his way to the bedroom to ready himself for the festivities.

As he entered the bedroom, Joan was naked and kneeling on the bed, her back to the door. Her chin rested on the high windowsill above their bed. He stopped, whatever she was doing it was absorbing and then with a shock he saw she was masturbating, intently looking at something outside. In a strange conspiratorial tension he closed behind her and saw that the object of her desire was a naked black young laborer, who was showering on the building site next door. The young man was heavily muscled and as the sun set he was blissfully unaware that he was being watched. His penis was large, huge even and as he soaped himself it was visibly getting larger.

Without a word, Richard slid his hand under the delicious buttocks of his wife and felt the moistness of her excitement. She flinched but did not do anything to disguise her situation and as he kissed her neck she reached back for him. He was already hard and dropped his trousers and slid easily into her from behind. He whispered lasciviously into her ear about the young man's genitals and licked her neck as he thrust. Then he held her hips and she thrust her buttocks toward him and they came in an explosion of sexual passion that they had seldom, if ever, reached before.

As suddenly as the adventure had started, so it finished. Joan backed off the bed.

'God I need another bath.' and dashed to do just that. Richard sat on the edge of the bed and received the children who charged down the corridor, complaining about their early bedtime.

The Solomon's were the first to arrive, Mrs. Solomon looking quite lovely and not at all as Richard remembered her. She still looked older than her husband, but she had a handsome face, a lean and attractive frame and she was beautifully dressed. Encouraged by this refreshing start, Richard effusively offered everything from their precious Champagne (for which they'd paid a fortune) to Coca-Cola, but all she would accept was water. Her conversation skills were like her drinking habits, extremely limited.

Hosi, as always, was charm itself. His flowery attention to Joan annoyed Richard from the outset, not least because Hosi displayed complete disregard for his wife, who surely deserved better. However, he had little time to ruminate on Hosi's slimy behavior as the Gombes and Coopers arrived in quick succession.

John Gombe's idea of informal was to leave off a tie, but still sport a fantastically expensive silk jacket. Anna looked dazzling, but at the same time vulnerable. Janice Cooper wore a snakeskin-like dress that matched her sinuous and sexy self. She obviously liked flaunting her predatory nature. Billy looked as if he was already drugged or drunk; it was hard to decide which. He could have walked into an air raid shelter, and been equally unimpressed by the decorations and attendant spit and polish.

Anna was particularly complimentary and begged to be allowed to go and see the children. They conceded with an apprehension that David in particular, would see her visit as an invite to the party.

Dinner itself was excellent. Joan had invented a mousse made from tinned salmon and fresh herbs which were washed down by a reasonable Chablis, followed by a Beef Bourguignon. The burgundy, in truth, had not travelled well but it sufficed as an accompaniment to the excellent food which was followed by a selection of cheeses (specially flown up from Lagos) and the last two bottles of burgundy, which somehow tasted much better than the first two.

Despite Richard's lack of libido, having been drained by his earlier adventure with Joan, Janice Cooper who sat next to him, behaved outrageously. She had to be discouraged from groping him under the table. On more than one occasion Richard leapt to his feet and busied himself, purportedly helping a surprised Peter. He idly speculated as he passed the other end of the table whether Joan was fighting off gropers from each side or were they allowed to dally and perhaps meet unexpected company at their objective. Certainly, with John Gombe on one side and Hosi Solomon on the other, put any woman's virtue at risk, though Joan seemed flushed with the attention.

Billy sat between Hosi and Anna and did his best to empty the house of alcohol. Mrs. Solomon sat quietly alongside Janice and John, hoping beyond hope that no one would notice that she was there. She was lucky; John Gombe on one side was pouring all his efforts into competing for Joan's charms, whilst Janice on the other was determinedly trying to get into Richard's pants. Opposite her, Billy was beyond speech, whilst Anna did her best to keep her on the fringe of the conversation, despite her reluctance to say a word.

As the alcohol took hold, so Richard became more amenable to Janice's advances and Anna became agitated as she got the drift of what was going on. The cheese course was punctuated by Billy collapsing head-first onto his plate, he reacted with a silly smirk and as he a rose he looked even sillier with a large piece of Camembert appended to his forehead.

They eventually left the table for liqueurs to be served on the patio. Joan put some music on the hi-fi and before a moment had passed, Gombe was dancing with Joan - smooching would have been a better word. Defensively Richard grabbed Anna, Hosi, dashed for Janice, which left the comatose Billy and silent Mrs. Solomon alone in the shadows.

Anna perfumed and cool felt like a paper doll in his arms, weightless and somehow empty and sad. Despite her beauty and her husband's power and wealth, she seemed uncomfortable at the feast. Here after all, was what Richard and Joan had always sought - wealth, fine food and wine, servants and no worries about what tomorrow would bring. Richard, the host to wealthy and influential people; basking in the decedent conditions of comparative wealth, youth and power, glamour even. A young wife who was without doubt a beauty desired by many, friends, perhaps acquaintances, who were beyond convention. Then there was Anna, a misfit, a discord, a call back to boring normality, a conscience they all wanted to avoid. Despite her own glamour, her coolness and distance was a dampener, a constant reminder of their responsibilities, one to another.

She allowed Richard to pull her close, she rested her head in the pit of his shoulder, her perfume was light and subtle, her hair lustrous and silky, her body sylphlike and gently feminine. She danced less stiffly than he remembered; indeed she followed every beat and step he made. She was the perfect dancing partner. As they drifted without a word, Richard now pleasantly relaxed, gazed over Anna's shoulder and saw Janice Cooper locked in a steamy embrace with Hosi Solomon, who despite his silent wife's sad gaze responded with enthusiasm, engaging her in grinding embraces and sensuous handling of her buttocks, thighs and breasts. He sniggered and cast his eyes to the darker shadows where John Gombe held Joan in an equally intimate, albeit more subtle embrace. The sight of his wife in a tangle with this obviously licentious black man didn't disturb him as it should have done. He watched and enjoined himself to their lechery.

"Richard," whispered Anna, "you have lovely children,"

"Yes, of course, "' he responded loosening their smooching embrace and looking into her eyes.

"Do you know how lucky you are?" she smiled, her smile almost apologetic, whimsical.

"Yes, of course we do." he responded and added as an afterthought, "We love the kids very much."

"I know you do, but can I…" she faded.

"Can you what, Anna? Whatever it is, of course you can."

"Can I say that you and Joan are a lovely couple and that you are not only lucky with your children you are lucky with each other." She took refuge in the small of his shoulder.

"Oh, I know that Anna, it's very sweet of you to say so."

She held him suddenly very tightly and whispered almost imperceptibly, "Don't loose it all, Richard. Don't keep us as friends, we… John is too… don't be too close. John will not help you to be in love with Joan." She stopped as tears welled from her eyes and he felt the dampness on his chest.

Richard was at first embarrassed, but held her close and then looked again in the shadows and saw Joan and John in a deep and unmistakably sexual kiss, their mouths were joined their tongues explored one another, his hands pulled her buttocks and hips to his. Richard closed his eyes, the ghosts of Sally and Leila danced sensuously together in his addled mind as Anna wept bitterly into his chest.

Billy fell off his chair, which brought the silent Mrs. Solomon to her knees and Janice to disengage from the attentions of Hosi. They all rushed to the scene of the drama, except Joan and John Gombe who languorously parted, gently and unashamedly pecking each other on their mouths in front of the assembled company. The party came to an abrupt halt, Anna seemed composed, Janice gathered up her drunken husband, Hosi took to the side of his devoted, but still silent wife. Richard and Joan bade their guests a civilized goodnight.

It was late and the whole day had taken its toll. They both thanked their equally exhausted steward and retired.

# CHAPTER 42

The news came on the following Tuesday. It came as a formal invitation for Richard to visit the Hospital site in Sokoto to have discussions on formalising the contract which Richard had been waiting for with bated breath for the last three months. All had been cleared with the State Government and the Contractors who were now anxious to finalise the arrangements for supply and final costing.

The Contractors, Gittings International, was a British household name with large interests in all the Commonwealth countries. Although the journey was long and tedious, Richard enjoyed the prospect of sealing the biggest contract Universal had ever received in Nigeria. He was cock a hoop with his own success and couldn't resist dreaming of the consequences for his reputation in the 'Universal' group. In London they would notice this leap among the African statistics, the bosses would speculate who was the initiator and the name of Richard Smiles would be mentioned in high places. He dreamed of things to come; promotion, bonuses, all manner of good things. Would a posting to a larger company come soon?

The car sped past the scene of the decimation of the goatherd, Mohamed taking more care than his boss. They arrived in Sokoto and went straight to the site where Richard was delighted to meet Bashir, who introduced him to John Larkin, the regional boss of Gittings International.

Larkin was about fifty. He was short and round, with strong features, huge arms and hands. When he shook hands, the strength of his grip was almost frightening. His plentiful hair was grey and he spoke with as cockney an accent as Richard had ever heard. He was, however, quite reserved and greeted Richard with a studied stare, as if he was calculating how to handle this young whippersnapper who'd changed the whole profile of the job. He looked hard and wore his experience in the calluses on his hands and the wrinkles in his forehead.

Richard for the first time understood that though he'd won his way this far, there would be nothing but excellence required by this tough professional. Charm was not going to win the day, he would listen and try to learn and Larkin could make this contract his testimonial or his professional funeral.

That professionalism set the tone for the rest of the day. There were few laughs, even smiles. It was detail, detail, detail. Bashir had departed and left Richard and Larkin together. Larkin brought in a number of his team, including Logistics and Purchasing, Quantity Surveyors, Detail Draftsmen and Section Supervisors. He examined Richard for hour after hour and when Richard was unsure, he piled on the pressure some more. Eventually at seven o'clock they stopped.

"Well, me 'ole duck, you've done okay. I must confess tha' I was not 'appy wif dis local supplier lark, you know wha' I mean? Bu' you seem to know your stuff okay, you know wha' I mean? Come on, I'll get us some chop and I'll treat you to a beer."

They left the site head quarters and drove to the Gittings staff housing where the six or so expats were billeted. Richard recognised them all from his day's examination and as soon as he arrived they welcomed him with warmth, recognising that here was a colleague who had passed the rigours of Larkin's inquisition.

Larkin insisted that Richard should stay in the guest quarters and assured him that they would be at his disposal throughout the contract. The room was comfortable, air-conditioned and with a quite luxurious bathroom. It was miles better than the government guesthouse. The cook was a jolly Palestinian who had drifted from Dar al Handassah, who cooked delicious whole small chickens stuffed with herbs, lemon and garlic.

The next day, they started work at first light. Richard spent two hours with the Quantity Surveyor going through costs and another hour or so going through detailed drawings with the resident Engineer, a small wiry Scot who could not have been more helpful. From him he learned that Larkin roamed West Africa for Gittings. Larkin was a terror to erring suppliers and employees alike. On the other hand Larkin was their champion with Head Office and a steadfast defender of all those he considered to be giving value. Never ever promise Larkin something one can't deliver, the consequences would be dire.

After a brief lunch in the site canteen, it was still only ten forty five, Richard sought out Larkin to bid his farewell, but found that Larkin was in conference. He waited an hour and eventually tapped on the door and entered. Larkin looked up and after a second's pause excused himself from the Nigerian and led Richard outside.

"I'm sorry to interrupt but I must be on my way, just wanted to say thanks and goodbye."

"Tha's alright son, good to meet'cha, you won't see much of me unless you've been a bad boy or de's a problem, see wot I mean, so good luck son, don' le' us down. I'll send a geeza dawn to see the progress at your place, okay? Look after yourself." His massive hand closed over Richard's, the shake was not quite so bone shattering this time. Larkin turned, "I've got the Minister of Health in 'ere wantin' a handover date already, cor blimey you wouldn't believe it would ya." His broad back disappeared into the office.

Mohamed raced back to Kano to visit the contractor on the Hajj pilgrim site near the airport. Although it was nearly nine months to the next Hajj, the Government was keen to complete the pilgrim camps in time for Christmas, three months early. The number of pilgrims increased each year as the value of incomes rose. They expected well over 200,000 to apply for the '73 Hajj. The government tried desperately to control numbers, but the political pressures to provide greater access to the Hajj was immense. The new pilgrim reception centre was being built to prevent the repeat of a catalogue of disasters of previous years.

There had been multiple loss of life through stampedes, massive sanitary problems as uncontrolled hordes of pilgrims camped willy-nilly around Kano and particularly the airport. Roads became clogged, the airport to all intents and purposes became a no go area to non-Hajj passengers. Flights in and out during the Hajj were up tenfold during the peak and that put huge strain on air traffic control, immigration, customs and all those associated with the airport.

Indeed, in the Hajj of '72 there had been a sad and devastating loss of life for the simplest of reasons. Hajj is in the first quarter of the year, usually in March, which is also the time of the Hamadan, a wind that prevails from the northeast and showers on to Nigeria millions of tons of Saharan dust over the country. Often the dust is so thick that visibility is massively curtailed. So it was in '72 when a chartered 707 returned to Kano, fully laden with two hundred pilgrims.

These pilgrims, it must be remembered, had little experience of international travel. Indeed, this would be their first and sadly their last experience of it. These pilgrims travelled cramped together in temporary high-density seating. They carried with them prayer rugs, kettles, primus stoves, food, blankets, pots and pans. Their luggage was managed as best the charter airlines could manage, but the pilgrims seldom allowed their worldly goods to be swallowed by a magic conveyor and insisted on carrying these great bundles of possessions on board. The cabin staff spent the whole of the journey back and forth, trying to store luggage and also preventing the pilgrims from lighting up their primus stoves on the aircraft floor to brew up their tea and provide their food. Such was the innocence of many of the pilgrims, they would find it difficult to unwrap an airline meal or use the aircraft toilet.

In any event the Captain decided to land, despite the poor visibility. The plane missed the runway and ground to a halt having lost part of the undercarriage. The crew opened the doors and instructed the passengers to use the emergency shoots, some did, but the great majority panicked, creating a dead logjam cutting off the escape of the majority. The emergency fire tender equipped with fire fighting foam was not available because some bright spark had decided to take the battery out for charging. As an expedient, another tender was rushed to the scene, alas, only carrying water. Some seven minutes had elapsed and still most of the passengers were praying or fighting inside the aircraft. The crew, despite heroic efforts, eventually abandoned the aircraft, being absolutely ineffective in trying to bring order to the chaotic pandemonium in the cabin. The Captain was almost dragged into the mêlée and only escaped after a tremendous personal struggle. No one quite knew when the fire started, other than seven minutes had elapsed since the shoots were deployed. The fire truck, the one with the functioning battery, started to spray water that spread the aviation fuel and large numbers of pilgrims tragically perished.

Soon an excited mob of awaiting relatives went on the rampage, seeking out the aircraft Captain. He went into hiding and was spirited out of the area and left the country, the following day. The outpouring of grief precipitated a political embarrassment that resulted in a massive overhaul of the pilgrim management programme.

So here was Richard, under great pressure to deliver the roofing systems. He had to supply a large variety of local contractors, many of whom were hopelessly incompetent. Many who would not pay their bills and others who were so intent on fiddling the system that it was almost impossible to work effectively.

His meeting this day was with the Chief Government Clerk of Works, an Alhaji Almahni, a man so incompetent that his abilities defied description, he had been appointed by his cousin, the Minister of Works for the Kano State Government

Almahni's office was almost totally submerged in paper. He seldom appeared for appointments and never had any answers to questions of any relevance. When Richard did find him, he almost inevitably excused himself as soon as a question came up which he found difficult, which was usually within five minutes. His reason was always the same.

"You must forgive me." He would say, "I must go, the Minister is calling."

Because of this absurd appointee, the whole thing got further and further behind. Almahni seldom completed progress reports to the Government department, who therefore released no money. Contractors stopped work because they had not been paid or otherwise submitted false claims as was their want, knowing full well that Almahni would be unlikely to know true from false. As time wore on the chaos mounted and the project got hopelessly adrift.

Amidst this shambles, Richard had one of the most difficult situations. He had been the nominated supplier for all the roofing systems as well as many of the fabricated louvers and doors. This was a massive project and he had taken the job at a very competitive price. He had to deal with fourteen different contractors, of who only five could be relied on and allowed credit. The others were a collection of native contractors who'd never before completed a job of any size or complexity. They had traded by barter. They had no idea about accounting and even less about co-ordinating their efforts to achieve a finished whole. The quality of the work was variable from just about acceptable to completely hopeless. Rates of progress that were meant to be co-ordinated were absolutely haphazard, so that in some parts of the site the walls were complete and up to schedule and in others ground works were still incomplete.

Richard's only support in all this was the splendid Usman Jalingo who dealt directly with the non-approved contractors, collected money (always in cash) and generally made sense of the senseless. The terms of the contract were that Universal was to deliver standard systems which would be distributed from the Government holding compound as the site developed. Each contractor would requisition his call off and Universal would then be informed what each contractor had called off and would collect payment. Sound in theory, absolutely disastrous in practice, particularly since the Department of Works was as hopelessly run as the rest.

By some miracle Almahni was in his office, even though it was nearly five o'clock. Usman was on seat and somehow had persuaded the Alhaji to wait. The Alhaji was bathed in sweat, his grimy fingernails bitten to the quick's. He nervously greeted Richard who, though tired and anxious, was placated by the calming presence of Usman.

"Good day Alhaji, I suppose the Minister is by now finished for the day, so we can chat"

Richard's opening salvo caused Usman to nod his disapproval.

"Sah, Meestah Smiles, the Alhaji and I have been discussing the problems on the site and how we can help each other." he beamed his usual warm and shining grin.

"Our problems, ugh-ugh, they beeg ones." confirmed the sweaty Almahni.

"You're not kidding. We've had all this stuff on the site for god knows how long and we've barely been paid enough to cover the haulage."

"It is not so bad. We will find a way, Sah." responded Jalingo.

"About time, if I might say." then mellowing, "But how?"

"The Clerk of Works, Alhaji Almahni, will allow us Sah, to go to each smaller contractor and give each one a technical help and we will count all the material on site and in the yard and report to Alhaji Almahni."

"And who's going to do all this work? It's not our job, with respect, Alhaji." he nodded in the direction of the hapless Almahni.

"But I beg you; we can do it in a week to ten days, maybe two weeks. We can then submit our report to the Ministry with the backing of Alhaji Almahni and we shall be paid. The Alhaji will be clearer and the Ministry may review those contractors who are not performing, Sah." He beamed another smile, "I will stay and do the counting, and Mbamane can help with technical advice Sah, he is a good man."

A long and detailed conversation followed as it became clear that Usman had found that the only way forward was to bail out his fellow Alhaji from under the pile of chaotic maladministration and in so doing restore Universal's fortunes. Almahni, who was aware that he was entirely out of his depth, was only too pleased to get Usman and Universal to dig him out of his very deep hole. What concerned him most was that he should receive appropriate acknowledgement for this initiative and that his face would be saved. It was all agreed.

Smiles remained concerned that Usman had been so keen to save Almahni. It was unlike him to push Richard in a specific direction without at least prior discussion. He called Usman back to the Hotel where Richard could relax with a beer and Usman with some refreshment.

"Why, why we save that idiot's hide, Usman? Why we take responsibility for that ass hole?"

"The Governor, he come today, he say fix or, chop! Chop! He throw out Almahni and his brother, but he is my brother Sah," he rushed on before Richard had the chance to respond, "and it is the only way for us to get some money, otherwise big palaver, go on for many years."

"Well I'm buggered, Almahni is your brother?" He thrust his head into his hands, "Jesus Usman why didn't you tell me before?"

"The contract ees a good one, Sah. We have to make sure we get our money, my brother will help us."

"Your bloody brother is the most useless man I have ever met and he can't even help himself, never mind us." He finished his beer and ordered another. "If this comes out that you colluded with these guys and that we've now got an inside track, we'll all go to jail. For God's sake this is the most politically sensitive contract in the whole bloody country and it's an unmitigated shambles due your hapless and useless bloody brother."

"Not so, Sah." Usman laid a restraining hand on his boss' arm. "We will make this work Sah, the Governor is aware of our efforts, although you must not know that, also the bigger contractors are taking over so that there will be only seven contractors, all except one we know and trust. After the report is finished and we know where all the site materials are, not only ours, all, then the Minister will fire the smaller less good men and put out their work to the others."

"I hope to God you know what the hell you're doing. A lot of people are strung out on a hope and a prayer."

"It will come right, Sah, Insh Allah."

'Usman, you old bugger, how many of these locals are your brothers?'

"Well Sah," he smiled his biggest smile, "there are many from my home in Bauchi who have influence, we are as one family."

"Well my friend," said Richard rising, "I hope you can trust me enough to let me know who in the family is helping who? However, Usman, in you I trust. Goodnight, I'll see you back in Kaduna."

"Goodnight, Sah, sleep well, it will be well Sah, it will be well." His agdaba billowing, Usman swept from the foyer of the Central Hotel.

Despite his nervousness and the certainty of the audit revealing their exposure on the Pilgrim contract, Richard felt bound to keep what he knew to himself. Edward Regan would go ballistic if he knew of their exposure and would insist on doing something that would cock up their future in Kano forever. His bond with Usman was strong, he trusted him despite his lack of sophistication. He could never hope to know how all this would work out, but he believed that Usman would deliver a solution through his band of brothers. It would be a Nigerian solution, but with Usman, at least it would be an honest one.

Sleep, however, came with difficulty. He prayed that Allah keep Usman safe.

# CHAPTER 43

The rains this year were poor, the country was bone dry and north of Kano the Sahara grabbed the land with her cruel, dry claws. Water holes became scarcer and the rural communities were becoming desperate. Animals were slaughtered before their time and what meat there was, was expensive and tough. The maize crop looked pathetic and dust was everywhere, in one's hair, even in the refrigerators. Water was cut off at regular intervals, so that not even the most affluent escaped the rigors of the heat, dust and lack of water. Great consternation was caused by the rumor that the Brewery might have to close due to the water shortage.

The golf course was like a desert. The concrete tee boxes standing like deserted pill boxes keeping watch over the brown sand "greens" which in turn punctuated the parched straw of the so called fairways. Despite the glumness and the heat, Sunday morning saw the usual gang assemble for the ritual monthly medal.

A caddy that carried the player's bag and always led the way into the rough, accompanied each golfer. This process of the caddy in front served two purposes, (1) to confront any snakes that were frequently lurking and (2) to allow the caddy to practice his skill of picking "his master's" ball up in his toes and preferring his lie. This was a particularly common skill of those caddies who had a permanent arrangement with "a master" who paid well and played well. The caddies supplemented their not unreasonable wages by wagering on their "master" who seemed always to escape the rough with impunity. The masters were not supposed to be party to this skullduggery; however, there was never a shortage of banter and suspicion.

On this particular Sunday the heat was blazing down. Richard, with his caddy, Ibrahim, assembled at the first tee with Malcolm, Bill Damper, Henry Ash and their caddies. They set off in the usually chaotic way, hats pulled down to shade their heads from the sun, wet towels attached to their bags and copious quantities of drinking water weighing down the caddies' already heavy loads. The humor was as usual, with a healthy derision for each man's golfing skill or lack of it. Richard's putting was a constant source of mirth for his companions.

As the morning wore on the heat really was unusually arduous, they learned later, up to one hundred and twenty degrees. Tempers frayed and even the caddies became uncooperative and surly. At the eleventh hole Richard played a shot that struck the very top of a tree. The shot, which was arrow-straight, collided with the tiniest of branches, but alas struck it full square and the ball dropped into the copse in an impossible lie. Richard, in a moment of rashness, swung his club violently at the narrow tree trunk in an attempt to wreak vengeance on the offending bough. Alas the club snapped and the club head flew like a boomerang at a right angle from the line of assault. Ibrahim already fed up with his morning's work received the spinning club head just under his right arm at about the second rib.

The noise was alarming as the wildly flailing club head scythed into Ibrahim's ribcage with sickening force. He let out a low- key sort of groan and collapsed in a heap onto the dusty, but hard ground. He lay still, quite motionless, not a sound came from him. The group too stood motionless, aghast at how easily an accident of such horror had happened. They rushed forward, Richard moaning.

"Sorry, oh shit! Terribly sorry old boy..."

"Oh Christ, I think you've killed the bugger." shouted Malcolm.

"You've done it now." wailed Bill Damper.

One of the other caddies started roaring with laughter the others sniggered.

"Don't laugh, you stupid buggers." cried Malcolm now crouched over the victim.

"Sorry, sorry, old boy." Richard kept repeating rather inanely.

"For Christ's sake shut up Richard. Let's see if the bugger's still alive and see what we can do. Stop whittering."

"Sorry, oh God sorry." Richard whittered some more.

Ibrahim came to life and almost immediately started groaning and writhing on the ground. His eyes rolled and he gripped his sore ribs and he kicked his heals in the dust. The other caddies laughed hysterically.

"That's better, a proper palaver, he'll be alright." Damper walked back to his bag.

The four-ball behind were getting fed up with waiting. Amongst the group was Dr Eli. Richard ran back and fetched the good doctor, who it must be said was more concerned with his approach to the green, ("brown") than administering first aid. He took one look at the prone caddy, told him to get up and immediately pronounced him fit to continue with his duties. Ibrahim was suitably upset and it was only a promise of an extra "dash" that persuaded him to continue. This he did, moaning at suitable intervals to remind Richard of the extent of the expected compensation.

The quality of golf had reached an all time low as the four struggled through the heat to get back to the bar. At the fifteenth Henry said he felt unwell, Damper replied that there could be no way out of paying his two Naira bet. On the sixteenth tee Henry complained again.

"Bloody hot old man, not long to go, a Star beer is on the horizon."

"I'm feeling bloody dreadful." moaned Henry.

"For Christ's sake be quiet, I'm about to drive." Responded Malcolm angrily.

There was a crash, or more of a crump really, as Henry hit the floor.

"For Christ's sake." shouted Malcolm, as his ball sliced horribly into the distant rough.

"Henry? Henry you all right?"

Henry didn't respond; he lay face down a dreadful colour.

"Fuck. He's dead." exclaimed Bill Damper.

"Don't be bloody silly." responded Richard, "I'll get Eli." and he trotted back once more.

"Dr Eli, Henry Ash's collapsed on the tee, could you come?"

"Have you given him some water? It's probably the heat and dehydration."

"I think you'd better come."

Henry Ash was stone dead. The seven golfers and eight caddies assembled on the sixteenth tee around the prone corpse of the late Henry Ash. Stalwart of the Kaduna Club and Rotary, all round good egg... gone, gone in the wink of an eye or a swish of a back-swing. It was all very upsetting.....What should they do next?

"I'll go back and play my eight iron, Henry's dead, heart attack, I daresay..." Eli moved off followed by his three unsure companions. "Send a car down for Henry and take him to the hospital, I'll call on the way home and see about the death certificate." His last instructions he called back, over his shoulder, his mind already focussed on the eight iron shot to come.

Damper, Malcolm and Richard stood staring down at the body of their friend. The caddies grouped just forward of the tee, death was bad juju. A minute or so passed,

"It's a case of a no return then." Said Damper with a sardonic smile.

"A no return indeed," Richard felt unwell. "I'll go organise the car, you guys wait I won't be long."

"Make some space, chaps," said Eli fresh from a par four. He set himself up to drive the 17th completely oblivious to the remains of dear Henry Ash that lay quietly simmering in the heat.

The car was driven out and dear old Henry was dumped unceremoniously onto the backseat. Malcolm accompanied the driver and the body back to the Clubhouse. Damper and Richard set out to walk in, Eli asked if the car could move on the right of the hole since he had a good card going and was anxious not to break his rhythm.

On arrival back at the Clubhouse they gathered solemnly and tucked into some Star beer, the ambulance having been called to take dear Henry off to the morgue. Richard tipped Ibrahim excessively and examined the lad's ribs, which looked viciously bruised. Henry's caddy crept in from the fringe; he tugged at Richard's sleeve.

"I beg you, Sah, I have not been paid, Sah, can I please now, and what should I do with the Master's clubs, Sah?"

"Here my boy, here's the fee and a dash too," Richard emptied his pocket into those grateful hands. They stayed and drank morosely; toasting Henry on his was to eternity. Richard would have to move and open the factory to fabricate a heavy gage aluminium coffin with a screw down lid for Henry's last journey home.

He had not been close to Ash. Henry had been a fixture at the Club and Golf Club and any other Club. He and his wife had been in Kaduna for many years. It had, nevertheless, come as a ghastly shock to see the man drop dead. The awful finality of it and Eli's matter of fact response had somehow been unreal. On his third beer with Damper and Malcolm, Malcolm suddenly broke into tears. Damper uncharacteristically said nothing and dragged on his cigarette and Richard patted the back of his friend's hand. They broke up silently with nothing to say and each made their way home for Sunday lunch.

Richard thought of Henry, his occasional golf partner, an unremarkable, but likeable man. In some ways he could have been described as a member of the old guard, but he was not one of those that Richard and Joan abhorred, he always was polite and respected the locals and never sneered at their differences. He'd expected to end his career in Nigeria after thirty years service with Barclays, where he'd been a competent and reliable Manager.

At home he broke the news to Joan, but only in response to her question.

"How was the golf, too damned hot I would have said?"

"Bloody awful actually, I nearly killed a caddy, broke a bloody golf club and dear old Henry Ash dropped dead on the sixteenth tee."

# CHAPTER 44

Richard was never sure if Henry Ash was related in any way to the rain Gods, but the day after his death the late rains came with a vengeance. The heavens opened and rain fell in torrents, for unusually long periods. The sky remained black virtually all day Monday, a rare happening indeed.

They celebrated Emma's first birthday party and it seemed to Richard that it was a hen party for Joan and her chums. The house was full of chattering young mums and Anna Gombe, her arms pathetically empty, her eyes hungry for a child of her own.

David, now three, was equally out of it and spent the afternoon dodging the rain and terrorising Mussa in the garden. His English still wasn't remotely as good as it should have been since his parents couldn't bring themselves to break his bond with Mussa. Mussa of course continued to speak his local dialect of Hausa and had no incentive whatever to speak English. Somehow both David and Mussa contrived to make themselves understood by Richard and Joan. The hapless parents never admitting their son's linguistic skills might be for ever impaired.

Things were going well at work. Usman's plan at the Pilgrim site was indeed coming up trumps and things were now run by a coalition of the contractors, suppliers, and a bright young accountant seconded by the Governor from the State Ministry of Finance. Alhaji Almahni still presided over the site office, but was encouraged by the powers that be, that he should catch every passing virus and stay home on sick leave.

The contracts were signed and sealed for the Sokoto Hospital, Gittings International had keenly negotiated prices, but it was still an excellent deal for Universal. Barring a complete disaster, Maiduguri would follow suit, so the future looked rosy.

The only fly in the Smiles' ointment was that Richard seemed to be continuously travelling to the northern reaches of the country. He and Mohamed were doing over a thousand miles a week, including very long days on the road.

Richard became a well-known face at the Government Rest house in Maiduguri. This was much the same as the one in Sokoto, even down to the cesspit outside the dining room window. It was here that he met one Brian Davis, a travelling salesman for an American equipment company. Over the evening meal Davis enquired if Richard rode horses.

"Well it's been a while, but sure I've done some riding." He had in fact been given riding lessons for about a month some twenty-two years before.

"Well that's great." enthused Davis, a tall, lean and fit young man. "I've arranged an evening outing with the local stables tomorrow, see you at four."

The 'local stables' turned out to be racing stables. The horses were big, very big and looked healthy and strong. It took Richard a considerable effort to mount his steed. His incompetence was apparent to all the stable lads who grinned and giggled at his hapless efforts. Once in the saddle, that turned out to be very small indeed, he found it difficult to engage the stirrups, which seemed almost under his chin they were so short.

He mumbled with as much dignity that he could muster, "We ride rather longer in England, don't you know."

The stable boys grinned.

Then he couldn't remember how to hold the reigns, the head boy showed him how. The horse was by now aware that the rider was an incompetent buffoon and had no right to be up there at all. His horse a gelding trotted off without so much as a bye your leave, with Richard bouncing hopelessly in the saddle, his scrotum painfully jamming against his inappropriate trousers. There were cries of "Wowah!" but to no avail. The horse obviously had a date somewhere and that was that. No matter how Richard tugged at the reins the horse just got more obstinate and broke into a canter further endangering Richard vitals.

At last the head lad cantered along side and turned the gelding round to join the other horses that were getting ready to depart in the opposite direction. Richard was embarrassed, but more concerned with the excruciating pain in his balls and hips, which he felt were about to become wrenched from his pelvis. He was already drenched in sweat, but somehow pride prevailed.

"Pretty frisky this bugger, perhaps I'm a little out of practice... it's been a while."

The stable lads grinned as they set off along the sandy tracks. At first they walked and Richard did his best to relax the reins and sit as quietly as he could, but then they trotted and then they broke into a canter and before you could say "oh shit!" they were galloping. Richard completely out of control, hung on for dear life. They galloped for what seemed miles, the horses in front kicking up no end of dust. The pain in his lower body was excruciating, his legs felt as if they'd never move again. There was a numbness developing in his pelvic region for which he was thankful.

Richard's mount seemed to enjoy the gallop and soon began to compete with the other horses going ever faster. The speed now was frightening and for one moment it appeared that his horse would pull away from the rest, but once more the Head Lad rescued him. They were mercifully brought to a halt, Richard dismounted, or rather fell from his horse, his legs turned to jelly, he could hardly stand. He made to lengthen the stirrups and again was assisted by the Head Lad when it became obvious he had no idea what he was doing.

"Isn't this great, these horses are really great, don't ya think?" called Davis from his comfortable perch atop a huge black and very beautiful stallion.

"Yes, great, absolutely." muttered the shaking Smiles. "Will we go back the same way?"

"No, boss, we go a mile walk then mile canter then we gallop round dat way" He waved his arms in a vaguely easterly direction.

Richard reluctantly remounted, this time taking special care to adjust his wedding tackle, patted the horse lightly and set off bravely in the middle of the pack. The stable lads chatted and grinned at him. Their language was a northern dialect all of its own and meant nothing to the reluctant jockey. He almost enjoyed the first mile walk but that did not last long. Soon they started to canter again, he did as little as possible in terms of guiding his mount and hoped to God that the animal would follow its fellow horses and that seemed to work. Richard concentrated on staying on. Again things were better; he got some sort of a rhythm, but the strain on his thighs and hips was beginning to peak once more.

The gallop - he hoped it would never come - but it did. They flew down a track between an avenue of trees. Richard hardly noticed the traders on either side with wares spread before them on small tables and rugs on the ground. Richard hung on desperately as they thundered on, the ground raced beneath him, he suspended his weight on his knees despite the pain, falling now could be fatal and he knew it. His horse once more took up the chase and pressed going at a wild gallop, in desperation Richard tugged at the reins wobbling dangerously as he did so. The consequence was not what he had in mind. The horse veered right, narrowly missing a tree whose lower branch hit Richard viciously in the face. By some miracle he was not unseated, he saw the traders scramble for their lives, their wares scattering in the dust. The horse bolted on as if crazed, the ground ahead was clear but uneven. Richard's hands drove down, down the neck of the horse puling in its head, but still it galloped on. The horse, for a reason all of its own, after what seemed like an eternity, slowed and stopped. Richard hung over its neck, the blood coursing down from his forehead and into his right eye. He was alive and more or less in one piece. The Gods had been kind.

The Head Lad and Davis arrived and without a word led Richard's mount, one at either side of the bridle. They walked the short distance back to the stables where the stable lads were keen to examine the horse, which it seemed was unscathed. Richard made his brief farewell to the Head Lad who slapped him on the back and grinned.

"Maybe boss come and race one day?" He roared with laughter.

"Not bloody likely." They shook hands and a much-amused Mohamed helped a shaking boss into his car.

He and Davis found a source of beer and drank the evening away, the American full of apologies for not making it clear that the rides were going to be a training session for high class race horses. He said he thought

Richard was a "sport" and, rather aggravatingly, addressed him as such for the rest of the night.

In his Rest House bed, Richard cursed his own stupidity. He could have killed himself, the horse, not to mention several local traders, all because he was too much of a coward to say "No". His legs, thighs and back ached, his head throbbed and the contusion above his hairline hurt like hell. So much for horses, best left to cowboys, and other lunatics.

"What happened to you? Have you been in an accident?" Joan looked at him without sympathy more with suspicious curiosity.

"Sort of, went for a horse ride." He dumped his bags.

"A Horse ride, you don't ride."

"I used to when I was about six."

"What happened did the horse kick you or what? Did you fall off.....? Don't tell me the other children wanted to fight for their favourite donkey." She laughed.

"Actually I was struck by an overhanging tree..... you know.... Branch, sort of thing."

She came closer and examined the welt that was purple and angry looking. As ever she efficiently treated his wound, now more tenderly.

"Are you blind? This was no twig, you've got a really nasty contusion, you were lucky not to damage your eye. Are you telling me the truth? This is nasty, haven't been in a car accident or anything, no bar room brawls?"

"Actually, I got sort of surprised, it was a bloody race horse, it bolted ... I've never been so scared in all my life."

She snatched his bag, smelt the horsy stink, she believed him.

"When will you ever grow up...Race horses, you're a silly bugger. ....Race horses" She laughed, and turned to attend her other children.

# CHAPTER 45

She announced that they had received another invitation to the Gombe's. She knew that Sally and Malcolm were also to be guests. Richard remembered the last dinner party at home and Joan's obvious attraction to John Gombe. He remembered too the warning that Anna had whispered to him on that same night.

"I don't think we should go." he said with as much nonchalance as he could muster.

"I've already accepted." shot back Joan.

"Then unaccept; we're not going."

"What's brought this on?"

"Nothing's brought this on," he snarled back, "I just don't like that son of a bitch."

"Oh, really. And why, may I ask, do you suddenly dislike this 'son of a bitch'?"

"You know perfectly well. I don't like him because he's trying like mad to get you into bed."

The slap resounded, his head spun, Joan stood unyielding. "Now who's the son of a bitch? Do you believe that I would go to bed with that, or any other man, do you think I would cuckold you, what do you think I am a tramp?" She tried to slap him again but this time he caught her hand, she burst into tears. "Is that all you think of me, you bastard? You don't know who you married, who bore your children, you shouldn't judge others by your own pathetic standards."

"And what does that mean?"

"Do you think I don't know about you and Sally, you miserable shit, I've known since the day you came home on leave, I can read you and your lecherous mind like a book."

He was speechless, there was nothing but silence. He had lost, game, set and match. His mind raced; what could he say? What had he let out of the bag? What should he do? Confusion and uncertainty reigned down on him in such magnitude that he thought he might fall over.

He turned silently and slumped into an armchair. She turned on her heel, slammed the hallway door with such ferocity that the whole house shook. It sounded like a gunshot and it hit its mark like one. Richard sat miserably alone.

Time passed, the children were put back to sleep, Peter returned to his quarters and the Magardi returned to their repose under the carport. Eventually, at close to midnight, Richard tiptoed to the bedroom. He undressed as quietly as he could but he knew she was awake in the darkness. As he slipped into bed, he received a vicious kick that struck his thigh like a hammer blow.

"If you think you're sleeping here, you can think again. Bugger off and sleep somewhere else." she turned, snapping the bed sheets over her.

"Look, darling, I'm sorry if you were offended by what I said, I didn't mean to say I don't trust you. It's just that John Gombe gives me the creeps and you were... well... kissing him..."

"At least I wasn't fucking him. By the way, how was Sally? Pretty sexy I would say."

Silence once more. Suddenly she sat up, switched on the bedside lamp, her eyes were red and swollen with tears. She looked vulnerable and plain.

"You might as well know that I asked Sally and she told me the lot, strangely I put it aside, not forgetting it, but it wasn't burning me up. But now it is, I know I flirted a bit and it was fun and yes, I think John is sexy, but it was and is only fun, particularly I might add when that whore, Janice Cooper, can hardly lay off your fly." She looked at him, "Have you shagged her too?"

"No, good God, no" he stared at the bed sheets; they didn't help him with anything to say.

"For what its worth, Sally told me it was her fault, but that you didn't take a lot of cajoling."

He coughed a dry embarrassed cough, he could still think of nothing to say.

She blew her nose and sniffled, "Well anyway, I don't like you much at the moment. You're an untrustworthy shit who's driven by 'you know what'. I enjoy our sex life and I do my best for you to enjoy it too. If you're just too greedy and mess it all up we'll both be sorry, especially you. So bugger off. It'll take me a while to see if I can take you back, I hope I can, because it was so good." The tears ran in floods, she threw her head under the sheet, "Bugger off"

He spent a grim night on the settee in the lounge, which did not have the benefit of air-conditioning. At first light he rose, exhausted and miserable. He dragged himself to the bathroom where he showered and shaved. He went into the bedroom where Joan was already up and dressed. She looked tired.

"Good morning," she smiled a thin smile, "remember there are children in this house who deserve a happy and loving home" She walked straight passed him and went to Emma's room to get her started for the day.

David, who seemed particularly full of noise and joie de vivre, in sharp contrast to his parents, dominated breakfast with shouts and chatter about school and the day ahead. The remainder of the week passed with a sense of emptiness between them, Joan with an attitude of armed neutrality kept Richard at bay. He was allowed back into the bedroom where there was no contact, physical or verbal. Richard unable to think of an approach that would in any way ameliorate the situation kept his own counsel, hoping upon hope that Joan would forgive him.

He dreaded the next meeting with Malcolm and Sally. Malcolm poor sod would be the only one to be unaware of what had come to pass. He struggled to understand how Joan seemed to have forgiven Sally. They seemed as friendly as ever. He didn't know if Sally knew that he knew that Joan knew; it was monstrous pressure. He felt he would never dare open his mouth ever again.

As Friday approached Richard accepted the inevitable that he would have to go to the Gombes' party. He dreaded the prospect. Would Joan punish him by flirting outrageously? He hoped not, he didn't think he could bear it. He resolved that he would steer clear of the booze so that at least he would keep his wits about him on what was bound to be a very trying evening.

Sally and Malcolm were to pick them up and have just one before they left Galadima Road. When they arrived they seemed much as usual, Sally looking stunning, Malcolm as ever quiet and calm. Joan emerged from the bedroom in a silk dress, it was the blue number she'd worn at Solomon's; she looked gorgeous.

Richard's plans for a rational and defensive evening, ended almost immediately. His pulses raced, here was the loveliest girl in the world, she was his, or was she? The girls made hoops and hollahs about each others' dress, made jokes about the men and seemed to be in cahoots to make Richard jealous. Malcolm seemed impervious to it all and drank his first, too large, scotch of the evening. They set out to the Gombes', the girls giggling away and Richard silent, convinced that disaster was not far away.

The lotus eaters' assembly was in full swing when they arrived. John and Anna, Billy and Janice Cooper, Freddie Solomon and his French trollop Gabby and another handsome huge black man with a tall woman at his side. Her back was to them. All they could see was her turban and wonderfully rich gown that fell from under her hair in a fabulous line to the floor. When they approached, the woman turned and Richard at least was taken aback to see that she was white. She was elegant rather than beautiful, a little older than them.

The Pataki's were, it transpired, the majority shareholders in one of West Africa's largest trading houses, Petain and Brandish. The man rejoiced in the name of Camion, apparently Sudanese and his wife was Italian, formerly the wife of the Brandish side of the business partnership. They reeked of wealth, from her gown to his watch, from his shoes to her turban. John Gombe made a great fuss of them and it seemed tonight as though Joan might escape his amorous attention. Janice Cooper behaved as eccentrically as ever continually making lascivious remarks about the sexual gifts of the black male and insinuating herself between Camion and John Gombe. Billy was at this stage still relatively sober and was charming and urbane to all. Freddie Solomon ignored the glamorous Gabby, who it seemed to Richard was in a constant state of misery. She complained continuously, albeit in her broad French accent.

When they sat down to dinner Maria Petawi sat on John Gombe's right and Anna to his left, each guest sat next to his spouse. Alarmingly Richard found himself between Joan and the dreaded Janice Cooper. He prayed to God that Janice would behave herself and not play her groping games under the table. During dinner Joan drank with a vengeance, so that by the time dessert was served she was loud and obviously the worse for drink. Billy was also flying fairly high by this time and they started an embarrassing conversation about marital fidelity. Billy asserting that his wife was over-sexed and needed other men, he added with a hurt sort of whimper, that he didn't much mind, as long as she didn't frighten the horses, so to speak. Joan piped up that women weren't allowed to be over-sexed but it was okay for men, adding with some venom "like my husband".

Anna Gombe tried desperately to change the conversation as Janice was about to launch into a comparative study of the sexual prowess of the men she had known, everyone thought it would be a safe bet that John Gombe would be on the list.

Joan, encouraged by the mayhem she had started, shouted "Bravo, lets get our notebooks out, what do you think Sally?"

"Brghhravo, brghhavo." encouraged Gabby, sensing mayhem just around the corner.

Sally remained quiet, marooned in ambiguity. Anna, as always the perfect hostess, shooed her guests away from the dinner table and precipitated a premature braking up of the dinner party which disappointed Janice and Joan who leered at each other and ran their hands up Richard's thigh meeting at a very sensitive point. Richard for his part sat with his knees very firmly together with his hands squeezed between them in a prayerful and suppliant fashion.

They meandered from the dinner table and gathered on the patio to watch a spectacular electrical storm. The lightening was brilliant and frightening as the sound of a million pounds of explosive crashed around their heads. The group seemed to have segregated by sex, the men at the bar end and the ladies grouped around the dining group at the other. The men talked about boring things like politics and the economy. The girls talked of men, sex and clothes. Both Janice and Joan were quite drunk, with Sally and Maria Patawi fast catching them up. Gabby stoked the fires of discontent as she slunk around the fringes of the conversation. As usual Anna was a sober and organizing influence, keeping the lid on a potentially wild event.

"Darling, men they are 'opeless, every night you must look after them.'" the Italian husky voice of Maria intoned. It was followed by a huge guffaw from Janice.

She countered in her upper crust tones, "What about us being looked after, darling, what about us?"

"Eet is 'opeless, that is why every other man in Eetaly 'as a mistress, I was agood mieestress to Chamoon, I was 'is partner's wife. 'Enrico 'ee was lovely guy, but 'ee 'ad a mistress, maybe two or three, I don' know, so I marry my Chamoon and now I make a vacancy for 'is mistress… it ees the way."

"I want another drink." announced Janice.

"Me too."

"Let's all 'ave one. Bon, c'est bon."

The Steward approached the ladies and a variety of cocktails were served. Richard noted anxiously that Joan was topping up yet again. The men, who'd heard the majority of what the ladies had to say, laughed and agreed that they would never understand women.

Chamoon was a very interesting man who'd been born in the Sudan, brought up in Ethiopia, educated in England and lived in the South of France, with houses in Italy, London and the Caribbean. His business interests extended from Italy to South Africa, mainly down the west coast of Africa. He seemed to be on first name terms of most of the rulers and more than a few dissident leaders. He spoke beautifully with a voice that was resonant and deep, with impeccable English that was touched by a hundred accents, but not any of them more than a smidgeon. His Nigerian interests were large, with five groups encompassing auto, electrical, civil engineering plant, a number of service companies in the ports and airports.

He seemed interested in everyone and listened intently to everything they said. He had a long discourse with every one, except Freddie Solomon, who he obviously knew and disliked. He talked to Malcolm about the strengths and weaknesses of various African economies. He talked to Richard about the great engineering projects in Nigeria and elsewhere in his realm and he shared with them all glimpses of the dark days to come, particularly in Angola.

Richard found Chamoon to be exotic and exciting. He judged that Chamoon was not more than forty-five, yet he was already a multi millionaire with enormous power and a life full of excitement and international influence. Richard could not resist the idea of perhaps getting an offer to work for this man, maybe as a leg man to start. He imagined traveling in the company aircraft and mixing with the Heads of State, it was heady stuff.

An hour passed as Chamoon held court, even John Gombe was quiet, seldom speaking and only interrupting to offer his best cognacs to his guests. The girls were now out on the patio as the storm had passed. They seemed to be having a ball. Joan was now, one of many, the worse for wear. They continued to hoot and celebrate each others jokes and comments, aimed no doubt at men. Maria seemed, from Richard's viewpoint, the most sober, but that wasn't saying a lot.

It was nearing twelve o'clock when there was a huge screaming guffaw from the patio, which was accompanied by a large simultaneous splash. The noise was such that it couldn't be ignored and the men dashed to see what had happened. There in the pool, fully clothed but in danger of sinking, floundered Joan and Janice, shrieking with laughter each time they surfaced.

'Damn it!' cried Gombe as he ran for a pair of liloes. 'They've fallen into the deep end.'

The men, apart from Gombe, did little but watch with amusement, tinged perhaps with a small degree of alarm. Joan swam the few strokes to the side and was helped out by Malcolm and Chamoon. Janice, for some reason no one could have expected, turned away from salvation and started to sink out of reach of the helping hands. Gombe threw the liloe, but she was now loosing her composure and thrashed about, ignoring the floating airbeds that were no more than three feet from her. It was Freddie who removed his shoes and dived in and with some difficulty dragged the now hysterical Janice to the side.

She was lifted out and looked an absolute wreck. Her hair was like rats tails, her make up ran and her dress hung to her like a rag. Billy staggered up when the drama was all but over and embraced his incorrigible wife with a touching affection.

"There, old girl, never were the best swimmers, were we?"

Joan sat, looking wrecked but still beautiful.

Richard was furious, "What the hell was that supposed to be? You could have drowned yourself for Christ's sake."

"A fat lot you'd care." She began to cry.

He took her in his arms, lifting her from her seat, held her very tight and whispered, "If you'd died, I'd have died. I love you, you crazy bitch."

The two soaked women and the heroic Freddy were led away to find dry apparel by Anna. Gabby declined to find anything remotely good in Freddie's efforts at saving Janice.

"Ee 'as always been a show-off; zat ees all."

Richard declined a change of clothes, but accepted another cognac, he was still mad.

"What on earth happened? Did they jump in?"

"No, they fell in."

"C'est la vie, eh" Gabby looked Richard straight in the eye, "she 'as spirit your wife, oui?"

"Oui, she has spirit aplenty."

He took Sally to one side as things calmed down and the first guests were beginning to make their farewells.

"How come you told Joan about us, are you crazy? You swore me to secrecy and now I'm in deep crap. I guess it's only a matter of time before Malcolm gets wind of it."

"She knew, I don't know how but she knew and we won't let Malcolm know, unless you do."

"What a bloody shambles, is she going to get over it, Sally? I love her?"

"She'll get over it, just be a patient boy, you're lucky this party's gone the way it has. She might have done something naughty to get you back. She even asked me 'how was it?'"

"What did you say?"

"I said you were rotten, your heart wasn't in it." She laughed, "Look out, here they come."

Joan sobered by her excursion into the pool, emerged dry and made up. She wore a blouse and skirt borrowed from Anna, which was one size too small. No bra would fit so her breasts were clearly visible through the tight blouse. The effect was electric, at least on Richard. It was time to take her home.

They bade farewell to their hosts and with the Hetherington's made their way home. The car was strangely silent, just Malcolm whittering on about the pool incident. Richard and Joan sat in the back still not touching. Richard tried to slip his arm around her but she shrugged him off.

At home they thanked Peter and asked the astonished Steward if he would hang Madame's dress, "I'll see to it in the morning." said Joan, marching independently to bed.

Richard followed, slid into bed beside his wife and risked another advance.

"You know I meant what I said at the pool, I love you."

"Hm," there was a silence, "I need this." she announced, "It's nothing to do with you, it's for me, do you understand?" She mounted him and had sex in a great release. There were no words, just humping, lustful, sex. When she had finished, he had not yet climaxed because he dared not too early, she dismounted, turned her back to him and without another word fell to sleep. He lay there frustrated but still, oh God how women can make you pay.

# CHAPTER 46

Their second tour of duty passed and relations between husband and wife began to heal, although it was clear to Richard that it would take time and that perhaps they'd never be returned to the pristine innocence of their early days. What was important was to leave the whole episode alone and let Joan bury her hurt, she still loved him he knew but the physical imperatives meant that recall was never far away. Neither for that matter was Sally Hetherington, who despite all this mayhem remained Joan's firm friend and confidant.

Sally's motives were a mystery to him. He wanted above all to enquire of Joan what she thought. He dared not. What was it between them that allowed Joan the generosity of forgiveness and Sally's sustained closeness to the Smiles'? Malcolm, as far as Richard knew, was the only one of the four who was ignorant of the past, or was he? Malcolm was such a nice, comfortable sort of man, he never seemed alarmed at Sally's frequently flirtatious behavior, or any other unusual behavior, come to that. His equanimity was unshakable and despite everything, they seemed extremely fond of each other.

The mystery continually perplexed Richard almost without relief. His only solace was that he believed that it was beyond understanding, and it should be left mysterious; as another unsolved wonder in the great secrets of the Mars – Venus theorem. It was all impossible and the only plan that Richard could imagine was to leave the enigma permanently unsolved. The dangers of enquiry were too great to risk.

There was only a month to go to their second leave and they looked forward to going home to the UK, although Richard had reservations about any length of stay in Tottenham. He quietly, but insistently, proposed that he and Joan could get away from the children somewhere in Europe. Paris or Amsterdam would be good. Joan did not dismiss the idea.

With three weeks to go, Richard rose to his usual morning routine and noticed on his first steps from bed that there was an unusual amount of dust and dirt on the floor. The trail of dirt led from inside his bedroom into David's room and up the corridor to the lounge. He called Peter, who expressed surprise. It soon emerged that they had received uninvited guests during the night.

"Jesus Christ, we've had burglars, and the buggers have been right into the bedroom while we were asleep."

Joan leapt from the bed as did David at all the commotion. Examination of the rooms revealed the loss of underwear, shirts, practically all of David's clothes, as well as a good fifty percent of Emma's. The portable radio was missing too.

"Magardi, where the hell are the bloody Magardi?"

"They have just gone Sah."

"Go and fetch the miserable sinners back now."

Peter sped from the house and returned in around five minutes with the robed guards with their bows and arrows, swords and god knows what other weaponry.

"Ask these prize warriors what happened last night."

Peter did as he was asked; the two guards shrugged and muttered amongst themselves. Peter persisted with his questions, but the Tuaregs just grunted, one to another.

"For Christ's sake," Richard interrupted the incomprehensible mutterings, "what the hell happened?" His voice had reached shouting pitch; he was angry, even angrier when Joan, still in her dressing gown, arrived to inform him that two hundred pounds of Sterling currency had been taken from her handbag hidden in the airing cupboard. He was furious.

"Well what have these pricks got to say for themselves?"

"Sah, they said they heard a noise in the night, Sah."

"What do you mean; heard a noise?  What did they do about it?  Bugger all I expect."

There was more mutterings in strange languages.

"'Sah, they heard a noise and they went round the house, Sah'"

"And what did they see, Sherlock Holmes and his mate?"

"I don't think this sarcastic humor is much help," interjected Joan.

"Will you shut up and leave this to me."

"You sod, sort your own damn problems."  She turned and marched back into the house.

"Peter, I'm waiting for some sort of explanation from our protectors here."

"They say, Sah, that they heard a sound and they went round the house, Sah.  They shone their torch all round the roof, Sah."

"Peter, why did they shine their torch on the roof?  Did they think we were being robbed by a fucking giraffe?"

"Please, Sah, what is 'Giraffe'?"

"Never mind, tell them we will go round the house now, now."

He led the group round the house and soon found the point of entry.  The thief had forced apart the burglar bars, removed some of the louver windows and made an easy entry.  He must have made a hell of a noise, taken a good deal of time and known the layout of the house.

He turned to the guards who shuffled uneasily, mumbling again in their own dialect.

"Well, you idle sods, explain to me how, if you heard a noise, you couldn't have located this major bloody hole in the kitchen window and how you could possibly miss a thief with a bloody great car jack?"

There was more multilingual mumbling.

"They say, sorry Sah, they do not understand."

"Please spare me the juju shit, these idiots were either asleep or they were in cahoots with the burglar.  Ask them, I want to know which it is?  Tell this pair of plonkers I'm going to fetch the police now, now."

The robed guards looked at one another, shifted from foot to foot.  They understood "police" all right.  They conferred once more.  More shuffling and whispering between the guards.

"Sah, they are very sorry Sah."

"Tell them to go away. I not want to see them again at all. Tell them I am sad that they did not keep trust, that they are lazy and not to be trusted. Tell them I shall tell their boss".

He walked away with a heavy tread, deeply disappointed that suspicion must fall on those who knew the whereabouts of the handbag. It had to be Joseph, the old Steward.

Joan was still cross at being excluded from the "men's conversation". After some conciliatory words from Richard, she sat with him to make a list of the missing items.

Although not the most valuable, the kids' clothes were the biggest loss, since there was no hope of replacing them in Kaduna. The good news was that they only had four weeks to leave for the UK and replacements were due anyway. Peter was very upset; aware perhaps that suspicion could easily fall on him. After all, he may have known the whereabouts of all the key items particularly, the Sterling cash. In any event, for certain he knew where the handbag was. Who knew whether he had a chance to look inside, there was ample opportunity.

Peter was clearly nervous and would not leave their presence, anxiously flitting about, obviously straining to hear their conversation.

"Peter would you leave us please?"

"Yas, Sah." He moved sullenly into the kitchen, closing the door behind him, leaving the door slightly ajar.

"Close the door please."

"Yas, Sah." It was closed with an audible bang.

"What do we do? Call the police? God help us and God help Peter if my experience down in Kaduna south is anything to go by." He rubbed his hands, aware that Mohamed was waiting to take him to work.

"Peter?"

"No way, no bloody way, I'd trust him absolutely."

They nodded, in assent.

"Peter." he shouted, Peter appeared like a genie. "Sit down, we want you to join us in finding who 'dee tiefman' is. We know it is not you because you are a good man and now part of our family, okay"

Tears came to Peter's eyes, he clenched his hands and palpably wanted to embrace Joan or Richard or both. It took him a moment to compose himself.

"Sah, I do not know, Sah. I beg you Sah, it ees not Mussa Sah."

"We never thought it was." smiled Joan, "In fact, it never crossed our minds." She touched his hand which still shook with anxiety.

"We think it's an almost sure bet that Joseph, your predecessor, has come back. It's almost exactly a year since I had to tell him to go away. What do you think?"

"I do not know Sah. I have heard of dees man. He is from a village near mine, Sah. I can find out, Sah, but maybe I cannot find out."

"I'm sorry Peter can you say that again, you can or you can't find out?"

"Maybe I can, maybe I can't, Sah. Maybe if he has dee money, he will spend it and people will know in the village, Sah. Maybe he will go away and we will not know, Sah."

"Do you think we should call the police? We should for insurance purposes, but Mister Smiles is afraid they might pick on you because you are our steward?"

"You should call them, Sah. They will be okay."

And so it was the policeman who visited Joan several hours later seemed fair and listened to her view that Peter was beyond suspicion. He spent half an hour with Peter in his neat quarters and emerged without so much as breaking a single finger of the interrogated. He reported back to Joan that he agreed with their reading of the situation and that he would pass his report to Minna Police department.

He could not guarantee a result but, "Eet is possible that maybe he will be seen with the goods, selling them. It is a beeg market however and it would be lucky if he was caught."

They would do their best. Then after an hour of discussion he sat down and wrote everything down in detail. He enjoyed a good lunch provided by Joan and a relieved Peter and departed about three in the afternoon. He strolled away at about one mile an hour, Joan felt they were unlikely to here more and that P.C.315 was not unduly perturbed by the burglary to the Smiles' residence.

Small children's underwear became an all-consuming subject over the next few days. David's clothing needs were satisfied by a whip round of the mums at his junior school. People were very kind and Joan mused that he was probably better clothed after the theft than before. Emma took a little longer, but young mothers they'd never even met turned up at the door to offer either things their kids had grown out of, or an item or two from overstocked wardrobes. All in all they were impressed by the way the ex-patriot community had rallied round to help. Richard was moved to put a note up on the Club notice board.

A week before their departure they were invited to the Hetherington's for dinner, where Malcolm announced that at last his promotion had been posted. They were to leave Kaduna in the near future, to take up the job as Senior Partner in Nairobi. There was much celebration, but it was tinged with sadness and relief. Joan was really quite upset at the thought of loosing her bosom pal and Richard would miss the phlegmatic and reliable Malcolm. Despite that, it was a good dinner, much grog, including two bottles of Champagne saved for just such an occasion. After dinner they talked and danced on the patio, Sally still taunting Richard to the very last with the almost connived approval of Joan who smiled enigmatically. The mystery continued.

The loss of their sterling was a blow, as the bureaucracy of the banks to acquire foreign exchange was daunting in the extreme. It would mean queuing for hours and tedious to-ing and fro-ing with no guarantee in the end that the money would be available. Then there was the visit to immigration. That took forever to get his re-entry permit. He was determined, however, to avoid the clutches of those corrupt sons of bitches in Kano immigration department.

Richard had booked his tickets, routing himself and Joan to Paris via London. This meant they could take a break in Paris if Grandma Page could be persuaded to look after the kids for a long weekend.

A Trainee Manager from London had been seconded to look after the business during Richard's absence. Young Jeremy Thompson was very bright, a Cambridge graduate, but possibly the most insensitive twit Richard had met since the days of Nigel Butter.

Richard knew that Jeremy was going to try to make a name for himself during his brief period of power and he also knew that Eke was going to be extremely un-cooperative if young Jeremy didn't behave a little better. During his ten days of familiarization training Jeremy was quick to understand the issues, but absolutely hopeless with people, especially the Nigerians. He was abrupt to a point of rudeness and extremely condescending when things didn't go to plan.

Richard was out when the Post and Telegraph man, Mr. Simon, came for his monthly dash. Thompson, just like the younger Smiles declined to countenance bribery, he sent Mr. Simon away with a flea in his ear. The phones mysteriously went down about twenty minutes later. Richard returned later in the afternoon to find Thompson ranting about corruption and incompetence of Managers who conspired to encourage it... Thompson was incredulous that Richard could countenance such a system and implied he felt it his duty to inform Head Office of these irregularities.

"Jeremy, don't be a prick all your life, this is the way things are. Imperfect I know, and let me say I agree with you wholeheartedly about condoning corruption, but brother, that's the way it is, pay up or no phones, believe me I've tried the alternative and it doesn't work."

"But Richard, I can't believe that this sort of thing is a part of the way you run this business; everyone said it is great chance to see one of the more successful companies operate. I can't say I think this is an example of progressive management."

"Frankly I don't give a shit, what you think. I can ring Edward and tell him I think you're too much of an impractical ass to be trusted with this business and believe me; he'll have your ass out of here in a day. So, be a good boy and do as I tell you and as Eke and Adegbulu advise."

"But..."

"No bloody 'buts'. You'll learn more from your local colleagues in six weeks than in a year from me. Just remember these guys have made this place tick for a long time and they will for a long time after you and I are forgotten, so no fucking buts, no buts at all."

Still Jeremy-'I'm a Cambridge graduate'-Thompson, looked high and mighty, he signaled, 'I'll do what I want to do when you're on leave, so there.'

In desperation and with Joan's permission he took young Thompson out to the Club and introduced him to all the "old farts". The ones who'd been in Nigeria for tens of years; and who still hankered back to the days of the colonies. Not all that surprisingly he seemed to get on well with these, even the half-wits, like the bullies from the textile business.

David took him to meet Coker at the hospital. He seemed unmoved, so there was nothing else but to take Jeremy out on the town, which meant getting him as drunk as possible and in so doing hoping the would share a 'all boys together camaraderie' that might make Jeremy see a little humility.

Unbeknown to Richard, Jeremy who had aspired to row for Cambridge, though he had failed to get his place in the University boat. He had been relegated to "Goldie", the second boat, only weeks before 'the boat race'. He had rebelled, dropped out and become one of the heaviest drinkers of his year. He still got a good "second" and more to the point had drinking skills of a very high order. Richard's plan backfired badly and it was Jeremy who leant the collapsed body at the door of Galadima Road, apologizing to Joan that her husband had become unwell. She was not amused.

Despite the failure of his experiment, he found Jeremy to be much more conciliatory during the last week. Somehow Richard's total failure at the drinking stakes had suddenly earned respect from the young man. The gangly Thompson acquired a grudging affection for Smiles and secretly rejoices in his superiority as a champion toper. As time passed towards their last day together Richard called a meeting with Adegbulu, Eke, Daniel from the Auditors and Jeremy.

Adegbulu, as always, accepted anything thrown at him with unflappable calm. Because he was such an obliging and quiet man he was easily overlooked. In truth he was a rock of sound advice and wide experience. His understanding of the business was encyclopedic and he knew every customer by credit control number, volume sales and any peculiarity going back to the foundation of the company in Kaduna, eighteen years previously. The only problem with him was he was so pathologically shy he would never speak unless spoken to. It had taken Richard nearly a year to recognize Adegbulu's virtues and he had evolved a way of getting the best out of him. He had instigated a weekly meeting that reviewed all incoming orders and credit control issues. He would ask Adegbulu to prepare a report on any exceptional matters and Adegbulu never did anything other than a meticulous job. Once he started on his prepared notes, item by item, he would open up and a fund of useful and relevant information would pour out.

He employed the same tactic today, having asked Adegbulu to report on the intakes and output forecasts for his leave period. Together with Eke and prompted by Richard, they put on a virtuoso performance. Richard made a point of including Jeremy, mainly on important items that he could not possibly know anything. This had the effect of Jeremy deferring to Adegbulu on a number of issues and to Eke on others. He was not made to look a fool but perhaps a little naked. Usman Jalingo charmed Thompson, as indeed he charmed everyone, so that by leave day Richard was reasonably confident that Jeremy would not screw up his patch. Nevertheless he rang Edward Regan and reluctantly asked his boss to keep an eye on the young high flyer.

Excitement in the household reached fever pitch as Mohamed loaded the car for the journey to Kano and the flight to London and six weeks of leave. So, with underwear borrowed from sundry places, the Smiles family set out back "home".

# CHAPTER 47

They arrived at London's Heathrow feeling very jaded indeed. Both the children had been fractious and noisy on the overnight flight and both parents had spent a sleepless night trying to control their brats. Emma, for some reason screamed her head off all the way home. Apart from suffocating their darling daughter they tried everything to keep her quiet. They'd spent the whole journey apologizing to fellow passengers in the stuffed aeroplane and receiving for their pains wan smiles and "tut-tuts".

They staggered through immigration and customs with the two children and their huge pile of luggage. Their caravan of trolleys, bags and children was almost through customs when a be-turbaned Sikh customs officer bade them stop.

"Good morning Sir, Madame. Where have you come from please?"

"Nigeria." snapped Richard.

"I would like you please to open your bags, please, Sir."

"You cannot be serious, you can....not be serious?"

"Yes, sir I am, please be opening the bags."

Richard threw the bags off the trolley onto the counter, took the keys from his pocket and then for no reason at all, except bad temper, threw the keys at the customs official,

"Open them yourself, help yourself, you officious little prick."

The Sikh, raised his eyebrows picked the keys off the floor, handed them to Richard and calmly instructed Richard to open the bags - all of them.

Richard passed the baby's bag over first where he sincerely hoped there resided some dirty nappies. Then he opened each of the cases filled with the miscellaneous underwear and a few gifts and craft items brought for their relatives.

"What is the value of this artifact?" enquired the Customs man.

"Nickels and dimes." snarled Richard.

"Do you have a receipt for this?" the be-turbaned one persisted.

"Are you serious? Do you know that we bought that off a door to door craft sales guy from Niger, he couldn't read or write as far as I know, let alone issue a receipt. Besides, we may have given him a meal and a couple of old shirts. Don't be ridiculous."

"Do you know the origin of this mask?" he persisted.

"No bloody idea. Mali, the bloke said, but who knows and for that matter who cares? For Christ's sake, we're standing here talking about some two penny, halfpenny mask. Can't you see the kids are shagged out and we're knackered? What are you, some kind of sadist?" He continued, "Look, why don't you keep the bloody mask? Go on, take it, take it home and I hope it scares the shit out of your Grandma. Now can we go please?"

Patiently the Customs Officer continued to rummage in the luggage, pulling out all manner of oddities, some cloth paintings destined for Muriel and one or two juju dolls that depicted little men with huge penises. The official was at pains to put them to one side where they could be plainly seen by the multitude of passengers meandering by.

"These artifacts are of substantial value and Her Majesty's Government seeks to stamp out the illegal export of national treasures, I may therefore impound theses articles."

Despite Joan's restraining hand, Richard lost his temper, "Okay sunshine, send back the Elgin Marbles, half the British Museum, keep the fucking gifts, I hope they make you very happy." He started to repack the cases leaving the presents to one side.

"Excuse me, Sir. You cannot just leave these things here, I shall have to make out a report and get a property notice of ownership and value."

He produced a sheaf of paperwork and Richard knew he was beaten. He exhaled and slumped to a seat on the counter. In Nigeria it was corruption in England it was bureaucracy. They both had the same numbing effect.

Joan ignored the collapse of her useless husband, summoned a smile and held Emma in her arms. "I'm sorry my husband's such a prat. He's been rude and I apologise."

The Sikh smiled back. She continued, "Really, those Nigerian nick-knacks were bought at the door of our home and they were bought for less than five pounds each. We'd certainly be happy to co-operate and leave them here, but would it be worth Her Majesty's Government's time? I doubt it. If you think we should pay duty please estimate what it is and we will gladly pay and be on our way."

The Customs man was undone. He shuffled off and returned in about two minutes with a cheerful colleague with a bright cockney accent. He looked at the objects in question, "Presents for the folks are they? This one's a bit saucy. Eh?" he chuckled, looking at the juju doll. "That's alright Madame, enjoy your leave and if you don't mind me saying, Sir, my colleague is only doing his job and doesn't need all that abuse, okay? Toddle-pip."

They staggered out with their kids, goods and chattels. Joan, despite her fatigue, was furious, "Why are you such an ass hole? Why do you have to be rude and impatient with everyone? It'll serve you right if some body locks you up one day, which you richly deserve. Do you know how much time you've wasted making your stupid points? You're a pain in the ass, that's what you are. No consideration for me, the kids, just your bloody great ego bestriding the world and to hell with the rest of us."

Their journey through interminable traffic jams did little to ease tempers and their arrival at Grandpa Page's was low key and strained. Immediately Richard entered the house he felt the clawing claustrophobia of its smallness. The stink of old George's cigarettes, of London grime and last week's Sunday lunch. Emily had aged in the year since they had last seen her. She looked gaunt, but at the same time fatter or flabbier. The grayness round her soft eyes betrayed the labors of another year pandering to the needs of her wretched husband.

Richard was disappointed that Uncle Arthur was not about, but they were reminded that it was Friday and that Arthur was unlikely to appear this side of midnight. Despite their massive fatigue there was only room for the children to be put to bed. Both Emma and David collapsed and fell into a deep sleep as only children can. The rest of the day was pure agony for Richard; who was in the doghouse with Joan, uncomfortable with George and so ashamed of himself he just wanted to find a corner and sleep. There wasn't one.

The put-you-up in the sitting room had not improved, so they didn't get a good night's sleep, despite their exhaustion. Joan, aware of Richard's discomfort, was on edge and their intimacy drained away in a pool of icy impatience. David missed the outdoor life and became fractious and miserable. He played off his Grandma against his parents, with a skill of which Machiavelli would have been proud. The visits to in-laws and relations swallowed up the following days. Emma was passed from female to female as each member of the Page tribe cooed and talked gibberish to her. Richard wondered how any child could develop any sensible speech at all in competition with this onslaught of "oodly doodlies" and "whoseaboofullthen".

Richard couldn't wait to be summoned to Head Office and escape this purgatory. He longed to talk of the business and maybe assess his chances of a move at the end of his third tour. At last the day came. He presented himself at the London Office of Universal Metals Plc in the heart of the West End. He had only one appointment with the HR people. He was received well by the Director of HR who was an urbane and engaging man. Much of their conversation was about wife and family and about Emma's health.

What did Richard expect of the future? Was he tied to Nigeria? How would he consider a move, at home or overseas? All these things were discussed. Richard became more and more convinced that something was in the air. He became quite excited, as his imagination ran away with visions of corporate grandeur. Despite this he tried to contain his euphoria and to remain clear and diplomatic.

What he wanted to shout was, 'Don't you people know how good I am? Haven't you heard about the hospital jobs? Don't you know that Universal Kaduna is one hundred per cent up because of me? Are you all deaf?' But he didn't, he sat patiently describing the lessons he'd learned and building a picture as subtly as he could, 'Here I am, I'm ready.'

"Well Richard, are you free for lunch?"

"Oh, yes, cleared the diary for the day."

"Good. There's someone who'd like to give you lunch, Frank Williams."

Did he hear correctly? Frank Williams, his heart leapt he gripped the chair involuntarily, oh wonder of wonders, to the feet of the almighty Frank Williams, oh joy unconfined.

"F..Frank Williams?"

"Yep. I'll get Mandy to take you to his office and I'll phone. He's expecting you."

They shook hands and the lovely Mandy, a Secretary of consummate looks, led him to an appointment with fame and fortune. As he focused on her gorgeous swaying behind his mind flew to other fields of executive bliss.

Frank Williams had the reputation of a lion, a man who worked hard and played hard, a man who was the most successful and youngest main Board Director in the Group. Richard had met him once, but much to his alarm he couldn't recall where or when. He hoped to God it didn't come up in conversation.

They walked the "golden mile", the corridor with the thickest carpet in corporate London. The walls were richly panelled with expensive works of art discreetly illuminating the way. Their footsteps sank silently into the carpet, the silence was eerie.

This was so far from the smell of factory lubricants and the clatter of machines; it was another world, a world Richard decided where he would fit, fit absolutely. William's office was close to Klitz's painting of the Radcliff Camera in Oxford. A tap on the door and Mandy waved him through.

"This is Liz Morgan, Mr. Williams' secretary."

Liz Morgan was forty, immaculately dressed, perfectly made up and absolutely in charge.

"Good morning Mr. Smiles." she extended her perfectly manicured hand, "Mr. Williams is expecting you, but he's on the telephone presently so perhaps you'll be good enough to take a seat."

"Thank you." he mumbled. This office was as grand an office as he had ever seen and this was the Secretary's. The walls were again panelled, but in a much lighter wood than the corridor outside. The furniture was expensive reproduction or even antique, he couldn't tell. There was a serenity that prevailed where the noise and grime of London was shut out. The impeccable and imperturbable Ms Morgan stood sentinel over her fiefdom. Even the phones rang with muted tones, here was order, here indeed were the corridors of power.

His anxiety grew, and despite the air conditioning his palms sweated. Frank Williams would see him once. It was do or die. One mistake and whatever opportunity there was behind that door; it would be his or lost and gone forever.

"Mr. Williams will see you now."

Frank Williams was a small neat man, with black hair, piercing eyes and with two fingers missing from his right hand. He spoke with a Cheshire accent and with something of a lisp. He looked directly at whomever he was addressing and was above all mercurial, quick and sharp. Time, to Frank Williams, was more than gold, each minute passed was an opportunity lost.

"Come in young man, take a seat." He came round the desk and extended his three-fingered hand. Richard tried desperately to shake it without any nuance of surprise or awkwardness. Williams slipped off his jacket, inviting Richard to do the same. Richard had no time to take in the grandeur of the office because Frank was already into his stride. He opened the file in front of him clearly labeled "Richard Smiles".

"You know what I do?"

"Well Sir,"

"Don't call me Sir, call me Fwank."

"Well apart from the fact that you control the European operations and also carry responsibilities for Mergers and Acquisitions, I'm afraid that's it," he hesitated, "Frank."

"Fair enough, that'll do for a start. Do you know how much the European Division contributes in turnover and profit to the group?"

"Around forty percent of turnover and forty seven percent of profit," another hesitation, "but maybe those figures are out of date."

"Yes and no, actually the profit figure is now approaching fifty percent. Do you know what Africa contributes?"

"Yes, about nine percent of turnover and very little profit."

"Well you should know your figures better than that because, you my lad have turned zero profit to some profit. Tell me about what you've been up to over the last two years."

Richard started nervously but got into the swing of it, gradually relaxing, even joking about some of the trials and tribulations of life in Nigeria. He chatted on for about a quarter of an hour. Frank interjected only once or twice with questions, but otherwise listened intently.

"Good, that's all very interesting stuff. When are you due to finish out there and come home?"

"I had imagined at the end of my next tour, October, that is if there's anything to come home to?"

"Well there won't be next October."

Richard's heart sank.

"I want you home by the first of April."

Richard's heart nearly leapt from his chest.

"Did you say next April? I'm not sure my existing boss, Edward Regan, will be too happy about that, but of course I'll do my best. .... May I ask what you want me to do when I return?" It was all too fast, what would Regan do? ....Who was Regan's boss?..... Yes, yes, yes, but what next.

"First, remember the statistics, if I want you home, home you'll come. Europe versus Africa is a mismatch. Second, we can easily get a replacement by then, I already have one Jeremy Thompson in mind." he smiled broadly. "What I want from you is hard work and some sharp thinking, in a job I can't name yet... but it will be a feather in your cap. All I can say right now is that it's a new venture and the job is pivotal to that success."

Richard was excited, confused and elated but uncertain. What job? How much? Where?'

"Where's your house now, near our Coventry plant?"

"I don't have one; we sold it before we went."

"Lousy advice you must have got."

"What about conditions, I mean Frank, of course I want to move onward and upward, but I need to tell my wife something. Actually, she's only just settling in over there." He wished he could have sounded less confused, but confused he certainly was.

"My boy the salary will be just one thousand over double what you earned when you left here two years ago. The location will be back in the

Midlands. Warwick is a good place to think about living near and you will be a subsidiary Director before your thirty third birthday."

He'd made it, his mind raced; Subsidiary Director at thirty three, Subsidiary Managing Director by thirty seven and a Main Board spot by forty. He could hardly believe it had happened.

Smoked salmon sandwiches and iced water were served for lunch. Richard was sworn to secrecy and told to go back to HR who would work out the details with his African boss, Edward Regan. Forty-two minutes after entering Frank Williams' office Richard emerged walking on air. Bollocks to Edward Regan. Wasn't life great!

Richard arrived back at the Page residence walking on air. Pleased as pleased could be.

"Darling, you won't believe it; I'm going to get a directorship as soon as we come back to the UK."

He hugged her but her response was not what he expected. There was no wild response, no reciprocation of the enthusiastic squeeze, just a limp, matter of fact, "Oh well done."

"What's more we'll be home by April and we can wash the dust of Nigeria off our feet."

"That's wonderful." Smiled Grandma Page.

"What do you mean? in April." Joan stood …unbelieving, confused.

"We're coming back to take up my new appointment in April."

"But we've got no where to live, we're all set up for another tour, you can't just pack up and come home…" She reddened, tears came to her eyes, "We can't do it, it's not possible we have nowhere to live."

"You can come here for a while." said dear Grandma Page.

Richard groaned inwardly. "We have plenty of time to buy a house and set up home, we're going to live near Warwick." He announced without thinking.

The blue touch paper that was Joan's emotional fuse was well and truly alight. She exploded.

"We're going to live near Warwick are we; we're coming back from Kaduna are we? God has spoken, ….and of course we'll all do as we're told. We'll change plans, countries, schools, houses and anything else that God dictates, thank you, you insufferably self centered shit."

Grandma Page sidled out of the room.

"But it's always what we wanted….."

Her slap rang, his head span, David screamed and Richard stood bemused and speechless. Joan turned and ran upstairs to the children's room and her cries of agony could be heard all over the house. Richard slumped into the armchair, David crawled up onto his lap and they sat in silence, both frightened in their different ways. They comforted each other.

"What's all this then," it was George, cigarette dangling from the corner of his mouth, the indispensable Sporting Life in hand. "I 'fink Joan's a bi' upset, what's it all abaa?"

"George, bloody women, I don't know... I've just had the biggest promotion of my life and the great news we're coming home sooner than we'd expected and your lovely daughter's gone berserk... I don' know George, I just don't know."

"Tell ye' what, let's go darn the Crown and 'ave a beer or three and celebrate, whadythink?"

"Good idea, Pop, Let's go." They set off in a new sense of comradeship, 'Pops' and 'Sonny' to drink a number of pints of 'London Pride' that of course Richard paid for. As each pint was consumed; the trenches of female opposition were deepened and reinforced. Their 'welome home' would be a rough one.

Joan cuddled Emma on the bed and received the relieved David to her lonely bosom. Oh why, oh why was Richard such a self-centered man, driven by his ambition, caring for nobody. He never dreamt that she had a view, he never thought about the home she dreamed of. He was a 'weekend father', yes he loved the kids, but only in his reserved way. They were fine as long as they were not in the way of what he wanted to do.

"Yes, mum, come in." Emily sat on the edge of the bed and stroked her daughter's leg.

"What's the trouble girl?... He's a good man, he's doin' well, he needs you to back 'im up, ya' know."

"I do, I do, but Mum he never shares with me he's always making decisions for me and the children, we never seem to talk things through."

"I know gal, but he's doin' well and you've got to look after 'im. ...... So be a good girl and try and see 'is point of view. Yo're a lucky girl, don't let it all get away."

Despite her mother's council Joan believed all men were bastards and she had better make her mind up to fight or she'd be submerged forever more in the wake of Richard's ambition.

Grandma Emily of course was delighted. The grandchildren would be close and safe.

The men arrived back, three sheets to the wind; George snorted a non-committal grunt and refocused on that day's "Sporting Life".

Uncle Albert, who'd arrived from work, thought it was brilliant that Richard was going up in the world and wondered what sort of car would be parked outside next year.

"A bleedin' Rolls, I shouldn't be surprised."

Over the next days Joan was reluctantly persuaded to go and look at the housing possibilities around Warwick and they were both surprised how house prices had risen since they had sold their home two years earlier. Indeed prices had almost doubled. Joan was dismayed at the sort of house that they could now afford, even with a handsome doubling of Richard's UK salary. They fought and bickered. Joan feeding on her anger, Richard for his part failed to understand how his wife couldn't share the excitement of his promotion.

They stopped at a small country pub, "The Black Lion" near a small village between Warwick and Stratford. They ordered a drink and sat miserably together in the empty bar. The Innkeeper was a rotund and jolly man born to his trade. He chatted to them, eliciting the purpose of their visit, their situation, number of children, counties of origin, Richard's job and much else besides, since strangers were everybody's business, particularly his.

" 'ave 'ee seen the Millhouse yonder that's up for sale, a bit down at heel, bu' a lovely aspect... school nearby an'all?"

"How much do they want for it?" asked Richard idly.

"Don' know tha'." said Fred their host, "Up for auction, tomorrow mornin'. You can look over it if ye' like, it's viewin' day sort of."

"No good I'm afraid," interposed Joan, "we've got to go back to London and the children."

" 'Old on a minute," Fred waddled from the bar and came back about three long minutes later with the auctioneer's brochure and description paper. "Look ye here this, what's it about, see what you think, my lady." He handed the brochures to Joan.

"Oh it does look gorgeous; oh look Richard isn't it pretty? Don't suppose we could afford it though."

It did indeed look the perfect picture portrait of an English country cottage, although a big one. It was not the whole of the Old Mill, but half of it, but the most interesting half, including an old mill wheel and stream running by. It had three bedrooms, only one family bathroom but stacks of room to build within the structure.

"It'll sell for a fortune." muttered Richard. "It's too expensive for us to even contemplate. Come on love, let's push off, there's a long way to drive."

They thanked their host and made their long journey back to London in tired silence, the Mill house papers stuffed in Joan's raincoat pocket.

The following day as they assembled for family breakfast, depression still hung over the disgruntled pair. Joan produced the Mill house papers and sighed, "Why don't we at least ring the Estate Auctioneer and see what he's expecting to get?"

"It's called a reserve, dear, a bloody reserve, that they'll easily get and we certainly won't be able to meet, not in a thousand years." Richard spat the words out demonstrating his aggravation and isolation. Who cared? It was all a pain in the ass.

He mooched around and promised to take David out. "Where to?" enquired Joan.

"Highgate Cemetery."

"Highgate Cemetery? Are you completely mad?"

"Highgate cemetery to see the tomb of Karl Marx. It suits my mood and at least it will be some sort of an education for David."

"You're absolutely barmy and you're not taking my son to any cemetery." She slammed the door.

Richard cursed and left the house to get a newspaper from down the road. He returned to find Joan getting the children ready to go out.

"Where are you going?"

"We're going to Waddington to see the Mill House. The reserve is twenty thousand and it has to go because of estate duties or something. Anyway the Auctioneer was very nice and told me to take our time and gave me his number and he'll meet us at the pub."

Richard was about to groan his disapproval when he saw Emily give him a wry smile. He mustered a smile, "Okay, let's go. Kids go the bathroom, David, nappies for Emma, quick march, off we go"

For the first time in many days they touched each other, nothing intimate, but a guiding hand on the back, both helped to pick up the same piece of luggage, their hands touched but they didn't recoil. They retraced their steps and at one o'clock they arrived at the "Black Lion", now full of locals consuming ale in a convivial and familiar atmosphere. The odors were different from the evening before, now there was the perfume of pipe tobacco and the whiff of cooking from the kitchen. Fred was glad to see them, ushered them to a small, family room and urged Richard to try his 'Speckled Hen' brew. He served them quickly, seemingly quite unperturbed by the children who so far behaved well. A splendid steak and kidney pie was served by Mrs. "Fred"; a woman as homely as her husband. She adored the children and stayed to chat to Joan.

Fred, in the meantime, in the time-honored manner of village landlords whispered the extraordinary detail of the Smiles to his 'regulars'. One at a time they ventured passed the family room, peering in and sizing up the potential newcomers. As Richard went to the bar and asked if he could phone the Auctioneer, Fred explained that there was no need, the Auctioneer, Mr. Jenkins, would pick them up at two.

With Richard somewhat the worse for wear from the "Speckled Hen" but Joan with a glint in her eye and the children happy, they followed Mr. Jenkins to the Mill House. The building was much bigger than they had imagined. It stood on the verge of a very narrow by-road, about half a mile outside the village of Waddington. An old willow tree sheltered the ancient mill wheel. Timbers were visible at intervals through the soft red brickwork and a slated roof followed the eyebrow eaves that once were thatched.

As they arrived the sun shone through, lighting a country picture, bathing it in magic. The Mill House was half the original great Mill that had stood on this site for five hundred years or so. The other half was occupied by an elderly couple named Watson, who'd lived there for twenty-two years. The contrast between the two halves of the large house was easy to see. The Watson's half was tastefully decorated, the exposed beams in the walls neatly delineated and the pointing between the ancient bricks was neat and tidy. The great oak door was well maintained with the cast iron fittings neatly blacked. The windows were clean and the curtains and window ornaments beckoned a welcome. A nameplate in cast iron, entirely in keeping with the medieval exterior, proclaimed "Waddington House" which suited its very substantial nature, for it was three storeys. The building stepped down to two storeys where Waddington House became the Mill House, adding to the individuality and charm of this ancient pile.

Mill House rather down at heel compared with its neighbor. The front door was nowhere near as grand, but still of framed panels of oak. The windows were wooden sashes of Georgian grace, but needed some repair. A path ran to the side of the house alongside the Millstream that had been protected by cast iron railings and hoops, which was a relief to the two parents.

Joan looked and loved the place. In an instant she saw it decorated and furnished. In her mind's eye there were bright curtains in the kitchen, sturdy fine pine furniture and the oak floor had been buffed and polished. For once this was hers to decide, she would make it hers because she wanted it. Richard would deliver, this time she would make it happen.

The garden was enormous, stretching at least one hundred and fifty feet back towards the farmland at the rear. Richard loved it too. How wonderful it would be to live here, not half an hour from Warwick, fifteen minutes from Stratford. It would be a fine address, and impressive place to entertain. Yes he loved it; it fitted his self image and his aspirations. A pretty village; a nearby infants' school; what more could they ask for? The down side was that the auction would probably yield much more for Mill House than they could afford. Secondly, it would take time and a lot of money to get the old house into a habitable condition.

Mr. Jenkins the Auctioneer explained at length that the house had been empty for two years since the death of the former owner. The heirs to the estate agreed that the house must now be sold and that a reserve price of twenty thousand would be their minimum expectation.

Richard explained their situation, mentioned his salary expectations and drew from Jenkins a view of the maximum mortgage he would be likely to raise, which he thought would be up to two and a half times salary, or eighteen thousand pounds. He didn't think raising such a mortgage would be a problem and assured Richard that he would be able to arrange such a loan on Richard's behalf.

The problem was that the auction date was set for the next Wednesday, could they bid on the expectation of raising the funds? Jenkins was very reassuring and said he thought it would be all right. Would they have to be at the auction? No, they didn't. They could bid on the phone or they could submit a sealed bid in advance that would be binding.

They agreed on the sealed bid idea and Richard and his excited wife retired to the car to talk through what they could afford. They pumped Jenkins for an idea of how many bidders he expected and what he thought would be a competitive bid, but he was very non committal, save that he hoped they'd be successful at something over the reserve.

Joan turned on her charm and eventually wormed out of him that only four other parties had been to see the Mill House.

They bid twenty one thousand pounds, which was more than they could afford. They drove back to London close to hysteria, would they or wouldn't they live in Mill House?

The days between their viewing and the auction dragged by. It was noticeable that Richard and Joan warmed to each other, sharing their hopes and anticipation for a new home and a new start. The sparkle was back, they touched each other; they held hands, they saw the Mill House in each others' eyes, they laughed and enjoyed just being together. Intimacy returned small step by small step, for the first time since their return they made love, despite the obstacles of the miserable put-you-up, it was warm, a mutual delight, freely given and taken. Apart from the excitement of the Mill House there was the adventure of getting away to Paris the following Friday, to celebrate or commiserate, but at least now they looked forward to the freedom of sharing each other.

As instructed, Richard rang the auctioneer at two p.m. on Wednesday. Joan hung on his arm, her ear pressed to the 'phone. Lewis was as charming as ever and sounded genuinely sorry that the Mill House had been sold to others for twenty four thousand two hundred and fifty pounds. There was a long silence. Richard put his arm round Joan and they both sobbed their disappointment alone in the hallway.

"Never mind, there'll be other places." He blew his nose.

"Why were we so daft as to dream we could get it?"

"We must never stop dreaming my sweet, so the search goes on."

The disappointment was deep, but it didn't drive them apart, it brought them together. The experience had taught them that despite everything a future without each other was unimaginable.

Emily, who'd never lived in anything other than a council house, saw their disappointment and did her best to cheer them up.

George grunted his views that "Twenty thousand is too much for an' 'ouse, cor blimey! It must have been Buckingham Palace."

Perhaps the Mill House was not to be theirs, but for Joan it would always be the place of salvation, the place where she fell in love with Richard all over again. It would always remain a magic place.

# CHAPTER 48

David played up before they left, but eventually they were free and away. They were to be in Paris for three nights. For such a stay Joan had seemingly packed enough clothes for three months. The journey was uneventful and they arrived late that afternoon in the small Hotel they'd booked in Montmartre. The room was tiny, almost completely filled by a huge double bed. There was nowhere to hang clothes, particularly the massive amounts that Joan had brought. The bathroom was also small, but at least it did have a bath, albeit of the sit in variety. Out their window was a charming view over the roof tops and if they craned their necks they could just catch a glimpse of the Sacre' Coeur.

They laughed about the peculiarities of Parisian hotels, tucked their suitcases under the bed, made love, dressed and wandered down the hill away from the main tourist area and had a delightful meal in a small bistro, they knew not where. They dined on oysters, jugged hare and lush French cheeses. They drank some delicious red wine and paid a gargantuan bill.

Hand in hand they walked back to Place Blanche, where they had a few drinks and some coffee on the sidewalk and eventually wandered innocently into a small cabaret club. The entrance fee was extortionate but what the hell, they walked in to the gloom and were shown to a table set in an alcove by the wall. A waiter immediately materialized out of the darkness, muttered something and placed a bottle of amazingly acid champagne on their table. Richard objected, but apparently it was all in the deal.

A slinky Chanteuse sang with a husky voice and the combo played with great musicianship. They sipped their ghastly Champagne and clapped when the singer ended her spot. It was then that they noticed that the club was full of men. There were one or two other women but at least half of those were hostesses.

Joan held his hand under the table as a tiny degree of apprehension overtook them. The next artiste was a stripper who, as far as Richard was concerned, was sensational. Joan at first objected and tried to leave but she was persuaded to sit and relax a little. One thing was certain; no one was looking at them. The stripper stripped, writhing over a chair and threatening to engorge a number of articles with a number of her physical attributes. It was very sexy, though Richard kept peeking to see what his wife's reaction was. She seemed fascinated and he felt her hand start to rub the inside of his thigh. She was as they say, turned on. Richard's response was almost too enthusiastic to control, but they played like adolescents feeling each other under the table.

The stripper was followed by a number of other acts, most of them bordering on being lewd. However, they enjoyed the decadence of it all, even consuming another bottle of the dreadful Champagne. They watched another gorgeous woman who was dressed as the devil down her right side and a peasant girl down her left. Her right half seduced her left half. The piece de resistance was a couple who simulated copulation, ending with the female administering oral sex; real or simulated it was hard to tell, much to the appreciation of the predominantly male audience. There was no rapturous applause at the end of the acts, simply a quiet almost reverent polite clapping, which reminded Richard of classical concerts held in Churches.

The love birds emerged from the club, their crotches sticky from prolonged foreplay. They dived into a taxi, arrived back at their hotel and ran to their room where they tore each others clothes off and made wild love to each other.

They woke to a dull drizzling Parisian morning. They ate mountains of fresh French bread with lashings of unsalted Normandy butter, washed down with cups of absolutely wonderful coffee. They made their way to Place du Tetre where the artists remained undeterred by the weather and spent an hour there, Joan diverting into the tourist souvenir shops to buy presents for the kids. They took the metro down to Isle de Cite, marveled at Notre Dame and strolled along the south bank as the watery sun peaked through. Their feet were tired and they enjoyed a light and forgettable lunch, Richard sinking several beers. They returned to their Hotel and, like a million honeymooners before them, made love and slept the late afternoon away. That night, they had tickets for the Lido and with a huge crowd of other tourists; they took their rather cramped seats for a pre-show dinner. Again, forgettable 'steak et frites'. They settled to the show, which for Richard was very much a reminder of the Casino du Liban, he could almost smell Leila's perfume. Go away Leila, go away, he silently implored but she remained stubbornly between them.

The show was full of bare breasted dancers, illusionists and even ice skaters. Waterfalls and lightening all added to the illusion of splendor, but it wasn't as good as the Casino du Liban.

On the other side of Joan sat a tall monacled Teutonic man, he was accompanied by a very attractive tall lady partner. Joan was wearing her best frock, a blue number with a low plunging neckline that accentuated her ample bust. She looked lovely, so lovely in fact her neighbor could not keep his eyes from peering down her cleavage. She put up with his close inspection for some time, but at the interval she swapped seats with Richard explaining that the lecher was becoming a nuisance. Richard grumbled but obliged to find that their neighbors did the same thing and now Richard was next to the tall willowy German lady. He thought no more of it, other than noting that she was a very handsome lady indeed. They settled down to the second half that was much like the first. Richard at first thought it was an accident, as he shifted his legs in the limited space, but there it was again. His ravishing neighbor was stroking his leg with hers. She was definitely playing footsy with him. He glanced sheepishly up and she smiled a conspiratorial grin. He didn't know what to do, excitement, guilt, all merged. Was he mistaken? No he definitely was not. He looked up again and then like a bucket of cold water he saw the lanky man, his monocle firmly clamped to his eye; wink a lewd wink. He jerked his leg away, and watched the rest of the show with his knees almost under his chin.

They left the Lido, it was still early but they were tired. They compared notes about their strange fellow Lido visitors and concluded that they were a couple of weirdoes.

The next day they did the Louvre, the Tuillerie Gardens and in the afternoon they ascended the Eiffel Tower. The weather was better and they loved the enchanting views from the top vantage point.

Their last night they spent on 'A Bateaux Mouches' which was absolutely delightful, the food was exquisite, the wines excellent and the music romantic. They could dance cheek to cheek as the great floodlit sights of Paris glided by. It was as perfect as they could wish.

"I'm sorry I won't be having another tour back to Nigeria." she whispered, "I shall miss Peter, Mohamed and Mussa."

"I shan't miss all the stress of trying to get things done, but I shall miss it too."

They talked about how they would mange their exit, there were still a hundred questions, buying a house, packing up, school for David, when should Joan come back, should she go back at all?

"Will you miss Sally and Malcolm?" she asked. It came like a kick to his stomach.

"Well they are moving on anyway."

"Yes, they are, and so must we." She looked into his eyes. "I've got over all that business now, you and Sally, but I have a confession to make too."

His heart pounded "Oh!... really" he responded with feigned calm.

"Yes, did you ever wonder why I didn't get mad and fight with Sally?"

"The biggest mystery of my life." His pulse pounded, what was coming? Had she been unfaithful too?

She snuggled closer to him and whispered in the tiniest voice, "She had me too."

He didn't understand, "What was that?"

She leant back, "Sally, she had me too, she made love to me as 'in bed'".

His feet stopped, they stood motionless on the tiny dance floor, he stared at his lovely wife. "Are you saying you had a relationship with

Sally?" He shook from his head to his feet. He tottered back to the table. "Waiter a cognac please."

"Two please." She sat opposite to him, looking composed and in control. Richard was speechless. This was something that had never crossed his mind, impossible, his sexy wife a damn lesbian. Had he got this right? Is this what she was saying?

The cognacs arrived. Richard gulped his down in one. Joan sat silently with an enigmatic little smile.

"Look," she said, "this is not the end of the world and it's not something that is so terrible. Sally and I just got a bit tiddly one lunchtime and we were comparing our wardrobes in their house. That's all."

"What do you mean that's all? For Christ's sake, if I said I'd been to bed with bloody Malcolm you'd wouldn't say 'well that's all'. How many times did you do whatever you did? Once, twice, a hundred times?"

"Once and a half actually, it really was just a get back at you. I don't know. I don't think I liked it all that much anyway. I am definitely a heterosexual and I love you."

After they returned to the Hotel Richard was still stunned as if he'd been hit on the head with a blunt instrument. He was numb. His mind raced but it raced nowhere. She tried to make love to him but he was cross and confused. He just couldn't find a way out of his disorientation and panic. He couldn't understand how his love, his familiar wife, the mother of his children, could do such a thing.

"Come on, if you're not susceptible to my feminine charms let's go downstairs and have a drink."

"I don't want a bloody drink." he sat petulantly on the bed. She sat on the windowsill looking out at the roof tops of Paris, seemingly determined to remain cool and in control.

"All right then," he eventually asked, "tell what happened, tell me how you and Sally could 'make it together'. Go on, I want to know the details, every fucking detail." The enemy of old returned, the jealous lust that had been so long conquered returned as if it had never been away.

"Are you sure, you want to know, it may upset you more?"

"Upset me more, are you kidding?" he snarled, "I want to know it all."

"Well I already suspected that you and Sally had been up to something, although I wasn't sure. We, by the way, were having a row because you were constantly buggering off to work, even when the kids weren't well. Sally, as you certainly know is a mischievous bitch, but I can't help liking her. Anyway, one night, when you were away, she tried to get me off with one of Malcolm's visitors, she really is wicked. It didn't work and I told her off. Then one day I was over there, Emma was asleep and we had a couple of gins and a sandwich lunch. Sally showed me her choice of dress for some Club do and asked me if I'd like to try it on, anyway I couldn't get into it. There I was stranded in my underwear and suddenly Sally's admiring my boobs and encouraging me to try one of her bras. Anything couldn't have been further from my mind until she started asking about our sex life, which by the way was pretty miserable at the time, which I confessed. She said who needed men anyway and before you knew it we were necking, from there it went into, well you know what…" She stared out of the window, as if he wasn't there.

"No I don't know. What? Tell me." He felt his sex rise. "Tell me everything, I want to know. I want to understand." He lied did he want to have a voyeuristic thrill? Did he want vengeance? He hated himself, and he didn't know why. How could he exorcise this whole bloody business, but his sex still rose.

"Well if you must know, in fact you do know how Sally is in bed. She was dominant and very sexy, she made me come and she made me make her too." Joan slurred her words, she enjoyed watch him squirm with jealousy.

"How, how did you make each other come?"

"What's wrong with you, Richard I'm trying to wipe the slate clean here and all you want is a sex story so you can go away and play with yourself." Despite her words she new she was turning the screw, he was suffering an ecstatic agony.

She unwound herself from the windowsill, pushed him back on the bed and undressed him. He didn't resist. He was hard, she took him in her hand, "Turned on are we? This is not the object Richard, I want us to be where we were yesterday, in love and together." She took his hand and slid his two fingers inside her, she offered her breast to his mouth, she played with his penis and she whispered, "Let's forget Sally, let's enjoy each other.  There is and never will be anybody else.  She pleased him every way she could, with every move she'd ever made, to ones she'd hitherto only imagined.  They made love for hours climaxing time and again, it was almost dawn when they gave in to sleep and the ghost of Sally Hetherington was exorcised.

# CHAPTER 49

They arrived back in London exhausted but renewed. Shagged out, some would say. They were greeted by their rowdy and excited son David who'd had a whale of a time, running his Grandparents ragged. Emily looked tired, David had obviously treated her like a constant play companion, another Mussa, at seventy-six she wasn't up to it.

The presents were received with glee, though George was unimpressed with a bottle of good cognac. Uncle Arthur though, mumbled his appreciation for his bottle of "Ricard" and confessed that he would love to go back to France. The last time he'd been there, he spent his time carrying dead bodies off the Dunkirk beaches.

"Din't see much of de' country." he mumbled, "Couldn't get off the beach." He blew his nose and that was the end of his war commentary.

Emily said with a great sense of understatement, "I can see the break did you a bit of good, enjoyed yourselves, I expect."

"Bognor." said George, "What's wrong with Bognor? Good enough for your mother and me."

"A bit cold this time of year." answered the diplomatic Richard. They laughed.

Their thoroughly chaotic situation demanded that Richard spend as much time as possible clarifying what he should and could do in relation to his new appointment. Frank Williams had only vaguely briefed the HR department and as was his custom, disappeared off to one of his ventures between Harlow and Hungary. Quite by chance, Richard once more found himself in the capable hands of Miss Joanna Elliot. Fortunately he remembered the name of the lady who'd been so efficient and considerate when his father, Percy, had passed away.

"Miss Elliot," he gushed as he handed over a large bunch of flowers, "this is just a small token in return for your wonderful support last year."

Miss Elliot, in her late fifties, plain and austere, was his forever. She sat him down in her modest office and led him through all the issues that could arise, from bridging loans to insurance, from travel for the family through returning personal effects from Nigeria, retrieval of stored household effects in the UK to continuity of pension. She was without doubt a treasure, the sort of treasure seldom appreciated. She turned down an offer of lunch, but agreed she'd love to take lunch soon when she had the opportunity to meet Joan. Two days later Joan was hustled up to the West End offices and did her part in buttering up Miss Elliot. Time had flown, still they had no idea where they were going to live and still they hadn't been down to Wales to see Muriel.

Muriel had aged. Loneliness had etched its miserable way into her defenses. Her eyes had lost a facet of their sparkle, although they saw it flicker strongly at the sight of the children. Her humor was as quick as ever, but with a laconic end, an echo of quips no longer shared. Here was a testament to love, an aching of things missed, but at peace from things locked forever in her memory. Her sadness tempered with thanks, her emptiness satisfied by the feast of passed joys.

She was overjoyed at the news that they were soon to return to England, it was as if a burden was lifted at the news. The stoop of advancing years visibly retreated, her back straightened, her step quickened. On this leave they had not been able to get a house near Muriel, they were some twelve miles away, but they took every care to be with her each day. There was barely time to settle, just one night out for Richard at his old rugby club, a dinner with some old friends and a couple of days devoted entirely to Muriel. Otherwise it was constant phone calls to Estate Agents, Head Office, and Nigeria.

Despite the resilience of her humor and her adoration of the grandchildren, Muriel had the inevitable moments of depression. Here was her only son, seemingly gone from her forever. Here was her only son, loving his own family, making his way; her only contribution now was as occasional babysitter and burden of worry to them. How could they care for her? Why should they?

Sometimes she was bitter and sharp.

"Go, go, find a home a hundred, a thousand, miles away from me, who cares?"

It was difficult for Joan, who was more sensitive to Muriel's loss than Richard. She understood how deep the void, how black the abyss. She was a woman who, like Muriel had decided at an early age to give her life to her husband and children. How awful it must be to see them taken away. Richard was so insensitive sometimes. He got away with a lot because of his charm and his gift of words, but often he was self centered and focused always on tomorrow, never on today.

Indeed they had to dragoon her into child minding whilst they made two further attempts at house finding in the Warwick area. Richard had seen several properties he liked, but Joan was adamant that they would live where she and the children had the best quality of life and she would not compromise her vision. This vision encompassed schools, reasonable proximity of shops, a community to share, yet near or in the countryside. These ideals were firmly cemented into place by the Mill House that matched almost to perfection her desires. The prospective home either met her finite list of requirements or not. Any efforts to compromise them were sternly rebutted. Richard's renowned shortness of patience was tried to, and passed its limit.

It emerged during their visit that Muriel's sister Brenda, was soon to retire from her nursing career. She had tended to the mentally retarded in the darkest parts of Liverpool for many years; she was a senior Sister who had always been very close to Muriel in spirit, if not in geographical proximity. Brenda had indicated that she would be happy to retire to South Wales and share the cottage that had ample room for two.

When Richard learned the news of Brenda's intentions, it came as a great relief. He genuinely believed that this event would be best both for Muriel and Brenda. He suspected too, to his everlasting shame, that this would take from his shoulders a burden he did not relish carrying.

Muriel though, aware of all the contradictions; and in a moment of quiet firmness, put their minds to rest; "I know I've been a bit of a bitch sometimes, but it's only because I want you with me more. I know that

that can't be and now that Brenda's coming, you needn't worry too much about me. I know you do, but we shall be fine." There was a relaxed silence as Richard and wife supped their tea. "You don't know how pleased I am that you're coming home, as long as you come and see me sometimes and maybe take your old mother for a break now and then." She smiled an impish smile. "Then we shall all be fine."

Joan moved from her chair and gave the old lady a warm embrace, "You are the kids' Grandma Smiles, we'll see lots of each other," she paused, "if we can find a damn house."

They all laughed, but it wasn't that funny.

The problems of their exit from Nigeria were difficult, the next tour would only be four months and someone had to be buying a house in the UK ready for their return. Things out there had to be packed up and at the same time they needed to get a stable base for David, whose first school was due in September when he would be four and a half.

Emily and George had the accommodation for the kids and Joan was content to stay there once more, however, there was a lot of domestic clearing up to do in Kaduna and no doubt Regan would put Richard through the mill and expect a meticulous handover.

Richard's first telephone conversation with Regan was not a pleasant one.

"Richard, I'm disturbed at the news, of course you realize that this will have to be negotiated through me."

"Naturally" Richard made faces at the 'phone, David howled with laughter.

"What's that?"

"Sorry Edward, kids, messing about."

"As I was saying, I expect that you maybe, only maybe mind you, be released by the half year, say June, what do you think?"

"Edward you've made it abundantly clear, it's not what I think that's important, it's you and Frank Williams. I will do as I am told."

There was a silence, "Uhm, I'll talk to Frank, I'm sure we'll work something out." Another silence. "Look here old man I've been quite delighted by your performance here and I was going to review your emoluments, quite generously actually and also I was going to send you to

Nairobi on a project actually, so it's all in the melting pot, see what I mean old man? There's a future for a good man here you know."

"Thank you Edward, but as we said it's between you and Frank, I can't discuss what he's offered but I'd like to take it. Edward it's a big chance for me."

"You're all the bloody same, come out here for me to train you and then off. You all bugger off because it's too bloody tough." Edward had lost it. He was mad and he was petulant. He continued, "What bloody job have they offered you anyway?"

"I can't say."

"You can't say, I'm your boss and if I want to know you'll bloody well tell me, do you understand?" He bellowed all the way from Lagos, the 'phone in Wales shuddered.

"I'm sorry Edward; you'll have to talk to Frank."

"That bastard's never there. He's a bloody cowboy, you wait and see, anyway you're on a posting here and you have a contract, if you've got any honor you'll abide by it."

"Sorry Edward you'll have to talk to Frank."

"I bloody well will." The phone went dead.

After innumerable consultations with the ubiquitous Miss Elliot, tickets were reconfirmed and the whole family got ready to return to Kaduna. They decided that they would remain in Nigeria together over Christmas and that Joan and the children would come back to the UK around the end of January, beginning of February. They would return to Grandma Page's and Joan would resume house hunting. Miss Elliot, or Joanna as she now had become, would ensure all support measures would be in place. Joanna would also keep in touch, on the "q-tee" as she put it, with Liz Morgan to monitor the diplomatic crisis between Frank and Edward. Not for one moment did anyone even entertain the idea that Regan would win this battle, and all proceeded accordingly.

The uncertainty of it all unsettled everyone, not least David who was confused about all this moving and rushing about and hearing all this talk about leaving his paradise in Galadima Road. Emma, at sixteen months, was too young to know what was going on but nevertheless sensed all the changes and began to loose her sleep pattern.

The "leave" had hardly been restful. They were exhausted before they set out for their last trip together to Kano and then Kaduna. Flights now departed from Gatwick airport, which meant a long and laborious drive through the southern suburbs of London. The traffic was as thick as treacle; they limped into the car hire return with bad tempers and balling children.

# CHAPTER 50

Jeremy Thompson had been a success. At least Eke and Adegbulu thought so. He had kept the place going well, even very well. Richard was slightly put out. He didn't resent the young man's successes and during the hand over week, he persuaded himself that he'd been the catalyst that liberated Thompson's talent. Richard was immediately aware that the younger man had mellowed in the short six weeks that had passed. He had been bright enough to listen, learn and put into practice sensible and useful improvements. He was obviously infinitely better than Richard at detail and had sharpened up a number of administrative procedures that Richard had simply accepted and perpetuated.

He was still a trifle arrogant for Richard's taste, but he seemed to get on with the locals extremely well. Whilst he was less familiar, indulged in less banter, he was consistent and reliable. The Nigerians praised these qualities beyond all others; they looked to the senior mangers to bring order and consistency to an otherwise chaotic world. It was something of a salutary experience for the returning Smiles to find that in this regard, he was far from perfect.

Still he was not unhappy and made an effort to get closer to Jeremy, he took him home for dinner and spent a little time drinking, but this time not competing. Jeremy expressed his pleasure at the experience but looked forward to returning home. Above all it had been a lonely for him, stuck in the Hamdalah Hotel with no social life.

The news of Richard's imminent departure had not yet filtered through and Thompson had no idea of Frank William's plan to return him as a permanent feature to Kaduna. In fact, Richard believed that Kaduna was an unsuitable post for a single person, particularly one with Thompson's drinking skills.

No sooner had Jeremy left for the UK than the order came to attend Edward Regan in Lagos. Richard knew the confrontation was coming and dreaded it. Richard sat through an unpleasant two hour meeting with his boss, who ranted on about loyalty, perfidy, trust, unseemly ambition and a number of other qualities either expected or absent. He then went on to offer a range of very generous incentives that would normally be very tempting. However, Richard had nowhere to go, even if he wanted to. He had pledged his future to the most powerful man in Universal. Any doubts or hesitation would result in his career prospects being consigned to the dustbin.

Regan had turned on the heat. He had even booked lunch for them at the Boat Club where they arrived with both men trapped in intransigent silence. They sat on the terrace and watched the muddy tide roll by. They ordered beer, breaking Regan's rules, and swigged in the lengthening silence.

"What's that?"

"What's what?"

"That over there; floating in the water."

Perhaps one hundred yards away, perhaps one hundred and twenty, there floating on the muddy surface was the unmistakable dead human body. It was clear, a male, stout and strong, black and muscled, but dead. Face down clad in a white singlet and blue shorts, it or he, floated by. The sight was awful. No one else, except Richard, seemed to dwell on it. The members had a look and then returned to their lunches or drinks. Richard remained stock still, fascinated and horrified.

"Is no one going to do anything?" he asked Edward urgently.

"What's to do?"

Then around the bend came a police launch, it approached the floating cadaver. The policeman took a grappling hook, turned the body over, said something to his colleague and pushed the body onward out to sea where it would be nobody's problem.

Richard sat, silent and shocked. Was life so cheap? Yes he knew it was. Another beer,

"No lunch, thank you Edward."

"Oh come on old boy, lovely prawns here; you won't often get the chance."

Richard had a strong desire to throw his beer over Regan. God what years out here did to you. He was going home and no one would change his mind. He wondered idly if anyone expected the floating body home for lunch, was there a youngster waiting for Dad to come home? Regan munched his prawns.

"Edward, I'm sorry you're pissed off about my impending move, but I'm afraid it's cast in stone, I'm going, and I'm going when Frank Williams says I must go. If you can agree a date with him, that's fine with me. But I'm going, so I don't want to get into a pissing contest with you, or be involved in some dispute between you and the great Frank."

Regan put up his hand.

"Let me finish my say, Edward. I think it best if you and I work hard to find a good replacement and organize a good hand over. There's a lot of business in the pipeline, so we don't want to screw it up, right? Look, I'm sorry it's all so rushed but that's life and I can't jeopardise my re-entry into the mainstream or I could be stuck here for ever."

As soon as the words were out of his mouth he regretted them. He tried to recoup.

"What I mean Edward…"

"What you mean Richard is that you think the African Region is for no-hopers like me." he sighed, "You may be right." he waved away the waiter, "You may be right, but it's where I'm going to end my service, a has-been who never was."

"Sorry Edward, sorry."

They drank up and left to return to the office, Richard looked back and saw the body now a speck floating away into the Bite of Benin.

They spent the rest of the day in a conference call to London, assessing potential candidates to succeed Richard. There were few, Thompson amongst them, apparently there was a fiancée in the wings but the London end weren't at all sure what his marital plans were. It was also agreed that Richard's departure would be gazetted the following week so that recruitment could be commenced.

He returned to Kaduna with relief. He felt he'd won his battle and that the air had been cleared and his own position clarified. He was now happy to focus on sustaining the business and leaving with his reputation in tact. Family matters, yes families do matter, would also need a good deal of sympathetic handling. No doubt that Joan would soon feel the strain of uncertainty close in on her. He needed to prepare to support her as best he could, but she would have to return to England without him and take on the responsibility of buying a house.

# CHAPTER 51

Back in Kaduna little had changed. Malcolm and Sally had gone on to pastures new, they had been succeeded by another couple who were altogether different. Younger, duller and the lady as plain, as plain could be. The Smiles' did their best to be kind and attentive but they seemed self reliant and almost suspicious of the Smiles'.

The Club continued to flourish. The Golf Club planned a new initiative to hold a northern Nigerian Golf Championship and no one else had expired since Henry's untimely exit. A few faces had changed, but otherwise corruption continued to flourish, chaos was at home and inter-tribal murders continued unabated. The rains had been good so the country looked greener. Social invitations began to arrive as news of their return spread.

The Solomon's, Gombes, and Coopers all invited them to dinner within a fortnight of their return and they accepted them all. Richard confident in the new found solidity of his marriage.

The Coopers dinner was the most extraordinary feast they'd ever been to. Billy Cooper had aged as his 'habits' continued to ravage his physique. He looked an absolute wreck. He'd put on a lot of weight, his skin looked yellow, as if he was stained by cigarette smoke, his eyes were bloodshot and his hands shook. As if to pretend that nothing was amiss he greeted his guests with charm and warmth. Janice seemed quite unchanged and cruelly unconcerned about the irreparable sinking of her husband. She wore a revealing low cut number that only succeeded in drawing attention to her inadequate breasts.

The Gombes were there, Anna as delicately beautiful as ever and John suavely attired and full of his own importance. He made for the Smiles' and started where he had left off,

"Welcome back Richard," he smiled staring at Joan. He turned to kiss her on the cheek and she in the tiniest of movements, indicated a coolness that was barely noticeable but at the same time inescapable.

The Cooper's house; once splendid, was a shambles. Furniture was strewn in bizarre patterns as if there had been a bar room brawl. Pictures hung at crazy angles and dust lay everywhere. In contrast, the bar set out on the terrace of a once lovely garden, was well stocked and organized. Two stewards plied the guests with any drink they asked for, from Tequila Sunrises to Harvey Wall bangers, Champagne was well chilled and Star beer was dispensed in iced mugs. The food was also copious, but for all its quality and serious quantity, it had been dumped onto a huge buffet with little thought. Booze was the focus of the household, money was plentiful, cleanliness was unimportant and food an incidental, but booze and more booze was the centre of this curious place.

The guests had been hand picked to do justice in this temple to alcohol. They drank the liquor with the enthusiasm of the committed, their conversation strident within minutes of arrival. The worn faces of old warriors that had been soaked in gin; like animated gargoyles, filled the surreal room. There were exceptions, Anna and Joan to name but two, but the majority threw themselves into the orgy of drinking and as the night wore on they got drunker and drunker. Booze spilled from waving glasses held by swaying topers onto carpets and shirtfronts and furniture. Janice Cooper hunted relentlessly for a man, any man. She had to move fast as alcoholic stupor blunted what sexual desire she hoped to find. Likewise, John Gombe circled the party of forty or so, making eyes and contacts with old conquests and attempting to attract new ones.

Richard ranked himself as a good middle order drinker and recognized on arrival that he was out of his depth; however, he was a top order trencherman and had little competition at the massive buffet. He ate handsomely, he and Joan with Anna alongside, retreated to another room with their captured food and an excellent bottle of French Claret and enjoyed an eccentric dinner, not five yards from the bacchanalian orgy next door.

Anna, they thought, looked sadder than ever, childless and helplessly trapped with her foreign and philandering husband. Locked away forever in the hopelessness of this prison, so far away from her home.

On the way home they held each other in the back of the car, "God, aren't we lucky, we've got each other and we've got a future."

She snuggled deeper into his shoulder.

"Not much future there tonight, all misspent past and pretty glum too. All too sad and all too dreadful, my love. I feel like the man in 'A Christmas Carol'. We've been shown the ghost of Christmas to come."

"I saw it a long time ago." she kissed him.

They were not surprised to learn a few days later that Billy Cooper had been flown back to England in a futile effort to save his wasted life. He died three weeks later despite the best medical support money could buy. Wealthy, well educated, intelligent and athletic, all had been thrown away to the demon drink. Talents and attributes that many would have given their lives for, drowned in so many pink gins. They never heard what happened to Janice Cooper. They imagined that she'd taken her inheritance and ensnared a submissive and alcoholic sex slave. The memory of the Coopers faded as quickly as a tropical twilight.

Richard charged around his responsibilities with a renewed vigor. His victory over Edward Regan, , drove him on to deliver what he had promised. He and Mohamed drove thousands of miles around the north to Sokoto and Kano and Maiduguri.. The contracts were monitored, the planning meticulous, the factory scheduled precisely and imported materials reviewed and cyclical orders put in place.

Despite all this, there came no official announcement of his impending move to the UK. He rang London as often as he dared, apparently there was a problem finding a replacement for Smiles. It was all very frustrating as the clock ticked on and they were marooned in a no man's land. Perhaps Edward Regan was winning after all, if no replacement was found, would they still ship him home? After all, it would be Regan who would decide if a candidate was suitable. Was the old sod being difficult to assert his authority, to dare Frank Williams to force a decision and jeopardize his regional performance, which would surely be a political win for Regan.

Richard told himself to trust in Williams. He had the power, there lay the glory. The strain began to tell, the long hours, the obsession with getting a hand-over that would be above any criticism made him tiresome and irritable. He was hardly ever home, working from early morning to late at night. When he did appear he was tired and irritable, had little time for the children and little sympathy with Joan who shared the burden of uncertainty. All the long journeys, miserable food and too many beers, exacerbated his hemorrhoids that were now a constant pain.

The break for Christmas was welcome but anticlimactic. Richard joined the workers for their Christmas party held in a makeshift tent at the Kikuri sports field. Nearly everybody turned up and there was a liberal dispensation of beer and palm wine. Richard thanked them all for their efforts during the year and told them he thought the future was secure. Eke and Mbamane translated for those who found English difficult, the men and women seemed pleased but didn't want the speeches, they wanted to get to the wine, beer and food. The food was barely recognizable to Richard. A market "Mama" having produced two massive cauldrons of goat stew and pots of yams and ochra and other grub, much enjoyed by the team. Richard gingerly took a plate of the goat stew that was surprisingly good, though he didn't care for the yam. Some of the men drank heavily and as if they were in a race, whilst others did not drink at all. Adegbulu stayed sedately at Richard's side, sheltering in his boss's shadow, avoiding mixing with the "workers" who he saw as a class below his station. Eke circulated easily, nodding and talking in any or all the dialects and languages of the hundred or so gathered. Richard marveled at his calmness and linguistic skills and how these talents settled so easily alongside his fierce tribal identity.

Richard set out to follow in Eke's wake, to circulate and wish every one individually a "happy Christmas", however he found it increasingly difficult to understand each fragment of conversation as he made his way through the increasingly drunken crowd.

Furthermore, the crowd seemed to be growing by the minute. Surely they didn't employ this many people. He pressed on talking to those he thought he knew.

"Well, happy Christmas to you and your family, are you traveling?"

"Sah, aynogodeeplace, fit fine proper, she be no der Sah."

"Good, have a good time." He moved on to exchange another incomprehensible nonsense with the next person.

He dutifully approached the next person, about the twentieth, the man shook his hand, exchanged a fairly understandable conversation about his wives and family, when Richard asked, "How long have you been working at Universal?" The man looked perplexed and spoke in deep pidgin. Richard again lost the thread, shook hands and moved on.

Eke, sidled up to him, "Mr. Smiles I think we should go now, Sir."

"Go? Now? Why? I haven't got round to all the employees yet. By the way, I think you should stick close, I don't recognize them all or recall their names."

"That is the problem, Sir, half these people are from the town Sir, and they do not work for us."

"Shit, Eke, how come you chose this location, what are we going to do?"

"Do, Sir?" Eke shrugged his shoulders. "We can do nothing; soon there will be hundreds more here."

"Dear God, are you telling me we're feeding the whole bloody town?"

"No, it's just that the word's got out and people will come. They will bring more palm wine and some will bring food, it will be a big party."

"Oh shit. Have all our people had something to eat and drink?"

"Yes, I think so, Sir. So, I think we should go now."

Richard waved; to whom he was not sure, they may or may not have worked for him. The number of strangers had confused him; he was no longer sure who was a worker and who was not. Everyone suddenly looked remarkably alike; he made a hurried exit across the field where Mohamed stood guarding the sparkling Peugeot.

On Christmas Day the children enjoyed their presents and so did Peter who was given a bonus and some new shoes. Alhaji Usman came with gifts for his Christian friends and received, with obvious delight, a copper plaque with Islamic inscription, which Richard had been assured, was authentic. He was relieved when Usman confirmed that this was indeed a saying from the Holy Koran.

Joan and Richard indulged the children the whole day. Richard took time out to read them the nativity story and they sang along with the

Christmas Carol service on the T.V. A full traditional Christmas lunch was served, albeit in the evening and Peter was invited to sit at the table. He politely refused.

They invited John and Anna over for Boxing Day lunch, more for Anna's sake than John's. She played with the children and they had a decent sort of day, John Gombe working hard to hide his boredom, though not quite succeeding.

It was in the following week that the breakthrough came, a call at home from Joanna Elliot assured Richard that his appointment would definitely be gazetted that next week and that he was authorized to make an announcement in Kaduna. It was a huge relief and they went to the Solomon's New Year's Eve party delighted to broadcast the news that they were on their way back to the UK. The party went with a swing; Joan was, as always, chased by Hosi Solomon.

Gabby was charming to them both and expressed her envy, 'Oh, 'ow I miss Monte Carlo.'

John Gombe spent most of the evening smooching with a young French woman, the wife of a new manager of C.F.A.O. the big French trading company in West Africa. Richard watched and had to remind himself that he was no longer in the game, but she did look delicious. Richard engaged dear Anna in a series of dances and had to break off a number of times to relieve Joan of the attentions of the ever-persistent Hosi. The food and drink was terrific and they enjoyed a lovely evening. At twelve o'clock they slipped away on to the patio and embraced and kissed and promised that tonight would be the beginning of an eternity together, wherever fate would take them.

"Come on let's go home and really celebrate the New Year." She teased him with her tongue. It was not to be, they were swept up in a conga, in handshakes and kisses and all the razzmatazz of what is expected at New Year parties. They danced and joked and flirted and drank into the early hours, it was a great New Year party.

They planned Joan's departure; their personal effects were packed with very few things left to warm the house after their departure. The house took on a bleak air, made worse by the shining cleanliness. It assumed the ambience of a Doctor's waiting room.

Richard still sustained his frantic work schedule, much to the bemusement of Eke and his staff who could see no reason why the boss drove himself so. But drive he did, despite the sickness that had invaded his body. Joan nagged him to go and see Eli, he never had time, he had meetings, clients to see, contracts to sign, and things to do. As the weeks went by Richard suffered like he'd never suffered, each day was agony, defecating was such a dreadfully painful experience he stopped eating in the hope that the less went in, the less came out.

Two weeks to go before Joan's departure, Richard rested prone in a warm bath, a lazy Saturday, a weekend of rest. They had been invited to the club for a farewell dinner for Joan that evening with those many friends and acquaintances they'd enjoyed over the last two years. The phone rang, it was a poor line, Peter struggled and Joan intervened.

"Yes, this is Mrs. Smiles... Who? I'm sorry... could repeat that please?"

Richard moved painfully up the corridor, he heard her, "Mr. Lewis, Mr. Lewis the Auctioneer, yes of course I remember... What? The Mill House? ... Are you sure? Yes, oh yes. What's your number? Yes, we'll be back to you or through Richard's Company, but definitely yes."

She listened some more, waving the curious Richard to one side. She put the phone down and leapt at him throwing her arms around him.

"Yes, yes.... oh there is a God and we should love him. The Mill House, those bidders couldn't come up with a completion, so would we let our bid stand? It's ours." She kissed him and squeezed him. He said nothing, but held her tight. This was wonderful news.

Despite his miserable stomach problems that seemed to get worse by the day, they worked feverishly to get Joan and the kids ready to return to the UK. She had to be in Waddington within ten days to sign the contracts on the Mill House. They had to arrange with their bankers, with the backing of Universal, a bridging loan to complete within a further twenty days. Joan's planned departure was brought forward and the following Wednesday, having supervised the packing up of all her personal effects, which were to be shipped overland and sea, they said a tearful farewell.

The surprising strength of feelings caught both Richard and Joan by surprise. It was all brought to a head as Joan and the children prepared to leave Galadima Road for the last time. Peter stood, his lower jaw trembling. Joan gave him a hug and they both started to weep. Mussa was also deeply upset and David ran to his side and asked if Mussa could go with them.

The journey to Kano was broken at the Zaria Club, purportedly for refreshment, but Richard went to the loo where he vomited violently. His miserable stomach and aching piles, the repetitive fevers, the now regular bilious attacks, scared him but he was determined that his illness, whatever it was, shouldn't interfere with the plans for repatriation. Joan of course had recognized some of the problems, but he'd been successful in masking the worst of his symptoms. The fevers had been the easiest to shrug off, as long as they didn't attack at night. Vomiting he confined to secret sessions and he was careful with his laundry.

On this occasion, however inopportune, he didn't get away with it.

"Richard you look ghastly, have you been sick again?"

"Nothing to worry about, it was something I ate." He replied lamely.

"Right, we're not going, we're going back to Kaduna and you're going straight to Dr Eli. Come on; drink up David we're taking Daddy home."

"Jesus, love, don't be ridiculous. Look, I promise I'll go and see Eli this very day, immediately I return from Kano. Promise!"

"Richard it's just not worth it. I've been worrying about you for weeks. It's just not worth it. I don't want the Mill House to live in as a widow and the kids want their Dad."

She tapped her foot absently and glanced at her watch. Time was getting tight. "If you don't go to Eli today, just don't bother coming home in any state, do you understand? If you put your stupid job before me and the kids that's it, do you understand?"

"Come on, we'll be late." He felt rotten.

The farewells were tense. Joan wept more out of anger than sadness and David simply wanted to go on the aero plane. Joan commanded that Mohamed take the "Master" as soon as possible today, to Doctor Eli.

He promised the Madame, gave both the children a small wrapped present, took Madame's hand, bowed, not quite kissing it. His tear dropped gently, to where a kiss would have been, she felt its moistness more poignant than any affected farewell, she embraced him.

"Mohamed, you have been our best friend, but now you must look after Richard, I beg you do not let him bully you, he must go to Doctor Eli." She took from the boot of the car the parcel she had brought, it contained a fine white Agdaba, It consisted of the finest lace embroidered suit that would be fine to grace any occasion.

She turned to Richard, "Look you obstinate bastard, we love you, but for once you're going to do as you're told." She hugged him, almost squeezing the breath from him, the agent and porter allowed one more cuddle with each child and they disappeared through the departure barrier.

# CHAPTER 52

The truth was that Richard new full well what ailed him, he was frightened not of the ailments but the treatment. All those jokes about piles as excruciating as having babies, and that the operation was so terribly painful, braver men than he had wept. He was ashamed to admit to himself that although he'd entrusted Joan to the medical powers that were available in Kaduna to have a baby, he was less than comfortable with the idea of the charming Hamdi routing around in his behind.

They arrived at the Surgery to find that Doctor Eli was not there and that he would return in an hour or so. It was the "or so" bit that bothered Richard. Had the Doctor taken his golf sticks? Apparently not, so there was hope. They waited, Mohamed obdurately refusing to leave the medical compound. Richard sat sweating as another bout of fever swept through him, biliousness welled up and he began to fantasies about what he was sure was his impending end.

He dreamed of Eke supervising the fabrication of his coffin, of Joan in raincoat and black veil, still looking sexy, greeting his body at the airport. He saw the Mill House, children playing in the summer sun and three settings for the Sunday lunch. Piles be damned, it must be cancer, the big C. Would it be worse how much pain and horror lay before him. He was afraid.

"Hello, Richard, you look a bit ropey." Dr Eli walked passed the bench of waiting patients, "Give me a minute and I'll be with you."

Their meeting was short. Richard explained his symptoms, reluctantly confessing his agonizing haemorrhoids. Eli tut-tutted away as he peered up Richard's rectum and asked Richard about the history of his sore bottom. He took blood samples. After less than ten minutes he told the exhausted and agonized Richard to wait outside. A further half hour elapsed.

"Richard, is your driver with you?"

"Yes." Funny question thought Richard.

"You are very unwell, brought about I must say by your own pigheadedness. I have seldom, if ever, seen worse haemorrhoids than yours You must have been in agony for months and how you've gone on without coming to see me defies all good sense."

"Sorry," mumbled Richard.

"I'm afraid you're going to be sorry. I want you to go home, pack a bag and report to Kikuri Hospital before seven. Not only is your behind a mess but you've succeeded in infecting your system. Septicemia could have killed you in another ten days or so. You have no choice now other than to undergo a regime to clear this infection up prior to a haemorrhoidectomy as soon as you are well enough."

"There's nothing else is there?"

"Isn't this enough?"

"No, I mean there's nothing else lurking? You know, cancerous?"

"Not as far as I'm aware, nothing indicates that. Look Richard, you've got enough to worry about, so stop fantasizing, I assure you that recovering from your present situation will be arduous enough"

"How long will all this take?"

"Depends how quickly your infection clears up, two to four days and then if you're fit enough the operation and then another week, and then some rest, say three weeks."

"Three bloody weeks is impossible."

"Has Joan gone yet?"

"Yes, today actually."

"We could send you home, particularly after the antibiotic therapy, if you like?"

"No, out of the question I've got about eight weeks left to finish here, I've got to be here."

"Right be a good boy." he handed Richard some pills and water which he took, "see you in Kikuri at seven."

"Seven it is."

Sister Theresa greeted him like an old friend and showed him to his room. He got into bed and felt relieved that at last there was an end in sight, albeit his bottom end and sureness about the future. Eli turned up at closer to eight than seven, armed with an array of medicines and the results of the blood tests. He administered an injection deep into Richards stressed buttocks and discussed dietary requirements with the good Sister.

"Be good, do as sister tells you. You can receive as many visitors as you like, but you'll be very tired and you need the rest. Remember, the more rest you get the quicker we can get on with your treatment."

Sister Theresa fixed up a drip and placed it painlessly into his arm and Richard slipped off into a deep and peaceful sleep for the first time in months.

The following morning Eke and Adegbulu appeared at the bedside of Smiles, Adegbulu looking particularly pained to find his boss in such a state. He looked embarrassed to find himself peering down at his bedridden superior; he wrung his Moslem hat, nervously shifting from one foot to another, staring down at the floor.

"Gentlemen, you find me at a disadvantage, but it won't be for long and I'm sure we can continue as normal. It'll be up to you to run things and seek my support for anything you believe I can help with. Until further notice I'd like us to meet each morning, here, and then perhaps one of you could pop in on your way home in the evenings."

They readily agreed. Eke announced that Regan was to fly up the following Monday and spend two or three days in Kaduna. Richard groaned inwardly at the thought.

"I'm sure that'll be very helpful." He smirked at Eke, who smirked back.

Adegbulu even more shy than usual, shuffled his feet and stared down at the floor, "Sah, it is my wife Sah, she has asked me if she or my family can do anything for you?" His embarrassment caused him to whisper.

"That's very kind of you....... and her, but I'll have everything I need, I'm on a strict diet." He grimaced and Adegbulu smiled back in sympathy.

Richard asked for the last year-end accounts as soon as they were ready so that he could complete his year-end report. Adegbulu sighed. He couldn't believe this man.

And so a routine was established, Richard worked in the morning and rested in the afternoons. The duty nurses administered injections at timely intervals, some more tenderly than others. On Saturday morning Eli, accompanied by Dr Hamdi, visited. Hamdi was as charming as ever and enquired about Joan and Emma with a diligence that would have led one to believe that they were his only patients.

They examined him, taking time to stick assorted objects up his excruciatingly sore behind. They declared that subject to confirmation of the results of a further blood test, the operation could go ahead on Monday.

He got through to Joan on that afternoon and made light of his situation, saying how much better he felt and soon he would be as fit as a flea again. Joan cried on the phone and offered to return to be with him. He laughed, told her not to be silly and that every thing would be fine.

On the Monday a lay Sister appeared with razor and warm water, at first Richard didn't quite understand, but grabbed the implements from her before she could administer the shaving round his scrotum. The Sister seemed amused but retreated after Richard's insistence that he could manage perfectly well.

Hamdi turned up and cheerfully explained what he was to be about and got Richard to sign the consent forms. The doctor took one more look at the offending anatomy and left to scrub up. The Sister returned this time insisting that she examined Richard's shaved wedding tackle and pointed out that the job was not a good one and had to be repeated. Richard once more insisted that he would do his own shaving, this time he was freed from the drip.

He was gowned up, one that tied in the rear and was surprised that he had to walk to the theatre. He self-consciously tried to hide his bare bottom as he walked the eighty yards or so to the operating theatre. When he reached there he removed his slippers and walked through the double doors into the theatre proper. It was big and bare. There was a small table, rather like a large ironing board with arc lights overhead. The team stood around like spacemen, masked, gowned and all wearing yellow Wellingtons. Then, as if in his worst nightmare a nurse approached from the rear and removed his gown, he stood there naked, shorn and defenseless. Hamdi beckoned him to lie on the ironing board and before he could count to ten... they could see his willy... oh I'm running over the rooftops and I can't pull my shirt down... he drove his open top red sports car, nearly running over... Who? The steering wheel is behind another passenger seat. When will we land? ... 'Smiles... Mister Smiles.'

Sister Theresa, her large generous face looked down on him, he lay in his room, struggling to come to terms with his confusion. God, his bottom hurt, oh God his bottom hurt.

"Do you know who I am?"

"Sister, of course I know you, God my bum hurts."

"It will, but we'll do our best to make you as comfortable as we can."

He lay back and a pain, something akin to the drilling of his behind with rusty razorblades, started and almost made him cry out. The good Sister Theresa explained that the pain would be difficult and that he had to be brave.

"Remember your wife, how brave she was with baby. This is not half as bad you know, so be a good boy."

Doctor Hamdi will come and see you in the next half hour or so and perhaps he'll let us give you something for the pain. The charming Hamdi did arrive, this time on time.

He asked how Richard was.

"In bloody agony actually, but the excellent Sister Theresa says it's nothing compared with having a baby, Jesus how does she know? Don't suppose she's had either."

Hamdi laughed, "'I'm going to have to look at the wound, we had a little local difficulty as we finished up, I just need to check a thing or two."

The patient rolled obediently to his side and the Doctor, assisted by the silent Sister, removed the wad of dressing from the operation site. The pain was indescribable. He did whatever he needed to do and replaced the dressing; again it was amazingly painful.

"Everything seems fine, I just needed to check."

"Why, I've only just got back, Christ it's hot, can't we put the air conditioning on?"

"Well that's the point, but nothing for you to worry about, it's just that the power failed just before we closed up and by some dreadful coincidence the generator didn't come on, but we had torches, so that wasn't ideal, but we finished as well as we could have expected."

"God help me, are you telling me you operated by torch light?"

"Yes, actually, but only the last twenty minutes or so, everything is fine, really!"

"I'll send the Matron down with some morphine right away. You can get some rest."

Morphine, oh morphine; what a balm, what a comfort, what an escape from the daggers in his ass. It carried Smiles from agony to an ecstasy of peace in a trice. Oh morphine, better than alcohol, more welcoming than a warm bosom, as calm and restful as a quiet dawn, as cool as spring water. No wonder people got hooked on it.

"Excuse me, Sah, there ees a gentleman who wishes to see you Sah. Sista Theresa says you must decide if you see him, Sah."

"Who is it?" Richard for once did not want to know how the factory was doing, why couldn't they leave him alone.

"A Meesta Rrregan, Sah."

Oh bugger, the boss, what a chance to tell him to come back in the morning, no I'd better see him.

"Yes, I'll see him, could you make sure he stays no longer than ten minutes." He winked at the diminutive nurse. She smiled back, nodding her assent.

Edward Regan stood looking awkward at the end of the bed. For once he was stuck for an opening. He was lost. Richard said nothing too, enjoying his superior's discomfort. He feigned sleep, his eyes all but shut, peering at Regan through the tiniest slits. After a long thirty seconds he took pity.

"Oh hello Edward good of you to come, hope all's well at the ranch."

"Fine, fine, how are you my boy, that's the thing, how are you?"

"I'll be fine, back in the saddle in a few days; I must say a saddle isn't very appropriate right now." He winced as another quiver full of arrows struck their target.

"I've spoken to Doctor Eli, who tells me you've been overdoing it, no need to sacrifice your health, old boy, no need at all."

"My fault, I suppose, self inflicted wound as they say. Sitting around on my ass too much." He grinned. "Never mind I'll get rid of these bloody piles if nothing else." Another wave of pain shot up his backside.

"I'll come back tomorrow, we'll chat when you're a bit stronger, anything you want?"

"No, thanks Edward, see you tomorrow." They shook limp hands and Regan retreated, glad to leave the sick room. Other peoples' pain was embarrassing.

Morphine on demand that was Richard's only desire, unfortunately it was not Sister Theresa's. She strictly rationed him over the next few days so that he became schooled in the business of pain management. He really didn't know what pain was, he'd broken the odd shoulder, collarbone and dislocated an ankle, he'd thought that was painful, but it wasn't. Nothing even approached the pain of those first efforts to evacuate his bowels.

If having a baby was as painful as this, the human race would have petered out centuries before.

Regan and Eke visited briefly over the next two days and then Regan returned to Lagos, comfortable that the business would survive, whether Smiles did was a matter of lesser concern.

At last and almost imperceptibly the pain crept away, Richard's appetite returned and he started harrying and hounding his subordinates again. He enjoyed a number of sessions with Usman Jalingo who attended as often as he could.

He was released the Sunday morning following and given strict instructions by Sister Theresa and Eli to rest and work only a few hours for the next three days and then do no traveling for another two weeks. He went home, greatly relieved, fetched from the hospital by a guard of honor of Mohamed and Peter in his best white uniform.

Returning home to the empty house was dispiriting, but Peter showing dazzling culinary skills cooked a splendid omelet, served with a bottle of Star beer. Only six weeks to go, how he missed Joan and the children.

He was down he knew, but he hated the sparsely furnished house with its empty quiet rooms. Six weeks seemed an eternity. He went to a lonely bed and willed himself to sleep.

Anna Gombe arrived the next morning at nine-thirty. Richard had already risen and toyed with his bullet like boiled eggs and cold toast. He was astonished to see her, he had quite forgotten about those "friends" who were no more than acquaintances, though he'd long had a soft spot for the gentle Anna. She tapped on the door and came timorously into the house.

"Oh, Richard we only just heard about you being so unwell, oh why didn't you ring us? John says I must pack you up and bring you home to stay with us."

"That's very sweet, but I'm okay, just a sore bum, too prosaic to mention really, anyway I'm over the worst now, but thank you and John, you're very kind."

"Anyway you must come to supper; we'll eat early, so that you can get away to rest."

"That would be nice, thank you."

"'May I drop a few things off, John thought you wouldn't come and stay." She walked to her car and brought in a huge bag of food, lots of fruit and fresh vegetables, the finest beef from their secret source, all manner of goodies, including smoked salmon and cans of impossible to find treats like asparagus tips. She bustled passed him into the kitchen where she engaged Peter in his native tongue, he'd never noticed before her facility with the local language.

"Will you stop for a cup of tea or coffee?"

"No, we'll pick you up at six, very casual, nobody else as guest, just you our friend. I must go." She gazed out the window where Mussa toiled his lonely patch.

How sad she was. It was as if she carried her sadness like a secret that she only shared with those she liked. Her reserve was such that she locked herself into a dark and lonely place in the midst of great wealth and social razzmatazz. A fish out of water, unrequited love, a Madame Butterfly marooned in the dryness of the Nigerian north.

Surprises did not stop there; the steward of the Solomon's appeared, enquiring when it might be opportune for Mr. and Mrs. Solomon to visit.

They did and suddenly the house in Galadima Road had enough fancy food to open a delicatessen. They also insisted that he be their guest at dinner the following evening. What was he to do with all the goodies?

All the news from Joan was good, the contracts had been signed, the bank had come up with the requisite money and the mortgage should be arranged finally during the week. Joan had persuaded the powers that be that she had power of attorney. Each phone call elicited great detail about his health and well being and each night huge amounts of money were expended on long and longing conversations.

# CHAPTER 53

Mbamane presented himself first thing in the morning. He sought a private audience with "Meestah Smiles". It was granted.

"Good morning, Sah!"

"Good morning my dear fellow, how are you?"

Mbamane still carried his crippled arm in a sling. The sling had no purpose, other than to stop the useless limb getting in his way. Richard admired the courage Gordon Mbamane had shown. Ever since the accident he had not complained or moaned or hung around expecting sympathy. He had learned to write with his left hand, he had come back to work, when he must still have been in great pain. He had created his new job through his courage and effort and now he had become an indispensable member of the team. He now was a most useful technical man having studied assiduously the products of Universal and prepared to go anywhere to do anything asked of him. True, he'd received a substantial sum by local standards as compensation, but the biggest compensation of all, was the way his boss trusted him. He travelled all over the country; by bus, or by hitch hiking lifts or plane, even by train, a singularly unreliable process. The pilgrim project at Kano had been brought to order by him, he was liked by all the contractors; and he and Alhaji Jalingo, as Usman, had now become, were a formidable team.

"I have come, Sah, to ask if you will come to my community Sah, to be our guest, all the Yoruba men invite you." He looked anxiously at Smiles who was not at all sure how to respond.

"That's very kind of you, when would you like to meet and is there a purpose, um, should I wear a tie?" It was a silly response but nothing else seemed to fit the bill.

"If it is possible then we would like to meet a week next Thursday at seven o'clock, Sah."

Richard still taken aback, 'I think that'll be fine, can you tell me anything else, you know what's happening, food and all that?'

"Yes, Sah. There will be a feast and we will meet to honor you, Sah."

"That's very kind my dear fellow, but a good supper will be fine, I look forward to it." He did not look forward to it, yams and goat were not what he needed and no doubt lengthy speeches and God knows what else. Mbamane left happily to report back to his fellows.

Anxiously Smiles enquired of Eke if he knew anything of Mbamane's plans. No he did not, he liked the man but he was "of his own people" which meant that Eke's reform had been a non-event. When Usman next appeared he enquired of him.

His response was much the same as Eke's, "They will honor you, Sah, it is good."

When the night in question arrived, Richard was somewhat surprised that Mbamane, dressed in his finest robes, accompanied Mohamed. The robes were not like anything that Richard had expected either. Mbamane was after all a technical assistant; he'd only seen him dressed in long pants and shirt or overalls. Here he was in his best tribal kit looking the 'bees' knees'. He wore an interlaced shirt which was quite brightly colored, with zig zag patterns, over the shirt he wore a robe not unlike an academic gown, but of rich quality cotton or silk, he could not tell. On his head he wore a conical but soft hat, which flopped over the side of his head rather like a collapsed ice cream cone. The overall effect was to give the man, even with his crippled arm, an air of authority and confidence, which Richard had not recognized before.

They drove to a part of the city that Richard had never visited before, though the journey was not that long and they arrived at an enclosed sports field. Richard was astonished to find that the place was quite full. There must have been four hundred people at least, as his eyes got used to the darkness he realized that four hundred males there may have been, but there were at least two hundred females in a separate group.

There was a central stage with an alter-like table and alongside it there squatted some drummers. Richard was led, still not comprehending, to a seat at the front of the excited male enclosure. All the people gathered seemed to be in their best regalia, there was no other European that he could see in the stadium.

There were fires and torches burning and in the flickering light he saw the faces, the light glinting off shining black faces, white teeth flashing smiles in the darkness, glimpses of the colored robes.

Mbamane explained that although Richard was to be honored, they first were to greet a very important guest. The Oba of Abeokuta, a very senior Oba, King, or City leader was visiting the Yoruba community in Kaduna. There would be a welcome from Otun Olabashu the local Chief.

Then Mbamane, with a fluency that Richard had never heard, launched into a history of the Yoruba people. How until the eighteenth century they had been the most civilized and advanced nation in Africa. The great cities of Ife and Benin, in the kingdom of Oyo that stretched from Benin to Dahomey that had streetlights and sewerage systems before London. The Yoruba culture was one of the greatest in Africa, a religion of hundreds of Deities, but a balanced and benign community of learning and strong social values.

All the kings or City leaders were "Oba", directly descended from Oduduwa, the first man sent by the Gods. The Yoruba culture was destroyed by the slave trade, when the invading Fulani captured thousands of peace loving Yoruba and sold them into slavery. They sold them to the British, the Portuguese, the Spanish and the French so that now there were derivations of the Yoruba faiths and religions all over the Americas - north south and in the Caribbean.

The gates opened as two huge Mercedes rolled into the stadium. The assembly rose as one man cheered and yodeled as the cars made a stately lap of the park. Eventually and to more great cheers the "Oba" and "Otun" stepped out. They were accompanied by the State Governor Col. Obada, himself a Yoruba. Drums, elaborately carved, burst into life with a staccato rhythm, dancers emerged, both men and women and began dancing to the frenzied beat. The drums were called "Bata" and the dance a "tambor". The "Oba" was a big man in a magnificent robe encrusted with beads. He wore on his head a conical bead encrusted hat. The "Otun" was not much less impressive on his zigzagged lace robes and hat. Just behind them came a smaller older man, again in colorful robes. He carried a staff, beaded with the effigy of a bird at its head. This man, Mbamane explained, was the "Diviner" and his rod was, not surprisingly, a divining rod.

As the entourage eventually took their seats, splendid armchairs covered in animal skins, the "Otun" made his way to the centre as the "tambor" came to an end and made a lengthy speech of welcome, in the Yoruba tongue. There was much yodeling and cheering at appropriate points. Richard sat, intrigued but isolated by the language.

The "Oba" was greeted with an enormous cacophony of cheering and yodeling. It sent shivers down Richard's spine. He spoke in a deep voice to his entranced audience; Richard remained spellbound, but ignorant. The speeches were long, very long, but the tension and enthusiasm was so spellbinding that there was no hint of tedium. Not a whisper came from the crowd, except when they cheered in unison. Not a single man or woman missed a single word. Finally, a buzz went through the crowd as the "Otun" announced the remainder of the program.

Mbamane slipped away and for the first time Richard felt uncomfortable, not threatened, but shut out by the language. After two long minutes, his minder returned and beckoned Richard to follow him. He was first introduced to "Otun" Olabashu, who welcomed the guest in accented but excellent English.

"You are welcome to our community, Sir." Intoned the 'Otun', "we welcome a friend to our people who has treated my brothers as equal. Mbamane has told us of your kindness and your wisdom, his brothers have also attested to your kindness."

Richard was taken aback, he found himself trembling slightly. Goodness this was a bit over the top, he gathered himself and replied, "You are too kind, Sir, it has been my privilege to live and work here over these past two short years. The support of Mbamane and his colleagues has been all I could have asked for."

"Come, follow me."

Richard, with Mbamane at his side, walked awkwardly along the front of the stand, under the gaze of the Yoruba hierarchy of Kaduna. The

"Otun" stopped and bowed deeply to the "Oba" and spoke in Yoruba, his arm extended and palm stretched back toward Richard.

"You are welcome among us, Mr. Smiles." The accent was a stunning Oxford public school. "My dear fella don't look so surprised, many of us were educated in your old country, don't you know. Anyway, good to meet you, it's not often, I must say, we get fella's like you being put up by juniors." He spoke to Mbamane in Yoruba, they spoke for a good three minutes. "Look old boy," he continued, "we'll have a chat after this ceremony is over. There's a feast and all that, we'll have a chat then."

Richard was ushered away not having said a word.

Perhaps twenty of the locals were presented for an audience with the "Oba". This took an hour or more. They all sat patiently, Richard being sorely tried by the mosquitoes.

Eventually the "Oba", "Otun" and "Diviner" moved to the central table where a number of men were brought and seemed to have a more confidential chat. This time with the "Diviner" walking around each person, then they were given a gift of some sort and they returned one by one to the joyful yodeling of the assembled company.

Richard was beginning to get anxious that this ceremony like most would go on for ever. His attention began to wonder. Then he was drawn from his reverie when two of the "Oba's" attendants approached and beckoned him to the centre. Now he was really unsure of what to do or expect.

It crossed his mind, as he walked between the two robed attendants; that he wanted to pee; why did this always happen at crucial moments.

He arrived, bladder suddenly at bursting point, bowed as he thought appropriately, the "Otun" took his arm and turned him to face the gathered multitude. God what if he wet himself in front of a thousand Yoruba.

The Chief spoke again in Yoruba, Richard recognized his own name. The Chief led him to the chair on the dais, next to the "Oba's" throne. There was much yodeling and muted cheers. The "Diviner" then came to the front and waved his divining rod.

"He is summoning "Elugga" the "Orisha" of the crossroads, it won't take a minute."

It didn't take a minute, it took an age. At the end of this communication with the 'Orisha' the Chief announced in Yoruba the fitness of Smiles to be initiated as a Yoruba honorary Chief or 'Otun'.

The 'Oba' then presented Richard with his own set of robes. They were of fine cotton with woven borders to the sleeves and a small, enclosed zigzag pattern to the back. He was invited to put them on then and there, which he did, perspiring heavily as he struggled to pull on the shirt. The 'Otun' helped to arrange his robe and adjust his hat, which made him feel slightly idiotic.

He then thanked the 'Oba' and the 'Otun' for the honor bestowed upon him and promised to uphold the dignity of his office. Then Mbamane summoned the rest of the Universal males and they came before the 'Oba' who gave his permission that Chief Otun Smiles could be carried behind the 'Oba' to the feast. There was Adebayo, Ayala Peter, and many others and they carried him in his chair to the feast.

True to his word, the 'Oba' did spend a few moments chatting to Richard, mainly about his son, soon to graduate from Oxford like his father before him.

Richard relieved himself with some difficulty taking care not to dribble down his ceremonial robes. The food was good. Beer and other drinks were plentiful. Col. Obada stopped and had a chat, expressing his sorrow that Richard was due to leave Nigeria. Richard responded politely that he too was sorry to leave.

He travelled home still in his ceremonial robes modestly tipsy. Peter greeted him with great ceremony and much good humor. It was not the same though, how he would have loved to show Joan his robes and his honor. The bed was cold and empty.

# CHAPTER 54

The heat shimmered outside his office, the shrubs and Flame Trees waved to him in all their glory. This was his last day at work, and rather like his first he found little to do. Daniel from the auditors called to wish him well, presenting Richard with a gift of a tie that Richard though touched to accept, would not be seen dead in.

There was a genuine sense of sadness as he toured the plant, he shook hands with each and every worker and he thanked them all for their support. Many could not have cared less, but there were those who did. Adebayo, his epilepsy now under control, got a trifle over emotional. Mbamane and his friends had written a speech of good wishes. Adegbulu twisted his little Moslem hat and mumbled a fond farewell. Rhoda, eyes firmly to the floor as she had his very first day, tearfully bade him goodbye and wished the Madame and the little ones well.

Usman Jalingo journeyed from Maiduguri to make his farewell, he arrived in time to pray, which he did outside the office. He told Richard that he prayed to God that Richard and his family (he recited all their names) would live in health and happiness and in God's protection. It was too much for Richard who hugged his huge Hausa friend and could not contain his tears.

The afternoon dragged slowly, he dreamed of the last two and a bit years, his triumphs, his failures, his ignominies. Of the 'wackers' who begged for compassion in his first week, one was never seen again. Benjamin had returned; been thankful, paid back his hundred Naira.

Edwin he assumed had a wonderful weekend and wondered off laughing up his sleeve. Richard hoped he hadn't made thieving too easy. Simon still collected his 'dash' to keep the phone connected; there had seemed no way round this particular scam. He wondered if every one paid. Simon must be quite rich.

"Well Eke, time to go, it's been a short time but a good time, thank you for all your help."

"We are sorry to see you go, Sah. I expect we shall learn to live with the new man from England," he looked up and smiled, extending his hand, "he will not be as good as you."

"I bet you say that to all the guys that pass through here......" He wished he'd think before opening his big trap.

Enigmatic as ever, "It will be the time for another young man, no doubt from England... but that is good. .......I shall look to see of your rise through the company, and I hope one day you will come back and see us."

They shook hands warmly, Richard resisted the compulsion to hug the reserved Ibo, it would only embarrass him. Then he did anyway, and it did just that. Eke walked straight-faced from the office; he waved over his shoulder as he went. The office was empty.

At Galadima Road all the bags were packed. Peter had prepared a snack lunch of cold pre-cooked chicken, which he ate without relish. Mohamed and Peter talked in hushed tones as he showered and changed for the journey. Peter was worried about his job and despite a number of reassurances from the boss, still fretted about his future. Richard had written a glowing testimonial and given him a contract for three months so at least he had security of tenure, even if the new man didn't get on with him.

He shook Peter's hand, urged him not to worry, not forgetting Mussa, who was surprised that Richard had even taken the time to say goodbye. He mumbled in his broad pidgin' what Richard assumed to be 'send love to David and Madame and the little one.'

They left the polished house like a doctor's waiting room, devoid of the Smiles' marks of home. A waiting room for what, another smart ass white guy, a smug superior has been, hopefully someone who cared.

They arrived in Kano for some last adieus to Chagoury and some others and then as the day faded, to the airport that was strangely deserted. Richard had been assured that the new service with Caledonian Airways was to depart from Kano that evening at nine.

There was no one to be seen, surely not another bizarre twist to this Nigerian Saga. He entered the concourse that remained in darkness, all was silent, he could see the lights from airline offices dimly illuminate the corridor, but no desks were open. Surely there was something amiss. Mohamed and his boss stood in the eerily silent concourse.

"Well Mohamed, what's up?"

"There is no one here, Sah."

"Damn it there must be. For Christ's sake, this ticket is dated today, the twentieth of March. I know it's a new schedule but surely they haven't cancelled it without letting me know?"

"Mr. Smiles, Mr. Smiles," A voice from the offices behind the concourse echoed through the empty building.

"I'm here." he shouted back

An airline official appeared, shook his hand, took his bag and checked him in.

"What's the problem?"

"No problem, Sir. Your flight will board in twenty minutes, it's a new schedule, the only problem for us is you're the only passenger."

"Well Mohamed, time to go."

Mohamed smiled his shy broad smile, his eyelashes accentuated by the slanting light, "We shall miss you, Sah."

"I shall miss you too, Madame I know misses you already, it has been a delight to call you friend. You be good to the next guy. I'm sure you'll like him."

They hugged and Richard quickly disengaged and walked slowly to the deserted departure gate, the airline man followed. "You can board any time you like now, Sir."

He climbed the aircraft steps and turned to look for a last time at Kano and there in the half-light the ever-faithful Mohamed waved a final farewell.

He took his seat in the strangely empty aeroplane; "God's gift to Africa?" He'd learned a little. But no matter what Eke learned; he and thousands like him stood in a life long queue, never moving forward. Waiting always to serve under some stranger parachuted in by the great 'Universal Metals'. A stranger in his own land whose skills and knowledge would always be under used. 'No wonder Eke was such a sad bugger,' he drank his gin and tonic.

But yet he felt sad, he had left something of himself behind, he dosed.

Two years, two years... Emma's birth... the burning of the Yoruba man... the kindness, the corruption,...the smile behind the sunglasses, the cockeyed buildings. The cruelty ...the police, keeping order by brutality and a kind of bizarre rule of law....fear. The poverty,.... the pride, the nobility of the durbar, the chaos of the Kano pilgrim camp, the delights of Baalbeck,..... Sally oh, Sally,...... the dedicated kindness of Mighty Mouse the selflessness of Coker, the agony of Mbamane, the bonds of Mussa and David, they all merged in his endless dream. Anna, poor Anna, lost forever, Hosi getting richer and richer with his silent wife and Chamoon Petawi striding the continent playing with pawns and kings. Henry Ash hit the ground with a sickly thump. Where would he end?

'Mr Smiles, I didn't wake you, but you've just got time for breakfast, we're landing in twenty minutes.'

England,...... Another day, another place, another Smiles.

Printed in the United Kingdom
by Lightning Source UK Ltd.
129483UK00002B/1-39/A